THE GOOSE GIRL AND OTHER STORIES

The Goose Girl and Other Stories

ERIC LINKLATER

selected & edited by
Andro Linklater

CANONGATE

This collection first published in 1991 by Canongate Press, 14 Frederick Street, Edinburgh EH2 2HB.

Copyright acknowledgements:
The earliest of these stories, 'Pathans' and 'The Wrong Story', were written in the late 1920s, but were not published until 1935 when Jonathan Cape included them in a collection entitled *God Likes Them Plain.* Other stories in this volume which appeared there for the first time were, 'The Abominable Imprecation', 'The Actress Olenina', 'The Dancers', 'The Duke', 'God Likes Them Plain', 'Kind Kitty', 'The Redundant Miracle', and 'Wineland'. 'The Crusader's Key' was published in 1933 by White Owl Press. In 1947, Rupert Hart-Davis published 'Sealskin Trousers', in a collection of that title, which also included 'The Goose Girl' and 'The Three Poets'. 'A Sociable Plover', 'The Masks of Purpose' and 'Escape Forever' appeared first in *A Sociable Plover* published by Rupert Hart-Davis in 1957. Acknowledgement is made to these publishers of their acuity, and to the Estate of Eric Linklater for its permission to reprint these stories.

The publishers acknowledge subsidy from the Scottish Arts Council towards the publication of this volume.

British Library Cataloguing-in-Publication Data
Linklater, Eric, 1899–1974
Selected short stories.
I. Title II. Linklater, Andro, 1944–
823.912 (FS)

ISBN 0 86241 325 7

Typeset by Falcon Typographic Art Ltd, Edinburgh & London. Printed and bound in Great Britain by Mackays of Chatham.

Contents

Introduction

TO JUDGE by his short stories, Eric Linklater was a convinced, unwavering pagan. In selecting these examples, my original intention was merely to represent the variety of his style and subject-matter, a quality for which he was often criticised, but which he himself blithely admitted, saying 'I have always been self-indulgent and plagued by fear of boredom, so I rarely write the same thing twice'. Yet it became obvious that for all their differences, they shared one fundamental relationship. Each bore the imprint of what could only be termed a pre-Christian imagination. This is not to say that my father was irreligious—he had, if not a Christian's faith, a fellow-author's warm regard for the Christians' God—but rather that he believed equally strongly in the existence of ungodly powers.

Such powers provide the energy within these stories. Some have substance, like the witch's fetch in 'A Sociable Plover' or the silkie in 'Sealskin Trousers'; some hark back to animistic myths and fairy-tales, as in 'The Goose Girl'; but most are aspects of the insubstantial magic of this world—love, beauty, ambition, drink, and language. These last, however, are not the small familiar thrills which in civilised society are sprinkled, as though from a cruet, to add savour to everyday life. They are agencies as powerful as witchcraft and as inescapable as fate. Robert Tyndall, the narrator of 'The Goose Girl' puts it succinctly, comparing the power of love to his memory of being carried away in a sailing-boat 'swiftly past a rocky shore though the wind had fallen and the sail hung loose. The moon was pulling the tide to sea and I was going with it. I was helpless in the grip of the moon, and I felt the excitement of its power'.

That fatalistic thrill comes from recognising one's doom, and in these stories it is a theme which recurs in a dozen different guises. Sometimes it breeds excitement, occasionally despair, and most often immoderate laughter, but once recognised there is no other course than to give way to it.

Such fatalism was not a conspicuous ingredient of Eric Linklater's own life, with one monumental exception. He was born in 1899, the son of a Merchant Navy captain and his strong-willed wife, who were so careless as to be domiciled at the time in the port of Penarth in

Glamorgan. Undeterred by this accident of birth, he decided at the earliest opportunity to be an Orcadian. His father, the youngest in a family of crofters who had farmed in Orkney for at least four centuries, returned there frequently for holidays, and to his profound satisfaction Eric calculated that he must have been conceived on the island. In time he too was taken there on holiday visits which enabled him to meet his grandmother, popularly regarded as a witch, and to catch the flavour of an era when gossip and folk-tales merged and, as Edwin Muir put it, 'there was no great distinction between the ordinary and the fabulous'.

When he was fourteen, the family moved to Aberdeen and, he wrote in his autobiography, 'with exemplary decision I became an Aberdonian as well as an Orkneyman'. And three years later, in 1917, as a pale, bespectacled youth whom Nature had clearly intended for a desk, he again created his own fate, this time by forging military documents in order to be sent to fight in Flanders as a private soldier in The Black Watch. His motive was expressed in contradictory forms: often he said it was from a desire to revenge his father, the sea-captain, who having saved his ship from a German submarine had succumbed to exhaustion and pneumonia; however, he also sometimes declared, and wrote so in his novel *A Spell for Old Bones*, that even the attraction of women paled beside the congested excitement of war.

Grudgingly in speech and more freely in a late autobiography, *Fanfare for a Tin Hat*, he admitted to being terrified by the mud, the bullying and the sudden slaughter of the Western Front. And a lifelong pride in The Black Watch testified to the depths that comradeship and shared danger touched in him. But there was something else. In training he had earned a marksman's badge, and early in 1918 with the Allies in headlong retreat, he was designated a sniper, lying out in advance of his company's hastily dug position to pick off advancing German soldiers of his own age.

'We had decided to fight, *à outrance*, against aggression' he wrote, 'and I, a microscopic projection of general insanity, shared to the full its insensate purpose, and with a robust perversion enjoyed the brief remnant of my active service. My few weeks as a sniper gave my life an excitement, an intensity, which I have never known since . . . I lived at a high pitch of purpose, a continuous physical and mental alertness that has never again suffused my mind and body.'

To be caught in that tide-rip of destiny was to be changed forever. For the long roll of names engraved on war memorials up and down the land, there was no need to understand what had happened; for the survivors the need was inexpugnable.

In April 1918, the Germans had their revenge for his sniping. He was struck in the head by a machine-gun bullet—leaping, he claimed, high in the air like a shot rabbit—and it was only by the depth of a war memorial's engraving that he escaped being added to the roll of honour. For the rest of his life, his skull was scored by a deep, transverse gutter, and his spirit by that intoxicated concentration upon killing, which in defence of one's country was admirable, in peacetime would have been criminal, and in memory held a primitive passion which nothing afterwards could obliterate.

It would be misleading to suggest that this experience alienated him; it was after all shared in some degree by several million of his contemporaries. What it did, however, was to confirm in him an atavistic streak which delighted in wildness—not chaos, but the unfettered play of natural forces in life and death.

In crude terms, it might be said that he backed nature against society, instinct against reason, but it would be truer to suggest that what he really enjoyed was the comedy of reason attempting to calm instinct, or society being embarrassed by nature. His primitivism co-existed with a highly cultivated intelligence, for Nature had not lied in giving the adolescent Linklater a scholar's face: after the war, he took an excellent First and every English prize in sight at Aberdeen University; his reading remained prodigious throughout his life, and as his collection of paintings by Peploe, Redpath, Eardley, and others, now hanging in the University testifies, he had a discerning eye for beauty.

In the circumstances, it is perhaps not surprising that he should have reconciled the two poles of his character by deriving an aesthetic enjoyment from the manner in which people responded to wildness. It was, he believed, an art, specifically the art of adventure, and in a book of that title, he cited among its exponents, doctors and poets, as well as soldiers and sailors. No one, however, practised the art more perfectly than the Vikings.

'They were unabashed by social obligation' he wrote in *The Ultimate Viking*, 'undeterred by moral prohibition, and they could be quite contemptuous of economic advantage and the safety of their own skin. But they saw clearly a difference between right and wrong, and the difference was aesthetic'.

Such people were 'artists in conduct', he suggested, and so too in their many different ways are the protagonists of these stories. (To say so is to fly in the face of Linklater's warning to readers of his short stories that 'He who looks for cousinhood of theme and consistency of treatment will be disappointed', but it is a son's bounden duty to contradict his father and put him right whenever opportunity presents.) Almost thirty years separates 'The Pathans', written in 1928, from 'The Masks of Purpose'; one concerns a squalid murder in India, the other the massacre in Glencoe, but the crux of each is the proper way to confront an inevitable fate, in this case death.

Doom comes in many other guises since wildness belongs pre-eminently to life, but the challenge remains the same, to behave fittingly. Should it come as joy, the appropriate response, as the title indicates, is to catch it as it flies. When it is drink, the art lies in sharing, and it is by this Viking yardstick that Kind Kitty shows herself fit for Heaven, indeed more fit than St Peter. The doom of the appalling Perigot is to be cursed, and it is because he shows himself so richly worthy of it that he is the hero, in the Viking as well as the literary sense, of 'The Abominable Imprecation'. By the same token, it is because they resist their fate, which is love, that Malis and Perdis, for all their virtues, deserve their fearful punishment in 'God Likes Them Plain'.

It was only in the 1930s after travelling in India, the United States and Italy, that Linklater finally settled in Orkney, by which time his early novels, *White Maa's Saga*, *Poet's Pub* and *Juan in America* had made him famous. He came in response to the rise of Scottish Nationalism and to the call put out by Hugh MacDiarmid for Scots writers to return to assist in their country's literary renaissance. After a brief, disastrous experiment as the Nationalist candidate for East Fife, he recognised that his proper contribution was to lend the renaissance his distinctively Orcadian voice. The islands had been, he remarked, 'the southernmost home of that pagan heroism which had changed the shape and temper of all northern Europe'. The Norse influence remained strong and was as congenial to his mature outlook as to his childhood daydreams.

The most dangerous of the ungodly powers to be found in these pages is language—nothing could be more dreadful than the curse of Shepherd Alken hurled at Perigot—and this is appropriate because it was Linklater's own doom. On the whole, his conduct was fitting. He submitted gracefully to grammar, tended faithfully to meaning, and gave rhythm its place, but where vocabulary was concerned he succumbed to a prodigal, joyful self-indulgence. Even his factual telegram to a friend announcing the birth of his second child became a verbal explosion: 'FACULTIES PARALYSED IN ANTENATAL SUSPENSE, PARTIALLY RESTORED BY BIRTH OF DOLICHOCEPHALIC GERANIUM COLOURED DAUGHTER, BUT NOW SUSPENDED IN LIBATORY POSTNATAL ALCO-HOLIC PARESIS'.

The penalty attached to his greed for words was a tendency, which appeared in some of his later writing, to over-ornate description. This, coupled with the foreign background of novels such as *Juan in America* and *Private Angelo*, had the unfortunate effect of obscuring the persistently Norse edge—savage, fabulist and intoxicated—which marked his fiction. As a result, some academic critics, determined to prune the diversity of Scottish literature to a mainland stump, have found difficulty in assigning him a place within the Scottish renaissance. MacDiarmid, it should be noted, encountered no such problem. Linklater's pleasure in wildness he recognised as coming from the same source as Dunbar's satire, Goodsir Smith's *Carotid Cornucopius*, and his own *A Drunk Man Looks at the Thistle*. From which it is clear that the influence of pagan heroism on the Scots imagination runs deep.

In these short stories, shorn as they are of excessive ornamentation, Linklater's quality can be found unadorned. Some of them may be familiar from anthologies, but more than a quarter of a century has passed since his stories were last collected, and so I trust that most will come as new.

When he died in November 1974, my father was buried in the Harray kirkyard in Orkney. But I continue to have my doubts about his Christian credentials. There was his choice of gravestone, for instance, a massive stone which, surely not by coincidence, was the same shape, and almost the same size, as the Standing Stones erected by Orkney's Pictish inhabitants. More poignantly, I remember walking with him through a birch wood in the spring before he died when he was obviously brooding on the finality of death. He found his answer, not in the Gospels, but where pagans have always looked for it, in the evidence of spring and the bright green buds. 'Of course there must be a life after death' he muttered, 'the trees tell you that'.

What follows is the outcome of that cast of mind.

ANDRO LINKLATER

The Goose Girl

When i woke among the currant-bushes I saw her coming out of the cottage door with her fist round the gander's neck. I heard them too, for she was yelling and the gander was beating the doorposts and beating her thighs with his great creaking wings. Like a windmill in the distance, like the slap of a rising swan's black feet on the water, like clothes on the line thrashing in a breeze: the gander was making nearly as much noise as she was, and she was shouting her head off. There was no leaping tune in her voice that morning. It was just the air in her lungs being driven through the funnel of her throat like steam from a well-fired boiler; and some of the words she was using were no prettier than what goes on in any stoker's mind. But I wasn't listening so much as looking. I had heard those words before, but I had never seen a woman's body like hers, so firm and long of limb, like a young reed in firmness and round as an apple where it should be, and white as a pearl. Against the gander's wings, which were a cold white like snow, her pallor was warm and glowing. Not reflecting light, but glowing with it. She was naked as the sky, and the sky, at four o'clock in the morning, was bare of cloud except for a little twist of wool low down in the west.

Now she gripped the gander's neck with both her hands, and even her hands weren't red like any other country girl's, but small and white. They were strong though, and I could see the hardness of her forearms. She was throttling the bird, and its beak was wide open, a gaping stretch of yellow skin, the upper mandible at right-angles to the lower. Its eyes were hidden in the ruffling of its little head-feathers. She dragged it through the door, gave a great heave, and threw it with a noise of breaking stalks into some overgrown rhubarb. A splash of dew-drops rose from the leaves and caught the light. For a moment she stood looking at the bird, her arms a little bent and her hair dishevelled, her mouth open, and her breast rising and falling. Then, abruptly, she turned and went back into the cottage, slamming the door behind her. I listened, I remember, for the sound of a key turning or a bolt going home; but in this part of the country they never lock their doors. It was lack of custom, not lack of feeling, that prevented her from giving this final emphasis to her act of expulsion.

The gander shook himself, hissing loudly, and broke more stalks of rhubarb as he made his way to a narrow path of little sea-shore pebbles. I had seen him before, half a dozen times with the girl, and always marvelled at the size of him, but now, from where I lay among the currant-bushes, he looked bigger than ever and his ruffled head-feathers stood out like a crown. His neck was as stiff as a broom-handle but twice as thick, and he turned his head this way and that with a twitch of the bill, an angry snap. His little black eyes were swollen and bright, and the broad webs of his feet fell on the path with the heavy tread of German infantry. He stopped when he saw me and stood for a little while, hissing like a burst tyre; but not in the way of an ordinary gander, with its neck low to the ground and its beak reaching forward. He stood upright, his head swaying back as if to look at me from a greater height, and when he had done with hissing he turned his back on me and went tramping through some rows of cabbage-plants to a gap in the low garden wall where the old turf-dyke on which it was built had collapsed and brought down the stone. It was a plain little garden with no colour in it except some yellow daisies under the cottage windows and a thin growth of honeysuckle beside the door. There was a fuchsia hedge on one side, not in flower yet, and gooseberries and black-currant bushes along the other walls, with a clump of grey-barked elder-trees in the corner. On one side of the dividing pebble-path rhubarb and spring onions, early potatoes and cabbage on the other: that was all. And the gander, marching like a Prussian, flattened the cabbages under his broad splayed feet as if there had been the weight of a man in him. Perhaps there was. He was no ordinary bird, that was certain.

I got up and followed him, cautiously, as he disappeared, and watched him swimming down the little stream that runs behind the cottage to the big loch a quarter of a mile away. I saw his head, still ruffled, still indignantly twitching, behind a bank of meadowsweet; and then he vanished.

I leant against the wall of a cartshed, thinking. The air was still, and the country looked as though no one had ever touched it. The day before had been wet and ugly, and I remembered with a kind of shame how unhappy I had been; and how clumsily I had behaved, getting drunk so that I could tell the truth. But now I felt uncommonly well—and I had done my duty. There's nothing like sleeping in the open air to prevent a hangover, and I had, after long delay, disburdened my mind. The evening before I had gone to see John Norquoy to tell him how his young brother had been killed on the shore of Lake Comacchio.

We had been together for a long time, Jim Norquoy and I, in the Seaforths to begin with and then in the Commando, and between Primo Sole in Sicily and that great cold lagoon of Comacchio, mud and water and a dancing mirage, we had had our fill of fighting. Jim was hit in shallow water, wading ashore after our boats had grounded on a mudbank just as the sun came up, and I carried him in. But he died on the edge of the land, and his last words were, 'You'll find it difficult to go back too, after all this.'

That was an understatement. I found it impossible to go back to the life I had known before, and when I came north to the islands, to tell his people about Jim and give him what immortality I could, by feeding their pride in him, I was looking for something for myself as well. No more school-teaching for me. I was never meant to be a teacher anyway, either by Providence or my parents. I had only wanted to live—I mean to live in such a way that life came in through my eyes and I could feel it on my skin—but never had I known how to go about it till the war came. And now, when the war was over, I was more at a loss than ever. I couldn't go back to an elementary school in Falkirk, and teach little boys the parts of speech and the more blatant pieces of history, for fear that one of them, some day, might ask me, 'What's it all for? What are we going to say when we've learnt the parts of speech; and if we learn all the history in the world, what would it mean?'

I was no coward, not in the physical sense, and I had been a good soldier—not as good as Jim, though I earned my pay—but when I looked at those questions in the solitude of my mind I knew that I couldn't face them in public. Nor did I want to. I wanted to live, but not to set myself up as a preceptor of living. As a small boy I had gone about in a state of perpetual astonishment; a book or a feather, a mouse or a fish or the dining-room table had all seemed equally miraculous, and I lacked the ordinary confidence in my own reality. I never went to bed without wondering what new shape I might inhabit by the morning. Almost from the beginning I was a disappointment to my parents. They had a position to keep up, and were ambitious too. They took it very badly when I was expelled from the school where my elder brother had been Head of his House and Captain of Cricket.

Now, after six years in the Army, I felt that I had served my apprenticeship to war, but I was still a novice in peace. So I couldn't, in honesty, set up as a teacher, and I had been looking for something else to do. I hadn't much to guide me except negatives. I didn't want to live in a town, for one thing, because I felt, at that time, the need to think; and peace to think, in my view of it, required the open sky.

I started badly, for after I had seen John Norquoy at a cattle market one day, I couldn't bring myself to go and tell him about Jim. I had wanted to make him, and all his friends, so proud of Jim that he would live for ever in their minds like a lighted lamp, to which their love would be as moths, gathering to his memory and beating its wings in the glow of him. Jim was my friend, and even the Seaforth Highlanders had never known a better man.

But when I first saw John Norquoy I realised that it wasn't going to be easy to talk about pride to him, for he knew enough already. That was evident, though it was quite an ordinary occasion. He was looking at a thin-faced cattle-dealer pulling the loose black skin on the rump of a two-year-old heifer. There was nothing of the braggart in him, nothing loud or boastful, but he had the same build as Jim, the same sort of head ten years older, the look of a man who knew what he was after and what it was worth. He was smiling, and there was the same irony in his smile, though he was only selling a beast, as I had seen in Jim's face, grey with the strain of battle, when we had to withdraw from the Primo Sole bridge because our ammunition was spent, and the infantry who should have relieved us hadn't been able to get forward in time. There was nothing I could tell John Norquoy about pride, and when I realised that I put off going to see him. I put it off for about three weeks.

I stayed with the village schoolmaster, a good man who had fought in the first war. I told him about my other difficulty, and he thought I could teach with safety in a country school. 'The children here,' he said, 'wouldn't worry you with awkward questions. They don't grow up with doubts in their minds. Life for them means birth and marriage and death, and they're all natural things. It means hard work and hard weather, and what amusement they and their neighbours can make for themselves. It means dancing and making love when they're young, and breeding a good beast and gossiping when they're older. And if, from time to time, they're troubled about the deeper significance of life, they keep their trouble to themselves. They know that it's an old trouble, and it wouldn't occur to them that you could cure it.'

But I didn't want to teach, either in country or town, so I spent my three weeks in idleness, but kept my eyes open. I had an open mind too, and no accomplishments. I was ready for suggestions; but not for going to see John Norquoy. I met Lydia one day, and talked to her for a quarter of an hour till her mother came out and called her in. The next time I saw her she had the gander with her, and she wasn't so friendly. I felt hurt and disappointed and a little angry, though I didn't realise then what she was really like. We pay too much attention to clothes, and hers were the sort you don't see in a town unless a strayed gipsy has come in. She had a small, beautifully shaped head, but her hair was tangled by the wind and greasy, and her features were so regular that I didn't notice, to begin with, how good they were. Her throat was lovely, long and as white as milk, but her neck was dirty, and when I saw her for the second time it was the same dirt, I'm fairly sure, that still darkened her skin. And yet I felt hurt when she wouldn't stay and talk to me.

I asked the schoolmaster about her, and he told me she was illegitimate, a state of being that's not extraordinary in country districts. Her mother was a grim old woman named Thomasina Manson, a crofter's only child, unpopular as a girl, who had lived a lonely and blameless life till she was about thirty-five, when she had gone to Edinburgh, and what she did there, except get herself into trouble, no one ever knew. It was generally supposed that she had been in domestic service, and when her baby was born, about three months after she came home, she told the doctor that its father came of the gentry. But that's all she told, and her father and mother, who had married late in life, never recovered from the shock. They were Plymouth Brethren, said the schoolmaster, sternly pious and pitiably dependent on their respectability. They died, one after the other, within a couple of years of Lydia's birth, and Thomasina was left alone to work the croft and bring up the child.

How, I asked, did she come to give it a name like Lydia?

The schoolmaster showed me a register of the village children. About half of them had been christened simply enough: Thomas and James and Mary, Ellen and Jean and William and David, and a few of the girls had clumsy feminine transformations of masculine names such as Williamina and Davidina and—like Lydia's mother—Thomasina. But the rest were a fancy array of Corals and Dereks, Stellas and Audreys, and so forth. 'Their mothers take a fancy to names they've seen on the films or in a magazine,' he said. 'They don't suit our island surnames, but they produce, I suppose, the same effect in the house as a piece of new wallpaper or a set of new curtains. They seem bright and cheerful.'

A moment later he said, 'When are you going to see the Norquoys? They know who you are, and they're expecting you. But they won't ask you to come, they'll just wait.'

'It's not easy,' I said.

'It won't be as difficult as you think. They won't show any emotion, you needn't be afraid of that.'

'I'm thinking of myself,' I answered.

I waited another ten days, and then, one Saturday morning, I went to town—four thousand inhabitants and a little red cathedral—and managed to get a bottle of whisky. I arrived at the Norquoys' about six o'clock, and though I hadn't told them I was coming, they seemed to be expecting me. News travels quickly here, and even a man's intentions become public property as soon as he has realised them himself, and sometimes before. So I sat down to a mighty farmhouse tea in the kitchen, and no one said a word about Jim. They asked me what I thought of the islands, and where I belonged to, and if my parents were still alive, and they all laughed when I mistook a young sister of John Norquoy's wife for one of his daughters. There were ten or a dozen people at table, and I had to be told very carefully who they all were, and they thought it a great joke when I couldn't remember. But no one mentioned Jim.

After tea John Norquoy took me out to see the animals. He had a couple of fine young Clydesdales, a small herd of black-polled cattle, a great surly white boar, and a few score of sheep on hill pasture. We walked in his fields for a couple of hours, and still no word of Jim. But when we came back to the farm he led me into the ben-room; a peat fire had been lighted in it, and going through the passage where I had hung my waterproof I took my bottle out of the pocket. Norquoy paid no attention to it when I set it down, but went to a little table in the window where another bottle, the same brand as my own, stood on a tray with glasses and a jug of water. He poured a couple of deep drams and said, 'It was very good of you to write about Jim in the way you did. We're most grateful to you, and we're glad to see you here. If you're thinking of staying, there's a bed for you whenever you want it.'

I took my drink before I answered, and then, slowly and little by little, I told him about Jim, and about the war, and what it means to go through five or six battles with the same friend beside you, and then to lose him in the last one. I realised, in an hour or two, that I was playing the bereaved brother myself, but couldn't help it by then. Mrs Norquoy came in, and their eldest boy, and her sister that I had taken for Norquoy's daughter, and then two or three neighbours. I went on talking, and they listened. I got most of the load off my mind, and if they didn't realise, by the end of it all, that Jim had been a soldier, well, it wasn't my fault. And every word I spoke was the simple truth. But when I got up to go Mrs Norquoy said,

'We're peaceful folk here, Mr Tyndall, and Jim was one of us. How he endured all that fighting I just can't understand.' It wasn't till a few days later, when I remembered her words, that I began to realise how much they had disliked what I had been telling them. They were peaceful folk, and they didn't approve of war.

But at the time I wasn't in the mood to catch a fine shade of meaning. Both bottles were empty, and I had had a lot more than my share. John Norquoy drank moderately and showed no sign of having drunk at all. He had listened carefully, with little change of expression, and the questions he asked showed that he was following and remembering all I said. But he made no comments on my story. One of the neighbours liked his whisky well enough, but carried it as solemnly as a cask. I was the only one who seemed to have taken any benefit from what we had been doing, and Norquoy insisted on coming with me as far as the main road. I was walking well enough, but talking too much by then, and I told him—without difficulty—what I had been waiting for the strength to tell. I got rid of the guilt on my mind.

For a black minute or two, splashing through the shallows of Comacchio, I had been glad when Jim was killed. Glad it was he and not I whom death had taken, for we knew, both of us, that our luck was too good to last, and one or the other must go before the end. And when I saw it was Jim I was glad, and the guilt of it had lain on me ever since. Norquoy said nothing that I can remember, though I think he tried to comfort me and I know that he wanted to take me home. But I wouldn't let him.

Soon after we had said good night it came into my head that I would like to take a look at the goose girl's house. Lydia's, I mean. The last time I had seen her she had been driving her whole flock, fifteen or sixteen of them with the great gander in front like a drum-major, past a big shallow pool in the stream, where the cattle came to drink, and the whole procession had been reflected in the calm water as if to make a picture. To see her like that, in a picture, had made her more real—or am I talking nonsense? Ideal may be the word, not real. Anyone who's fit to be a teacher could tell you, and tell you the difference between them, but I'm not sure myself. But whatever the word should be, I looked at her on the other bank of the stream; she was wearing an old yellow jersey and a dirty white skirt and her legs were bare among the meadowsweet, and I looked at her reflection in the picture, and that night I dreamt of her, and in my dream she was trying to tell me something, but I couldn't hear her.

So I turned off the main road towards her mother's house, and before I got there I realised how drunk I was. I'm not trying to excuse myself, but the whisky had been mixed with a lot of emotion, and as the result of one coming in and the other going out my knees were beginning to buckle, and when I came to the cottage I had one hunger only, and that was for sleep. There was a south-easterly breeze blowing, chill in the middle of the night, and to get into shelter I clambered over the garden wall, and the softness of the dug soil on the other side seemed very comfortable. I fell asleep under the currant-bushes, and what woke me was Lydia's screaming and the clattering of the gander's wings as she threw it out of the house.

Well, after I'd seen the bird go marching off, and disappear downstream, I went round, as I said before, to the lee-side of the cartshed and smoked a cigarette. I had been lying on the packet and they were pretty flat, but I rolled one into shape again, and while I smoked I thought, and came to a conclusion.

I fingered my chin, and it was smooth enough. I had shaved about five o'clock the afternoon before. I felt fresh and well. Sleeping on the ground had done me no harm, for I had grown used to that, and the night had been mild. My clothes were damp with dew and soiled with earth, but I took off my coat and shook it, and cleaned myself fairly well with some cut grass. Then I went down to the stream, and kneeling on the bank I washed my face and rinsed my mouth, and drank a few handfuls of water.

The door, the unlocked door, opened easily enough and I made no noise going in. I stood in a little passage with some old coats hanging on the opposite wall, and an uncarpeted wooden stair before me that led to a loft. To the right there was a door into the kitchen, where the old woman slept in a box-bed, and to the left was the ben-room with a closet on the inner side where Lydia slept. The ben-room door was closed with a latch, or a sneck, as they call it here, and my hand was steady. I opened the door without a sound, but only two or three inches, and looked in.

Lydia had put on a long white nightgown, an old-fashioned garment with coarse lace at the neck, and she was sitting at the north window, the one that opens into the yard. She held a looking-glass in both hands, and was staring at her reflection. Her right cheek—the one I could see—was pink.

She jumped up with a gasp of fear, a hoarse little noise, when I went in, and faced me with the looking-glass held to her breast like a shield. 'What do you want?' she asked, but her voice was quiet.

I closed the door behind me and said, 'If you had asked me that a week ago, I couldn't have answered you. I might have said *Everything* or *Nothing*. I didn't know. But that was a week ago.'

'What does that matter to me?' she asked. 'Why have you come here?'

'Because now,' I said, 'I do know.'

'You have no right to come into my room,' she whispered.

'I want you to marry me,' I said. 'I want a wife.'

She flushed and asked me, 'Why do you think you can find one here?'

Then I told her, or tried to tell her, why nothing had any force or weight in my mind, after seeing her as I had seen her that morning, but to live with her in the love of a man for his wife, in the love of possession without term or hindrance. She turned pale, then red again, when I said that I had seen her wrestling with the gander, and tried to push me out. But I caught her by the wrists, and spoke as a man will when he is wooing, in fumbling and broken words, of her beauty and the worship I would give her. Fiercely, but in a voice as low as a whisper still, she cried, 'I want no one's worship!'

'Last night,' I said, as urgently but as softly as she spoke herself—for the old woman was sleeping only a few yards away—'Last night my mind was full of bitterness and grief. There had been little else in it for a year or more. But I emptied it, last night, and this morning you came into its emptiness and took possession. And I'm not going to live again like a man who's haunted. I'm not going to live with a ghost in my mind, with a ghost walking on my nerves as if they were a tight-rope, a ghost outside the window of my eyes and just beyond my fingers! I want reality. I want you, in my arms as well as in my mind, and I want the Church and the Law to seal you there.'

She answered nothing to that, and I went on talking, but I don't think she listened very closely, for presently she interrupted and asked me, 'Where did the gander go?'

'Down the burn towards the loch,' I told her.

'That's where he came from. He came here about a month ago, and killed the old one. The gander we had before, I mean.'

'He won't come back,' I said. 'He's had enough of you, after the way you handled him.'

She turned to the window, the one that opens into the yard, and looked out, saying nothing. I went behind her and put my arms round her. She tried to push me away, but with no determination in her movement, and I talked some more. She listened to me now, and presently turned and faced me, and said yes.

The next morning I began my new life of work and responsibility.

I bought a boat, a heavily built, round-bellied dinghy, ten-and-a-half-foot keel and in need of paint, for £18. 10*s*. Two days later I took a summer visitor out fishing and made fifteen shillings for six hours' easy work. It was a good fishing loch, and there were visitors in the islands again for the first time since 1939. I could look forward to three or four days' work a week, and as trout were selling for 2*s*. 9*d*. a pound I sent home for my own rod and tackle, and did quite well on my unemployed days in addition to enjoying them. I could have done still better with night-lines and an otter at dusk and a little caution, but I like fishing too much to cheat at it.

I was still living with the schoolmaster, for £2. 10*s*. a week, but our relations became a little cooler when his wife discovered that I was sleeping out. That didn't worry me, however, for my happiness that summer was like the moon and the stars, shining and beyond the reach of malice.

It puzzled me a little that I couldn't persuade Lydia to settle a date for the wedding, as I thought there might be a proper reason for it before long, but when I once spoke of it more seriously than usual, she said, 'We're perfectly happy as we are. I don't see why we should bother. Not yet, at any rate. And I'll have to explain to mother, and she's difficult sometimes.'

'I'll do any explaining that's necessary.'

'No, no! You must leave that to me. You won't say anything to her, will you?'

I said I wouldn't. She asked very little of me—she never has asked much—and neither then nor now could I refuse her anything. She had made a good pretence of surrendering, but my surrender went deeper. I had become the roof and the walls within which she lived, but she was the soul of the house. I thought of Jim whenever I looked up at the Kirk hill and saw Norquoy's farm on the slope of it, but to think of him didn't make me feel guilty now. I was no longer obsessed by him, and if a new obsession had taken his place, I had no cause to grumble against it. So June and July went quickly by in that happiness and in good weather, though not settled weather, for the island skies are always changeable, till one day in mid-August, when I came ashore in a rising wind, colder than it had been for weeks, the old woman met me and without a word of greeting said, 'You'd better come home to your tea.'

'That's very kind of you,' I said, and pulled the boat up and took out the two trout which were all I had caught. 'Would you like these?' I asked.

'It's a poor return for a day's work,' she said, though they were good fish, the better one a little over the pound, and slipped them into the pockets of the old raincoat she was wearing without a word of thanks. She had a man's cap on her head, and boots like a ploughman's. We walked along the road together, not saying much, and tea was a silent meal but a good one. She or Lydia had newly baked bere bannocks and white bannocks, there was sweet butter and salt butter, and I ate a duck's egg and the half of a stewed cock-chicken. Then, when we had finished, she said, 'Lydia tells me that you're wanting to be married.'

'It's what I've been wanting for the last two months and more,' I told her.

'She couldn't agree, and you wouldn't expect her to, until she'd spoken to her mother about it,' said the old woman grimly. 'She's a good girl, and it's a treasure that you're getting.'

I told her, humbly, that I was well aware of that.

'You've been a soldier, she says?'

'For six years I was.'

'I'm glad of that,' she cried, nodding her head. 'It's an ill world we live in, and there's times when the soldiers are all we can depend on, though it's a fool's trade if you look at it squarely.'

I had nothing to say to that, and she went on briskly: 'Well, if you're going to be married you'll be married in a decent manner, with the neighbours there to see it, and something good enough for them to remember too.'

'A wedding,' I said, 'is a woman's affair. I'm willing to be married in any way that suits Lydia. If she wants a big wedding, we'll have it. I've got about a hundred and sixty pounds in the bank—'

'We're not asking you for money,' said the old woman. 'It's not a pauper you're marrying, no, faith! nor anything like poverty neither.'

She went to an old black wooden desk that stood in a corner of the kitchen, with a calendar pinned above it, and took a bank pass-book from a pigeon-hole stuffed with papers. 'Look at that,' she said, and held it open in front of me.

I was flabbergasted. It had never occurred to me that they could have any money at all, but the pass-book showed a credit of £1,207.

'Eight hundred and fifteen pounds of that is Lydia's own money,' said the old woman. 'Five hundred pounds came to her when she was born, and the rest is the interest which I've never touched and never shall. Her money will be hers to spend as she wants when she's of age—you've got three years to wait, so you needn't go to market yet—and the wedding I'll pay for out of my own.'

She gave me a dram then, and took one herself. Just the one

each—it was the first time I had tasted whisky since that night at the Norquoys'—and then she put the bottle away in a cupboard with some fancy tumblers and glass dishes. She went out to the byre after that, to milk their two cows, and left Lydia and me together. Lydia had hardly spoken a word since I came in.

The following Sunday the banns were read in the Parish Church, and a few days later the old woman showed me the invitation cards she had had printed for the wedding. She hadn't done it cheaply, that was clear. They were a good thick board with gilt edges, and they read:

Miss Thomasina Manson
requests the pleasure of your company
at the wedding of her daughter
Lydia
to Mr Robert Lacey Tyndall
in the Ladyfirth Parish Hall
at 6 p.m. on Wednesday, September 6th
R.S.V.P. *Dancing*

I said they had a very dignified appearance, and so they had if you weren't so hidebound by convention as to be startled by the prefix to the mother's name. The old woman was very proud of them, and propped one up on the chimney-piece. Then Lydia and I sat down at the kitchen table and began to write in names and address envelopes. The old woman had prepared a list, and there were two hundred and eighteen names on it. But by then I was beyond surprise.

I had no difficulty in dissuading my own parents from coming. I had always been the unwanted member of my family, and I had disillusioned them so often that they could guess the disappointment they would find in my wedding. They had grown accustomed to my disappointing them. I had never enjoyed teaching in an elementary school in Falkirk—that was due to my falling in love, at the age of nineteen, with a female Socialist with red hair and the sort of figure that, in a jersey, is like an incitement to riot—but they were shocked by my choice of a profession. They were less perturbed when, later, I went to sea as a deck-hand on a tramp steamer. They didn't like that, but they regarded it as an escapade. In comparison with the rest of the family I was, of course, an utter failure, for both my brothers had gone to Oxford and done well there, and my sister had married the junior partner in a highly regarded firm of stockbrokers. When Archie, my elder brother, was given an O.B.E. my father was much better pleased than when I got my D.C.M. Neither he nor my mother made any serious offer to come to the wedding. I used to get drunk, when I was younger, and once or twice I had caused them serious embarrassment, so I suppose they thought I should get high, loud, and truculent, and make a spectacle of myself. My father sent Lydia a dressing-case, for which she could discover no purpose at all, and me a cheque for £25. But he missed something by not coming himself.

The old woman wore a black dress that had belonged to her mother, and a man's cap. Not the old ragged tweed one she usually wore, but a new black one such as countrymen sometimes wear at a funeral. She sat in a high-backed chair beside the band, and it was easy enough to guess her thoughts. 'I bore my child without benefit of clergy or the neighbours' goodwill,' she was thinking, 'but my child, by God! will have all the favour and fair wishes that money can buy. My child will be wedded as well as bedded, and no one will forget it.'

And no one who saw her will forget Lydia that night. I realised that I still had things to learn, for though I had doted on her beauty, now I was humbled by it. By her beauty and her dignity. I stood beside her, while the Minister was reading the service, and felt like a Crusader keeping his vigil. The schoolmaster was my best man, though his wife hadn't wanted him to be, and I could hear him breathing, hoarsely, as if in perplexity. He ate little more than I did at supper, and I could eat nothing. I danced twice with Lydia, and the rest of the time stood like a moon-calf while people talked to me. But Lydia was never off the floor, and all night her mother, in the high-backed chair beside the band, sat with a look that was simultaneously grim and gloating.

There was a great crowd there, the fiddlers were kept hard at it, and the wedding was well spoken of. Nearly everyone who had been invited had come, and thirty or forty more as well. All the Norquoys were there, but John and his wife left about two o'clock. Before he went he said to me, 'I'm very glad that you've become one of us, and I hope you'll settle down happily here. You were a good friend to Jim, and if I can help you in any way, be sure and tell me.'

'There's no one can help me more,' I told him, 'than by wishing that as I am tonight, so I may continue.'

Lydia came to say good-bye to them while we were speaking, and after they had gone she said, 'Jim Norquoy was always my mother's favourite among the boys in the parish. She used to tell him that he mustn't be in a hurry to get married, but wait till I grew up and see what he thought of me before going farther afield.'

The schoolmaster came and asked her to dance, and I went outside. The hall was hot and men's faces shone as if they had been oiled, but the night air was cool. There was no wind and the sky was a veiled purple with a little haze round the moon. I could hear the slow boom and dulled thunder of the Atlantic on the west cliffs, four miles away. West of the cliffs there was no land nearer than Labrador, and for a few minutes I felt dizzy, as if I hung in space over a gulf as great as that. The old woman had meant to marry her to Jim, but Jim had died, and I had fallen heir to his portion. 'You won't find it easy to go back,' he had said, as if he knew that another fate would claim me. Nor had I gone back to my own country, but come instead to his, to do what I had to.

I remember sailing once, near Oban, in a little yacht I had hired, and getting into a strong tide and being carried swiftly past a rocky shore though the wind had fallen and the sail hung loose. The moon was pulling the tide to sea, and I was going with it. I was helpless in the grip of the moon, and I felt the excitement of its power. The sensation came back to me as I stood outside the hall where the band was playing, and listened to the Atlantic waves, driven by the wind of invisible distant clouds to march against our cliffs. I was moon-drawn again, though I could not see my star. But I knew then that I had come north to the islands, though innocent of any purpose, to take Jim's place, who should have married her but had been killed instead. That was my doom; and I wanted no other. In a little while I went in again and saw the old woman. She was satisfied.

It was nearly seven in the morning when the wedding finished, with the drink done, the band exhausted, and the guests hearing in their imagination the lowing of their cows waiting to be milked. Lydia and her mother and I walked home together, and as soon as we arrived the two of them changed into old clothes and went out to the byre.

Her wedding, however, wasn't the only time when I saw Lydia well-dressed. She had gone to the town day after day, and bought clothes in plenty. Her more ancient garments were thrown away, and her everyday appearance was now smart enough by country standards. She told me one night that it was her mother who had insisted on her dressing like a scarecrow, and often enough wouldn't even let her wash her face for fear of bringing men about the house.

The weeks passed with nothing to spoil our happiness, and I got a job under the County Council, driving a lorry. The mornings and the evenings grew darker, and after a great gale had blown for three days from the north-west the winter came. It was cold and stormy, but after the wildest days the sky might suddenly clear for an evening of enormous calm with a lemon-coloured sky in the west and little tranquil clouds high in the zenith. After the harvest had been gathered and the cattle brought in, the country became strangely empty and its colours were dim. But I liked it. Wherever you stood you had a long view of land and water, and though the sky might be violent, the lines of the hills were gentle.

When I came home one evening about the middle of November, the old woman told me that Lydia wasn't well. There was nothing seriously wrong, but she would have to stay in bed for a few weeks, and she wanted her—the old woman—to make up a bed for herself in the ben-room. I would have to sleep in the loft.

'The doctor has seen her?' I asked.

'No,' said the old woman. 'I don't believe in doctors.'

I had a general knowledge that accidents might occur in pregnancy, but no precise information, and I couldn't make a physiological picture in my mind. I thought of blood and mortality, and the old woman saw that I was frightened.

'Don't fret yourself,' she said. 'She's not going to die yet, nor for many a long year to come. She'll be a brisk, stirring woman long after you're in the kirkyard.'

'Is it only rest that she needs?' I asked then, thinking vaguely of some anatomical bolt or washer that might have shaken loose, and needed immobility to re-establish itself.

'Rest,' said the old woman, 'a long rest and a lot of patience. Now go in and see her, but don't worry her with questions.'

Lydia was pale and she had been crying, but when I knelt beside the bed she put her arms round my neck and told me, as her mother had done, that I mustn't worry. And I didn't worry long. Two or three days, I suppose, and then it began to seem natural that she should have to stay in bed. I took to reading to her when I came home from work. My mother had sent a lot of things that belonged to me, including a box of books. I never had many books, I can't remember having had much time for reading when I was younger, but there were some good stories of adventure that I had enjoyed: *Typhoon* and *The Nigger of the Narcissus*, *Kim*, and *The White Company*, and Trelawny's *Adventures of a Younger Son*, *Kidnapped*, and *The Forest Lovers*, and *Revolt in the Desert*, and so on. I've read them all to Lydia at one time or another, and she seemed to enjoy them. I liked reading them again. It was Conrad who was responsible for my going to sea after I had had a year of teaching in Falkirk, and couldn't stand it any longer. I made three or four trips to the Baltic and the Mediterranean in tramp steamers, and a voyage to Australia as a steward in a Blue Funnel boat. But when the war began I had had enough of the sea, so I joined the Army. Lawrence of Arabia may have had something to do with that, or it may have been Kipling.

Only one thing happened to annoy me in the next two or three months, and that occurred one morning when I was taking a load of road-metal to a secondary road we were patching, and drove past the old woman's cottage. It was a dark day, as dark as gunmetal, and the rain was blowing across country in blustering squalls. As I came near the cottage I saw Lydia crossing the road, leaning against the wind with a half-buttoned waterproof flapping round her, and a zinc pail on her arm. I pulled up hard and jumped out.

'Are you trying to kill yourself?' I shouted. 'You're supposed to be in bed, aren't you?'

For the first time since the morning when I'd seen her throwing the gander out of doors, she was angry. Her face seemed to grow narrower than usual, and her lips as hard as marble. She stared straight at me—her eyes are grey, with sometimes a flash of blue in them—and said fiercely, 'I can look after myself. You go about your business, and I'll take care of mine.'

'You're supposed to be in bed,' I said again, stupidly and sullenly. There were some eggs in her pail. They had a hen-house across the road, and she had been feeding the hens and gathering what eggs the draggled birds had the strength to lay in that weather. 'It's madness for you to be stooping and bending and carrying buckets of meal,' I said.

'I wanted some fresh air,' she said. 'I can't stay in bed for ever.'

'Your mother ought to know better, even if you don't. I'm going in to see her,' I said.

'You'll do no such thing!' she cried. 'You leave mother and me to manage our own affairs. Don't you interfere, or you'll be sorry for it. And now go! Go, I tell you. You've got work to do, haven't you? Well, go and do it!'

She was ten years younger than I and a good head shorter, but her words came like the smack of an open hand on my face, palm and knuckles, this way and that, and I stepped back, muttering some limp excuse, and got into my lorry again.

I brought her some oranges at night, that I'd bought from a sailor, and we said no more about it. But two or three days passed before she asked me to read to her again, and then for another six or seven weeks we were calm and happy, though the loft was a cold place to sleep in, and sometimes when the moon shone through the sky-light I woke up to see the rafters and their black shadows, and thought for a moment or two that I was still in the Army, making the best of it in a deserted farmhouse, and once I stretched out my arm to feel if Jim was beside me.

About the middle of February I began to worry about arrangements for her lying-in. Or, to put it more accurately, to worry because no arrangements had been made. I talked with the old woman, who wouldn't listen to me, or wouldn't listen seriously, but I didn't say anything to Lydia in case I should upset her again. And then, before we had come to any decision, I got a telegram from Edinburgh to say that my father had had a stroke, and would I come at once. Archie, my elder brother, was with some Government commission in Washington, and Alastair, the younger, was still in the Army in Rangoon. I didn't want to go, I had never got on well with my father, but the old woman said that if he died without seeing me I would be saddled with regret, like a heavy curse on me, for all the days of my life, and Lydia was plainly shocked, as if by the sight of some fearful wickedness, when I said that he could die as happily by himself as with me holding his hand. So, after a day of argument, I went to Edinburgh, and for a week my mother and I were uncomfortable in each other's presence, and my father slowly recovered. I had been wrong when I said that he wouldn't want to hold my hand. He did. I sat by his bedside for two or three hours every day, and sometimes, with a lot of difficulty, he managed to speak a few words. I was glad, then, that I had done what Lydia wanted. One day my mother told me that he meant to give me a present, and when I went upstairs he smiled and pointed to a leather case that lay on a chair beside him. It was his favourite gun, a fine piece by Holland, far too good for a man who lived in a cottage and drove a lorry for the County Council.

I said good-bye to them in a hurry when a letter came from Lydia to say that she had given birth to a daughter the day after I left her. 'I am very well and so is she,' she wrote, 'and I didn't want to disturb you with my news when you had so much to harass you already. But now, if your father is no longer in danger, I hope you will be able to come home again.'

I said good-bye, but I didn't leave them for another fortnight. My father had a second stroke, and while I was sitting in the train and waiting for it to start, my sister came running along the platform, looking for me, to tell me I mustn't go. He lived for more than a week, but never regained proper consciousness, and then I waited for the funeral. I read Lydia's letter again and again, and two others that she wrote, both of which were full of news about the child. 'I think she may be the most beautiful baby in the world,' she said.

In my mind, when I saw her, there was no doubt at all. She had the perfection of a doll that some dead sculptor—a sculptor too great to be alive in this world—had carved in love from a rosy-veined alabaster. She was very small, and perfect. She was sleeping, and

I had a monstrous fear that she might never wake. I put out my hand to touch her, but Lydia caught my wrist and shook her head. 'Let her sleep.'

I made no mention of something I found, a day or so after my return, for I couldn't be certain, then, that there was any meaning in it, and if there was I didn't want to think about it. The sight of it, in the grass, struck deep into my mind like a forester's wedge that splits the fibres of a tree, and for a minute or two I stood trembling. But there was no sense in it, and I didn't want to curse myself with a madman's doubt. I wanted to be at peace, and dote upon the child, so I denied the meaning of it and let it drown in the daily ebb and flow, the tidal waters of common life. It sank into the darker parts of my mind like a body into the deep sea with a sack of coal lashed to its ankles, as I had seen a sailor buried once. Committed to the deep, as they said.

The child grew quickly, and at six months she was like an Italian picture of a cherub, her head covered with small tight curls, paler than gold, and eyes the colour of a hare-bell. The old woman said she could understand already every word we said, and neither Lydia nor I was very serious about contradicting her. For we all thought of her in a way that I can't suppose is usual even in the fondest of parents. It wasn't only with pride of possession and a flood of affection whenever we looked at her, but with a kind of glee that never grew stale or sour in the remembrance of its excess.

In May I gave up my job but told the Road Surveyor that I should be glad to have it again in October. He wasn't too favourably disposed to my plans at first, but I had served him well; he was a fisherman himself and knew the compulsion of it, so after a little argument he agreed to let me go and take me back again when autumn came. I painted my boat, put my rod together, and had a week's fine sport before the first of the summer visitors arrived. Then, for three or four days a week till September, I watched my patrons fish, and calculated by the end of September that my own average, on the intervening days, was about as good as the best of theirs. But I fished longer hours than they did, and the price of trout was still high.

Sometimes I used to wake up at night, with Lydia beside me, and see the darkness about us like the mouth of a huge engulfing fear. I had no right to be so happy. No one had such a right. It was like oil on the top step, it was like a German white flag with a sniper lying beside it, it was like a spider telegraphing *Walk-into-my-parlour* over his lethal gossamer. I would lie in the darkness, open-eyed, for perhaps an hour, drenched in fear, but in the morning, waking and turning to

Lydia, and then playing with the child for half an hour, my happiness would come back like the returning tide. I couldn't help it. They were both so beautiful.

Once, when the child was about fifteen months old, I woke in the first phase of one of my frightened moods, and saw her standing up at the end of her crib. She had taken off her nightgown and she was poised with her head tilted up, her arms out and her hands resting on the side-rails of the crib as if she were addressing a public meeting; or facing her judges, unafraid. There was a late moon that night, and though the window was small there was light in the room. But that wasn't the light that irradiated the child. Her light, unless I'm the simple victim of some cuckoo-born delusion, came from within. Now Lydia's body, on that first morning when I saw her throwing the gander out of doors, was gleaming like mother-of-pearl, or a pearl on velvet, with a light of its own; but never since then had I seen her better than a milky white.—As white as milk and as smooth as curds, but not with that radiance.—Yet now the child, naked in the darkness, was gleaming with such a light. It was no brighter than the moonlight dimmed by white curtains, but it wasn't in the overflow of moonlight she was shining. It was in a light of her own.

I slipped out of bed, quietly so as not to waken Lydia, and said to the child, 'You'll catch cold, standing up like that. You ought to be asleep.' She looked at me for a moment, as if surprised to see me there, and then twined her arms round my neck and kissed me. I put on her nightgown and obediently she slid down between the blankets.

A year went by and part of another. I came, I suppose, to take my good fortune for granted, and my happiness perhaps lost something of its fine edge and became a rounder contentment. Time, when I look back, seems to have gone very quickly and as smoothly as the water curving over a weir in a polished flow without break or interruption. We were on friendly terms with our neighbours, I saw the Norquoys and the schoolmaster every week or two, and gradually I came to think of the islands as my own place, my proper environment in which I had become an accepted part. But my real life was lived on the old woman's croft, at home. My senses were livelier there, my feelings more profound, my consciousness of life more widely awake.

The old woman could work as well as a man. She could plough and harrow, and between us, when harvest came, we cut and bound and stacked four acres of oats. Lydia looked after the poultry, and singled turnips, took her fork to hayfield and harvest, as well as doing housework and tending the child. We were rarely idle and often our work was hard, though I don't remember that we found it unduly hard because we did it all in our own time, and we had no master to drive us or reproach us or thank us. I couldn't spend so much time fishing as I had done when I first lived there, but I enjoyed working on the land so long as it wasn't continual work.

In the winter months, when I drove a lorry again, I used to read in the evenings. Both Lydia and her mother liked the tales of adventure best. I had some other books, by Jane Austen and Dickens and Galsworthy, that I had never read myself, but we didn't care for them. It was a tale of far-off lands, with the noise of a dangerously running sea, or the thud of a sword going stiffly home, the crack of a rifle, that the women liked. There was something fierce in them, an appetite for deeds, that couldn't show itself in their ordinary life, but was there all the time and came out of hiding a little when I read to them. But domestic scenes, and comedy and conversation, bored them.

Well, this good easy life continued—it wasn't physical ease that characterised it, not in those northern winters, but we were all contented—till the child was in her third year, and then one summer day when there fell a flat calm and the loch lay like a mirror, pocked with rising trout, but not one that would look at a fly, I came ashore at midday and on the road a little way past the house I saw five carts standing, three of them loaded with peat and two empty. The loaded ones, coming home from the hill, were John Norquoy's, and the horses between their shafts stood motionless, with drooping heads, their shoulders dark with sweat. The empty carts belonged to a neighbour of his who had started earlier and was on his way back to the hill for a second load. His horses were restless, tossing their heads and pecking at the road with steel-shod hooves. But their drivers paid no attention to them. John Norquoy and two others were squatting on their heels, on the road, and two were leaning against the nearest cart, and in the midst of them, her hands behind her back like a girl reciting poetry at a village prize-giving, was the child. She was talking, and they were listening.

I waited for a little while, some forty yards away, but none of them turned a head in my direction, and when I went up and spoke to them, some looked sheepish and embarrassed, but John Norquoy, still on his heels, said to me, 'I could wish you had stayed away and not interrupted us. It's a real diversion, listening to her.'

I picked the child up and asked her, 'What were you talking about?'

'I was telling them a story,' she said, and when I set her on my shoulder she turned and cried to them, 'Good-bye now!'

I don't fully know why, but this small incident annoyed me at the time of it and worried me later. I told Lydia and her mother what I had seen, and said they would have to take better care of the child, for I wasn't going to have her grow up to believe she must always be the centre of attention. I didn't like to see a child showing-off, I said. 'Perhaps,' I went on, 'we ourselves are to blame, for we've always made much of her—too much, I dare say—and let her see that we're proud of her. But we'll have to change our ways if they're going to have a bad effect.'

'We could change our ways a dozen times without changing her,' said Lydia.

'That's nonsense,' I said. 'A child is the product, very largely, of what she's taught. I used to be a teacher myself—'

The old woman interrupted me with a cackle of laughter. 'It would take more than you,' she said, 'to make an ordinary bairn out of that one.'

Then I lost my temper, and for the first time we had a proper quarrel. We had had differences of opinion before, and sometimes grown hot about them, but this was different. Now we grew bitter and said things to each other that were meant to hurt, and did. The argument didn't last long, but at night, when Lydia and I were alone, it flared up again. It was she who began it, this time, and when I saw that she was bent on making trouble—her face put on its fierce and narrow look, her lips were hard—I smacked her soundly on the side of her head, and before she could recover I laid her across my knee and gave her an old-fashioned beating with a slipper.

A week or two passed before she forgave me. Or, perhaps, before she openly forgave me. I knew her fairly well by that time, and I don't think she bore a grudge against me for the beating, but because she didn't want to admit defeat she maintained an appearance of hostility till the affair could be regarded as a drawn battle. Then for a week or two we were in love again with a new fervour.

It was towards the end of February, a few days before the child's third birthday, that the gander came back, and I realised that fear of his return, an unregarded but persistent fear, like the white wound-scar on my leg that I never thought of unless I was tired or there came a hard frost, had always been with me.

There had been a heavy snow, piled into great drifts by a strong wind, and for a few days work on the roads came to a stop and I had a winter holiday. The sun came out, the sky cleared to a thin bright blue, and the land lay still as death under a flawless white surface that gave to every little hill and hollow the suavity of ancient sculpture.

The loch within a fringe of crackling ice, a darker blue than the sky, was framed in white, and a few swans like small ice-floes swarm in a narrow bay. On land there was nothing stirring, and the smoke rose straight from the chimneys of diminished houses.

I had gone out with my gun—the fine piece by Holland—to try and shoot a late hare, and after following tracks in the snow for an hour or two I had got a couple. I was on my way home again when I saw, by the burnside a few hundred yards from the house, the child in her blue cap and her little blue coat. The burn, bank-high, was running strongly, and I hurried towards her with a sudden feeling, as of a man caught among thorns, of nervousness and annoyance that she should be there with no one to look after her.

She stood with her back to me, in her favourite position, her hands clasped behind her, and not until I had come within a few yards of her did I see the gander. He was afloat in a little smooth backwater of the burn, but as soon as he caught sight of me he came ashore, his broad feet ungainly on the snow but moving fast, and I thought he was going to attack me. The child turned and I called to her: 'Come here, Nell! Come here at once!'

But she stayed where she was and the gander came up behind her and opened his wings so that she stood by his breast within a screen of feathers as hard as iron and as white as the snow beyond them. It must have been the whiteness of the fields, with the bright haze of the sun upon them, that dazzled me and deluded me into thinking that the gander had grown to three times or four times his proper size. His neck seemed a column of marble against the sky, his beak was bronze, and his black eyes reflected the sun like shafts from a burning-glass. A low rumbling noise, like the far-off surge of the sea on a pebble-beach, came from his swollen throat.

I'm not a coward and I couldn't have been frightened of a bird. It was snow-sickness, I suppose, that set my brain swimming and undid the strength of my knees, so that I thought I was going to faint. I remember seeing the same sort of thing happen to a soldier in Italy, in the mountains in winter-time. He was a friend of my own, a big fellow as tall as myself. He stumbled and fell, and the strength went out of him. We thought he had gone blind, but after we got him into a house and had given him some brandy, he was all right.

When I came to myself and knew what I was doing, I was on my hands and knees, crawling, and my hands were on fire with the friction of the snow. I had to crawl another twenty or thirty yards before I felt fit to stand up, and then I staggered and stumbled as if I were drunk. I wasn't far from home by then, and I rested for a while in the barn.

When I felt better I went into the kitchen. The child was there already, and as soon as I came in she ran towards me, and pushing me into a chair climbed on to my knee. She began to pat my face and play with my hair, as if trying to comfort me.

Presently I went out again, and found my gun and the two hares where I had dropped them. There was no sign of the gander. They were big hares, both of them, and I took them into the back-kitchen and got a basin, and cleaned and skinned them. But all the time I was thinking: Well, this is the end of pretence. There's no point or purpose in denial now. But what am I going to do?

The women were on the other side, so I couldn't talk to them. Lydia was in love with me, as I with her—there was no doubt about that—and the old woman liked me well enough; but now I knew the dividing-line between us, and I couldn't cross it. But I had to talk to someone.

John Norquoy wouldn't do. I had made a confession to him before, and it was too soon to make another. Nor would he believe me if I did. I had no great faith in the schoolmaster either, but I had to do something, say something to someone, and after tea I set out for his house, walking heavily through the snow, and if he was surprised to see me he didn't show it, but made me welcome. He had spent three or four idle days, with only a dozen children able to come to school, and in his own way he too may have been glad of a chance to talk for a while. His wife left us to ourselves.

I didn't know how to begin, but he helped me. He had been reading a book whose author was trying to prove that modern war was the result of conflicting demands for oil; and he, full of brand-new information, was ready to argue that war had always had economic causes, and no other causes. I didn't believe him, and said so. It was ideas that made war, I said. If an economist went to war, with material gains in view, it was because he was a bad economist, a quack and a charlatan; for any practical economist knows that war is likely to waste far more than it can win. 'But if men believe in ideas, of power and glory, or religious ideas, or even social ideas,' I went on, 'they may go to war for the simple reason that idealists don't count the cost of what they want. They go to war, that is, in despite of the economic arguments against it. And they're always against it.'

We talked away on those lines, getting warmer all the time, and the schoolmaster, really enjoying himself now, went back into history, back and back, till he had proved to his own satisfaction that the Peloponnesian War was due entirely to the imperialism of Athens, and the determination of the Athenians to brook no interference with their mercantile marine.

'And did Agamemnon and Menelaus,' I asked him, 'go to war to win the right of exploiting mineral resources in the windy plains of Troy?'

'If we really knew anything about the Trojan War,' he said, 'we should probably have to admit that that indeed was the cause of it; or something very like that.'

'It's not the generally accepted cause,' I said.

'According to the fable,' he answered, 'the purpose of the war was to recover, from the person who had carried her off, the erring wife of Menelaus. And who was she? Zeus, who never existed, is said to have visited a fictitious character called Leda in the guise of a swan, and the result of their impossible union was a legendary egg out of which a fabulous being named Helen was incredibly hatched. Helen, says the story, grew to miraculous beauty, married Menelaus, and ran away with Paris. You can't seriously regard a woman who wasn't even a woman, but only a myth, as the cause of a war.'

'It lasted for ten years,' I said.

'I've been talking history,' he said. 'You really shouldn't try to answer me with mythology.'

'How does a myth begin?' I asked.

'How does a novelist go to work?' he demanded.

'By drawing on his experience, I suppose.'

He got up impatiently and fetched a bottle of whisky and two glasses from the sideboard. Then he went out for a jug of water, and when he came back I said, 'What's worrying me is this. If a man discovers something within the scope of his own life that will eventually be a cause of war between nations, what can he do about it?'

'What could such a thing be?' he asked.

'I can't explain.'

'But it's impossible,' he said. 'War hasn't a simple origin or a single cause that you can take in your hand like a trophy to be fought for in a tournament. You have to consider the whole economy of the rival countries, their geographical situation, the growth of their population—'

'And their ideas,' I said. 'Their leaders' desire for power, or a new religion, or a woman.'

'You're going back to your myth,' he said.

'You fought in one war, I fought in another. My experience of war is that you fight for five years, and at the end of it you see your best friend killed beside you, and you're glad—you're glad, by God!—that it's he who's dead, and not you. I don't want another war.'

'Well,' he said, 'whatever starts the next war, it won't be a woman. You can put that fear out of your head.'

'I'm not so sure,' I said.

The argument went on for a long time, and gave me no satisfaction. But talking did me good, and we drank a lot of whisky. When I got home I felt calmer, but very old, as if I were a character in a Greek play who saw the enormous tragedy that was coming, and could do nothing but wait for it, and then abide it.

Lydia and her mother were in bed, and I got a lantern from the back-kitchen. I lighted it and went to the stable. Meg, the old black mare, was twenty-seven or twenty-eight, and we dared not let her lie down in her stall for fear she could never get up again, so every night I put a broad canvas sling under her belly, to take the weight off her legs, and she slept standing. She woke as I went in, whinnying softly, and turned her head to watch me.

I stood on a wheelbarrow in the empty stall beside her, and reaching to the top of the wall, where the rafters go in, took down what I had hidden there, and never looked at since, nearly three years before. I had made a parcel of it, with string and brown paper, and now it was covered with thick cobweb. I brushed off the web and cut the string. For a moment or two I held in my hands the cigarette-box—covered with a fine Florentine leather stamped in gold, that I had taken from one of those little shops on the Ponte Vecchio—and then I opened it.

Inside lay the broken shell of a big white egg. I fitted the larger fragments together, and judged it to have been about seven inches long and rather more than four inches in diameter at the widest part.

That was what I had picked up, after coming home from my father's funeral, in the long grass under the ben-room window. It may seem funny to you, but you're not in my position.

The Dancers

Mr G. P. Pomfret was a wealthy man and the centre of as large a circle of friends and relations as the junior partner in a prosperous brewery might reasonably expect to be. But, until he disappeared, he was not famous. Then he became a household word, and the five members of his family—consanguineous, allied, and presumptively allied—who disappeared with him, all earned pages in those indefatigable supplements to our national biography, the Sunday newspapers. For with Mr Pomfret there also vanished Mrs Pomfret his wife; Lt.-Commander Hugo Disney and Mrs Disney (*née* Pomfret); Miss Joan Pomfret; and Mr George Otto Samways, her fiancé.

The circumstances of their joint occultation were remarkable, and as the geographical environment was sufficiently and yet not immeasurably remote from the more advertised holiday haunts of man, the affair took to itself a halo of romance that was entirely different from the hectic nimbus that ever and again makes some obscure police-court luminous.

It has been said that Mr Pomfret was wealthy. He had inherited a large number of shares in an excellent brewery and with them a sanguine and speculative temperament. His fortune persuaded the members of his family, initial and contributory, readily to accept a certain imperiousness of temper which Mr Pomfret occasionally exhibited; and so when one evening early in June he said, from the top of his dinner-table, 'I intend, subject to your approval, to take you all with me on a somewhat unusual holiday', his household (including Lt.-Commander Hugo Disney) and the solitary guest (Mr George Otto Samways) accepted the invitation in the manner of a royal command.

'Where are we going?' asked Joan, adeptly peeling her peach.

'To Orkney, my dear,' replied Mr Pomfret, and surveyed with benign amusement the expressions of surprise which impinged upon or flitted across the faces of his domestic audience.

Lt.-Commander Disney alone showed no amazement. 'That's excellent,' he said heartily. 'I've meant for long enough to go back there.'

Orkney is worthy of some attention. The islands have a romantic appeal as the home of lost races. The Vikings settled there, and before the Vikings there was a mysterious people, Picts or such, little men who vanished but left many traces of their occupation. At some time Culdee monks from Ireland went there; and went again as silently. Stewart earls ruled the islands like young pagan emperors. When the Great War began the British Fleet chose Scapa Flow, in the heart of the Orkneys, as its headquarters and battle haven. Later the German Fleet also rested there; but at the still bottom, not on the wind-flawed surface of the waters.

It was, however, the excellence of the trout-fishing which led Lt.-Commander Disney to applaud Mr Pomfret's decision. He had spent the less active intervals in three years of naval warfare in Scapa Flow, and had become acquainted with the opportunities of sport which the island lochs offered to a fisherman robust enough to disregard occasional inclemencies of weather. Frequently he had spoken to Mr Pomfret of brown trout and sea trout, praising their strain of fishy pugnacity and the delicate savour of their flesh; praising too the lure of sunny waters under a canopy of brilliant sky all painted with cloud galleons, porpoises and swimming dolphins of cloud, and at evening glorious with the barred crimson and gold, the errant greens, the daffodil hues, the rosy outflung feathers, of the sun sliding bedwards behind the enormous wall of the Atlantic. And these conversations, moving like yeast in Mr Pomfret's brain, had finally given rise to this momentous decision.

It is unnecessary to consider the manner of the journey north, which was complicated. Mr Pomfret had rented for two months a large house called Swandale, in one of the seaward parishes in the northern part of the Mainland of Orkney; it was considered advisable to take, as well as his family, a motor car, his chauffeur, and three maids. The first week or so of their residence passed pleasantly enough. They were enraptured with the scenery, the vast stretches of ever-changing sea, the majestic cliffs loud with the ceaseless activity of gulls; they watched the diving gannets, the ludicrous earnest puffins, the graceful terns, and hysterical oyster-catchers. They were delighted with the shy and independent islanders. They enjoyed the novelty of peat fires blazing in an open hearth. Lt.-Commander Disney and Mrs Disney fished with notable success in the neighbouring lochs. Mr Pomfret walked and inquired diligently into local traditions and history. And Mrs Pomfret read the works of Lord Lytton, to which she was ineradicably addicted. Joan Pomfret and Otto Samways occupied themselves in ways apparently satisfactory, and certainly remote from the rest of the family.

The holiday would probably have continued on these pleasant

and harmless lines had it not been for the imaginative temperament (excited by love and romantic surroundings) of Miss Joan Pomfret. It suddenly occurred to her that they were rapidly approaching Midsummer Day.

Now the summer solstice has, or had, its appropriate festivals. In the northern parts of Britain the sun used indisputably to reign supreme, and, at such times as his presence blessed the earth almost throughout the circle of day and night, it was proper to honour him with dancing and other devout festivities. In Orkney he succeeds at Midsummer in banishing the thief of night for all but a dim hour or so from the dominion of his majesty. There is light on the islands, benign and irresistible, except for one or perhaps two shadowed hours in the cycle of twenty-four.

Something of this was in Joan's mind when she said over the marmalade one morning, 'Daddy, the day after tomorrow is Midsummer. Let's celebrate it properly.'

'How, my dear?' asked Mr Pomfret, putting down the toast which was within an inch of his mouth.

'By a midnight picnic. We'll spend the night on an island—on Eynhallow—and see the dawn come up before the afterglow is out of the sky. And we'll dance when the sun shows himself again.'

'I haven't danced for years,' said Mrs Pomfret pathetically, 'and don't you think the grass would be damp?'

'Tut!' said Mr Pomfret. 'Grass damp? Pouf!' Spousal resistance invariably excited him to action, and he had, it may be remembered, a sanguine nature.

'I should like a chance to watch the birds on Eynhallow,' said Lt.-Commander Disney. 'They're interesting in the early morning. And we could take plenty of rugs, and a flask, you know, in case it is cold.'

'Of course we could.' Mr Pomfret was in a singularly eupeptic mood that morning. He felt positively boyish. 'Do you remember, Mother'—he called Mrs Pomfret Mother when he felt particularly young and could think good-naturedly of her growing a little mature—'Do you remember that bicycling tour I did once in Cornwall? Excellent fun it was, Hugo. It must be twenty-five years ago, and I often wish that I had found an opportunity to repeat it. This idea of yours is splendid, Joan, my dear. Dancing to the Midsummer sun—Ha! I shall show you all how to dance. Hugo, my boy, will you see about a boat?'

Eynhallow is a small uninhabited island between the mainland of Orkney and the island of Rousay. It is surrounded by unruly tides, but to the fishermen who know them it is not difficult to land, provided the weather is calm. Those definitely in favour of the expedition were Mr Pomfret, Lt.-Commander Disney, Joan, and naturally, since Joan would be there, Otto Samways. Mrs Disney shrugged her shoulders and said, 'It will mean the first late night I've had for a fortnight and the first woollen undies I've worn for years. I don't mind, though.' Poor Mrs Pomfret sighed and returned to *The Last Days of Pompeii*.

Hugo Disney persuaded a local fisherman, John Corrigall, that it would be more profitable than lobster-fishing to sail the Pomfret party to Eynhallow and call for them on the following morning, and so the preliminaries of the excursion were successfully completed. John Corrigall was privately convinced that they were all mad—except Mrs Pomfret, whom he found to be an unwilling victim—but refrained from saying so, except in the privacy of his own family; for a madman's money is as good as that of a man dogmatically and indecently sane, and, indeed, more easily earned.

On Midsummer Eve then, after dinner, the Pomfrets set sail. They carried baskets of food, for a night in the open is a potent ally of hunger, but no instrument of fire, such as a primus stove, for that, Joan said, would be an insult to the omnipotence of the sun, who should rule alone. They took rugs and cushions, and Mrs Pomfret wore a fur coat and Russian boots. They set a portable gramophone—for they were to dance—in the stern of the boat, and Otto Samways carried two albums of records. There was a heavy cargo aboard when John Corrigall hauled his sheet and brought the boat's head round for Eynhallow. He landed them, without more incident than a faint protest from Mrs Pomfret, on a shingle beach, and left them.

And that is the last that has been seen of them.

When Corrigall returned to Eynhallow in the morning, he found the island deserted. He shouted, and there was no answer; he walked round the island, which is small, and found no trace of the midnight visitors. He sat on a rock and struggled heavily with thought, and then, because he was anxious to get back before the tide turned, he sailed home again.

It is, of course, an ingrained belief in the mind of the northern Scot that the English are a flighty, unreliable race. They travel far from home when there is no need to travel, they are wantonly extravagant (John Corrigall had been paid in advance), and their actions spring from impulse instead of emanating slowly from cautious deliberation. They are volatile (as the English say the French are volatile), and their volatility makes them difficult to understand. So John Corrigall said nothing, except to his wife, of the disappearance of the Pomfrets. He had no intention of making a fool of himself by raising what was possibly a false alarm, and the whole day, which might have been profitably spent on investigation, was wasted.

In the evening, the chauffeur, an energetic man when aroused, went to make inquiries, and was astounded to hear that his master had apparently vanished. With the decision of a man who had lived in cities and learnt, before he took to driving one, the art of evading motor-cars, he told a little girl who happened to be at hand to summon the village constable, and ordered Corrigall to make his boat ready for sea. The latter protested, for the wind and tide were at odds and a pretty sea was breaking round Eynhallow. But the chauffeur was like adamant, and drove the constable and John Corrigall to the shore, helped to push out the boat, and after a stormy crossing landed, wet through, on the island. A thorough search was made, and not a sign of the Pomfrets could be found; nothing, that is, except a little tag of bright metal which was found lying on the grass, the significance of which was unknown to Corrigall and the policeman, who had no experience of modern toilets, and to the chauffeur, who was virtuous and unmarried. Later it was identified simultaneously by the maids as the end, the catch or hatch as it were, of a stocking-suspender such as many ladies wear. If Miss Joan had been dancing vigorously, it might have sprung asunder from the rest of the article and fallen to the ground, they said.

The three maids became hysterical soon after they learnt of the mystery; John Corrigall went home to his bed, convinced that it did not concern him; the constable was useless, having encountered no such case in his previous professional experience; and it was left to the chauffeur to devise a course of action.

He persuaded the constable to cycle to Kirkwall, the capital and cathedral city of Orkney, and report to such superior officers as he might discover there. He insisted on the local telegraph office opening after hours, and sent an expensive message to the newspaper which guided the thought and chronicled the deeds of the town in which Mr Pomfret had prominently lived. And he made a careful inventory of everything that the unfortunate party had taken with them. Then he sat down to compose a long letter to the newspaper already mentioned.

The assistant-editor of the paper made instant and magnificent use of the chauffeur's telegram. Times were dull, and his chief was away on holiday. The chief sub-editor was a man of consummate craft and no conscience. Between them they splashed a throbbing, breath-taking story over the two main news columns. They flung across the page a streaming headline that challenged the hearts of their readers like a lonely bugle sounding on a frosty night. Eynhallow became a Treasure Island encircled by northern mists, and the sober citizens who read this strange story of the disappearance of people whom they knew so well (by sight), whose motor-cars they had envied, and whose abilities they had derided, felt creeping into their souls an Arctic fog of doubt, a cold hush of suspense, a breath of icy wind from the waste seas of mystery. Which was precisely the effect intended by the enterprising assistant-editor, and the highly competent sub-editor.

This was the beginning of the story which subsequently took all England by the ears, and echoed, thinly or tumultuously, in ribald, hushed, or strident accents, in railway carriages and on the tops of buses, at street-corners and over dinner-tables, at chamber-concerts and through brass-band recitals, in all places where two or three newspaper-readers were gathered together, and finally in one or two topically-inclined pulpits and behind the footlights of the variety stage.

The assistant-editor sent hurrying northwards a young and alert reporter, and it was not his fault that an emissary of a great London evening paper arrived in Orkney before him. For the latter travelled by aeroplane, the evening paper being wealthy and its editor having been noticeably impressed by the provincial report. The first general information, therefore, that Britain had of the Great Pomfret Mystery was a brightly written account of the long flight of Our Special Investigator.

Within twenty-four hours every self-respecting news-sheet in the country had published a map of Orkney, on which the approximate position of Eynhallow was surrounded by a black circle. The more erudite contributed brief historical sketches of the islands, and a few discovered that a church or monastery had once been built on the particular islet of mystery. Brief descriptions of Mr Pomfret with at least the names, Christian names, and ages of his party appeared in all the papers. Two offered ready-made solutions to the problem, three laughed at it, and one rashly cited as a parallel case the vanishing crew of the *Marie Celeste*.

On the following day a Paymaster-Commander wrote to say that he had once, during the War, motored from Scapa to Swandale (Mr Pomfret's house) and distinctly remembered seeing Eynhallow. 'A charming, sea-girt, romantic-looking island', he wrote, 'with the appearance of having withstood a thousand storms and blossomed with a thousand green springtimes.' Subsequently an Admiral, who had also been in Scapa during the War, corroborated this, writing to say that he had seen the island himself. Thereafter its actual existence was not doubted.

In a short time photographs began to appear, photographs of Mr Pomfret and his family, one of Lt.-Commander Disney in uniform, and a charming picture of Miss Joan Pomfret playing in a local tennis tournament. The two reporters sent long descriptive stories about nothing in particular, and their respective sub-editors garnished them with suggestive and arresting headlines. Several papers remembered that the *Hampshire*, with Lord Kitchener aboard, had been sunk on the other side of Orkney, and 'A Student of Crime' wrote to suggest that a floating mine, one of the chain responsible for that dire catastrophe, had survived to be washed up on Eynhallow, and had blown the Pomfrets into minute and undiscoverable fragments. No sound of an explosion, however, had startled Orkney, and no trace of such a convulsion was apparent on the island. A photograph of John Corrigall and his boat appeared, an artistic camera study with an admirable sky effect. Several stories of mysterious yachts cruising in the vicinity were mooted, and the yachts were all satisfactorily identified as trawlers.

On the second Sunday after the disappearance, when the mystery had been deepened by time and even the most ingenious could offer no likely solution, an eminent clergyman, a staunch supporter of temperance, publicly warned the country against the danger of owning breweries. Mr Pomfret, he said, was widely known as a brewer, one who had made his fortune out of beer, that enemy of man and canker in the home. And Mr Pomfret had disappeared. Divine vengeance, he said, cometh like a thief in the night. Today we are here, in the midst of our wickedness, and tomorrow we are plucked up and cast into the oven. Let all, he concluded, who own breweries consider the appalling fate of George Plover Pomfret, and mend their ways by honest repentance while there is yet time.

And then the London paper had a scoop. Its reporter discovered that during all this bustle of conjecture, doubt and query, investigation and disappointment, a German professor had quietly been living, as a summer boarder, in a farmhouse not two miles distant from Swandale. His own explanation of his presence so near the scene of supposed tragedy was that he was collecting and examining survivals of Norse influence in the Orkney dialect; but his story, especially when it was printed alongside his own photograph, met with derisive incredulity, and in the natural excitement that followed this disclosure there was not a little sturdy denunciation of the Hidden Hand. The professor was detained in custody, and was released only on the telegraphic intervention of the German Foreign Secretary, who personally vouched for his honesty and innocence. This again deepened the suspicions of many newspaper readers.

The local police, meanwhile, reinforced by an inspector from Edinburgh and a detective from Scotland Yard, had quietly and systematically established that there were no clues to the whereabouts of Mr Pomfret and his friends, and no solution to the mystery of their disappearance. It was impossible for anyone to get on or off the island without a boat, and no boat could easily have landed, owing to the state of the tide, between the hour at which the Pomfrets were disembarked and the morning visit of John Corrigall. No strange vessel had been seen in the vicinity. The Pomfrets could not have made a raft, as some hundreds of people had suggested, because they had nothing out of which to make one, except two luncheon baskets, a gramophone, some records, and a box of gramophone needles which were, it must be admitted, too small to nail together pieces of driftwood, supposing suitable planks to have been present on the beach. Nor, unless they had been attacked by an epidemic mania, a surging and contagious Sinbad complex, was there any particular reason why they should have wanted to make a raft. No clear evidence even of their presence on the island, except an integral portion of a lady's stocking-suspender, was found, and some people suggested that John Corrigall was a liar and that the Pomfrets had never gone there. But the circumstantial evidence of the servants was in Corrigall's favour, and he had not, it was found, the mental ability successfully to dispose of six adult bodies.

Investigation of a practical kind came to an end. There was no one to question and nothing to find. Even the spiritualistic mediums who offered their services were of no real assistance, though some of them claimed to have established communication with Miss Joan Pomfret, who told them that everything was for the best in the best of all possible Beyonds. Mrs Pomfret, it was reported, had said, 'Sometimes it is light here and sometimes it is dark. I have not seen Bulmer, but I am happy'. There was a little discussion on the significance of *Bulmer*, till a personal friend suggested that it was a mis-tapping for the name of Mrs Pomfret's favourite author; but the general mystery was in danger of being forgotten, dismissed as insoluble.

It was about this time that Mr Harold Pinto left Kirkwall in the Orkneys for Leith, sailing on the S.S. *St Giles*. Mr Pinto was a commercial traveller, more silent than many of his class, a student of human nature, and in his way an amateur of life.

When the *St Giles* was some four hours out of Kirkwall he stepped into the small deckhouse which served as a smoking-room, and, pressing a bell, presently ordered a bottle of beer. There were, in the smoking-room, two other commercial travellers with whom he was slightly acquainted, the reporter of the provincial newspaper which had first heard of the Pomfret case, an elderly farmer who said he was going to South Africa, and a young, bright-eyed man, carelessly dressed, distinguished by a short, stubbly beard. He looked, thought Mr Pinto, as though he might be a gentleman. His nails were clean; but his soft collar was disgustingly dirty and his clothes had evidently been slept in. He asked for Bass, at the same time as Mr Pinto, in an educated and pleasant voice, but when the beer came he merely tasted it, and an expression of disgust passed over his face. He took no part in the general conversation, though Mr Pinto noticed that he followed the talk actively with his eyes—very expressive eyes they were, full, at times, of an almost impish merriment.

The conversation naturally centred on the Pomfret Mystery, and the reporter very graphically told the story from the beginning, embellished with certain details which had not been published. 'There are some things,' he said, 'which I wouldn't willingly tell outside this company. It's my private belief that old Pomfret took drugs. Don't ask me for proof, because I'm not going to tell you. And there's another thing. Joan Pomfret once asked the gardener at Swandale—he's a local man—whether he knew of any really lonely places near by. The sort of places where there were likely to be no casual passers-by. I didn't send that piece of news to my paper because I'm still waiting for the psychological moment at which to make it public. But you'll admit that it's significant.'

The other commercial travellers both contributed theories, at which the reporter scoffed, but Mr Pinto was almost as silent as the young man with the beard.

'Mass suicide won't do,' said the reporter, 'however much you talk about crowd psychology; and mass murder, followed by the suicide of the murderer, won't do either. None of them was likely to run amok. And where are the bodies? One at least would have been washed up before now. No, it's my opinion that there's an international gang at the bottom of it, and one of the party—at least one—was either a confederate or a fugitive from the justice of the gang.'

The man who was going to South Africa said that he had a cousin who had once disappeared in Mashonaland. He was about to tell the story more fully when the two commercial travellers and the reporter discovered that they were sleepy—it was nearly midnight—and went hurriedly below. And after a minute or two the man with the cousin in Mashonaland followed them.

The young man with the stubbly beard sat still, staring at nothing with eyes that were alert and full of comprehension. He seemed to be listening to the throb of the steamer's screw and the answering wash of the sea. His lips moved slightly when a wave, louder than the others, ran with a slithering caress along the ship's side, and he smiled engagingly, looking at Mr Pinto as though he expected an answering smile.

'The Möder Dy,'[1] he said, 'laughing at fishermen's wives. All summer she laughs lightly, but the laughter of her winter rut is like icebergs breaking.'

Mr Pinto, remarking that it seemed to be a fine night, stepped out on to the deck.

'Oh, a glorious night,' said the young man with the beard, following him. 'Look at the clouds, like grey foxes running from the moon.'

'Indeed, there is one extraordinarily like a fox,' replied Mr Pinto politely.

'She is hunting tonight,' said the young man. 'Foxes and grey wolves. And see, there's a stag in the west. A great night for hunting, and all the sky to run through.'

Mr Pinto and his friend had the deck to themselves, and Mr Pinto began to feel curiously lonely in such strange company.

'Listen,' said the young man, pointing over the rail. 'Do you hear a shoal of herring talking out there? There's a hum of fear in the air. Perhaps a thresher-shark is coming through the Firth.'

Mr Pinto, convinced that he had a lunatic to deal with, was considering an excuse for going below when the young man said: 'I saw you sitting silent while those fools were talking about Pomfret's disappearance. Why did you say nothing?'

'Because I didn't think any of their theories were good enough,' answered Mr Pinto, feeling a little easier, 'and because I had no theory of my own to offer.'

'What do you think? You must think something?'

Mr Pinto blinked once or twice, and then diffidently suggested, 'There are more things in heaven and earth, you know; it sounds foolish, after having been quoted so often and so unnecessarily, but . . .'

'It does not sound foolish. Those others were fools. You, it seems, are not yet a fool; though you will be, if you live to grow old and yet not old enough. If you like, I will tell you what happened to George Pomfret and his friends. Sit there.'

Mr Pinto, rather subdued, sat; and the young man walked once or twice up and down, his hair flying like a black banner in the wind,

[1]'Möder Dy'—the Ninth Wave.

turned his face up to the moon to laugh loudly and melodiously, and suddenly said: 'They landed on Eynhallow in the quietness of a perfect evening. The tide was talking to the shore, telling it the story of the Seven Seals who went to Sule Skerry, but they could not hear it then. A redshank whistled "Oh Joy! look at them!" as they stepped ashore. But they did not know that either. They made a lot of noise as they walked up the shingle beach and the rabbits in the grass, because they made a noise, were not frightened, but only ran a little way and turned to look at them.

'Mrs Pomfret was not happy, but they let her sit on the rugs and she fell asleep. The others walked round the island—it is not big—and threw stones into the sea. The sea chuckled and threw more stones on to the beach; but they did not know that. And the sea woke birds who were roosting there, and the birds flew round and laughed at them. By and by the shadow of night came—it was not really night—and they sat down to eat. They ate for a long time, and woke Mrs Pomfret, who said she could never eat out of doors, and so they let her sleep again. The others talked. They were happy, in a way, but what they talked was nonsense. Even Joan, who was in love, talked nonsense which she does not like to think about now.'

'Then—' Mr Pinto excitedly tried to interrupt, but the young man went imperturbably on.

'Disney said one or two things about the birds which were true, but they did not listen to him. And by and by—the hours pass quickly on Midsummer Night—it was time to dance. They had taken a gramophone with them, and Joan had found a wide circle of turf, as round as a penny and heavenly smooth, with a square rock beside it. They put the gramophone on the rock and played a fox-trot or some dance like that. Disney and Norah Disney danced together, and Joan danced with Samways. Two or three times they danced, and old Pomfret made jokes and put new records on.

'And then Joan said, "These aren't proper dances for Eynhallow and Midsummer Eve. I hate them." And she stopped the gramophone. She picked up the second album of records and looked for what she wanted; it was light enough to read the names if she held them close to her eyes. She soon found those she was looking for.'

The young man looked doubtfully at Mr Pinto and asked, 'Do you know the music of Grieg?'

'A little of it,' said Mr Pinto. 'He composed some Norwegian dances. One of them goes like this.' And he whistled a bar or two, tunefully enough.

The young man snapped his fingers joyously and stepped lightly with adept feet on the swaying deck.

'That is it,' he cried, and sang some strange-sounding words to the tune. 'But Grieg did not make it. He heard it between a pine-forest and the sea and cleverly wrote it down. But it was made hundreds of years ago, when all the earth went dancing, except the trees, and their roots took hold of great rocks and twined round the rocks so that they might not join the dance as they wished. For it was forbidden them, since they had to grow straight and tall that ships might be made out of them.'

The young man checked himself. 'I was telling you about the Pomfrets,' he said.

'Joan found these dances that she loved, and played first one and then the other. She made them all dance to the music, though they did not know what steps were in it, nor in what patterns they should move. But the tunes took them by the heels and they pranced and bowed and jumped, laughing all the time. Old Pomfret capered in the middle, kicking his legs, and twirling round like a top. And he laughed; how he laughed! And when he had done shaking with laughter he would start to dance again.

'"This is too good for Mother to miss," he said, "we must wake her and make her dance too." So they woke Mrs Pomfret and there being then six of them they made some kind of a figure and started to dance in earnest. Mrs Pomfret, once she began, moved as lightly as any of them except Joan, who was like thistledown on the grass and moonlight on the edge of a cloud.

'And then, as the music went on, they found that they were dancing in the proper patterns, for they had partners who had come from nowhere, who led them first to the right and then to the left, up the middle and down the sides, bowing and knocking their heels in the air. As the tune quickened they turned themselves head over heels, even Mrs Pomfret, who held her sides and laughed to see old Pomfret twirling on one toe. And the gramophone never stopped, for a little brown man was sitting by it and now and again turning the handle, and singing loudly as he sat.

'So they danced while the sky became lighter and turned from grey to a shining colour like mackerel; and then little clouds like roses were thrown over the silver, and at last the sun himself, daffodil gold, all bright and new, shot up and sent the other colours packing.

'And everybody shouted and cheered like mad, and for a minute danced more wildly than ever, turning catherine-wheels, fast and faster in a circle, or shouting "Hey!" and "Ho!" and "Ahoi! Ahoi! A-hoi!"

'Then they sank to the ground exhausted, and the Pomfrets looked at their partners who had come from nowhere; and were suddenly amazed.

'"Well, I'm damned!" said old Pomfret, and all the little brown men rolled on the grass and laughed as though they would burst.

'"Oh, they're the Wee Folk, the Peerie[1] Men!" cried Joan, delightedly, clapping her hands. "Peerie Men, Peerie Men, I've found you at last!"

'And again the little men laughed and hugged themselves on the grass. By and by, still laughing, they drew together and talked among themselves very earnestly, and then the biggest of them, who was as tall as a man's leg to the mid-thigh, went forward, saying his name was Ferriostok, and made a little speech explaining how delighted they were to entertain such charming guests on Eynhallow; and would they please to come in for breakfast?

'Some pushed aside the stone on which the gramophone had been standing and, as though it were the most natural thing in the world, the Pomfrets went down rock stairs to a long, sandy hall, lit greenly by the sea, and full, at that time, of the morning song of the North Tide of Eynhallow. They sat down, talking with their hosts, and then two very old little men brought stone cups full of a yellow liquor that smelt like honey and the first wind after frost. They tasted it, curiously, and old Pomfret—he was a brewer, you know—went red all over and said loudly, "I'll give every penny I have in the world for the recipe!" For he guessed what it was.

'And the little men laughed louder than ever, and filled his cup again. One said, "The Great King offered us Almain for it eleven hundred years ago. We gave him one cup for love, and no more. But you, who have brought that music with you, are free of our cellar. Stay and drink with us, and tonight we shall dance again."

'No one of them had any thought of going, for it was heather ale they drank. Heather Ale! And the last man who tasted it was Thomas of Ercildoune. It was for heather ale that the Romans came to Britain, having heard of it in Gaul, and they pushed northwards to Mount Graupius in search of the secret. But they never found it. And now old Pomfret was swilling it, his cheeks like rubies, because Joan had brought back to the Peerie Men the music they had lost six hundred years before, when their oldest minstrel died of a mad otter's bite.

'Disney was talking to an old grey seal at the sea-door, hearing new tales of the German war, and Joan was listening to the Reykjavik

[1] Peerie—little.

story of the Solan Geese which three little men told her all together, so excited they were by her beauty and by the music she had brought them. At night they danced again, and Joan learnt the Weaving of the Red Ware, the dance that the red shore-seaweed makes for full-moon tides. The Peerie Men played on fiddles cut out of old tree-roots, with strings of rabbit gut, and they had drums made of shells and rabbit skins scraped as thin as tissues with stone knives. They hunt quietly, and that is why the rabbits are frightened of silence, but were not afraid of the Pomfrets, who made a noise when they walked. The Peerie Men's music was thin and tinkly, though the tunes were as strong and sweet as the heather ale itself, and always they turned again to the gramophone which Joan had brought, and danced as madly as peewits in April, leaping like winter spray, and clapping their heels high in the air. They danced the Merry Men of Mey and the slow sad Dance of Lofoden, so that everybody wept a little. And then they drank more ale and laughed again, and as the sun came up they danced the Herring Dance, weaving through and through so fast that the eye could not follow them.

'Now this was the third sunrise since the Pomfrets had gone to the island, for the first day and the second night and the second day had passed like one morning in the sandy hall of the Little Men; so many things were there to hear, and such good jokes an old crab made, and so shockingly attractive was a mermaid story that the afternoon tide told. Even the sand had a story, but it was so old that the Peerie Men themselves could not understand it, for it began in darkness and finished under a green haze of ice; and since the Pomfrets were so busy there they heard no sound of the chauffeur's visit and the Peerie Men said nothing of it. They had taken below all the rugs and cushions and hampers and gramophone records, and brushed the grass straight, so that no trace was left of the Midsummer dancing—except the tag of Joan's stocking-suspender, which was overlooked, so it seems.

'The old grey seal told them, in the days that followed, of all that was going on by land, and even Mrs Pomfret laughed to hear of the bustle and stir they had created. There was no need, the Peerie Men found, to make them hide when more searchers came, for none of the Pomfrets had any wish to be found. Disney said he was learning something about the sea for the first time in his life (and he had followed the sea all his life), and Norah sang Iceland cradle-songs all day. Old Pomfret swilled his ale, glowing like a ruby in the green cave, and Joan—Joan was the queen of the Peerie Men, and the fosterling of the old grumbling sand, and the friend of every fish that passed by the sea-door. And at night they danced, to the music of the tree-root fiddles and pink shell-drums, and above all to that music which you think was made by Grieg. They danced, I tell you!'

The young man tossed up his arms and touched his fingers above his head; he placed the flat of his foot on the calf of the other leg; twirled rapidly on his toes. 'Danced, I say! Is there anything in the world but dancing?' And he clapped his heels together, high in the air, first to one side and then to the other, singing something fast and rhythmic and melodious.

Mr Pinto coughed nervously—he was feeling cold—and said: 'That is an extraordinarily interesting story. But, if you will pardon my curiosity, do you mind telling me what reason you have for thinking that this actually happened to Mr Pomfret and his friends?'

'Reason!' said the young man, staring at him. His hair blew out on the wind like a black banner, and he laughed loud and melodiously.

'This reason,' he said, 'that I am Otto Samways!' And he turned, very neatly, a standing somersault on the deck and came up laughing.

'They sent me away to buy something,' he said, 'and when I have bought it I am going back to Eynhallow to dance the Merry Men, and the Herring Dance, and the Sea Moon's Dance with Joan.'

And once again he sang, very melodiously, and turned a rapid series of catherine-wheels along the deck.

'To buy what?' shouted Mr Pinto, as he disappeared.

'Gramophone needles!' bellowed the young man, laughing uproariously.

Sealskin Trousers

I AM NOT MAD. It is necessary to realise that, to accept it as a fact about which there can be no dispute. I have been seriously ill for some weeks, but that was the result of shock. A double or conjoint shock: for as well as the obvious concussion of a brutal event, there was the more dreadful necessity of recognising the material evidence of a happening so monstrously implausible that even my friends here, who in general are quite extraordinarily kind and understanding, will not believe in the occurrence, though they cannot deny it or otherwise explain—I mean explain away—the clear and simple testimony of what was left.

I, of course, realised very quickly what had happened, and since then I have more than once remembered that poor Coleridge teased his unquiet mind, quite unnecessarily in his case, with just such a possibility; or impossibility, as the world would call it. 'If a man could pass through Paradise in a dream,' he wrote, 'and have a flower presented to him as a pledge that his soul had really been there, and if he found that flower in his hand when he woke—Ay, and what then?'

But what if he had dreamt of Hell and wakened with his hand burnt by the fire? Or of Chaos, and seen another face stare at him from the looking-glass? Coleridge does not push the question far. He was too timid. But I accepted the evidence. and while I was ill I thought seriously about the whole proceeding, in detail and in sequence of detail. I thought, indeed, about little else. To begin with, I admit, I was badly shaken, but gradually my mind cleared and my vision improved, and because I was patient and persevering—that needed discipline—I can now say that I know what happened. I have indeed, by a conscious intellectual effort, *seen and heard* what happened. This is how it began . . .

How very unpleasant! she thought.

She had come down the great natural steps on the sea-cliff to the ledge that narrowly gave access, round the angle of it, to the western face which to-day was sheltered from the breeze and warmed by the afternoon sun. At the beginning of the week she and her fiancé,

Charles Sellin, had found their way to an almost hidden shelf, a deep veranda sixty feet above the white-veined water. It was rather bigger than a billiard-table and nearly as private as an abandoned lighthouse. Twice they had spent some blissful hours there. She had a good head for heights, and Sellin was indifferent to scenery. There had been nothing vulgar, no physical contact, in their bliss together on this oceanic gazebo, for on each occasion she had been reading Héaloin's *Studies in Biology* and he Lenin's *What is to be Done?*

Their relations were already marital, not because their mutual passion could brook no pause, but rather out of fear lest their friends might despise them for chastity and so conjecture some oddity or impotence in their nature. Their behaviour, however, was very decently circumspect, and they already conducted themselves, in public and out of doors, as if they had been married for several years. They did not regard the seclusion of the cliffs as an opportunity for secret embracing, but were content that the sun should warm and colour their skin; and let their anxious minds be soothed by the surge and cavernous colloquies of the sea. Now, while Charles was writing letters in the little fishing-hotel a mile away, she had come back to their sandstone ledge, and Charles would join her in an hour or two. She was still reading *Studies in Biology*.

But their gazebo, she perceived, was already occupied, and occupied by a person of the most embarrassing appearance. He was quite unlike Charles. He was not only naked, but obviously robust, brown-hued, and extremely hairy. He sat on the very edge of the rock, dangling his legs over the sea, and down his spine ran a ridge of hair like the dark stripe on a donkey's back, and on his shoulder-blades grew patches of hair like the wings of a bird. Unable in her disappointment to be sensible and leave at once, she lingered for a moment and saw to her relief that he was not quite naked. He wore trousers of a dark brown colour, very low at the waist, but sufficient to cover his haunches. Even so, even with that protection for her modesty, she could not stay and read biology in his company.

To show her annoyance, and let him become aware of it, she made a little impatient sound; and turning to go, looked back to see if he had heard.

He swung himself round and glared at her, more angry on the instant than she had been. He had thick eyebrows, large dark eyes, a broad snub nose, a big mouth. 'You're Roger Fairfield!' she exclaimed in surprise.

He stood up and looked at her intently. 'How do you know?' he asked.

'Because I remember you,' she answered, but then felt a little confused, for what she principally remembered was the brief notoriety he had acquired, in his final year at Edinburgh University, by swimming on a rough autumn day from North Berwick to the Bass Rock to win a bet of five pounds.

The story had gone briskly round the town for a week, and everybody knew that he and some friends had been lunching, too well for caution, before the bet was made. His friends, however, grew quickly sober when he took to the water, and in a great fright informed the police, who called out the lifeboat. But they searched in vain, for the sea was running high, until in calm water under the shelter of the Bass they saw his head, dark on the water, and pulled him aboard. He seemed none the worse for his adventure, but the police charged him with disorderly behaviour and he was fined two pounds for swimming without a regulation costume.

'We met twice,' she said, 'once at a dance and once in Mackie's when we had coffee together. About a year ago. There were several of us there, and we knew the man you came in with. I remember you perfectly.'

He stared the harder, his eyes narrowing, a vertical wrinkle dividing his forehead. 'I'm a little short-sighted too,' she said with a nervous laugh.

'My sight's very good,' he answered, 'but I find it difficult to recognise people. Human beings are so much alike.'

'That's one of the rudest remarks I've ever heard!'

'Surely not?'

'Well, one does like to be remembered. It isn't pleasant to be told that one's a nonentity.'

He made an impatient gesture. 'That isn't what I meant, and I do recognise you now. I remember your voice. You have a distinctive voice and a pleasant one. F Sharp in the octave below middle C is your note.'

'Is that the only way in which you can distinguish people?'

'It's as good as any other.'

'But you don't remember my name?'

'No,' he said.

'I'm Elizabeth Barford.'

He bowed and said, 'Well, it was a dull party, wasn't it? The occasion, I mean, when we drank coffee together.'

'I don't agree with you. I thought it was very amusing, and we all enjoyed ourselves. Do you remember Charles Sellin?'

'No.'

'Oh, you're hopeless,' she exclaimed. 'What is the good of meeting people if you're going to forget all about them?'

'I don't know,' he said. 'Let us sit down, and you can tell me.'

He sat again on the edge of the rock, his legs dangling, and looking over his shoulder at her, said, 'Tell me: what is the good of meeting people?'

She hesitated, and answered, 'I like to make friends. That's quite natural, isn't it?—But I came here to read.'

'Do you read standing?'

'Of course not,' she said, and smoothing her skirt tidily over her knees, sat down beside him. 'What a wonderful place this is for a holiday. Have you been here before?'

'Yes, I know it well.'

'Charles and I came a week ago. Charles Sellin, I mean, whom you don't remember. We're going to be married, you know. In about a year, we hope.'

'Why did you come here?'

'We wanted to be quiet, and in these islands one is fairly secure against interruption. We're both working quite hard.'

'Working!' he mocked. 'Don't waste time, waste your life instead.'

'Most of us have to work, whether we like it or not.'

He took the book from her lap, and opening it read idly a few lines, turned a dozen pages and read with a yawn another paragraph.

'Your friends in Edinburgh,' she said, 'were better-off than ours. Charles and I, and all the people we know, have got to make our living.'

'Why?' he asked.

'Because if we don't we shall starve,' she snapped.

'And if you avoid starvation—what then?'

'It's possible to hope,' she said stiffly, 'that we shall be of some use in the world.'

'Do you agree with this?' he asked, smothering a second yawn, and read from the book: '*The physical factor in a germ-cell is beyond our analysis or assessment, but can we deny subjectivity to the primordial initiatives? It is easier, perhaps, to assume that mind comes late in development, but the assumption must not be established on the grounds that we can certainly deny self-expression to the cell. It is common knowledge that the mind may influence the body both greatly and in little unseen ways; but how it is done, we do not know. Psychobiology is still in its infancy.*'

'It's fascinating, isn't it?' she said.

'How do you propose,' he asked, 'to be of use to the world?'

'Well, the world needs people who have been educated—educated to think—and one does hope to have a little influence in some way.'

'Is a little influence going to make any difference? Don't you think that what the world needs is to develop a new sort of mind? It needs a new primordial directive, or quite a lot of them, perhaps. But psychobiology is still in its infancy, and you don't know how such changes come about, do you? And you can't foresee when you *will* know, can you?'

'No, of course not. But science is advancing so quickly—'

'In fifty thousand years?' he interrupted. 'Do you think you will know by then?'

'It's difficult to say,' she answered seriously, and was gathering her thoughts for a careful reply when again he interrupted, rudely, she thought, and quite irrelevantly. His attention had strayed from her and her book to the sea beneath, and he was looking down as though searching for something. 'Do you swim?' he asked.

'Rather well,' she said.

'I went in just before high water, when the weed down there was all brushed in the opposite direction. You never get bored by the sea, do you?'

'I've never seen enough of it,' she said. 'I want to live on an island, a little island, and hear it all round me.'

'That's very sensible of you,' he answered with more warmth in his voice. 'That's uncommonly sensible for a girl like you.'

'What sort of a girl do you think I am?' she demanded, vexation in her accent, but he ignored her and pointed his brown arm to the horizon: 'The colour has thickened within the last few minutes. The sea was quite pale on the skyline, and now it's a belt of indigo. And the writing has changed. The lines of foam on the water, I mean. Look at that! There's a submerged rock out there, and always, about half an hour after the ebb has started to run, but more clearly when there's an off-shore wind, you can see those two little whirlpools and the circle of white round them. You see the figure they make? It's like this, isn't it?'

With a splinter of stone he drew a diagram on the rock.

'Do you know what it is?' he asked. 'It's the figure the Chinese call the T'ai Chi. They say it represents the origin of all created things. And it's the sign manual of the sea.'

'But those lines of foam must run into every conceivable shape,' she protested.

'Oh, they do. They do indeed. But it isn't often you can read them.—There he is!' he exclaimed, leaning forward and staring into the water sixty feet below. 'That's him, the old villain!'

From his sitting position, pressing hard down with his hands and thrusting against the face of the rock with his heels, he hurled himself into space, and straightening in mid-air broke the smooth green surface of the water with no more splash than a harpoon would have made. A solitary razorbill, sunning himself on a shelf below, fled hurriedly out to sea, and half a dozen white birds, startled by the sudden movement, rose in the air crying 'Kittiwake! Kittiwake!'

Elizabeth screamed loudly, scrambled to her feet with clumsy speed, then knelt again on the edge of the rock and peered down. In the slowly heaving clear water she could see a pale shape moving, now striped by the dark weed that grew in tangles under the flat foot of the rock, now lost in the shadowy deepness where the tangles were rooted. In a minute or two his head rose from the sea, he shook bright drops from his hair, and looked up at her, laughing. Firmly grasped in his right hand, while he trod water, he held up an enormous blue-black lobster for her admiration. Then he threw it on to the flat rock beside him, and swiftly climbing out of the sea, caught it again and held it, cautious of its bite, till he found a piece of string in his trouser-pocket. He shouted to her, 'I'll tie its claws, and you can take it home for your supper!'

She had not thought it possible to climb the sheer face of the cliff, but from its forefoot he mounted by steps and handholds invisible from above, and pitching the tied lobster on to the floor of the gazebo, came nimbly over the edge.

'That's a bigger one than you've ever seen in your life before,' he boasted. 'He weighs fourteen pounds, I'm certain of it. Fourteen pounds at least. Look at the size of his right claw! He could crack a coconut with that. He tried to crack my ankle when I was swimming an hour ago, and got into his hole before I could catch him. But I've caught him now, the brute. He's had more than twenty years of crime, that black boy. He's twenty-four or twenty-five by the look of him. He's older than you, do you realise that? Unless you're a lot older than you look. How old are you?'

But Elizabeth took no interest in the lobster. She had retreated until she stood with her back to the rock, pressed hard against it, the palms of her hands fumbling on the stone as if feeling for a secret lock or bolt that might give her entrance into it. Her face was white, her lips pale and tremulous.

He looked round at her, when she made no answer, and asked what the matter was.

Her voice was faint and frightened. 'Who are you?' she whispered, and the whisper broke into a stammer. 'What are you?'

His expression changed and his face, with the water-drops on it, grew hard as a rock shining undersea. 'It's only a few minutes,' he said, 'since you appeared to know me quite well. You addressed me as Roger Fairfield, didn't you?'

'But a name's not everything. It doesn't tell you enough.'

'What more do you want to know?'

Her voice was so strained and thin that her words were like the shadow of words, or words shivering in the cold: 'To jump like that, into the sea—it wasn't human!'

The coldness of his face wrinkled to a frown. 'That's a curious remark to make.'

'You would have killed yourself if—if—'

He took a seaward step again, looked down at the calm green depths below, and said, 'You're exaggerating, aren't you? It's not much more than fifty feet, sixty perhaps, and the water's deep.—Here, come back! Why are you running away?'

'Let me go!' she cried. 'I don't want to stay here. I—I'm frightened.'

'That's unfortunate. I hadn't expected this to happen.'

'Please let me go!'

'I don't think I shall. Not until you've told me what you're frightened of.'

'Why,' she stammered, 'why do you wear fur trousers?'

He laughed, and still laughing caught her round the waist and pulled her towards the edge of the rock. 'Don't be alarmed,' he said. 'I'm not going to throw you over. But if you insist on a conversation about trousers, I think we should sit down again. Look at the smoothness of the water, and its colour, and the light in the depths of it: have you ever seen anything lovelier? Look at the sky: that's calm enough, isn't it? Look at that fulmar sailing past: he's not worrying, so why should you?'

She leaned away from him, all her weight against the hand that held her waist, but his arm was strong and he seemed unaware of any strain on it. Nor did he pay attention to the distress she was in—she was sobbing dryly, like a child who has cried too long—but continued talking in a light and pleasant conversational tone until the muscles of her body tired and relaxed, and she sat within his enclosing arm, making no more effort to escape, but timorously conscious of his hand upon her side so close beneath her breast.

'I needn't tell you,' he said, 'the conventional reasons for wearing trousers. There are people, I know, who sneer at all conventions, and some conventions deserve their sneering. But not the trouser-convention. No, indeed! So we can admit the necessity of the garment, and pass to consideration of the material. Well, I like sitting on rocks, for one thing, and for such a hobby this is the best stuff in the world. It's very durable, yet soft and comfortable. I can slip into the sea for half an hour without doing it any harm, and when I come out to sun myself on the rock again, it doesn't feel cold and clammy. Nor does it fade in the sun or shrink with the wet. Oh, there are plenty of reasons for having one's trousers made of stuff like this.'

'And there's a reason,' she said, 'that you haven't told me.'

'Are you quite sure of that?'

She was calmer now, and her breathing was controlled. But her face was still white, and her lips were softly nervous when she asked him, 'Are you going to kill me?'

'Kill you? Good heavens, no! Why should I do that?'

'For fear of my telling other people.'

'And what precisely would you tell them?'

'You know.'

'You jump to conclusions far too quickly: that's your trouble. Well, it's a pity for your sake, and a nuisance for me. I don't think I can let you take that lobster home for your supper after all. I don't, in fact, think you will go home for your supper.'

Her eyes grew dark again with fear, her mouth opened, but before she could speak he pulled her to him and closed it, not asking leave, with a roughly occludent kiss.

'That was to prevent you from screaming. I hate to hear people scream,' he told her, smiling as he spoke. 'But this'—he kissed her again, now gently and in a more protracted embrace—'that was because I wanted to.'

'You mustn't!' she cried.

'But I have,' he said.

'I don't understand myself! I can't understand what has happened—'

'Very little yet,' he murmured.

'Something terrible has happened!'

'A kiss? Am I so repulsive?'

'I don't mean that. I mean something inside me. I'm not—at least I think I'm not—I'm not frightened now!'

'You have no reason to be.'

'I have every reason in the world. But I'm not! I'm not frightened—but I want to cry.'

'Then cry,' he said soothingly, and made her pillow her cheek against his breast. 'But you can't cry comfortably with that ridiculous contraption on your nose.'

He took from her the horn-rimmed spectacles she wore, and threw them into the sea.

'Oh!' she exclaimed. 'My glasses!—Oh, why did you do that? Now I can't see. I can't see at all without my glasses!'

'It's all right,' he assured her. 'You really won't need them. The refraction,' he added vaguely, 'will be quite different.'

As if this small but unexpected act of violence had brought to the boiling-point her desire for tears, they bubbled over, and because she threw her arms about him in a sort of fond despair, and snuggled close, sobbing vigorously still, he felt the warm drops trickle down his skin, and from his skin she drew into her eyes the saltness of the sea, which made her weep the more. He stroked her hair with a strong but soothing hand, and when she grew calm and lay still in his arms, her emotion spent, he sang quietly to a little enchanting tune a song that began:

I am a Man upon the land,
I am a Selkie in the sea,
And when I'm far from every strand
My home it is on Sule Skerry.

After the first verse or two she freed herself from his embrace, and sitting up listened gravely to the song. Then she asked him, 'Shall I ever understand?'

'It's not a unique occurrence,' he told her. 'It has happened quite often before, as I suppose you know. In Cornwall and Brittany and among the Western Isles of Scotland; that's where people have always been interested in seals, and understood them a little, and where seals from time to time have taken human shape. The one thing that's unique in our case, in my metamorphosis, is that I am the only seal-man who has ever become a Master of Arts of Edinburgh University. Or, I believe, of any university. I am the unique and solitary example of a sophisticated seal-man.'

'I must look a perfect fright,' she said. 'It was silly of me to cry. Are my eyes very red?'

'The lids are a little pink—not unattractively so—but your eyes are as dark and lovely as a mountain pool in October, on a sunny day in October. They're much improved since I threw your spectacles away.'

'I needed them, you know. I feel quite stupid without them. But tell me why you came to the University—and how? How could you do it?'

'My dear girl—what is your name, by the way? I've quite forgotten.'

'Elizabeth!' she said angrily.

'I'm so glad, it's my favourite human name.—But you don't really want to listen to a lecture on psychobiology?'

'I want to know *how*. You must tell me!'

'Well, you remember, don't you, what your book says about the primordial initiatives? But it needs a footnote there to explain that they're not exhausted till quite late in life. The germ-cells, as you know, are always renewing themselves, and they keep their initiatives though they nearly always follow the chosen pattern except in the case of certain illnesses, or under special direction. The direction of the mind, that is. And the glands have got a lot to do in a full metamorphosis, the renal first and then the pituitary, as you would expect. It isn't approved of—making the change, I mean—but every now and then one of us does it, just for a frolic in the general way, but in my case there was a special reason.'

'Tell me,' she said again.

'It's too long a story.'

'I want to know.'

'There's been a good deal of unrest, you see, among my people in the last few years: doubt, and dissatisfaction with our leaders, and scepticism about traditional beliefs—all that sort of thing. We've had a lot of discussion under the surface of the sea about the nature of man, for instance. We had always been taught to believe certain things about him, and recent events didn't seem to bear out what our teachers told us. Some of our younger people got dissatisfied, so I volunteered to go ashore and investigate. I'm still considering the report I shall have to make, and that's why I'm living, at present, a double life. I come ashore to think, and go back to the sea to rest.'

'And what do you think of us?' she asked.

'You're interesting. Very interesting indeed. There are going to be some curious mutations among you before long. Within three or four thousand years, perhaps.'

He stooped and rubbed a little smear of blood from his shin. 'I scratched it on a limpet,' he said. 'The limpets, you know, are the same to-day as they were four hundred thousand years ago. But human beings aren't nearly so stable.'

'Is that your main impression, that humanity's unstable?'

'That's part of it. But from our point of view there's something much more upsetting. Our people, you see, are quite simple creatures, and because we have relatively few beliefs, we're very much attached to them. Our life is a life of sensation—not entirely, but largely—and we ought to be extremely happy. We were, so long as we were satisfied with sensation and a short undisputed creed. We have some advantages over human beings, you know. Human beings have to carry their own weight about, and they don't know how blissful it is to be unconscious of weight: to be wave-borne, to float on the idle sea, to leap without effort in a curving wave, and look up at the dazzle of the sky through a smother of white water, or dive so easily to the calmness far below and take a haddock from the weed-beds in a sudden rush of appetite.—Talking of haddocks,' he said, 'it's getting late. It's nearly time for fish. And I must give you some instruction before we go. The preliminary phase takes a little while, about five minutes for you, I should think, and then you'll be another creature.'

She gasped, as though already she felt the water's chill, and whispered, 'Not yet! Not yet, please.'

He took her in his arms, and expertly, with a strong caressing hand, stroked her hair, stroked the roundness of her head and the back of her neck and her shoulders, feeling her muscles moving to his touch, and down the hollow of her back to her waist and hips. The head again, neck, shoulders, and spine. Again and again. Strongly and firmly his hand gave her calmness, and presently she whispered, 'You're sending me to sleep.'

'My God!' he exclaimed, 'you mustn't do that! Stand up, stand up, Elizabeth!'

'Yes,' she said, obeying him. 'Yes, Roger. Why did you call yourself Roger? Roger Fairfield?'

'I found the name in a drowned sailor's pay-book. What does that matter now?' Look at me, Elizabeth!'

She looked at him, and smiled.

His voice changed, and he said happily, 'You'll be the prettiest seal between Shetland and the Scillies. Now listen. Listen carefully.'

He held her lightly and whispered in her ear. Then kissed her on the lips and cheek, and bending her head back, on the throat. He looked, and saw the colour come deeply into her face.

'Good,' he said. 'That's the first stage. The adrenalin's flowing nicely now. You know about the pituitary, don't you? That makes it easy then. There are two parts in the pituitary gland, the anterior and posterior lobes, and both must act together. It's not difficult, and I'll tell you how.'

Then he whispered again, most urgently, and watched her closely. In a little while he said, 'And now you can take it easy. Let's sit down and wait till you're ready. The actual change won't come till we go down.'

'But it's working,' she said, quietly and happily. 'I can feel it working.'

'Of course it is.'

She laughed triumphantly, and took his hand.

'We've got nearly five minutes to wait,' he said.

'What will it be like? What shall I feel, Roger?'

'The water moving against your side, the sea caressing you and holding you.'

'Shall I be sorry for what I've left behind?'

'No, I don't think so.'

'You didn't like us, then? Tell me what you discovered in the world.'

'Quite simply,' he said, 'that we had been deceived.'

'But I don't know what your belief had been.'

'Haven't I told you?—Well, we in our innocence respected you because you could work, and were willing to work. That seemed to us truly heroic. We don't work at all, you see, and you'll be much happier when you come to us. We who live in the sea don't struggle to keep our heads above water.'

'All my friends worked hard,' she said. 'I never knew anyone who was idle. We had to work, and most of us worked for a good purpose; or so we thought. But you didn't think so?'

'Our teachers had told us,' he said, 'that men endured the burden of human toil to create a surplus of wealth that would give them leisure from the daily task of bread-winning. And in their hard-won leisure, our teachers said, men cultivated wisdom and charity and the fine arts; and became aware of God.—But that's not a true description of the world, is it?'

'No,' she said, 'that's not the truth.'

'No,' he repeated, 'our teachers were wrong, and we've been deceived.'

'Men are always being deceived, but they get accustomed to learning the facts too late. They grow accustomed to deceit itself.'

'You are braver than we, perhaps. My people will not like to be told the truth.'

'I shall be with you,' she said, and took his hand. But still he stared gloomily at the moving sea.

The minutes passed, and presently she stood up and with quick fingers put off her clothes. 'It's time,' she said.

He looked at her, and his gloom vanished like the shadow of a cloud that the wind has hurried on, and exultation followed like sunlight spilling from the burning edge of a cloud. 'I wanted to punish them,' he cried, 'for robbing me of my faith, and now, by God, I'm punishing them hard. I'm robbing their treasury now, the inner vault of all their treasury!—I hadn't guessed you were so beautiful! The waves when you swim will catch a burnish from you, the sand will shine like silver when you lie down to sleep, and if you can teach the red sea-ware to blush so well, I shan't miss the roses of your world.'

'Hurry,' she said.

He, laughing softly, loosened the leather thong that tied his trousers, stepped out of them, and lifted her in his arms. 'Are you ready?' he asked.

She put her arms round his neck and softly kissed his cheek. Then with a great shout he leapt from the rock, from the little veranda, into the green silk calm of the water far below . . .

I heard the splash of their descent—I am quite sure I heard the splash—as I came round the corner of the cliff, by the ledge that leads to the little rock veranda, our gazebo, as we called it, but the first thing I noticed, that really attracted my attention, was an enormous blue-black lobster, its huge claws tied with string, that was moving in a rather ludicrous fashion towards the edge. I think it fell over just before I left, but I wouldn't swear to that. Then I saw her book, the *Studies in Biology*, and her clothes.

Her white linen frock with the brown collar and the brown belt, some other garments, and her shoes were all there. And beside them, lying across her shoes, was a pair of sealskin trousers.

I realised immediately, or almost immediately, what had happened. Or so it seems to me now. And if, as I firmly believe, my apprehension was instantaneous, the faculty of intuition is clearly more important than I had previously supposed. I have, of course, as I said before, given the matter a great deal of thought during my recent illness, but the impression remains that I understood what had happened in a flash, to use a common but illuminating phrase. And no one, need I say? has been able to refute my intuition. No one, that is, has found an alternative explanation for the presence, beside Elizabeth's linen frock, of a pair of sealskin trousers.

I remember also my physical distress at the discovery. My breath, for several minutes I think, came into and went out of my lungs like the hot wind of a dust-storm in the desert. It parched my mouth and grated in my throat. It was, I recall, quite a torment to breathe. But I had to, of course.

Nor did I lose control of myself in spite of the agony, both mental and physical, that I was suffering. I didn't lose control till they began to mock me. Yes, they did, I assure you of that. I heard his voice quite clearly, and honesty compels me to admit that it was singularly sweet and the tune was the most haunting I have ever heard. They were about forty yards away, two seals swimming together, and the evening light was so clear and taut that his voice might have been the vibration of an invisible bow across its coloured bands. He was singing the song that Elizabeth and I had discovered in an album of Scottish music in the little fishing-hotel where we had been living:

I am a Man upon the land,
I am a Selkie in the sea,
And when I'm far from any strand
I am at home on Sule Skerry!

But his purpose, you see, was mockery. They were happy, together in the vast simplicity of the ocean, and I, abandoned to the terror of life alone, life among human beings, was lost and full of panic. It was then I began to scream. I could hear myself screaming, it was quite horrible. But I couldn't stop. I had to go on screaming . . .

Joy As It Flies

SHE HAS GIVEN beauty a new category, he thought, for she appears to be edible. She is the word made fruit, rather than flesh, and with sugar and cream she would be delicious. Her neck would taste like an English apple, a pippin or nonpareil, and her arms, still faintly sunburnt from the mountain snow, of greengages.

'How old are you?' he asked.

'Nearly nineteen,' she answered, 'and I'm very mature for my age. We had lectures on all sort of things at Lausanne. Really up-to-date lectures on genetics, and Cocteau, and the ballet, and—oh, everything!'

'And what's your opinion of Cocteau?'

'Well, I don't think the lecture on him was a very good one—what are you laughing at?'

'I'm sorry.'

'I never pretended to know *much* about him, did I? But I do know who he is, and what he is, and that's something.'

'It's a great deal.'

'Then you shouldn't have laughed at me.'

'You make me feel light-hearted: that's the trouble.'

'You mustn't be light-hearted about the match, or everybody will be furious. A Rugby International is very serious.'

They stood idly, in a moving throng of people, in the cold sunlight of March in Edinburgh. If they should step over the sharply drawn line between light and shadow, into the shadow of the tall stand, the darker air would be as cold as January. But the several thousands of people, hearty and red of cheek, who were streaming into the ground to see a match between England and Scotland, thought their northern climate could not be bettered. They brought their own warmth, a genial excitement, a general euphory that made men's voices ring louder and more kindly than usual and girls look vivid and pretty though they were not.

Latimer, when he woke that morning after a night in the train, had had no expectation of watching Rugby football. His mind had lately been occupied by a domestic issue of the greatest importance, and he had come unwillingly to Edinburgh on business that could not be postponed or delegated. For nearly two hours he had argued stubbornly with an elderly and cantankerous Writer to the Signet who, having got his way with most of the disputed clauses, became suddenly jovial, insisted on taking Latimer home with him to a luncheon-party of ten people, and there persuaded him, easily enough, to go to the match. There were seats for all of them, but in different parts of the stand: two quartets and a pair.

'Latimer,' said the crusty old man, mellowed now by food and a second glass of port, 'you're an Englishman and England's going to be beaten. But you're my guest, so we'll need to provide you with pleasure of some kind. You'll take Corinna, and sit with her . . .'

'Oh, look!' she exclaimed, catching his arm and pointing to an ancient victoria, a shabby survival of carriage-days, that on creaking wheels rolled slowly towards them. It was drawn by a thin brown horse with enormous chestnuts depending from the inner faces of its large flat knees, and the cabman, in a greenish bowler and a short fawn-coloured coat, was small and old, pale of cheek but pink of nose, with a long unhappy upper lip. Three young men, who had done themselves too well at lunch-time and now regretted their extravagance, got hurriedly down, embarrassed by the attention they had attracted, and after quickly paying the cabman went off to their seats. The cabman, sour and dispirited, sat with the reins loose in his hands, and made no move to turn and go. The brown horse hung its head, and the pale sunlight showed the dust that lay thick upon the faded blue upholstery of the old carriage.

'Isn't it heavenly?' said Corinna. '*How* I wish we could go for a drive!'

'There's nothing to prevent us,' said Latimer.

'There's the match. Uncle Henry would be livid if we missed it. We can't miss the match, can we? But it would be fun!'

'You can look at footballers every winter for the rest of your life; but cabmen are dying out.'

'So a carriage-drive might be an historic occasion?'

'It might.'

'You don't want to see England beaten. You're trying to escape.'

'That may be the reason. Or it may be the light-heartedness I spoke of before.'

'We can't really go, can we?—Oh, he's driving away! Shout to him!'

'Cabby!' shouted Latimer.

'Where to?' asked the old man as the carriage tilted, the springs protested, they got in, and dust rose from the stained blue cushions to meet them.

'I don't think it matters.'

'Drive to the Castle,' said Corinna, 'and stop on the Esplanade. There'll be a view to-day.—Oh, isn't this the most wonderful thing that's ever happened?'

'I'm not quite sure how it did happen. I'm not sure if it should. Do you think, perhaps, that we ought to go back? Your uncle—'

'Must we?' she asked.

She had leaned heavily against him as the cabman wheeled abruptly on to a main road, and an antic fear had momentarily possessed him that he could not refrain from taking her into his arms and embracing her, regardless of the many latecomers to the match, now hurrying past on either side, who were already looking over their shoulders with amused or curious glances at the ancient carriage and its occupants so strangely going the wrong way. The impulse had seemed, for an instant, beyond control, and very properly it had frightened him. Only forty-eight hours before he had been sitting at his wife's bedside, his hands gripped fiercely by hers in her recurrent torment, and in his anxiety he had offered to the future all manner of extravagant bargains if she and her baby should survive their peril and their pain. For Latimer was in love with his wife, a lively black-haired girl, and the composure of his love was alarmed, as if a volcanic pulse had shaken it, by so urgent and unruly a desire to close with a young stranger. His conscience was perplexed, and over its surface ran the ruffle of fear lest he make an exhibition of himself. It was bad enough to be seen riding in a victoria, absurdly seated in an absurd vehicle trundling away from the football-ground that everybody else was moving towards; but to be caught embracing a girl, a lovely and seemingly edible girl of eighteen, under the bright intolerant sky of Edinburgh—oh, madness! Disaster shook its panic finger, goblin-eyed.

Out of his fear, then, he suggested going back, but when Corinna reproachfully asked, 'Must we?', he looked at her lips, become suddenly childish, and the blank disappointment of her gaze; and brusquely commanded his emotion. It was trivial enough, he found, he could rebuff it. As firmly as if fear had been a ball in a squash-court bouncing to his forehand, he drove it from him and said confidently, 'I was only thinking of your uncle—of my rudeness to him—but we shan't be missed, I'm sure. And you can see an International next year.'

'I've been taken to football matches ever since I can remember, and to go for a drive instead . . .' She turned and waved her hand to three small boys who whistled derisively from the pavement-edge. 'They're jealous,' she said. 'Everybody is jealous of us. Look at that deadly-dull woman leaning out of a window! Oh, what dull lives people lead! There ought to be more horses in a town, they smell so beautifully.'

On the causeway-stones the wheels rattled, the hooves of the thin brown horse beat in steady rhythm an old-fashioned tune, and leather loosely slapped its hide. When the off-wheels were caught in a tram-line the carriage lurched and threw Latimer and Corinna close together, but in the same moment her attention was taken by a seagull, come inland from the Forth, that balanced solemnly on the rim of a large gilded mortar over the door of a chemist's shop; and he, having snubbed the panic impulse, now dreaded no mischance but felt stirring in his mind a high nonsensical pleasure.

'There are more dull people,' she said as they passed two women in respectable drab clothes, one of whom was old, and a narrow-shouldered man of depressed appearance. 'I couldn't bear to be middle-aged! I couldn't bear to be anyone else!'

'Some of us have our compensations,' he told her.

'Oh, but you're different.'

'Though it's true that many are unlucky. I once heard a man say, "I never got much fun myself, but some of my friends have had an amazingly good time."'

'How terribly sad!'

'So it seemed to me, but he didn't think so. He was a well-fed, apparently contented person.'

'But how could he be?'

'You don't know what secrets he had. You don't know anything about other people. You don't know what terrible strands of interest hold together those two dowdy women and the man with bottle shoulders.'

'Do you?'

'They may have a plot to strangle him after supper tomorrow, while he has a better plan to hit them on the head, with a stone in the toe of a stocking, after tea.'

'That's not typical of life in Edinburgh.'

'But you can't deny the possibility. You can't even tell me what the seagull saw that was sitting on the edge of a golden mortar outside a chemist's shop.'

'Do you think there was anything in it?'

'A rag and a bone and a little wooden box.'

'What was in the box?'

'The telephone number of an old man who's forgotten what nobody else ever knew.'

'Goodness! You have got good eyes. Now tell me what he's looking at.' She pointed to a sailor who was staring into a fishmonger's full window.

'It can only be one thing, can't it?'

'Something horrible?'

'I'm afraid so. There's a flounder on the slab with his dead wife's ring in its mouth.'

'What a shock for the poor man! But perhaps she was a bad woman?'

'The worst woman in the world.'

They drove past houses set back from the road behind little gardens emptied by the winter, and looked at black or curtained windows, and the sky above them was as clear and cold as a great zircon. The old carriage groaned and rattled, and tall tramcars swaying on their shallow rails went shrilly past. Here and there, idly, Latimer read the name of a street: Roseburn, a shepherd's lyric deafened by stone, the remote Victorian echoes of Kew Terrace and Osborne Terrace, then a flour-mill and the vanished rural chaffering of the Haymarket, and so into shabbier thoroughfares till they saw mounting high and precipitous before them the darkly gleaming Castle rock. And all the way they spoke of nothing grave, of no material subject, and little even of themselves but for Corinna's recollection, now and then, of some ludicrous girl at school or a mistress's peculiar discipline and her outwitting. Latimer talked nonsense with an imagination as fluent as a hill-stream after rain—or a fortune-teller's patter in a booth—and Corinna's voice, like a swallow hunting evening flies, went to and fro in effortless arcs and charming cadences after topics so minute as almost to be invisible. But subsequently, when Latimer tried to remember what subjects had held them in conversation, he was inclined to believe that somehow they had touched—oh, lightly, it is true, but with conscious fingers—eternal themes and the poets' deeper chords.

He had made a joke about Byzantium—the architects of Edinburgh have sometimes had unlikely motives—but was it all a joke? He had described his sailing to the Fastnet in a leaking yacht improvidently manned, and made of dangerous misadventure a ludicrous tale; but surely in its burden had been the immemorial menace of the estranging sea? Corinna, talking of a concert solemnly attended by twenty schoolgirls, had described a plump and bespectacled friend's untimely woe, whom Gluck's *Orpheus* reminded that she had not prepared her necessary twenty lines of the *Aeneid*, Book IV, which they were reading—and then, oh surely then! they had fallen silent to think of Queen Dido in eternal grief upon the Africk shore. Such notes they had struck, he was sure of it in after years, though honesty could find no certain words to substantiate his faith. But a vibration of remembered light suffused his memory, as of goldfinches' wings above a thistle-field in the sun; and a sonorous echo of emotion, like a bell at sea, kept it alive.

They drove slowly up Castle Hill, and leaving the victoria on the Esplanade climbed to St Margaret's Chapel and looked northward over the Forth to the lands and the hills of Fife, dove-grey and glinting with gold. Corinna was confident of her geography and told him where the Bonny Earl of Moray had been slaughtered on the sea-wet rocks.

'Physical beauty was very rare in earlier times,' said Latimer. 'Beauty needs good food, and our ancestors fed poorly or foolishly. And because beauty was so rare it inspired a romantic devotion, while nowadays our appreciation is aesthetic—'

'Is it?' asked Corinna.

'Yes, I believe so. And aesthetic appreciation—'

'Is a little bit bogus, isn't it?'

'I don't think so.'

'Well, you're not really good-looking, but I like you.'

'I'm very glad. But are you being logical?'

'Oh, logic doesn't affect *people*!'

Slowly they walked down the Esplanade again, and climbed into the waiting carriage. 'We'll be in Murrayfield before the match is over,' said Latimer . . . .

That was ten years ago, and he had not seen her since. War had invaded their uneasy climate, and Latimer, going to France in 1939, had retired hurriedly from Dunkirk a few months later, and served thereafter, sometimes dangerously on the field and sometimes in the mingled strain and camaraderie of a Divisional Headquarters, in North Africa and Italy. He had been more fortunate than many. He had recuperated pleasantly from a winter wound in Amalfi, and after demobilisation returned to his previous occupation without grave reluctance. His wife had suffered from the tedium and the huge accumulation of war's minor difficulties more deeply than he, and it was she who proposed, in the first autumn after the fighting stopped, that they should spend a few weeks in the relatively untroubled air, and among the splendid fleshpots, of non-combatant Ireland.

When the war was over, the victorious but thin-ribbed English discovered that Ireland, for so long a synonym of hunger and discontent, had become something like an Egyptian granary. The victims of old oppression had meat upon their tables and butter in their lordly dishes, while the heirs of the haughty Ascendancy, of the barons in their Pale and the squires in their parks, fed sadly on offal from the Argentine and the confected fats of chemical industry. So week after week, in their hungry thousands, the famished conquerors were humbly crossing the narrow sea to fill their bellies with neutral beef and mutton that had not—they now were thankful—been sacrificed to any common good.

After three weeks in Kerry, the Latimers were spending a few days in Dublin before returning home, when he, going into their hotel one evening, was halted outside by a girl who held in front of him a wooden collecting-box.

'What's it for?' he asked.

'For the language,' she said.

'What language?'

'The Irish language, of course.'

'I don't understand. Why should you collect money for a language?'

'So that we can teach it. It's to pay the teachers.'

'And who's going to be taught to speak it?'

'Every one of us. Or so they say.'

'Do you think that's a good thing?'

'I do not!' said the girl. 'I wouldn't speak it myself!'

'Here's half a crown for honesty,' said Latimer, and climbed the steps.

In the lounge he discovered his wife in a group of six or seven people seated round a table on which were twelve or fourteen cocktails, for which two warm and hearty men were disputing the privilege to pay. He was not much surprised. He knew that his wife had arranged to meet an old school-friend and her husband, and he was well aware of her faculty for gathering company, both old friends and new, with a celerity that he could never match. But he was astonished beyond measure when, in the midst of inaccurate but genial introduction, he perceived, with her back to the light, Corinna.

'You know her, don't you?' said his wife. 'She told me that you're old friends. Her husband is Nick's cousin, but he's not here and Nick hasn't come either. So like the Irish, isn't it? Darling, we've all been drinking far too much, you must hurry and catch us up.'

'This is a surprise,' he said.

'You haven't changed a bit,' she answered.

'But you have.'

'My hair,' she said. 'I used to hide behind it. But then I realised what a nuisance it was, and had it cut off.'

'It suits you,' he said, and looked at her with a sudden greed of attention while the great artery above his heart beat with a perceptible and disconcerting vigour. The soft roundness of her face had become an exquisite tension between cheek-bone and jaw, her eyes seemed the larger in consequence, and her short hair, finely curling, showed the delicate firmness of her head.

'It's incredible,' he said.

'That we should meet again?'

'That Time should be your beauty-parlour.'

'That's Italy!' she said. 'Your wife told me you were in Italy. You've been practising compliments in Rome.'

'On the contrary, I assure you. I was in Trieste with Tito's votaries.'

'Tony spent most of the war with the Northern Patrol and running convoys to Russia. His notion of being romantic is to build a roaring fire, close all the windows, and create a fug that brings the tears to you eyes.'

'Tony's your husband?'

'Yes. I'm an old married woman now. I've got two children.'

'We have three.'

'What a lot can happen in ten years! A war and two families!'

'I've had a very quiet ten years, except for a battle or two.'

'Well, so have I. There wasn't much hectic gaiety in being a wife and mother in the south of England during the war. It's only in the last few weeks that I've got my hands clean.'

'Do you remember driving to the Castle in Edinburgh?'

'Of course.'

'Do make the conversation general!' cried Mrs Latimer. 'We're all trying not to listen, but my own ears are vibrating furiously, and I'm not the worst. Where have you been, darling?'

'I went to see Michael again.'

'Is he any more cheerful?'

'Someone has asked him to write an article about a very brilliant young Irish dramatist, whose name I can't remember, and he's had to refuse because he isn't quarrelling with him at present. Apparently no Irishman can write about any other Irishman unless they're in a state of open hostility.'

'How very odd. So incense doesn't make the heart grow fonder?'

For half an hour they spoke of the meals they had lately eaten. Food, food and drink, was the English topic in the first years of their victory—the world had rarely seen a hungrier triumph—and in their laurelled heads were childish dreams of sugared cakes. They spoke of steaks with reverence, of cheese with sober joy. Ireland, said one of them, was in danger of acquiring a population of new Protestants, as hunger, that once had stripped her, now drew to her green acres her over-taxed and undernourished neighbours. Ireland of the many famines, now glistening with fat, was England's dream of joy; and the conquerors talked of cream.

Then Corinna said she must go. She had to call for her husband; they were dining with a cousin of his.

'Let me take you,' said Latimer.

'Don't be late,' said his wife. 'We have a table at Jammet's.'

They went out, Corinna cool but he embarrassed.

With shuddering decision a taxi-cab was pulled abruptly to a halt, and the driver leaned towards them. He was an oldish man, burly of frame, with a friendly purple face and a watery eye. Latimer gave him the address, and got in. As violently as he had stopped, the driver started again, and a moment later nearly ran a cyclist down.

'He isn't very clever, is he?' said Corinna.

'Does it matter?'

'It may, if he meets someone as stupid as himself. I don't want to die with you.'

'Did your Uncle Henry ever discover that we didn't see the match?'

'No, I don't think so.'

'You didn't tell him?'

'I never told anyone.'

'Nor did I.'

'I've often tried to remember what we talked about. We talked all the time, and I've forgotten everything we said. What did we talk about?'

'Queen Dido and Byzantium.'

'It doesn't seem likely, but tell me more.'

'Dublin is ten years west of Edinburgh. We've less time than we had.'

The driver swerved widely to pass a halted tramcar, and in the lurching cab, filled momentarily with yellow light, Corinna fell into Latimer's arms, and made no move to escape again when his hands closed upon her shoulder and her side. The minutes passed—three, four, or five—before she moved away and said, 'We must be nearly there. Do I look as though you had been kissing me?'

'You look as if God had been kissing you,' he answered a trifle breathlessly.

'I don't think Tony would believe a story like that,' she said, and took out her powder-box. Then peering through the window, exclaimed, 'But where are we? We haven't come the proper way! I'm sure we haven't!'

She beat upon the sliding glass that divided them from the driver, and when he drew it open, asked him sharply, 'Do you know where we are?'

'I do not!' he said with wild vexation in his husky voice. 'I'm lost entirely.'

'Well!' she said. 'What do we do now?'

The driver, aware that he owed them some explanation, turned his purple face and shouted, 'It's drunk I am! As drunk as a pig!' And angrily closed the sliding glass.

'But this is dangerous,' she said, and let Latimer take her hand.

'He's going very slowly now. We shan't come to any harm,' he answered.

Again the driver opened the slide between them, and now in a more affable tone declared, 'But it's all right for you! I'm not charging you for this.' And pulled down his flag.

'Is that any comfort?' she asked.

'It's the handsomest thing I ever heard! *Bonosque soles effugere—*'

'Darling, you're not drunk too?'

'No, of course not. I'm misquoting Horace. Or is it Martial? I believe it's Martial.'

'But what does it mean?'

'You learnt Latin at school, didn't you?'

'What difference does that make?'

'None at all, none at all. But we haven't time to talk about education, have we? Listen to what I'm saying, it's most important. *Solesque*—no, that's wrong, you've put me off. *Bonosque soles effugere atque abire sentit, qui nobis pereunt et non imputantur.*—There now! Aren't we in luck?'

'How do I know, unless you tell me what it means?'

'Just what the driver said. No one's going to charge this to our account. Ireland, God bless it, is neutral still!'

The driver, deciding to try his luck in the opposite direction, turned right-about in the breadth of the street without slackening speed, and threw Corinna on to Latimer's breast before she could decide whether that was her intention or not. He, clasping her and advantage firmly together, began without loss of time to kiss her fondly, repeatedly, and with such enthusiasm as was bound to provoke a reciprocal warmth. The driver, looking this way and that but scorning to ask the help of any passer-by, turned east, west, north, and south to find a familiar landmark and the address that he had long since forgotten.

He looked for it in Ballsbridge and the neighbourhood of Glasnevin cemetery. He had a notion it might be in Ringsend, and not long after was out past Kilmainham Gaol and on the road to Mullingar. But open country frightened him, and he turned in a great hurry and drove at high speed past Guinness's Brewery, then loitered thoughtfully on College Green, and slowly, like a man in a trance, patrolled O'Connell Street and Grafton Street. He circumnavigated Merrion Square and went twice round St Stephen's Green to see if it was there. He remembered Rathmines and with fresh hope increased his speed again, but was perplexed by many streets that looked the same, and with a salmon's instinct in the spring turned north again to dawdle by the Liffey. Memory stirred more strongly in him, but a memory quite irrelevant, and for a long time he waited by the gate of the Rotunda Hospital, where he had been born. When at last he returned to Latimer's hotel and deposited Latimer, alone, he was nearly sober.

Latimer paid him off, and turning to go in encountered for the second time the girl with the collecting-box to whom he had spoken earlier in the evening.

She held the box in front of him, a little wearily. 'For the language,' she begged.

'Go home,' he told her, 'for you're wasting your time. There are no words for it in any language. Joy's inenarrable, as every cabman knows!'

Kind Kitty

Thay threpit that scho deit of thrist, and *maid* a gud end.
Efter hir dede, scho dredit nought in hevin for to duell,
And sa to hevin the heiway dreidles scho wend.

DUNBAR

NINE OUT OF every ten people in Edinburgh never look at anything but the pavements and the shallow shop-windows and the figuration of neighbours as belittled as themselves. This is for safety, and to keep their wits from wandering; because whoever will raise his head suddenly to the Castle may see Asgard looming in the mist, and the hills above Holyroodhouse, that one day are no more than slopes for children to play on, the next are mountains that thrust huge shoulders through the clouds and bare their monstrous brows in the heights of the sky. So also if you look down at the houses that press numerously against the outer walls of Holyrood you may see nothing but a multitude of mean roofs. But you may as easily surprise a coven of witches dancing in the smoke, and warlocks leaping on the chimney pots.

This was a sight that Kind Kitty saw whenever she came up out of the Canongate to sit on a seat in the gardens under the Calton Hill, with a little flat bottle of whisky in her pocket, and a bonnet with a broken feather precariously pinned to her dirty grey hair.

Kind Kitty was never afraid to look at the hills and the air-drawn heights of the town, for though they might steal her wits away she had no wealth or position that needed her wits' attention, and nothing to lose, though her thoughts took holiday for days on end, but a dozen hens and the wire-netting that confined them. It was the odour of hens that strangers first noticed, and most urgently disliked, when Kitty sat down beside them in the gardens. It overcame the other smells that accompanied her, of smoke, of clothes incredibly old, of a body long unwashed, of yesterday's beer and the morning's dram. It was a violent unexpected smell, and Kitty's casual neighbours would soon rise and leave her. Then she would grumble through her old blue lips, and peer after them malevolently with her red and rheumy eyes, and unwrapping a piece of newspaper from the little bottle she would take a quick mouthful of whisky. 'Tae hell with you, then, for a high-minded upstart,' she would mutter, and wipe her mouth, and a water-drop from the end of her nose, with the back of her bony hand. But in a minute or two she would forget the insult, when her bleary eyes were captured by witches and warlocks dancing in the smoke, or by a flank of the Pamirs that pushed its stony ribs against the firmament. Then she would think of life and death, of the burnside in Appin where she had been born, of the great soldier, Sir Hector McOstrich, and the lovely wicked Lady Lavinia. The weave of life, like gunmetal silk shot with bright yellow, shone for her, at such an angle, with the remote and golden-lovely frailty of sunset after a rainy day. Misery in the morning was forgotten, and squalor after noon, beneath that aureate sky, returned like rain to the deeps of the earth.

But sooner or later the sunset would fade from her thoughts, the hills diminish, the warlocks dissolve into bitter vapour, and her belly protest its emptiness with loud exclamatory repetition. Then, with a twitch to her bonnet, a hitch to her dusty skirt, and a pull at her broken stays, she would rise in a sudden temper, and muttering furious complaints against the littleness of small whisky bottles, she would hobble back to the Canongate, and stop to stare balefully at The Hole in the Wall, whose doors were not yet open. 'The mealy-mou'ed thowless thieves,' she would mutter. 'The bletherin' kirk-gaun' puggies!' And she would spit on the pavement to show her contempt for the law, and those who made it, that public-houses should be closed while thirst still grew unchecked.

It was drink, not food, that her empty stomach clamoured for. She ate little, and took no pleasure in such tasteless stuff as bread and potatoes and tinned beef. But for beer and black stout and whisky she had so great a love that her desire for them was unceasing, and her relish for their several flavours more constant than any carnal love. Except for a shilling or two that she was sometimes compelled to pay for rent, and a few coppers that went on corn for her hens, she spent all her money on drink and still was dry-mouthed for three or four days out of seven. She had the Old Age pension, and ten shillings a week was paid her, though unwillingly, by Sir Hector's grandson, who was not a soldier but a stockbroker, and bitterly resented such a burden on his estate. This income might have been sufficient to preserve her from the most painful and extreme varieties of thirst had she been content to drink draught ale, and that in solitude. But Kitty was both extravagant and generous, she liked whisky and good company, friendship and bottled beer, and twenty shillings a week was sadly insufficient for such rich amusement. Many of her friends were poorer than herself, and none was more wealthy, so their return for Kitty's entertainment was always inadequate. They would sometimes treat her to half a pint of beer, more rarely to a nip of whisky, but usually they repaid her with cups of tea, or half a herring, which gave her no pleasure whatever. She never calculated the profit and loss of good-fellowship, however, and so long as her neighbours had lively conversation and a cheerful spirit she would share her last shilling with them.

But a friend of hers, an old cast whore called Mima Bird, found a ten-shilling note one Christmas, and buying a dozen bottles of Bass invited Kitty to come and drink six of them. The nobility of this entertainment inspired Kitty with a great desire to emulate it—not in vulgar competition, not for the ostentation of surpassing it, but simply to give again, and enjoy again, the delights of strong liquor and warm fellowship—so after much thought, and with high excitement, she formed a plan and made arrangements for a Hogmanay party that would put the Old Year to bed with joy and splendour.

New Year's Eve fell on a Saturday, and on Friday Kitty drew her Old Age pension and cashed the ten-shilling order that came from young Mr McOstrich. But a pound was not nearly enough to furnish such a party as she intended. She went to see James Campbell, the landlord of The Hole in the Wall, and after long discussion came to an agreement with him, and pledged her whole income for the first two weeks in January in return for thirty-three shillings in ready money and the loan of five tumblers. These were the best terms she could get, for Campbell was a hard man.

But Kitty did not waste much time in bemoaning so heavy a rate of interest. She had no reverence for money, as respectable people have, nor concern for the future; and her mind was occupied with entrancing preparations for the party. She bought two bottles of whisky, two dozen bottles of beer, and a dozen of stout. Nothing like so huge and extravagant an array had ever been seen in her dirty little kitchen in Baxter's Close, and the spectacle filled her with excitement that yielded presently to a kind of devotion, and then became pure childlike joy. She set the beer, orderly in rank, on the table, with the two whisky bottles on the mantelpiece, and the porter like a round fender before the empty fire. Then she stood here and there to admire the picture, and presently rearranged the bottles and marshalled the beer, like a fence, in front of the wire-netting that closed her dozen hens in a small extension of the kitchen that might, with a more orthodox tenant, have been the scullery. The hens clapped their wings, and encouraged her with their clucking. Then she made patterns and plans on the floor, now a cross, before which she signed herself with the Cross, and now a rough plan of Tearlach's Hall, in Appin, where Sir Hector and Lady Lavinia had lived in pride and many varieties of sin. Her old hands took delicately the smooth necks of the bottles, she patted into place a label that was half-unstuck, she made a shape like a rose, the bottles standing shoulder to shoulder in the middle, and the tears ran down her cheek to see the loveliness of that pattern. Weary at last, replete with happiness, she fell asleep with a bottle of whisky in her arms.

When morning came she woke in pride to be confronted with such riches, and her demeanour, that only her hens observed, was uncommonly dignified. Setting the bottles on the table, according to their kind and now without fantasy, she carefully considered her arrangements and debated their sufficiency for the imminent party. Was her house properly furnished for entertainment? There were five tumblers that she had borrowed, one that she possessed, a bed where four might sit, a chair, a stool, and more drink than had ever been seen in one room in all her memory of Baxter's Close. What else could be needed for the pleasure of her guests?

A thought entered her mind that she first repelled and then suffered to return. Some of her visitors might like something to eat. If that were so, it would be a great nuisance, and for a little while Kitty thought impatiently about the frailties of humankind and the monstrous demands that people made for their contentment. But presently she counted her money and found she had still four shillings left. So she put on her bonnet and went out shopping.

The wind blew coldly down the Canongate, with a flourish of rain on its ragged edge, but Kitty, with money in her purse and in her heart the intention of spending it, was too important to notice such small discomfort, and going first to a baker's she bought for two shillings a Scotch bun. With that fierily sweet and bitter-black dainty under her arm she turned and walked slowly, over greasy pavements, to a corn chandler's in the High Street, where for ninepence she obtained a large bag of Indian corn for her hens. Then she returned to the Canongate, and having purchased threepennyworth of cheese she entered The Hole in the Wall, at the very moment when its doors opened, and made a satisfying meal of a shilling's worth of draught beer and the bright wedge of American cheddar.

The afternoon was slow in passing, but Kitty amused herself with ingenious new arrangements of the bottles, and with feeding her hens, and soon after six o'clock her first guest arrived, who was Mima Bird, the old whore. Then came Mrs Smiley, who made a small living by selling bootlaces; Mrs Hogg, who should have been well-off, her husband having had both his legs shot off while serving in the Black Watch, but he spent all his pension on threepenny bets and twopenny trebles; old Rebecca Macafee, who had been a tinker till she married a trawler's cook, who deserted her, and varicose veins kept her from the country roads; and Mrs Crumb, who has a good job as a lavatory attendant, but had to support a half-witted husband and three useless sons. These were Kind Kitty's oldest and favourite friends, and when she saw them all sitting in her kitchen each with a dram inside her to warm her stomach and loosen her tongue and flush her cheeks—each with a glass of beer or stout in her hand and another bottle beside her—then she was so happy that all of a sudden she cackled with laughter, and rocked to and fro on her stool, and began to sing an old song in a loud hoarse voice:

'O Sandy, dinna ye mind,' quo' she,
'When ye gart me drink the brandy,
When ye yerkit me owre among the broom,
And played me houghmagandy!'

'It's better among the broom than in the Meadows on a cauld winter night, or up against the wall of Greyfriars Kirk with a drunken Aussie seven foot high,' cried Mima Bird.

'Ay, but they'd money to spend, had the Aussies,' said old Rebecca, 'and faith, they spent it.'

'It was a fine war while it lasted,' sighed Mrs Hogg, whose husband, for three good years, had been more use to the Black Watch than he had ever been to her.

'The boys did well enough,' said Kitty, 'but the generals and the high heid yins were a pack of jordan-heidit losingers.' And she thought, sadly and lovingly, of Sir Hector McOstrich, who would have shown them how to win battles had not shame, not war, untimely killed him. But far-off thoughts could not long endure the loud immediacy of her cummers, whose laughter grew more frequent, whose tales and jolly memory became with every passing minute more rich and lively and delectable. Now and again their laughter would wake even the corn-fed hens to responsive clucking and scratching; and in the smoky light of a dingy lamp the coarse and weather-beaten cheeks of the six old women, their wrinkled eyes and creasy necks, were lovely with a life invincible. The air was full of the rich odours of beer and stout, and ever and anon its heavy layers would lift and waver before the genial shock of a great crackling belch. Kitty gave them another dram, and thick slices of black bun.

'If whisky was a river, and I was a duck,
O whisky! Johnny!
I'd dive to the bottom and I never would come up,
O whisky for my Johnny!'

sang old Rebecca. 'When that man I was married on, and a hog-eyed lurdan he was,' she said, 'would come home from sea, he was so thick with salt it would fill you with thirst to smell him half-way up the stairs.'

'You must have robbed a bank to give us a party like this,' said Mrs Crumb. 'It beats the High Commissioner's garden-party at Holyrood just hollow. Why, we've drink to every hand, and the very best of drink at that, but there, so they tell me, the ministers' wives are fair tumbling over each other, and tearing each other's eyes out, to get to the eatables and the drinkables, and them nothing but lemonade and ha'penny cakes.'

'It's the very best party I ever was at,' said Mrs Hogg.

'It's the only one I've ever been to,' said Mrs Smiley, and that was a lie, but she thought it was true and began to cry, and got another dram to stop her.

So the evening wore on, and by half-past eleven there was nothing left in the glasses but dry feathers of froth, nothing in the bottles but a remembering air. By then, however, it was time to go out and join the multitude, coming from all directions, that was crowding the pavement before St Giles and filling the night with a valedictory noise. These were the common people of Scotland, come to tread underfoot, as bitter ashes, their lost hopes of the Old Year, its miseries they had survived, and to welcome the New Year with hope inexpugnable and confidence that none could warrant and none defeat. The procession of the months would give them neither riches nor wisdom, beauty nor holiness, but under every moon were many days of life, and life was their first love and their last. So the bells rang loudly as they might, the little black bottles were offered to friend and stranger—for all were brothers out of the same unwearying and shameless womb, and many were drunk enough to admit the relationship—hands were held in a circle by unknown hands, songs were sung, and a boisterous dance was trodden. The New Year was made welcome like a stranger in the old days of hospitality, though none knew whether he was whole or sick, or loyal or lying.

Now when the old women, who had spent such a fine evening with

Kitty, came out into the night, the cold air beat on their foreheads and made worse confusion of their befuddled minds, so that four of them lost control of their legs and nearly all cognisance of the world about them. Mrs Smiley lay in the gutter and slept, and Mrs Hogg, lying curiously across a barrel, slept also. Mrs Crumb, walking in a dwaum, clung to the arm of a kind policeman, and old Rebecca, having bitten the hand of an officer of the Salvation Army, vanished in the darkness of a near-by close. But Kitty and Mima Bird staggered valiantly along and came near enough to St Giles to be caught in the crowd and to join their cracked voices in song, to lurch bravely in the dancing, and to crow their welcome to the infant year.

It was late the next morning when Kitty woke on her dirty and disordered bed. Her boots had made it muddy, her broken bonnet lay on the pillow beside her. How she had reached home she could not remember, nor did she worry her aching head to try. Her mouth was parched and sour, her eyes smarting, her stomach queasy. She lay for a long time before she had the strength or courage to move, and then agonisingly sat up, her head splitting beneath a great jolt of pain, and wretchedly set her feet to the floor. She groped among the debris of the feast, holding bottle after bottle with shaking hands to the dim grey square of window to see if any sup remained. But they were all as empty as though a hot wind of the desert had dried them, till at last, hidden by the greasy valance of the bed, she found one that held—O bliss beyond words!—a gill of flat beer. This she drank slowly and with infinite gratitude, and then, taking off her boots and putting her bonnet in a place of safety, she returned to bed. 'What a nicht wi' Burns!' she murmured, and fell asleep.

In the middle of the night she woke with a raging thirst. Headache and nausea had gone, but her whole body, like a rusty hinge, cried for moisture. Yet water was no good to her. She filled her rumbling belly with it, and it lay cold and heavy in her stomach and never penetrated the thirsty tissues. Her tongue was like the bark of a dead tree, her mouth was a chalk-pit, her vitals were like old dry sacks. Never before had she known such thirst. It seemed as though drought had emptied her veins, as rivulets to dry in the high noon of summer, and her bowels resembled the bleached and arid canvas of a boat that has drifted many days beneath the parching pitiless sun of Capricorn. In this agony, in this inward and ever-increasing Sahara, she lay till morning, while her very thoughts changed their direction with a creak and a groan.

But when the time came for it to open, she went to The Hole in the Wall and pleaded with James Campbell for a little credit, that she might save her life with a quart or two of beer. He, however, refused to let her have a single drop, not a sparrow's beakful, till she had paid into his hands, on the following Friday, her Old Age pension and her ten shillings from young Mr McOstrich. Then, he said, out of pure Christian kindliness he would let her drink a pint or so on consideration of her pledging to him another week's income. Nor could he be moved from this cruel and tyrannous decision.

It seemed to Kitty, as she walked home, that her body at any moment might crumble into dust and be blown away. She opened her mouth to suck in the wind and the rain, but the wind changed in her throat to a hot simoom, and choked her with a sandstorm of desire for the slaking gold and cool foam of bitter beer. She sat in her dark room gasping for assuagement, and tormented by the vision and the gurgling noise of ale cascading into glass. The marrow dried in her bones.

But despite the unceasing torture she would not yield to the temptation to beg sixpence or a dram, supposing they had it, from her friends. To sorn like a tinker on those whom she had so lately entertained like a queen was utterly impossible. Her spirit was too proud to stoop so low for comfort. Her torment must continue. She had nothing to sell, nothing that anyone would conceivably buy, not even her hens, for they were long past laying and too thin to be worth the plucking. She was shipwrecked, and she must endure till time should rescue her.

But she had not so long to wait for relief as she feared, for about six o'clock in the evening, when The Hole in the Wall was open again for those who had money, her hens began clacking and chacking as though they were mad, and anyone who had been there might have seen Kitty's head fall to one side, and one hand slide stiffly from the arm of her chair. She was dead, and it was thirst that had killed her. Thirst had sucked out the vital essence of her life, and left nothing but dry tubes and a parched frame behind. Her body was dead and as dry as a powdery sponge in a chemist's shop.

Some time later her soul felt better, though not yet at ease, when she found herself walking along Death's Road to the worlds beyond this world. She was still thirsty, but not agonised with thirst. She was worried by the flies and the midges on the lower part of the road, and she was angry to find herself dead; for she had enjoyed being alive. But she kept bravely on her way, knowing the proper thing to do, and she felt exceedingly scornful of the innumerable travellers who grumbled at stones in the way—for it was not a motor-road—and complained about the lack of sign-posts, and sulkily lay down in the shadow of a hedge to wait for a bus that would never come.

The road climbed slowly round the side of a hill whose top was lost in a luminous mist. After a few hours Kitty became reconciled to death, and trudged on with growing curiosity. The farther she went the lonelier the road became, till for a mile or two she saw no one at all. Then, at a fork in the road, she found a group of some twenty people, very well dressed for the most part, who were discussing which way they should go. For on the left hand the road led downhill to a valley shining in the sun, but on the right it climbed steeply and narrowed in a few hundred yards to a mountain track. The majority of the disputing travellers favoured clearly the low road, but a dubious minority furrowed their brows and looked without relish at the upward path. The debate came to an end as Kitty drew near to them. A well-bred female voice, like a ship's bell in the night, exclaimed: 'The idea is absurd. As though such a wretched little path could lead to anything or anywhere!' 'Unless to a precipice,' added a tired young man. And the party, with scarcely a glance at Kitty, turned downhill with resolute steps or a shrug of the shoulders.

'Tyach!' said Kitty, and went the other way.

The path she took was not unlike the little road that leads to Arthur's Seat. The resemblance comforted her, and so did the mist, which was like a Scots haar with the sun coming through it. The track bent and twisted and crossed a depression between three hills. It rose into the mist. She walked for a long time in a sunny vapour, and lost her breath, and grew thirsty again.

Then the view cleared, and on the forefront of a great plateau she came to a high wall, with a tall white gate in it, and beside the gate a house with an open door, two bow-fronted lower windows, and three upper ones, from the centre of which jutted a green holly bush. So Kitty knew it was a tavern, and taking no notice of the ivory gate in the wall she walked gladly in, and rapped on the bar. But when she saw who came to answer the summons, she was so astounded and so abashed that she could not speak, though a moment before she had known very well what she meant to say.

It was a lady with high-piled golden hair who came to serve her—but the gold was dim, the colours of her dress were faded (it had been fashionable when King Edward VII was crowned), her mouth had forgotten laughter—and Kitty, seeing not only all that had changed but that which was unchanged, knew her at once.

'Well,' said the lady, 'and what can I give you?'

'Oh, your ladyship!' stammered Kitty, and twisted her dirty old hands in joy and embarrassment.

Then, before either could speak again, a tall thin man came in through the outer door with a basket on his arm. He had a nose like a hawk's beak, a pair of fine moustaches like the wings of a hawk, he wore a deer-stalker's cap and an old Norfolk jacket, and the basket on his arm held a loaf of bread, a beef-bone, and some vegetables. He put the basket on a table and murmured to the lady with the dimmed golden hair, 'A customer, my dear? Things are looking up, aren't they?'

'Sir Hector!' said Kitty in a trembling voice.

But though she recognised them, they did not remember her, for she had lived longer than they had, and life had used her inconsiderately. It was only after long explanation, after much exclamation, that they knew her, and saw faintly in her dissipated features the sweet young lines of Kitty of the Burnside. Sir Hector was visibly distressed. But Kitty, giving him no time to speak his pity, indignantly asked, 'And what are you doing here, in a pub at Heaven's gate, who never soiled your hands with work of any kind on earth below? Is there no respect in Heaven? Or has someone been telling lies about you, and dirty slander, as they did in Appin, and London, and Edinburgh too?'

'We have been treated with understanding and forgiveness,' said Lady Lavinia; and Sir Hector loudly cleared his throat and added, 'It was a situation of great difficulty, a very delicate situation indeed, and we have no complaints to make. None whatever,' he said, and took his message basket into the kitchen.

But Kitty was sorely displeased by the indignity of their condition, for in her youth they had been great and splendid figures—though shameless in their many sins, dissolute in all ways, and faithful only to their mutual love—and in her loyalty she vilified the judgment of Heaven, that kept them beyond its gate. She swore that if they were not good enough for God's company, then He could do without her also. She wouldn't go to Heaven. Not she, she said. Not though God and all His holy angels came out to plead with her. 'Be damned if I'll consort with you,' she would say, and that would teach them what other people thought of their treatment of a great gentleman like Sir Hector, and a lady like Lady Lavinia.

So for a few days Kitty stayed in the inn by Heaven's gate, and the beer there was as good as she had ever tasted, and her heart was glad to be in such grand company. But she could not restrain her curiosity to see what Heaven was like, and one morning she knocked on the ivory door, and when St Peter opened it she did her best to slip inside. But St Peter pushed her back, and asked her who she was. Nor did he seem much impressed when she told him.

'And how did you get here?' he asked.

'Well,' said Kitty, 'it all began with a Hogmanay party in Baxter's Close in the Canongate . . .'

'That's enough,' said St Peter. 'We want none of your kind here.' And he shut the door in her face.

Now having been refused admission, Kitty's curiosity became overwhelming, and she made up her mind to enter Heaven by hook or crook. So she walked up and down muttering angrily, till she thought of a trick that might beat St Peter's vigilance, and the following morning she knocked again on the ivory door.

St Peter frowned angrily when he saw who it was, but before he could speak, Kitty exclaimed, 'There's an auld friend of yours in the pub ootbye that's speiring for you, and would like you to go and have a crack with him.'

'What's his name?' asked St Peter.

'I just canna mind on,' Kitty answered, 'but he's a weel-put-on man with whiskers like your own.'

'It's not like any friend of mine to be spending his time in a public house,' said St Peter.

'You wouldna deny an auld friend because he likes his glass, would you?'

Now at that moment Kitty had a stroke of luck, for beyond the wall a cock crew loud and piercingly, and Kitty said quickly, 'You'll remember that once before you cried out you didna ken a man you kent full well. You'll not be wanting to make the same mistake again, I'm thinking?'

At that St Peter's face grew dark red with rage and shame. But he tucked up his gown and went swiftly out and over to the inn, leaving the gate of Heaven open. And Kitty, as soon as his back was turned, scuttled inside.

It seemed to her that Heaven had a rather deserted look. She had expected to see well-dressed crowds and a fine air of prosperity and well-being. She had hoped to associate with lords and ladies, or at least with wealthy people of the kind that lived in Heriot Row and did their expensive shopping in Princes Street. But the only people she saw were almost as shabbily dressed as she was, and even they were few in number.

She stopped and spoke to a mild little man who sat on a green chair beneath a white-flowering tree. 'The others will have gone for a picnic?' she asked. 'Or they'll be busy with their choir practice?'

'There are no others,' he answered. 'At least, not here. Some of the farther regions, that people of an older birth have chosen, are well enough populated, but here we are very few in number. So many on earth today have lost their faith . . .'

'The glaikit sumphs!' said Kitty, and continued her walk, but without much enjoyment. She was saved from boredom, indeed, only by discovering, in the shelter of a little wood, a henhouse with a run attached, in which a score of finely feathered Rhode Island Reds were gravely scratching, their ruddy plumage a very pretty contrast to green leaves and white sand. While Kitty stood watching them with interest and admiration, she was surprised, and somewhat perturbed by the approach of Our Lady and a young woman in a khaki shirt and cotton breeches.

Kitty most reverently curtsied, Our Lady as graciously smiled, and the young woman in the breeches went into the hen run. Presently she reappeared with a dejected look on her face and two small eggs in her hand.

'Now really,' said Our Lady, 'that's *most* disappointing. Two eggs today, three yesterday, and four the day before. They're getting worse and worse. I do think you might persuade them to do better than that, Miss Ramsbottom.'

'I'm giving them the very same feeds that were recommended by the Government College of Dairying and Poultry Management,' said Miss Ramsbottom unhappily.

'Well, if that doesn't suit them, why not try something else?'

'But I don't know anything else. We weren't taught anything else in the Government College. It took us so long to learn . . .'

'You let me look after them, Your Ladyship,' said Kitty. 'I kept a dozen hens in a back kitchen in Baxter's Close, in the Canongate in Edinburgh, and fed them on anything I could find, or on nothing at all, and they laid like herring-roe for eight or nine years, some of them, till the poor creatures were fairly toom, and nothing could be done with them at all. But with bonny birds like these we'll have eggs dropping all day, like pennies in the plate at a revival meeting.'

'All right,' said Our Lady, 'I'll give you a trial and see how you get on. And if there's a choice—though there hasn't been for a long time past—it's the brown eggs that I prefer, especially for breakfast, though the white ones are good enough for omelettes, of course. Now come along, Miss Ramsbottom, and I'll find something else for you to do.'

So Kitty was given work in Heaven, and for several weeks she was happy enough to be looking after such handsome and well-disposed fowls, for under her care they became not merely prolific but regular in their habits. Two circumstances, however, kept her from settling down in whole contentment, one being the lack of congenial company, the other the fact that in Heaven there was nothing to drink but light wines and beer, and the beer was poor in quality.

She took to wandering far afield, and found that regions more remote from the gate were fairly thickly populated. But many of the inhabitants, to her disgust, were foreigners, and even among those of Scottish or English origin she found few with whom she had much in common. Yet she continued to explore the upper reaches of Heaven, for having met Our Lady she was seized with ambition to encounter God the Father and the Son of Man.

It was after a very long walk that by chance she saw God. He was sitting in a pleached arbour drinking wine with a bald man in doublet and hose, his head the shape of an egg, and another in sombre garments, with a broad bony forehead, untidy thick hair, and a wild mouth. Their voices were loud and magnificent, and a pleasant lightning played about the forehead of God the Father.

'I wrote your true morality,' said the bald man, 'when I made Parolles say *Simply the thing I am shall make me live*.'

'And I,' said the man with the bony forehead, 'I wrote your pure wisdom in the third movement of my Emperor concerto, when I put the Hero—the Conqueror, the Fool—in the middle of a ring, and fenced him round with dancing countryfolk and laughter that would not stop.'

'So you're my Moralist, and you're my Philosopher?' said God the Father. 'And what was I when I said *Let there be light?* Simply the Artist for art's sake?'

'A pity you hadn't also said *Let there be understanding*,' said the man with the bony forehead.

'Then would you have robbed poor dramatists of their trade,' said the bald man.

Now this kind of conversation, though it appeared to please its participants, had no interest for Kitty, and without waiting to hear more she went on past the pleached arbour, and came presently to a little rocky foreland in the cliff of Heaven, and looking over the edge she saw something of the world below.

She had never known till then what evil there was upon the earth. But looking down, through the clear light of Heaven, she saw lies and tyranny and greed, misery like a dying donkey in the sand and greed like a vulture tearing its vitals. She saw hunger and heard weeping. She saw a fool in black uniform who had made his own people drunk with lying words and threatened all Europe with war. She saw bestial stupidity consume the horde of humanity like vermin on a beggar's skin. And then she found that she was not alone on the little foreland, for in a cleft of the rock was the Son of Man, weeping.

So Kitty, in a great hurry to escape unseen, came quickly away from there, and without waiting to look at anything else returned to her henhouse and the comforting plumpness of her Rhode Island Reds. She was hot and leg-weary after her long walk, and very depressed by what she had seen of the farther parts of Heaven. She wanted to sit down in a comfortable chair, and take off her boots, and drink a quart or two of good strong ale. She needed ale, and plenty of it, to soothe and reassure her. But as luck would have it, the beer that night was thin as a postcard, sour as vinegar, and there was very little of it. Kitty lost her temper completely, and let anyone who cared to listen know just what she thought of Heaven and the only brewer—since men brewed their own—who had ever succeeded in swindling his way into it. At dinner time the next day she repeated the whole story, for again the beer was small in quantity and less in quality, a cupful, no more, and little better than swipes.

She rose from the table in fury, and went straight to the gate, which was unattended. She threw it open, and without any feeling of regret heard it slam behind her.

But in the tavern below the wall, with a tankard of their own brewing before her, she soon found good temper again, and told Sir Hector and Lady Lavinia a fine story of the hardships she had had to endure.

'Not that I wasn't real pleased to be working for Our Lady,' she said, 'and a fine time *she* had while I was there, with two good brown eggs to her breakfast every morning, but apart from her the company was poor—no gentry at all—and there were sights there that I wouldna care to see again, and talk that made no sense, and the beer was just a disgrace. It's maybe all right for them that like it, and God knows I wouldna say a word against the place, but I think I'll be better suited here, if you'll keep me. I can peel the tatties and scrub the floor and clean your boots, and if you won't grudge me a nip and a pint when my work's done, I'll be far happier here than in ahint that wall of theirs. And I wouldna find it easy to get by yon birkie with the keys again,' she added.

There then, in the inn at Heaven's gate, Kind Kitty found her proper place. There she is still, doing a little work and drinking a good deal, and whomsoever Death takes from this world, whose legs and faith are strong enough for the hillward path, will do well to stop there and drink a pint or two for the good of the house and his own comfort. For Kitty's presence is sure proof that the ale is still good. Had its quality failed she would have gone elsewhere long before now.

The Duke

STANDING INHUMANLY tall, on the hill called Ben Bhragie, was the statue to the old Duke. It was a monument to crime, a memorial to greed and folly. In his name and by his authority the happiness of a broad countryside had been laid in ruins, and misery domesticated. Many thousands of people had been robbed of land that was theirs by the right of immemorial usage, and evicted with every circumstance of brutality from the homes their fathers had built and they had plenished. Leaving behind them a blazing roof, carrying what they could of their small wealth, encumbered by the aged and the weak and by crying children, the stricken Highlanders had been driven from their native valleys like refugees before a barbaric invader. Yet no foreign power was hostile to them. Their enemy was their own chieftain. In nine years fifteen thousand of them had been turned out of their snug inland farms and exiled on a barren coast where, from weedy rocks and a sour turf, they might compete for a starved living with coneys and gulls and harsh weather.

Had they been savage and debased, their fate would still have been pitiful. Had their hills been the home of bandits, their villages of corruption, such punishment might still be thought severe. But they had been, on the contrary, a people given equally to virtue and to valour. Peaceful in their private lives, as soldiers serving their chieftain or their king they had been famous for their audacity in attack, for the sternness of their courage in adversity. On their farms they had lived in quiet simplicity, in the field—in France and on the Peninsula—they had won for the Ninety-Third Highlanders a glory more proud than Roman eagles. They had deserved well of all men, even of their enemies, and their enemies indeed remembered them with respect. But their chieftain had betrayed them because they owned land that he coveted. That was their crime. They tilled their farms, and lived on the product of their toil, but he, who was already a leviathan of wealth, made little or no profit out of them. Sheep would pay him better. So he told his agents to drive them out, and bring flockmasters from the south to replace them. That was why his statue was raised so inhumanly tall on Ben Bhragie.

The Castle was set pleasantly among fields. Planted with trees, they were acquiring the mellow and accomplished appearance of a nobleman's park. The Castle was square, with towers at the corners, but preparations were being made to enlarge it, to add a wing, another tower, and a massive and ornate front. Foundations were being dug for the wing, piles of timber and cut stones were lying about, when the Duke—the son of the statued Duke, and himself now old—came north from London with a duty to discharge. Britain was at war with Russia, and the Queen's army needed men for the Crimea. The Duke was a patriot, and he had promised to recruit some hundreds of his own clansmen. The offer was warmly welcomed by Her Majesty's ministers, for no finer fighting men could be found, and the Duke assured them that they would soon have another battalion to throw against the Russian redoubts.

Hurried preparations for a great recruiting meeting were made in Golspie, a village on the coast, a mile or two south of the Castle, and notices were sent round the neighbouring parishes to warn people of the Duke's presence and apprise them of their duty to attend. These orders were respectfully received, and on the morning appointed at least four hundred men assembled in Golspie, at a place where the street broadened and where two recruiting sergeants were already walking up and down. Tables had been set on trestles, and there were chairs behind them, including a handsome leather-furnished armchair for the Duke. The crowd regarded these arrangements without much apparent emotion. They were quiet and well-behaved, talking together in little groups, and gradually coalescing into a closely packed throng as more and more late-comers arrived, and the pressure grew of women and children on the flanks of the assemblage. These were more inclined to be noisy, calling shrilly to each other in Gaelic, till their menfolk sternly bade them be quiet. Absolute silence lay on the crowd when the Duke arrived.

He came in a carriage drawn by a pair of fine grey horses. His factor was with him, there was an officer wearing long Dundreary whiskers, and a minister of the Church of Scotland who had served his patron well by telling the crofters that eviction from their holdings was an act ordained by God, as a just punishment for their sins, and they must suffer it patiently and without resentment. Other members of the Duke's household, clerks and underfactors, had already arrived, and the recruiting party arranged itself behind the trestle-tables, a sergeant on either flank and the Duke enthroned in the middle.

They became busy with certain matters preliminary to the enlistment of the clansmen. Pens and ink-bottles were set out, piles of attestation papers laid on the table. The factor produced a black

speech, referred again to his bounty, and trembling with indignation declared that their behaviour was such an insult as he had never in his life received. But he would give them one more chance. Who would join the colours? Who were not afraid to be men, and who were simply cowards?

The silence on the crowd seemed to grow more heavy. It lay on them like a roof, and beneath its weight they seemed to contract, to grow in upon themselves. They stood like men made of stone. Even the sound of their breathing was subdued.

The Duke still waited for a forward movement to break their ranks. But no movement came. Then in a passion he shouted, 'This is the first and only time in history when the men of Sutherland have refused a call to duty! Your fathers and your grandfathers would be ashamed to own you. They were heroes, and you are dastards. Whenever there was danger, wherever there was war, the Highlanders—your brave ancestors—were first against the foe. And do you, their sons, hang back and hold to the skirts of your womenfolk like poltroons? What are you frightened of? Of the enemy? Your fathers faced the world in arms. Are you frightened of getting hurt? You'll be well looked after if you're wounded. Your country will treat you generously and see that you never want. Great Britain doesn't forget those who serve her! Your wives and children will be properly cared for while you're away. I myself will make it my sacred charge to see that no one suffers the smallest hardship whose breadwinner is fighting his country's battles.'

Like a black ripple on the sea, a sound of bitter laughter ran through the crowd. It passed, and silence followed. It passed as quickly as a catspaw of wind, blowing down from the cliffs, will overrun a narrow bay. But brief and small as it was, it disconcerted the Duke, who sat down, heavily and suddenly, and gripped the arms of his chair, and stared at the crowd with some obscure emotion in his soul and in his eyes.

Then an old man came out from the heart of the crowd. It opened slowly, like a dark leaf opening, and he came out and stood in the open space between the men of Sutherland and the recruiting party. He stood straightly and firm on his feet, not a big man, but tall enough to have a look of authority, though his face was lined with sorrow and his eyes were the eyes of a man who had seen disaster more often than triumph. He took off his bonnet—it was old and faded—and spoke in a high clear voice, in the accents of one whose natural talk was the Gaelic, but in words that did not fail him though he had to put his thoughts into English.

'Your Grace,' he said. 'We are indeed the sons of our fathers who fought so often for their King, and fought so well that you and all men remember them with pride. We are their sons, I say, and because of that we remember their fate who trusted to your promises, and to the promises of your ancestors. It was near this very place that your maternal grandmother, at forty-eight hours' notice, mustered fifteen hundred men and chose out of them the nine hundred she wanted for the King's service. And they went willingly, as volunteers, because they trusted her, and she would make, I am thinking, the same promises that you have made. But what did they find when they came home again, or when their few survivors came home? They found their fathers and their wives, their sisters and their children and the widows of their comrades, sitting desolate and hungry and homeless on the cold seashore, whom they had left in fine houses, with cattle about them and ploughed fields in the inland glens. They found the good land that was theirs a desolation, a wilderness in the hands of strangers, and no sound in the air but the bleating of sheep, where once they had heard the bagpipe and the clarsach and the women singing. That is what your promises are worth, and that is why they deceive us no longer, because we are wiser than our fathers! Here is Donald Ross, with the mark on his forehead where the blazing beam fell from the burning roof of his mother's house, when your factor drove them out! There is John MacDonald, who lived, he and his family, on a diet of boiled grass and limpets for three long years, because he had been robbed of the farm that was his fathers' farm for six hundred years; and his four men children died of hunger and cold. If you had left them on their land they would have lived, and they would have been the Queen's soldiers, and every man of them might have killed ten Russians apiece! But they are dead, and you cannot enlist them now, though you offer sixty pounds a head for them. Nor will their father go at your command, and for your promise, because he knows what your promise is worth and what your bounty is like. You say the Czar of Russia is a tyrant and a despot, and that may well be the truth. But we in Sutherland say this, that if the Czar of Russia took possession of Dunrobin Castle and of Stafford House next term, we would not expect worse treatment at his hands than we have had at the hands of you and your family for the last fifty years. So go back to Her Majesty and tell her that you have found no men for her service, because you and your servants have driven them away from their hills and their glens, and the few that remain among the ruins and the rubbish of the county will no longer listen to your lying words. Go back to Her Majesty, and say that you have no men left in your land, but if she wants venison or mutton she can have it in plenty. For it was sheep and deer that you preferred to men, it is sheep that live on all the good land today, and sheep are all you can now command!'

Once or twice during this harangue the Duke had made an effort to interrupt and silence it. But words failed him, or the strength to speak them, and he sat, with a face as white as parchment, and twitching hands, till it came to an end. Then he rose abruptly, staggering against the table so that the sovereigns jingled in their plate, and walked unsteadily to his carriage. He looked at no one, neither at the old man who had spoken so daringly, nor at the men behind him, nor at his own people. His head was bent, his eyes saw nothing but the trodden earth before him. He would not wait for the others, but got into his carriage and was driven at once to the Castle.

Till he was out of sight the crowd was quiet enough. But when he had gone they began to grow more lively. The factor and the minister and Major Hatton were left with the tables to clear, and they hardly knew whether to clear them at once or to wait awhile to see if matters mended. But the factor prudently packed the money, the sovereigns and the pound notes, back into his bag, and made the two sergeants stand in front of him while he did so. Then there was a little laughter, and the children on the outskirts of the crowd began to imitate the bleating of sheep. The women followed suit, and some of the younger men. *Baa-a-a-a-a*, they cried, and laughed, and bleated again.

The minister tried to stop them, shouting angrily, but they bleated in concert, and the air was full of the silly noise of the flocks that had dispossessed them. They followed the recruiting party back to the Castle, baa-ing like shorn ewes. Their dignity was forgotten now, in which they had stood so long unmoved and silent, but they remembered how to laugh, and they saw that the years had given them reason to laugh, as well as to mourn. *Baa-a-a-a-a*, they cried. If the Duke and his hirelings preferred sheep to men, then they must like the foolish noise of sheep. They bleated again.

The flocks on the mountains heard them, and bleated too. Uneasy wethers carried the crying westward. It spread from Golspie to Lairg, and up Loch Shin. It crossed Ben More, and ran along the sides of Loch Assynt. It came to the Atlantic shore, so that over the whole country there was heard the sound of mockery. The south country shepherds in their bothies, nervous and ill at ease, called to their dogs. And in Dunrobin Castle the Duke stopped his ears with trembling hands. But he could not keep out the noise of his defeat.

The Masks of Purpose

ONE

A ROOM IN Kensington Palace on a January morning in 1692. Bright winter-light from a tall window that let in the reflection of sun on snow, and the warmth of a wood fire slowly burning to white ash and rebuilt on piles of ash. The elegance, on plain walls, of a tall portrait by Kneller, and opposite the picture a door hidden by a heavy tapestry from Ghent.

Elegance was reiterated, underlined, in the costume of the two noblemen who sat there: the one in formal pose at a writing-table, the other straddling a tilted chair. They wore periwigs that fell in a foam of curls below their shoulders and gave off a scent of powder; long coats to the knee, with heavy sleeves on which great cuffs reached back to the elbow; cravats of Dutch lace, three or four pairs of silk stockings against the cold, and pretty, silver-hilted swords. Nothing in their costume betrayed their country—unless all did—for they came of a poor land that for fifty years had known scant luxury and little peace.

He at the table was Sir John Dalrymple, called the Master of Stair, and now King William's Secretary for Scotland. A stranger who could recognise intelligence, and be impressed by it, would have admired the manifest intelligence of his face; but might have cared less for its complacency. Those who knew him in his private life found his conversation ripe and abundant, his temper genial; but every Jacobite denounced him as a turncoat, every Presbyterian detested him as a trimmer. His intelligence was too cold, and he hated extremity on either side: perhaps nothing but extremity. He was a Lowlander from the south-western parts of Scotland, and had little knowledge of the Highlands, but a deep, intrinsical dislike of them. He knew some of the chiefs of their clans, and despised them for their arrogance, the barbaric finery they flaunted, and their witless loyalties. They were the extremest dangers to the life of reason, good sense, and constituted order for which he wished, and his temper froze in hatred of the anarchy of their mountains, the treason in their glens. But now, to deal with the barbarians—whose present mockery of King William and his policy aggravated their natural faults—he was entertaining a Highland chief whom he trusted for one good reason, and only one. He was astute, and his loyalty would lie where advantage lay.

Astraddle on his chair—as if to belie or make light of the bland dignity of his look, his stately, heavy-lidded assurance—sat easily, in his own device of comfort, John Campbell, Earl of Breadalbane, a man in his fifties who had never feared either the complexity of double-dealing or the simplicity of violence. He had made war in his own right, lived with a foot astride political division as now he straddled his chair, and prospered comfortably by shrinking from no iniquity that would serve his ends. Among the papers on the Master's table was a secret report that gave him credit for 'neither honour nor religion but where they are mixed with interest', and described him as 'of fair complexion, of the gravity of the Spaniard, cunning as a fox, wise as a serpent and supple as an eel'. In these attributes, however, the Master—King William's Secretary for Scotland—saw a reflexion (though coarsely blurred) of his own abilities; and felt pleasantly aware that a clever man may confer more confidently with opposing cleverness than with the unpredictable mind of a simpleton.

He shuffled his papers, made sure that the secret report was well covered, and read again a letter referring to Breadalbane's late employment by the Government. He, having wide influence and great power in the Highlands—his lands stretched from Loch Awe to Loch Tay—had been busy with official bribery, and now claimed to have bought general peace, and won for King William the allegiance of a dozen disaffected chiefs who had previously acknowledged no king but James; all this for the trifling sum of £12,000, and that not spent, but only promised. He would, however, give no precise account of what he had promised.

Without impatience, the Master tried again. 'I know Lochiel,' he said, 'better than the others. How was he? Did he come easily?'

'Except in their manner, there was little difference between him and Keppoch. Hard bargainers, both of them.'

'But Lochiel is your cousin—'

'My cousin indeed, but a Cameron first. He thinks of his clan before he remembers cousinhood.'

'How much did he cost you?'

'Does that matter?' asked Breadalbane. 'The money is spent—or promised—the Highlands are quiet, and between friends that's the only way I know of accounting.'

'How long will they stay quiet? There are reports—not here, but I have seen them—that say some of the chiefs were willing enough to take the new King's money, but most would welcome the old King back again.'

'They have taken more than money. They have taken their oath of allegiance.'

'Have you ever known a Highlander bound by an oath when he saw the advantage of breaking it?'

'They have their own way of judging a thing,' Breadalbane admitted.

'And their own habit of accountancy,' said the Master.

'It is a habit that has lived with me too long to suffer change,' replied Breadalbane smoothly.

'But even in your country they have taken note of your—shall I call it singularity? There has been comment—widespread comment—and some criticism. Unfriendly criticism.'

'You have a report on that too?'

'No, no. We do not ask for reports on what our friends are doing. But gossip—who can restrain it?—gossip sometimes comes my way, and there was talk, I remember, of a dispute in your castle of Achallader.'

'Old MacIan of Glencoe said the chiefs, so he had heard, were refusing to be bribed, and I was putting the money in my own pocket.'

'It was something of that sort.'

'MacIan is the damnedest rebel of them all, and a thief by trade.'

'That I know.'

'He was with Claverhouse at Killiecrankie, with Cannon at Dunkeld, and with Buchan at the Haughs of Cromdale: three times in open battle with your Government! But we fell out before that, about cattle, not politics. And that debate was renewed after Killiecrankie, when, on his way home, he took a score of milking cows, with my mark on them, and drove them into that black glen of his. Cattle-thief and rebel, there's MacIan for you! And if you prefer his word before mine—'

'Indeed, and I am not such a fool. I was giving you the talk of the country, and that is all.'

'To what purpose?'

'There is still discontent and hostility in those abominable hills, and I must know what keeps it alive. It was in August that we offered full pardon to all who had been in arms against the Government—to all who would take the oath of allegiance before New Year's Day—and how did they reply to generosity? They turned their backs, and pretended indifference. They were arrogant, not grateful. They refused to take shelter till the last moment. They had told you their price, but still put off signing the bond. Some of them waited till the Old Year was dying in its ultimate daylight before they came in—intransigent, contemptuous, and stubborn to the end.'

'They may have been waiting for their orders. From the King across the water.'

'Did they ask for his approval of surrender?'

'So it is said.'

'Then our policy of buying their allegiance was moonshine from the start! And those of the chiefs who took payment—'

'They all took it: or promise of payment. All to whom I offered it.'

'That was my meaning. And those whom you had promised to pay went home, and rattled their gold in anticipation, if not in fact, and laughed at the Government whose exchequer they would spoil.'

The Master rose, and going to the window looked out for a minute at the bright snow. Then, turning his back on the sunlight, his face in shadow, said bitterly, 'I had hoped they would refuse the oath. That some, at least—Lochiel, Keppoch, and Glengarry—would refuse, and give us the excuse to teach them a lesson they would not easily forget; and that others might learn from their misfortune. Now is the time for it, now in mid-winter, and the troops are there ready at Inverlochy. We should have given them a mauling. It is all they understand. But for a year past we have been blowing hot and cold: now menaces, now fair words and bribery. We have blown about like weathercocks, and lost our chance.'

Breadalbane turned his chair, and now leaning back, his legs outstretched, looked at the ceiling and said, 'You use a word that I seem to remember. I think it was I who first spoke of the propriety of mauling them, and the very sound reasons for mauling.'

'But you changed your mind when it was proposed to buy their submission, and you were asked to arrange the purchase-price.'

'It isn't I who frame your policy. I am your friendly agent, no more than that. And even so I said it was nonsense to throw good money into certain houses.'

'You spoke against Keppoch and Glengarry—'

'Against all Clan Donald. Burn and destroy that pestilent tree and all its branches: that was my advice.'

'Are you still of the same mind?'

'What use is it now, when they have all come in?'

'If we could block the last loop-hole, against the last latecomer?'

Breadalbane sat up straight and answered, 'If there is one, only one, then, whoever he may be, leave nothing standing or alive. Burn crops and houses, take their cattle, kill all that can cry for mercy, for if you leave infants crawling on the floor they'll shout defiance when they've grown to it.'—With prying, importunate eyes he leaned towards the Master and asked softly, 'Who is still to come?'

'That mountebank Lochiel was nearly late, but just got home in time.'

'Lochiel may outlive both of us: he's less of a fool than you suppose.'

'Glengarry has refused.'

'Glengarry has a strong house to sit in. We must wait awhile to deal with him.—Is there no one else?'

'One other.'

'Who?'

'MacIan of Glencoe was late.'

'It should have been a greater man, but we'll take MacIan and be thankful for small mercies. MacIan and every one of his rieving, thieving, cattle-hungry clan. Would God there were more of them! But they have roofs enough to make a good bonfire in Glencoe.—When did you hear this?'

'Last night, when Argyll was here.'

'Would they not register MacIan's oath?'

'It has come to that in the end. Here are the letters he brought.'

Breadalbane pulled his chair to the table, and he and the Master sat shoulder-close to read. Neither saw the slight, dividing movement of the heavy tapestries that covered the doorway, and if the Master had observed it he would have turned away to make sure of seeing nothing more; for he knew and was tolerant of the curious habits of his King. But now he had no need of pretence, for he was absorbed in the matter before him: in papers on the table that held the destiny of a small Highland clan. He looked up once, to narrow his eyes against the glare of sun-lit snow, and think how much deeper it would lie in dark Glencoe; and on the other side of the tapestries the King so enlarged the paper-knife slit of their division that it became a peep-hole for an eye that gleamed, enquiring, like an oyster on a shell half-opened.

'He went first to Inverlochy,' said the Master, 'but Hill, who commands there, quite properly said he had no authority to take his oath. He must go to Inveraray and swear his allegiance before the Sheriff. The weather was bad—is it ever anything different in the Highlands?—and he and his following were delayed by heavy snow. They had a difficult journey to Inveraray, and when they arrived they found the Sheriff away. Drinking the New Year in with his friends, I am told.'

'You mean Ardkinglas?'

'Colin Campbell of Ardkinglas: that's the man. He came back on the 5th or 6th, and even as late as that was persuaded to take MacIan's oath. Is he known to be a weak man?'

'He is a man with many friends. A kindly creature.'

'But very ill-advised. He sent the certificate of MacIan's allegiance to Edinburgh, for submission to the Privy Council, and also, more sensibly, wrote a full account of what had happened, and sent it by special messenger to Argyll.'

'Did the Council reject his certificate?'

'It appears that the Privy Council never saw it. But the certificate—here it is—was crossed out and cancelled.'

'Who did that? Argyll?'

William of Orange, joint-sovereign of Britain with Mary, daughter of James II, had grown up among enemies; early in life he had discovered the advantage of judicious murder, and been prompt to reward the murderers. A malignant destiny had cast him for opponent to *le Roi Soleil*, God's self-appointed deputy on earth, Louis XIV of France; whose hope of conquering the Netherlands he spoilt by letting in the sea and turning several provinces into a swamp. A fishy victory, characteristic of a life in which he was often successful without glory, indomitable without pride, and prudent without principle. A hint of perversion, a tendency to constipation, were reflected in the melancholy of his long, pale face, and his cynicism may have been the bitter flower of self-knowledge. By temper and circumstance suspicious, he had acquired the habit of covering his natural expression with an almost visible mask of repellent, cold indifference. A profoundly unattractive man, he suffered as profoundly from self-consciousness, and when his wife died, whom he had loved and to whom he had been vulgarly and blatantly unfaithful, his sorrow was over-whelming. Self-hating, he had no pity for others; but could feel remorse.

He had no pride—nothing of royalty's pride—and went about the Palace unattended, often in slippers of list, for quietness. He distrusted the Master of Stair, his Secretary for Scotland, with good cause, and spied on him, or eavesdropped, as often as he could; but in his judgment of what he heard he was handicapped by his ignorance of Scotland.

Now, having gathered that some new mischief was being plotted, he retreated, soft-soled, from the tapestried doorway into the anteroom, and composed himself and his features for the confronting of his Secretary and the assured cunning of Breadalbane. When unprepared, or with his few intimate friends, William's face always betrayed the nervous, questing suspicion of his nature: a twitching nose with a flare of pink in the nostrils, a close-pursed mouth, a fretful eye. But for public appearance he had devised a drill: he would pass his hand, four or five times, across his cheeks and mouth and brow, pressing hard to deaden them against normal impulse; and so, as if he had put on a mask, he could assume a look of sculptured calm. A cold, repulsive calm.

This he now did, in the anteroom, and advancing with a little dry cough to the tapestries of the doorway, brusquely parted them, and stopping at the entrance stood there without speaking: not intending his silence to be offensive, to imply rebuke, but because now his whole consciousness was behind his greedy eyes, that were picking up all they could.

Breadalbane and the Master rose quickly from their chairs, and bowed deeply towards him. 'Your Majesty,' they said.

'What's new in Scotland?' he asked. 'More mischief?'

'Of the chiefs, or chieftains, with whom we have been negotiating, Sir, two only have failed to take advantage of Your Majesty's clemency and secure themselves by swearing allegiance. One is Macdonald of Glengarry, who is holding out in his castle of Invergarry, and who, till better weather comes and we can send artillery against him, must wait for justice; the other, a lesser man in every way, is MacIan of Glencoe—'

'Not less in bulk or stature,' interrupted Breadalbane. 'Old MacIan is as near to seven foot as six, and broad as a door and thick as an ox.'

With an impatient gesture for silence, the Master continued: 'This MacIan, chieftain of a sept of Clan Donald, has an evil reputation of old continuance. He is a rebel by nature and habit, and in his usual practice a cattle-thief and pillager.'

'And how,' asked the King, 'do you propose to deal with him? Are you going to ask for more money—strip my exchequer of another two or three thousand pounds—to bribe him into loyalty?'

'No, Sir,' said the Master. 'Subject to Your Majesty's approval, my lord of Breadalbane and I are in agreement that we must use force and punish the people of Glencoe.'

'Where is it?' asked the King. 'What troops can be led against them?'

'There are troops at Fort William in Inverlochy; and more, if they are needed, at Inverness.'

'How far away?'

The Master looked enquiringly at Breadalbane, who answered, 'If they ferry across Loch Leven, Argyll's Regiment at Inverlochy are within twenty miles of Glencoe. And Inverness to Fort William is no more than seventy miles; less, I think.'

'So to punish them will cost less than bribery,' said the King.

'That is good. I had thought you wanted more money. But punishment is better. What will you do?'

As if to wipe from his face a film of doubt or fatigue, the Master passed his hands over his cheeks, pressing them down from the centre line of his nose—it was a gesture not unlike that which the King had made in the anteroom—and apparently moved by a similar uneasiness, Breadalbane stifled a yawn with a hand that moved firmly down from brow to chin. On both faces the expression hardened and was fixed, as if they had put on invisible masks which, being assumed, became visible by their obliteration of all tenderness, humanity, and natural feeling. Now the King, already masked, looked through his frozen calm of obligation at two men who wore no semblance of day-by-day humanity, but faces that were the artefacts of statecraft and their purpose.

'I am going to ask you, Sir,' said the Master, 'to sign this document. It is the customary letter of fire and sword. Scotland must be cleansed of MacIan and his brood. They must be wholly and utterly destroyed—and I ask for your authority on the order I have drafted.'

'Is it necessary to go so far?'

'These people, Sir, are no better than the wild Indians of North America. Call them, not Highlanders, but Iroquois or Mohicans, and you would better realise their nature. There is no room for them in our world, that must be ruled by law and shaped by an ordered custom. We must be rid of them.'

'Indeed, Sir,' said Breadalbane, 'they are a cursed nuisance to any landowner who tries to keep his estates in good shape and preserve his people against violence and murder. That by heredity and inclination they are rebels against your rule, is well known; but only we who live neighbourly with them suffer year by year the depredations by which they sustain themselves. They are cut-throats, foot-pads, cattle-lifters, blackmailers—one and all of the same vile stock—and the only way to deal with it, is to uproot and burn it.'

'What are their numbers?' asked the King.

'Not many,' said the Master, and looked to Breadalbane for confirmation.

'MacIan can put fifty fighting-men in the field,' said Breadalbane. 'Of old dodderers, women and children, add two hundred more.'

'In battle,' said the King, 'I have seen more than that fall before the armies met in main assault.'

'In truth, Sir,' said the Master, 'it is a very small matter; but if we destroy entirely this incurable clan of malefactors, we may win the large reward of pacifying all Highland Scotland. For when greater men see what will befall MacIan, they will think twice—twice, thrice, and again—before they utter a word or do anything to offend Your Majesty.'

'That may be the conclusion,' said the King, 'or it may not. You told me you could win them over by bribery, and you were wrong. But this is cheaper than bribery, and now you may be right. Where's the paper, and where do I sign?'

'Here, Sir,' said the Master, as the King sat himself at the table. 'And will you, Sir, counter-sign at the top as well as at the bottom?'

'Why?'

'To mark the urgency of the instructions, and fortify your order. It is customary, Sir, in such special circumstances as these.'

Slowly and deliberately the King read the order, and then, saying 'I suppose you know your business better than I do,' signed at top and bottom.

Over his shoulder he handed the document to the Master, and with a restive, enquiring hand pulled from the sheaf of papers on the table a couple of letters, and read them too.

Presently he asked, 'What are these? Here's one, dated December in which you write, *Delenda est Carthago*. And another, written this year, where you advise somebody, "I hope the soldiers will not trouble the Government with prisoners."'

The Master showed no sign of the embarrassment and deep discomfort that he felt, but answered in a firm voice, 'They are copies, Sir, of letters that I wrote when it appeared that none of the chiefs would accept your mercy and take the oath; and when, so it seemed, we would have to undertake military action on a large scale. In no sense are they orders, but merely an expression of my own opinion, written to advise and help the officers to whom they were sent.'

'You give advice in a very peremptory tone,' said the King, and rose from his chair. He paused at the doorway to ask, 'Do you think Cato was a happy man? Or does that not matter?' And without waiting for an answer, left them.

'What has Cato to do with it?' asked Breadalbane.

'It was he who used to say, perhaps too often, *Delenda est Carthago*.'

'If a man can't abide the consequence of policy, he should stay at home and grow cabbages.'

The room seemed to have grown warmer, and moved by the same feeling of discomfort ebbing, relief emerging, Breadalbane and the Master, almost simultaneously, pulled from their long coats handkerchiefs edged with lace, and like men now at ease after hot exercise in the sun, mopped their tired cheeks and brows. The masks of purpose vanished, and such weakness, geniality, or normal impulses as they possessed were again apparent.

'That went more easily than I expected.'

'Does he always come soft-footed and take you by surprise?' asked Breadalbane.

'He doesn't stand on ceremony.'

'I should sleep uncomfortably under his roof.'

'He is the King we need. He has strength of purpose. And he has signed the order.'

'It's a good king who does what he is told. And I shall lose less cattle this year, without MacIan in my arm-pit. Who, do you say, should have the task of destroying Carthage?'

'The orders will go to Hill, at Inverlochy, but Hill is not the man we want. Too old, and he has been too long in the country. Leave an Englishman in the Highlands, in command of Highland troops, and within three or four years he's half a Highlander himself, and thinks his men are children whom he alone can handle, drill, and understand—and therefore must comfort and sustain. We need a stiffer man than Hill.'

'Have you asked Argyll for candidates?'

'There was no thought of making a positive choice until we had the King's approval, but we spoke of the matter, and Argyll—if you approve—inclines to think Campbell of Glenlyon may serve the turn.'

'Poor Robin! He's fed off the crumbs from my table these three years past. He can't afford to say no: that's one thing in his favour. He's been a gambler all his life, and thinks every day of the year is a new card dealt by fortune—no nonsense about good works, desert, or merit—so there's another good mark. And he's now so steeped and pickled in drink, though he still carries himself like a gentleman, and looks, from a distance, a very pretty gentleman, that he's lost all fear of foresight and dread of memory. Yes, Glenlyon may be your man.'

'If, then, you and Argyll agree—'

'When do you see him again?'

'Let us meet tomorrow.'

'Dine with me, in my lodgings. I have a saddle of five-year mutton, and two or three dozen of old Margaux,' said Breadalbane. 'Yes, it is a good King, though I dislike the quietness of his tread—and we shall be his good servants.'

TWO

On a sky as taut and clear as the skin of a black grape a half-moon and stars that quivered in the frosty air with, as it seemed, the energy of their own brilliance, lighted the white Shepherds of Etive and the dark straits of Glencoe. They showed a landscape of majestic fantasy that now, in the moonlight and the stillness of frost, looked like the chance exposure of nature's abundance and natural extravagance: as if geology, in a mood of prodigal invention, had shaped the mountains and the glen and the long sealoch for pleasure alone and the fulfilment of a romantic vision.

The half-moon did, indeed, discover wealth of a sort; for in some respects the glen was rich. Not, however, in a material way. Not by ordinary accounting. The houses that sheltered MacIan's little clan numbered no more, or scarcely more, than forty; and only one of them was built with stone walls. This was MacIan's own house of Carnoch on the shore of Loch Leven, and now it stood empty. All the rest were built of turf—of turf walls and a roof of great clods of heather—about a frame of wattle-and-daub, wooden door-posts, and a roof of rough-hewn beams with a hole in the middle to let out the smoke of a peat-fire that burnt against a stone reredos. There was no comfort in these humble dwellings: no comfort more than shelter against rain or snow or the howling winds that swept the glen. But, incongruously, they enclosed a measure of luxury.

The men had their weapons: targe and broadsword and dirk, often a targe richly patterned, and blades well forged and firmly fitted to comely hilts. Their clothes were rough and scanty, but they had their great plaids that gave them bedding in the hills as well as at home, and though they stank in the breeze when their wearers, with a gesture, folded and threw them over their shoulders, they flaunted bright colours and bold patterns.

The women went bare-foot, but their minds were stored with song and story. They laboured constantly, but laboured with music in their ears, and all their labour went with song. Their minds were rich with a knowledge, so close to them it seemed like memory, of ancestors who reached back in a dancing, desolated, loud-singing line to him who had fathered the first Lord of the Isles—and farther still, in kinship of the imagination, to legendary heroes. No woman and no man lived in herself or in himself alone, but all were bound by the same thongs to a community and to history. They were whole and separate, yet variations on a theme; and the theme was rich.

They knew hunger in the spring, but fatness in the autumn. They knew the shrinking of an unfilled belly, and the joy of filling it full. They had no priest in the glen to tell them of the wrath of God, and the memories of old teaching that survived, all assured them of the mercy of Jesus and the unceasing kindness of his Mother. They had poor beds to lie on, and many were lousy; but their faith gave them soft pillows and let them sleep without scratching.

Poverty on the surface, riches in the depths. Within the clan there was no ill behaviour—nothing serious, nothing but boys' mischief—and the blood they spilled beyond the clan did not harden their hearts, for to do battle with their enemies was part of their nature. Between their hills they guarded peace, and beneath their poverty lay a hoard of secret riches.

The night of the half-moon a man came out of his own turf cabin, where the rush-lights gleamed about a spinning-wheel and his son knelt weeping at his mother's knee, and trod deliberately—not quickly, but with deliberation—to the house of John, MacIan's older son. The great hills on either side were thickly quilted with snow, but in the valley there was only a thin coverlet that dissolved beneath his feet, and left his foot-prints black and visible. He came to John's house, which, like all the others, was turf-built, but larger than most, and being distinguished by an upper storey was called a loft-house.

He opened the door and went in, saying 'Hail to the house and household.' Immediately there was a stir of interest, and those within came from their corners and their several tasks to hear what he had to say. He was a man called Red Angus, and he had a reputation in the glen for his skill in piping, for his aptitude in singing 'mouth-music'—that serves for dancing when there is no instrument, or no one to play an instrument—and for his knowledge of old stories and new riddles. He had not come to ask riddles, however, but to bring news.

He sat down beside John, MacIan's son, and was given ale. He said, 'My child Hamish, who is a good boy and not much inclined to lying, went out in the gloaming to look for an old ewe that had not come home with the flock, and he could not find her. But high up on the side of the hill, in the corrie above the loch, he met a great beast with a hide of dark hair and yellow eyes, and a long mouth full of snarling teeth. He struck it with his stick, and ran for his life, and now he is at home and crying on his mother's knee for the fear he felt.'

'What sort of a beast would that have been?' asked John.

'I am thinking it would be a wolf,' said Red Angus.

'There are no wolves here in Lochaber. Not now,' said John. 'The very last of them was killed, by Lochiel himself—was it ten years ago? No, more. It was twelve years ago—and no one in this glen, now living, has ever seen a wolf.'

'Your father will have seen one.'

'I do not think so.' He called his own son, a boy of ten or eleven, and said, 'Run to my father's house, and tell him what Red Angus has been saying. Then ask him if he ever saw a wolf in the glen.'

MacIan had left his big house of Carnoch because it was too near the Loch Leven ferry, and he was afraid of being surprised by soldiers from Fort William. He, who all his life had been fearless, was now grown nervous and melancholy, and he chose to live in a little narrow valley that lay south of the glen, where, in a turf cabin, he was less conspicuous. He had taken some furniture from Carnoch, and when the boy arrived he found MacIan and another old man—a winter guest, a Stewart of Appin—seated on good chairs at a round table, with claret before them and candles lighting the wine.

Such refinement was incongruous on a bare mud floor, in the smoke of an open fire, and the boy stared with astonished eyes at the unexpected scene. There were women in the room, some carding wool, others spinning or knitting, and one of them said MacIan must not be interrupted while he was talking to his guest.

He was telling the man from Appin of his desperate journey to Inveraray in the last days of the old year, to take the oath before it was too late. 'The word,' he said 'did not come till the year was slipping away like the last of the ebb, but I would not go till I had the word. I could not listen to the King in London till I had permission of our own King.'

He had gone first to Inverlochy, to swear his oath before Colonel Hill, the commander of the garrison; but Hill had sent him to Inveraray, to make submission to the Sheriff, the civil power; and he had started his journey in a snowstorm.

He had crossed the ferry and gone by the Appin shore in gale weather; he riding a good garron, and four gillies running beside him. The weather grew worse—none but themselves, neither beast nor human, was abroad—and when they came into Campbell country they found worse enemies than snowdrifts and the wind. They were held prisoner for a night, and then let go. But the old year died as they came to Taynuilt, still thirty miles from Inveraray, and the grim Pass of Brander between. A blizzard met them the next day, more drifts, and on Loch Awe beside them the white snow melted in the white spindrift of the waves. It was the second day of January before they reached Inveraray, and the Sheriff, Colin of Ardkinglas, to whose clemency Colonel Hill had recommended MacIan, was not there. He had gone to stay with friends, to bring in the New Year in the proper convivial way; and not until the 5th of January did he return.

He was a kindly man, and though he thought it now beyond his authority, he at last consented to register MacIan's oath, and promised to send the papers to Edinburgh; and that was done. But since then MacIan had heard nothing, and the winter journey had so taxed his strength that what remained was no match for his anxiety. He lay back in his chair, inert and massive: a huge, heroic figure whose spirit was exhausted.

The man from Appin listened silently to the story, and muttered through bearded lips some dubious consolation. MacIan roused, and poured more wine, and saw in the candle-light the waiting boy.

'What brings you here?' he asked.

The boy repeated, well and clearly, the story Red Angus had told. 'And my father,' he concluded, 'wants to know if you yourself ever saw a wolf in the glen.'

'If the wolves are coming back, there will be worse to follow,' said the man from Appin.

'Where did the boy see it?' asked MacIan.

His grandson told him—it was, he said, high up in the corrie that runs down to the point of Loch Triachtan—and MacIan, his eyebrows and his brush of a moustache looking behind the candles like snow-drifts on the rough, red hill of his face, answered slowly, 'It was there that my father killed the last wolf in Glencoe. He killed three in his lifetime, and I as a boy saw the bodies of two. Twice I have seen a running wolf on the Moor of Rannoch, but never in the glen.'

'Nor, in my lifetime, have they been seen in Appin,' said his guest with proper complacency.

'Bid your father,' said MacIan, 'to tell Red Angus that his son Hamish was dreaming, but to think no worse of him for that. In the deep snow, in the whiteness of the snow, even a grown man's wit can wander, and no one should believe what a boy has seen. There are no wolves in Glencoe, but before long there may be worse than wolves.'

The boy ran home, and found his father's house now full of people who had come to hear Red Angus telling stories, and singing mouth-music. To begin with, when he spoke of a wolf on the hillside, the women of the house had risen and closed in upon him like ghosts of themselves, they were so stricken with fear. Ancestral memories awoke of yellow eyes in the dark, sharp fangs, and long slavering tongues. Of wolves in the snow, fierce with the hunger of winter. And for a little while there had been a tremulous stillness in the house.

But then Red Angus, with another mug of ale in him, had said, 'I left the boy crying at his mother's knee, and I thought he was crying with fear of what he had seen. But perhaps he was crying for remorse, because he had thought of a fine big lie to tell, and indulged himself by telling it. There may be no wolf at all, except in his imagination—and now, if we are talking of imagination, did I ever tell you what the Cuckoo said to the Cockle on the strand? I listened to them once, and this is what the Cuckoo said . . .'

He sang a Gaelic verse in a high-pitched, bird-like voice, and the melody of the words was so closely tuned to the little, leaping air that his audience, quick to respond and with instant recognition, all felt as if spring had already come and a cuckoo was mocking them from a copse of hazels. It was about then that other people from the clachan began to come in. They had seen Red Angus on his way to John's loft-house, and thought with simple, unerring logic that there would be good entertainment if he were to spend the evening there. So a dozen or more discreetly followed him, and presently Red Angus sang a little song that imitated the harsh voice and curious conversation of a corncrake; and another whose bubbling words and lilting tune were the very likeness of a song-thrush meditating in the early dawn its mating impulse and warning other cock-birds to keep their distance.

He sang it again, and a girl cried, 'Let us have dancing now!' There were other young people who took up her cry, and Red Angus sat down on a three-legged stool, and filling his chest with air, compressed his lips and forced from his lungs a draught of wind that carried a torrent of wild, nonsensical words which mimicked the notes and noise of a piper playing a reel for dancing. And every man in the house took his partner, and on the well-packed mud floor trod heel and toe. They danced featly and closely, in a maze of movement, a whirl of lifting feet and turning legs and waving hands. They danced with a spring and a flourish, all moving together and avoiding each other as cleverly as starlings, in a flock of starlings, turning and wheeling in the evening sky. They danced till they filled the air with smoke, though the fire in the middle of the floor had been burning, when they started, with a clear warmth out of old, black peat; and when the smoke got into Red Angus's lungs, he began to cough, and the mouth-music came to an end.

Then a daughter of the house went to her father's side, and knelt beside him, whispering close in his ear. She was a girl of eighteen or so, whose husband had lately been killed in a brawling, unnecessary fight with some of Breadalbane's people. He may well have been in the wrong, for he was in Breadalbane's country and the bullocks he was driving may not, as he claimed, have been his own beasts that had strayed. No complaint was made against the Campbells, but his death was deeply mourned; for he had been a stalwart young man of lively temper and good natural gifts. He had left the girl Shiona with a baby two months old, and she had wept for a week; and then, being young, put memory behind her. She had always, as a child, kept close to her father, and now, kneeling beside him, she begged him to sing the song he had made about the fight at Killiecrankie.

Her father, though almost as tall and broad as MacIan himself, was a quiet and modest man. He had made the song for his own pleasure, and sung it, till now, only for the entertainment of his own family. But Shiona besought him to sing—she was a tall and lovely girl, with dancing eyes and lips of promise and full breasts—and when others clamoured too, to hear the song, her father stood and began his lay.

It started quietly. A simple recitation of the facts. There were two armies facing each other in the rocky glen through which the rushing Garry ran brown and swift. The army of the King in London, red-coated, exact in discipline, but drawn-up on lower ground. Above them, smaller in numbers, the Highland host, and the wind that flung, this way and that, the silver birches in the glen, fluttered their tartan plaids, and the music of their pipers danced and re-echoed from the rocks and sang above the burden of the river. The midsummer sun was sinking—now John's tune grew livelier—and when the sun that had dazzled the impatient eyes of the host was spilling itself on the western hills, the Highlanders, trotting like hill ponies, began their advance. The redcoats fired their volley! Now there were open spaces in the ranks, as when a winter gale blows through an old pine-forest and takes the tallest trees. But the Highlanders stood, firm of foot and clear of eye, with arm-muscles braced and muskets level, and fired an answering volley. Then, with a shout, threw down their smoking firelocks, and with broadswords flashing high, charged down-hill.

Oh, charged! Down-hill with tartans in the breeze like sails full-bellied in a gale of victory, and broadswords flashing, slashing, cutting through and asunder, breaking the serried line and driving men and horses, disciplined men and frightened horses, into the brown current of the fierce river, and voices shouting a chorus of triumph. Their enemies scattered like the winnowed chaff, and the mood of triumph filling the rocky glen like the Garry in flood—till, of a sudden, they heard the knell of hope and the tidings that filled their hearts with desolation. For at the very top of triumph, their leader the Graham—the Graham, great lordly laughing Claverhouse himself—had been struck by an errant ball and died on the field. So victory, the whirlwind charge of Highland victory, reaped no harvest but the death of its proud commander. Great Claverhouse was dead, and victory an empty cask. . . .

They heard his song, and rewarded it with long silence; but Shiona put her arms about her father's neck and kissed him on the forehead. 'Better Claverhouse than you,' she said. And then, as when the making tide begins to flow, in ripples leaping up the sand or runlets filling a dry channel through the rocks, they all began to talk. A story here, of Claverhouse or the fight at Cromdale. A story told, with laughter, about the redcoats. An argument, warmly debated, about Lochiel, who had gone to London and enjoyed himself at court, but suffered the King—the second James—to make a butt of him and mock his Highland ways. Lochiel, who had killed the last wolf in Lochaber! Lochiel, who had fought with an Englishman till their swords were broken, then fought with bare hands, and tumbling on the ground Lochiel had fastened his teeth in the Englishman's throat and killed him as if he had been a wolf himself. 'The sweetest bite I ever had,' he said.—Another tale, of little modesty, about a woman whom Lochiel had met at court; and then by strange analogy the history of a cow in Glen Ure that fell in love with a red stag and took to the hills. The stories reached farther and ran deeper back in time, till the heroes of old legends, Finn and Oisin, and Deirdre of the Sorrows, and birds and seals, were rubbing shoulders with men they knew, with their own fathers, and the politicians in London. And in whatever was told they were all concerned, for all were akin. In temper and abilities they were individual and apart, but in nature they were one.

The fire burnt low and it grew cold. Again a girl called for a dance, and Red Angus made his mouth-music till his lips were dry and his throat sore with the effort. But they danced till the air was warm again.

One of the two or three good pipers of the clan had come in, who sat with John, drinking ale; and when the younger people had had enough of dancing, he stood and tuned his drones. He began to play a little indeterminate air, but soon proclaimed the notes of a pibroch for which he was famous. It was called *The Children of the Dead*, and commemorated an old clan battle in which the MacIan of his time, and most of his chosen warriors, had been killed; but the children of the next generation had grown taller and stronger than any young men who had ever played in the glen before; and because in their childhood their mothers had sung them to sleep with prayer for reprisal and invocation to vengeance, they grew up with knowledge of their destiny. They grew into a generation of warriors, and when the time was ripe they fell upon their fathers' enemies and destroyed them utterly.—It was a long pibroch, and when it was finished some of the guests began to feel it was time to go home; and when some got up, the others followed their example.

It was, indeed, not far from the dawning of another day; and the boy, John's son, who had gone to MacIan's house to ask about wolves, was the only one in the company who felt discontented. For when he came home the house was full of singing and dancing, and everyone had forgotten the fear with which the evening began. He had had no chance to tell them, with all the authority of MacIan behind him, that no one in living memory had ever seen a wolf in the glen.

It was not till late in the following morning—not until nine o'clock or thereabout—that any movement could be seen about the houses. There was very little out-door work to be done in winter, and no one believed in the virtue of early rising for its own sake. But by ten o'clock the chimneys were smoking, and even Red Angus's wife no longer believed in the wolf that her son had met when the old ewe, for which he had searched in vain, was seen grazing contentedly with the rest of the flock. The meadow-grass that grew richly in the seaward parts of the glen was left uncut, for the most part, and when snow fell both sheep and cattle could still find some grazing in the low-lying fields by nuzzling through the snow.

The day, so late begun, was fair and still. The sun was silver-gilt, the snow unflurried by any wind. In this winter calm there was more movement than usual—a sort of holiday movement—between the several clachans, or main hamlets, of the glen. There was a cluster of dwellings about MacIan's house on the lochshore, two others on the river bank, and a fourth beyond Loch Triachtan where the glen lay narrowly between a steep mountainside to the north, and a turmoil of high hills to the south, that were called the Top of the Peaks and the Shepherds of Etive.

In sun-lit pleasure, in gossip and idleness, MacIan's people spent that calm and empty morning; and in the afternoon, succeeding this innocency of friendly visiting, the whole clan stood rooted in fear about their houses when a man came running to say that a column of red-coated soldiers was marching in from the Loch Leven ferry.

THREE

In the Master of Stair's room, in Kensington Palace, the Earl of Breadalbane sat alone.

The Master—King William's Secretary for Scotland—had received him with a cordiality somewhat straitened by annoyance with his sovereign. He had been promised an audience an hour before, and found the King so closely engaged with the Queen and a pair of architects that he had neither time nor wish to speak of Scotland. The Master had hoped for some conversation with William before they met Breadalbane, and heard from him the latest news of their strategy in the Highlands: not because he still distrusted Breadalbane—that he now resolutely denied—but because, with a statesman's simple faith in his own judgment, he had thought it best, for the King's sake, not his own, that he should be the first to inform William of their plans, and explain the significance of their troop-movements; after which Breadalbane, without confusing intelligence, could add what details were necessary.

But the Master's purpose had been spoiled by the King's determination, suddenly ripened, to re-build Kensington Palace in a style better suited to the Queen's pleasure and his own dignity. It was a plain, uncomely building that he had bought from the Earl of Nottingham, and the need for alteration and extension was manifest. He wanted, moreover, to gratify the Queen—whose first request had been for a formal garden—but he was not inclined to spend so lavishly as she anticipated. He had engaged the interest of Sir Christopher Wren and Mr Grinling Gibbons, who were now preparing plans for the enlargement of his house.

When the Master waited on him, he found both their Majesties closely intent on the drawings that Sir Christopher and Mr Gibbons were explaining. The King held up a warning hand, and remaining some distance apart from them the Master obediently waited. The Queen, seated, showed clearly her admiration of the scroll that Sir Christopher held for her inspection. He was a short, slightly built man of sixty or so, whose features declared a simple happiness, a sweetness of temper, that consorted a little oddly with the well-known strength of his intellect and its many abilities. In spite of his mild, unassuming look he appeared, for the moment, to dominate the scene, and on the long roll of paper that the Queen was examining he had drawn the elevation of a Palladian building of vast size and great magnificence. The Queen was a modest and retiring woman, but enthusiasm had broken down her shyness, and with an almost girlish excitement—she was barely thirty, and since girlhood her occasions of happiness had not been many—she exclaimed with delight as her finger pointed to colonnades and gracious doorways. Sir Christopher, accepting with innocent pleasure her approval of his design, leaned over to explain a detail of his drawing, and the King, behind her, asked sharply some question about the size of the building. The temper of discussion changed. Sir Christopher was on the defence, and the King attacking. Presently, as it seemed, he dismissed the whole project.

He had raised his voice, and at the other end of the room the Master had heard his question. The Master, conspicuously detaching himself from business that did not concern him, was slowly walking to and fro. The small noise of his footfall prevented him from overhearing the royal conversation—and the King, he hoped, would observe his discretion—but his eyes, in sidelong glancing, missed no movement or change of expression. He saw the King's sudden displeasure, Sir Christopher's discomfiture, and the Queen's ingenuous revelation of disappointment. The King, it was manifest, was complaining that the new palace would cost too much. Sir Christopher, with the sad hope of saving something from the ruin of his splendid plan, was improvising a new proposal, new estimates. And the Queen was silent, looking like a girl who had been robbed of her birthday necklace.

While the King argued with Sir Christopher, Mr Gibbons approached to show her a sheaf of his drawings. These she studied closely, and gradually her look of pleasure returned. She grew animated, compared one with another, and pointing to the dull chimney-piece of the long dull room in which they were talking, exclaimed with audible delight, in her small invalid's voice, to see how Mr Gibbons could improve it. She called to the King, who was watching Sir Christopher as, quickly and with increasing confidence, he scribbled in outline the elevation of a smaller, plainer building; and the King, taking from her two or three of Mr Gibbons' drawings, went to a window to examine them in a better light.

He seemed puzzled, or surprised, by what he saw; and asking a question, caught sight of the Master, whose presence he had forgotten. He came, impatiently, to tell him, 'I shall be with you—with you and Breadalbane—as soon as I can. A quarter of an hour, not more. But I cannot leave the Queen now, or she will command a new palace fit for *le Roi Soleil*; and I am not *le Roi Soleil*.'

The Master bowed and withdrew. He returned to his own room and said to Breadalbane, 'The road is blocked by a new palace.'

'Our road? And whose palace?'

'He and the Queen are still talking to Christopher Wren and Grinling Gibbons, in a litter of plans and diagrams. They are going to rebuild this dull and inadequate house—and indeed, as you can see, it's no place to roof a king and house a court.'

'But Wren can wait an hour, can't he?'

'He could; but the Queen is waiting for immediate fulfilment of her wishes; and the King daren't leave her alone for fear that she and Wren, between them, design too much for the exchequer.'

'How long, then, are we to wait?'

'A quarter of an hour, he said. But we'll be lucky if he comes within the hour.'

'I've told you all I know, and all that has been done. There's nothing more we need discuss.'

'No, nothing. All we need now is his knowledge and approval.'

'And till we get it, we can cool our heels.'

'A man who is building a new house, whether he's a London tradesman or a Roman emperor, has no thought for anything else.—But give him an hour.'

They waited forty minutes, and then the King, unannounced and unattended, came in through the curtained doorway, still carrying in his left hand a little sheaf of drawings. 'Well,' he asked, 'what are you doing in Scotland? Can you promise me peace there now?'

'That is the purpose of our coming, Sir. My Lord of Breadalbane—'

'You have made a good arrangement?'

Breadalbane, bowing, spread on a table—smoothing its creases flat—a map of Glencoe and the neighbouring country. 'There, Sir,' he said, 'is the home of the robber-clan that must be rooted out. As Your Majesty will see—you, Sir, who know more of the art of war than I shall ever learn—there are few roads of access to the glen, and few roads of escape. My own people will keep the Glenorchy passes, while Menzies of Weem watches the roads to Perthshire. My lord of Argyll prevents escape through Appin, and Colonel Hamilton will come down into the upper end of the glen by the Devil's Staircase.'

'Who,' asked the King, 'will be the executioner?'

'Glenlyon, Sir. Captain Robert Campbell of Glenlyon, a kinsman of mine.'

'When will he go in?'

Breadalbane, with a question in his eyes, looked to the Master, who nodded slightly.

'He should be there today, Sir.'

'In what strength?'

'With a hundred and twenty.'

'Is that enough?'

'Colonel Hamilton will send four hundred on the day of execution—

in the darkness of a very early day—and with those watching the passes there will be, in all, some nine hundred soldiers.'

'Against how many? I forget.'

'MacIan can put fifty men in the field.'

'You should be enough,' said the King drily, and taking the map went to a chair by the window to study it more closely. He sat down and looked, from one to another, at the several papers he held: in the one hand the map of Glencoe, in the other a batch of drawings by Grinling Gibbons.

Breadalbane repeated, with more detail and particularity, the troop-movements that had been planned to prevent escape from the glen, and pledged his faith in the zeal and purpose of Hamilton and Glenlyon, whose hands would be executive.

The Master waited, and when Breadalbane had finished, said quietly, 'This is the proper season of the year to take and exterminate them. It means a rigid climate for the soldiers to march in, but it's the only time these rebels cannot escape; for now, in these weeks of winter, no human constitution can endure to be long out of doors. All that's necessary and possible can now be done in a few days. Now in the winter-time, in the long cold nights, is the time to maul them: the only season when we can be sure that a Highland clan cannot escape us and carry their wives, bairns, and cattle into the mountains. This is the time when fire and sword will make sure of all. *Delenda est Carthago*, and winter will do what escapes us. They deserve no kindness, Sir.'

The King made no reply, and the Master, looking more closely, saw that he had dropped the map of Glencoe and was studying the drawings of Grinling Gibbons. Offended and irate, he stood still and silent; and presently the King said, 'Do observe these drawings by Mr Gibbons. They are very clever, aren't they? You see how they imitate the good Dutch painting of Brouwer, Jacob Ruisdael, and Pieter de Hooch. Those grapes, these flowers and pomegranates, apples and pears and flowing ribbons—they are like reality and like Dutch painting. And when he carves them in wood—limewood is his favourite—they will be cut out, whole and entire, and show their roundness, their perfection. I like the work of Grinling Gibbons. What do you say, Mr Secretary?'

'It is most ingenious. But, Sir—'

'Wren is a great man, though small in body, just as I am. But he is unreasonable. He thinks the world was made as a platform for architects to build upon. He thinks all England is only a foundation for his palaces. After the Fire he wanted to rebuild London to make fine views: no concern for value of the land and commerce, but a radiation and fine views and St Paul's in the middle. Well, you cannot trust him, can you? But Gibbons is different. Gibbons will decorate what you tell him to decorate. I like Gibbons, he doesn't take money out of your pocket till you tell him what you want to spend. These are truly pretty, are they not? He was born in Amsterdam.'

'Very pretty,' said the Master. 'But in the matter of Glencoe—'

'I thought we had dealt with that.'

'So we have, Sir, if you will approve what my lord of Breadalbane and I have devised.'

'I approve in principle. It is only you who know in detail what must be done.'

'Then will you, Sir, sign this further letter to Livingstone—'

'Livingstone?'

'Who commands in chief at Inverness, Sir.'

'Yes. Yes, of course. I knew that.'

'A letter, Sir, that exhorts him—and through him, his sub-ordinate officers—to trouble the Government with no prisoners.'

'Is that advisable?'

'It is necessary, Sir.'

'Is that all you want me to do?'

'That is all, Sir.'

'Well, the Queen is waiting for me. The Queen and Sir Christopher and Mr Gibbons. God knows what mischief they'll be up to, if I'm not there. Where is the letter, and where do I sign?'

'Here, Sir.'

'They're to take no prisoners?'

'They would only be an encumbrance, Sir.'

'And mean more expense, I suppose.'

'A lot more expense, Sir.'

'Well, I suppose you know best.'

A little grudgingly, as it seemed, the King signed the letter, and picked up the drawings by Grinling Gibbons. 'They're very pretty, aren't they?' he said.

'Very pretty indeed, Sir,' said the Master. And he and Breadalbane bowed deeply as the King went out.

FOUR

Go north and a little west of north from London—go all the length of England and half the length of Scotland—and five hundred miles from Kensington, as a carrier-pigeon might fly, you will come to Fort

William at the south-western end of the Great Glen that almost cuts Scotland in two and lies like a gutter between the snow-capped mountains of Inverness and the silver-tipped heights of the northern Highlands. A chain of narrow lochs divides them, and near their Atlantic entrance, under the vast and gloomy shadow of Ben Nevis, George Monk had built a fort, in 1655, to hold in subjection, under Cromwell's discipline, the clans who roosted in the woods and hills of wild Lochaber. It was still, in 1692, a very rude and simple fort, though it had been strengthened and enlarged, but its strategic importance far exceeded the height of its walls; and now, to keep the peace, it housed a garrison of Argyll's Regiment.

Its Governor and Commanding Officer was an old soldier in his sixties, an Englishman, a Colonel Hill who had served his country for forty years and more, and got little reward but pay in arrears, promotion deferred, the distrust of his superior officers, and endless service under the wettest hills in Scotland. He had learnt his trade under Monk, and in the way of a good soldier he had acquired love and a half-understanding of the people he had conquered and disabled; and a whole desire to serve them, so far as he knew how. He had made friends among the Highlanders, and continued to serve his Government. With a shrug of his shoulders he had proclaimed Richard Cromwell—that shadow of a discredited name—with Lochiel and Glengarry beside him to substantiate the shadow; but when the King came into his own again—the second Charles, with French whores and monstrous wigs to enhance his royalty—he had surrendered his fort to Lochiel with perfect geniality. He was a soldier and a gentleman; and while infinitely despising politicians, felt an almost superstitious fear of them.

He had helped Lochiel, when Lochiel came at the last moment to take his oath. He had tried to help MacIan, though he knew all MacIan's ill deeds and disaffection. And now, when he knew something of the Government's final purpose, he knew also that the Government and his Commander-in-Chief no longer trusted him, but were sending instructions behind his back to his Lieutenant-Colonel, his second-in-command at the fort, a man called Hamilton.

The old Colonel had been too long in the service to remain unaware of such transgressions of routine. From Livingstone, his Commander-in-Chief in Inverness, he had heard of the King's command that the tribe of Glencoe, 'that sept of thieves', should be extirpated. By the Master of Stair he had been told that Argyll, Breadalbane, and Menzies of Weem would guard all routes of escape from Glencoe, and a detachment of Argyll's Regiment must 'cut off' MacIan and his clan. The Master had written again to say, 'When anything concerning Glencoe is resolved, let it be secret and sudden.'

But to Livingstone the Master had written, with open hatred leaping from the paper, 'I am glad that Glencoe did not come in within the time prescribed.' And Livingstone had written to Hamilton repeating the Master's pleasure that MacIan had been too late, 'so that the thieving nest might be entirely rooted out;' and warning Hamilton that he and all under him would be judged by the efficiency with which they dealt out death.

February lay black and wet on the western lowlands. No snow about the ferry-landings on Loch Leven—snow never lies there long—but deep snow on Ben Nevis, its pallor half-seen through grey, snow-filled clouds, and snow on the high Shepherds of Etive, and on the heights of Morven across Loch Linnhe. An arctic cold on the mountain tops, a frozen wind shrilling round the walls of the wet, black fort, and the old Colonel in his cold quarters listened to a clerk as old as himself who told him of the latest letter delivered to Hamilton, his Lieutenant-Colonel, from his Commander-in-Chief—from Livingstone, who was younger than himself, and had succeeded that ill-tempered but honest man, General Hugh Mackay—and with a sick acceptance Hill swallowed the insult to his private dignity, the affront to the discipline of his profession.

A Major Forbes, in Argyll's Regiment but properly loyal to his Colonel, came in to report his return from Edinburgh. He had travelled by the shore-road round Appin, and said he had seen, at the ferry-landings on Loch Leven, a detachment of his regiment on their way to take up quarters in Glencoe; and all in the detachment—all but a few Lowlanders—were men from Breadalbane's country. That was on February 1st.

It was Hamilton, not Hill, who had ordered the move; and a day or two later the old clerk who was still faithful brought Hill a copy of Hamilton's instructions to a Major Duncanson who commanded four hundred men lying in an advanced position on the north shore of the loch. It was Hill, in obedience to his Commander-in-Chief, who had ordered the advance; but Hamilton had underlined the order with savage detail. Yet Hill made no complaint. Hill said nothing, but brooded in cold impotence over the insult to his dignity and the impending brutality in Glencoe.

A week went by, and more than a week. Ten or eleven days. Then the old clerk gave him a copy of an order that Duncanson had sent to Glenlyon—Glenlyon, who had now been living with MacIan and his people for nearly a fortnight—and while he was reading it, Major

Forbes came in again. Duncanson's order began: 'You are hereby ordered to fall upon the rebels of Glencoe, and put all to the sword under seventy. You are to have a special care that the old fox and his sons do upon no account escape your hands. . . .'

He looked up and asked, 'What do you want now?'

'Major Duncanson's detachment, sir, is already on the move.'

'I have given no orders!'

'No, sir. That I knew. But they have begun to march round the head of the loch.'

With a trembling hand he picked up Duncanson's order again, and read further in it: 'You are to secure all the avenues, that no man escape. This you are to put in execution at five of the clock precisely; and by that time, or very shortly after it, I'll strive to be with you with a stronger party. If I do not come to you at five, you are not to tarry for me, but to fall on. . . .' It was now February 12th.

'He had no order from me!' he said again, and rose from his chair, his old body quivering with rage. He began to shout and storm in feverish ineffectual fury. 'But what can I do?' he demanded. 'Resign my commission? And what good would that bring?'

No good at all. The punitive column would still march in, and he would lose his long-promised knighthood, all his back-pay, and the pension that was due to him after forty-five years of service. And he had four unmarried daughters.

He sat down in his chair again, and put his head in his hands. 'God damn it, Forbes,' he said, 'this is all the thanks we get! We who are soldiers make peace, and the politicians make war again. But say nothing of the anger I have shown, for I am an old man and anger is natural to me. Go to your quarters—you are wet through—and put on dry clothes, and take a dram for the safety of your health.'

When Forbes had gone he opened a cupboard and took from it a bottle of whisky: the wine of the country. From a pocket he pulled a great silk handkerchief, and wiped his face, for his eyes and cheeks were wet with tears; and after he had wiped it his face looked different, as if he had pulled on a thin, transparent mask of tired and cynical indifference. His features were the same, but, as it seemed, stiffened by artifice in an expression of forlorn but unfeeling detachment from the gross and squalid world in which he lived. For a long time he had known what was intended, and could foresee what would happen; but with an old man's folly he had maintained a pretence that it would not happen, and could not happen, without his command. But now he admitted recognition of the deed, and disowned it.

He drank, from a horn cup, the whisky he had found for his

comfort; and the mask fell into a tighter, more natural fit on his old and flabby face.

FIVE

There were a hundred and twenty soldiers, in red coats and grey trews, in the column that came marching into Glencoe on February 1st; and though, like their unsuspecting hosts, they were, for the most part, Highland-born and bred, there were those among them who looked from side to side, with the wary, calculating eyes of men in a strange, unfriendly country, at the steep white hills that so narrowly confined their path, and threatened to close about them like a trap.

Leading the column was a short, square-shouldered man, with quick and restless eyes, whose commonplace, ill-tempered features had been disciplined by twenty years' service to a harsh, professional severity. He, Sergeant Barber, was indifferent to the menace and grandeur of the hills, but observant of all he saw that might be of military significance: a cleft in the hills where men might climb, a house that covered a field of fire, a chattering ripple where the river could be forded. He was a good soldier, in a regimental way, but little more. A stentorian word of command, a seeing eye, a retentive memory; a native bravery fortified by long habit, a sense of rough justice; but nothing else of human sort except an uncertain geniality in drink and a singing voice, wholly unlike his drill-yard bellowing, in which, when gently drunk, he sang bawdy London songs.

Behind the column, walking easily and seeming to pay no heed to it, were its commanding officer, Campbell of Glenlyon, and a couple of dull-looking, sturdy, junior officers, both called Lindsay, and neither memorable for physical attraction or gifts of the mind: young men who, if need be, might die with propriety, but could not hope to live with distinction.

Their commander, Captain Robert Campbell, had, as it seemed, a different constitution, and certainly a different spirit. Despite his humble rank he was a man of nearly sixty, and notwithstanding his years and a dissolute life he was a man of comely and dignified presence. Race maintained him, race held at bay his sins, excesses, weaknesses, and stark incompetence. He was a gambler who had always lost, a drunkard who had never felt shame or remorse for the squalid misdeeds of drunkenness, and a man of good birth who had never caught sight of the obligations of birth. In his youth he had had a strange and sinister beauty: a long straight nose above girlish, pouting lips, bright cheeks and cold dark eyes, a long, narrow, piercing chin, and a look of remoteness from the jostling crowd. Now, at sixty, his fair hair was only lightly brushed with grey, his eyes were still bright though bloodshot, and his features looked like a varnished replica of his youth's appeal; with a multitude of little cracks in the varnish, as on some old picture. But his chin was lean, unsoftened by fat, and his long nose had kept its pallid dignity, though his nostrils were dark with snuff.

To his subalterns he talked, of trivial subjects, with the careless ease of a man who neither sought nor found in company anything but his own amusement; and though his breath met the air with a strong scent of brandy, he walked as well and nimbly as his young companions.

When they had marched a couple of miles, Sergeant Barber halted the column, as he had been told to do, and waited for his commanding officer. Glenlyon, with one of the young Lindsays, came forward, walking leisurely, and acknowledged the Sergeant's salute with a friendly smile.

'Tell the men,' he said, 'that we shall now march at attention, and if MacIan himself comes to meet us they will be halted—Mr Lindsay will give the order—and remain at attention. I want all drill-movements to be carried out as smartly as if General Livingstone were inspecting us. Some of our rearward files are marching like cows heavy in calf, so you had better stay with the other Mr Lindsay and use your voice to maintain the pace. Is that understood?'

'Yes, sir.'

'Then let us go on.'

Now Glenlyon, stiffening his shoulders and affecting a little pomp in his carriage, set himself at the head of the column, and the advance was continued. The news of their approach had meanwhile spread throughout the glen, and John, MacIan's elder son, with a score of men hastily armed—little time was needed to buckle on a sword-belt and take a leather targe from the wall—waited for them near John's own house. He knew Glenlyon—Alastair, his brother, was married to a cousin of the man—and when they recognised each other Glenlyon halted the soldiers and came forward alone. John went to meet him, and from a distance asked loudly, 'What have you come here for? There is no quarrel now between us and the King.'

'No quarrel at all,' said Glenlyon, 'and I was about to greet you civilly and wish you good day.—Good day to you, cousin, and how are the kindly folk of Glencoe?'

'No more comfortable for seeing a company of red-coats in the glen.'

'It's little comfort we have had in Fort William, where there are soldiers packed together like herring in a barrel. And that is why we have come to you, to beg shelter for a week or two.'

'What is the need for so many soldiers in the fort?'

'It is no secret, cousin, that Glengarry still refuses the King's peace, and sooner or later we shall have to try persuasion with him. But not, I hope, before the weather mends—and in the meantime the poor soldiers must have roofs to sleep under.'

'There are not many roofs here.'

'You have one of the richest glens in Lochaber, cousin. Rich by nature, and richer still by acquisition.'

For a long minute John stood silent, pondering Glenlyon's meaning and the intention of his words.—Three years before, Coll Macdonald of Keppoch, with some of the Glencoe people in his train, had harried and despoiled the lands of Glenlyon—stripping them of horses, sheep, and cattle to the value, it was said, of more than £8,000, Scots money—and the herds and the flocks had been driven to Glencoe, and there divided between the partners of the raid. Glenlyon himself had lost six heavy mares of English breed, more than two hundred cattle, and as many sheep. If he had come for revenge or reprisal, under cover of the King's name, he had some reason for revenge.

Having considered this, John said slowly, 'There is no memory of unfriendship between us except for a small matter, some years ago, that was done openly, as an act of war in time of war. And no blame can hang on that.'

'No blame at all,' said Glenlyon heartily. 'I was never a man that brooded on misfortune in the past, nor do I worry over what may fall out in the future. The present is enough for me, it covers me like a tent—and within its tent, at this moment, I have a flask of French brandy. Let us sit and talk awhile.'

There was a grey boulder beside them that lay like a dead and frozen stag on the moor, and sitting down Glenlyon pulled a flask from his pocket. John, with grave politeness, drank his health, and Glenlyon, taking a deeper and more casual swig, handed him the flask again. For courtesy John put it to his lips, but did not drink.

'Tam Lindsay, my subaltern, has a billeting-order, signed by old Hill at Inverlochy—'

'Colonel Hill is our good friend,' said John.

'That I know well, and with Hill's authority behind us, you need have no fear. None at all. Give us house-room for a week or two, and that's all your burden; for which you'll be paid: or, to be blunt about it, you'll get a promise of payment—for God damn all governments, they're the same, whatever the colour, in their reluctance to hand out good money.'

'My father,' said John, 'has not been living in the big house of Carnoch for some time past. Will you be wanting to go there?'

'No, not there. But there's a house called Inverrigan, a mile this side of it, that belongs to your tacksman; and the house over there—'

'Achnacon.'

'They'll do for me and my two subalterns, and the soldiers you can billet as you please. They'll go four or five to a house, there's none of them a giant and very few as big as you, cousin.'

'I am glad you do not want my father's house. He is living down there in the small glen. You can see the roof.'

'We shall interfere neither with MacIan nor with you and Alastair, except for asking you to join us in a hand of cards now and then, or the sharing of a bottle. Tell your clan that we have come as friends, cousin—we are Highlanders all, speaking the same tongue—and now that we owe the same allegiance, there need be no doubt or discontent between us. God knows I am the last man on earth to start a quarrel, and the first to forget it.'

'You will be wanting to speak to my father,' said John.

'Let me go to him alone. I want neither your escort, nor my own men. I shall go by myself, and put myself between his hands.—Hey, hey! Lindsay!'

He shouted to his subaltern, who came at a quick, awkward pace, intent on prompt obedience yet trying hard to look at ease, and Glenlyon said, 'Let me present my lieutenant, Tam Lindsay. There is another of the same name, whom you will meet presently. And now, cousin, if you will confer with my brace of Lindsays about the billeting of the men, I shall go and offer my respect and duty to MacIan.'

'Shall I not come with you?' asked John.

'In a glen so friendly as this, a man can walk alone.—A dram before I go?'

John refused, and Glenlyon, putting the flask to his mouth, swallowed twice and said, 'We can suffer a Dutch king so long as he lets us drink French brandy.' Then, cocking his bonnet, walked with a lilting swagger that denied his years towards MacIan's house.

MacIan stood by the door in trews and belted plaid, but bareheaded and unarmed. At either end of the house were women, anxious of look, some wringing their hands and quietly weeping, others standing dour and truculent; and in the background were little groups of rough-clad men with sword at side and targes hanging from their left arms, who stood as suspicious and quick to move as red deer on the hill.

Glenlyon, unperturbed, walked jauntily towards MacIan, and when a couple of yards from him swept off his bonnet, lightly bowed, and cheerfully exclaimed, 'Hail to the house and household! Good day to you, MacIan. I am here as a suppliant for hospitality, knowing you have never yet denied it.'

'I am told,' said MacIan, 'that you bring a hundred soldiers to enforce hospitality.'

'A hundred and twenty—and all dependent on your good will.'

Glenlyon repeated his explanation of their presence, and MacIan, as John had done, replied, 'Colonel Hill has been a good friend to us.'

'A good friend, also, to me and my poor red-coats,' said Glenlyon. 'There is nowhere else he could have found for us billets as warm and comfortable as your glen can offer, nor company so kind and cheerful.'

MacIan, who had been almost inert in his anxiety—who had sat in his chair like an old man defeated by the enmity and rubs of time—had roused at once when he was told that the soldiers were already in his glen. His spirit came back when the enemy appeared, and now, before the door of his house (his head above the lintel) he confronted Glenlyon with the monumental dignity of his great stature, and with the assurance of an ancient bravery face to face with all it could lose, and contemptuous of loss. But, simultaneously, with the wary mind of a chieftain whose clan depended on his wits as well as on his strength.

'We are all in the King's peace,' he said. 'I have taken the oath, and the paper went to the Council in Edinburgh.'

'That I know as well as you,' said Glenlyon. 'I have had a word or two with John about it, and there is no breath of trouble between us.'

MacIan, huge and silent, looked gravely at him, and Glenlyon pulled on his bonnet. 'The evening wind blows shrewdly,' he said, 'and I am not so warmly thatched as I used to be.'

MacIan's expression changed. Solicitude showed on his face, and concern for a guest. 'You will be tired,' he said. 'Come in. Come in and take bite and sup with me. Enemies we may have been in the past, but if you speak truly now, and come seeking hospitality, we must be friends for all that.'

He stood aside, and Glenlyon, stooping under the low doorway, went in to a darkness lighted only by a fire of dry, black peat that gave out no smoke. But MacIan called loudly to the women of the house, and demanded candles and wine and food. They waited in silence while the women hurried to and fro, and presently there were four candles on the round table, their flames reflected in two old, thin silver plates. MacIan's wife put down a silver platter heaped high with slices of kippered salmon, another piled with oat-bread, a china plate of cheese—no butter at this time of year—and glasses, and two flasks of wine.

They sat, and Glenlyon said, 'It's true, as I have been told, that this is as rich a glen as can be found in all the west.'

'No, no,' said MacIan, pouring wine. 'We are a poor people, living only by God's grace, and that on the very ledge of extremity.'

'By God's grace and your own dexterity,' said Glenlyon.

'We have much to be thankful for,' said MacIan, and put three or four pieces of kippered salmon on Glenlyon's plate.

'With salmon from the river and your own abundance of mutton, there's no danger of starvation here.'

'There are worse places for pasture. I have a score or two of sheep, and a few cattle too. But that is all.'

'You couldn't feed heavy horses in the glen?'

'No, no. There is no feed for a heavy horse. Only the Highland garron can survive the hard life here.'

'So the six English mares that Coll Keppoch took from my fields did you no good?' asked Glenlyon.

'Now when would that be?' asked MacIan.

'Three years ago—a little more than three.'

'That I cannot remember. I once had an English mare—it would be about three years ago—that a friend left here, in payment of a debt—it may have been Coll Keppoch, indeed—but she lived no time at all. There was no winter feed for her, and never again would I try to keep an English horse. You can be assured of that, Glenlyon.'

'Indeed I am, MacIan. I am fully assured.—But your judgment of Bordeaux is also good. This is as good a wine as I have ever drunk in the Highlands.'

'Fill up your glass, there is no lack of wine, thank God. All in my house is yours—and let us think no more of English mares and the mistakes we all have made in the past.'

'I say damn the past, MacIan, and damn the future too! Let us live within the confines of a day, like butterflies that come out on a summer morning, or the disciples of Jesus Christ, if they did as they were told.—Your very good health, MacIan!'

Some three or four hours later MacIan was put to bed by his wife and two elderly cousins who lived in the house: thickset women with mournful eyes and high, chattering voices; and when they had undressed him, he, for a moment recapturing the solemn sense of his importance in the family, stood upright in his shirt and invoked on them the blessing of Almighty God before he fell senseless on his pillow. Glenlyon was carried to the billet he had chosen, at Achnacon, by two of the wild-seeming clansmen who had watched his arrival with swords ready to their hands—small, tough, long-haired, wild-cat-like fellows—and now bore him gently to his couch with perfect sympathy for a gentleman's habit and his helpless condition. He slept in his clothes, but early in the morning he was out and about, with blood-shot eyes and the snow-bright light shining on his cracked and varnished but well shaved chin.

He watched Sergeant Barber drilling his company, and walked briskly by their ranks to call attention to an ill-fitting uniform or some small failure to clean a musket thoroughly. He took pleasure in watching a line wheel right or left, to offer a presumptive flank, and with the pertinacity of an artist insisted that the movement be repeated until quick performance and perfect symmetry were achieved as if by nature.

After an hour's drill the company would be dismissed to a meal of porridge and dried fish; and paraded again to rehearse more elaborate movements. In perfection of discipline lay the army's only hope of defeating the superior forces of continental monarchies, or the exuberance of a Highland charge, and Glenlyon, like a gambler seeking always the perfect hand of cards, was indefatigable in his pursuit of perfection in drill. His two subalterns were of small help, but Sergeant Barber believed as firmly in drill as the most rigorous of the Children of Israel in the Decalogue; and in the isolation of its new training-ground their detachment of Argyll's Regiment grew daily more vigorously exact in the handling of arms, more precise and strict in movement.

Glenlyon, who preserved a vestige of sensibility under his varnished skin, was sometimes embarrassed and inclined to tetchiness by the constant attendance of the women and children of the glen; who watched with admiration the manoeuvring of his company, and often cheered its smarter evolutions. But Sergeant Barber accepted such attention as a reasonable and proper tribute to his power of command.

Nearly every afternoon there were games of shinty on the level fields. The low ground was frozen but bare of snow, and shinty was a game that, at its most severe, could draw blood. The stick that was used was bevelled on either side, to loft the ball with both a forehand and a backhand drive, and the ball was a solid sphere carved from bog-oak that flew like a cannon-ball when hard hit. But because it was a game no injury was accounted base in motive, and the wildest charges were accepted as the necessary tactics of the game. All the young men of the glen were players and most of the soldiers.

The troops who had followed Glenlyon came, for the most part, from Campbell country, and a good many, who lived about Glen Orchy, Loch Awe, and Loch Fyne were near neighbours of MacIan's people; they had no difficulty in understanding each other, their speech was the same and their habit of life identical. The Lowlanders in the regiment—about a score of them—were at some disadvantage, but their fellow-soldiers and their hosts both made much of them, as if to assure them that their inferiority was superficial, and counted for nothing; and they could grumble among themselves and be comforted by the example of Sergeant Barber, whose command of the Gaelic tongue was limited and barbaric, but whose command of men was whole and undisputed.

Within a few days of their arrival, the red-coats became part of the little community of Glencoe, and their hosts, having quickly forgotten their initial fear, were lavish in their hospitality and frankly pleased to have guests whose talk and tales abated the long dullness of winter. The soldiers were pleased—as soldiers always are—to be under independent command, and remote from the over-crowded, exacting discipline of Fort William, where senior officers went to and fro in the thunderous atmosphere that gods and colonels gather round them. The soldiers' pleasure was, moreover, much enhanced by the better rations they drew in Glencoe: their hosts had been told the billeting-allowance they would be paid, but not a woman in the glen counted the cost of the dried fish and mutton hams they put before their guests. The glen indeed was richer than many a Lowland parish, with salmon out of the river and the loch hanging from cottage rafters, and cattle—not all of them bred at home—that had to be killed for lack of winter feed, and sometimes an old stag or a young hind brought down from the hill; though the deer in the neighbourhood were not many. It was not the Highland way to count the cost of entertainment, and many a meal-chest would be empty long before the spring brought grass and milk to fatten the children again, and new-run fish to replenish vacant larders.

But what was wealth except for spending, and who would balance security against the pleasures that strangers brought, who could sing new songs in the mother-tongue, and tell old stories of their common ancestry in the heroic past, and dance so featly, and take their turn at the chanter or the harp?

There were *ceilidhs* every night, and the Campbell soldiers who wore the King's red coat discovered a natural fellowship with the little MacIan sept of Clan Donald, their immemorial enemies. In the last light of short winter days they played at shinty, they wrestled, they threw the hammer and competed with the caber and the shot: they lived together like contending cousins, and when night fell they sang and danced on the beaten floors of the warm and smoky cabins in which they slept.

Sergeant Barber, much respected for his manifest authority and expert discipline on the parade-ground, went from house to house, drank more than his share, and won the Highlanders' generous applause for singing in a sweet tenor voice the bawdy, common songs of London, that no one but himself could understand, but whose tunes were noted and remembered.

Glenlyon and the two Lindsays played cards and drank every night with John and Alastair, MacIan's sons, and with the tacksman of Inverrigan and him of Achnacon. They drank, without stint, the wine and spirits that their hosts put on the table, and Glenlyon, who was a gentleman by instinct though rarely in behaviour, brought down from Inverlochy a butt of claret and some great stone pigs of whisky. Glenlyon, in the two weeks he spent in the glen, never went sober to bed, and none of MacIan's folk who sat with him was any better.

For two weeks, within a day or so, nothing happened to spoil amity, nothing roughened the placid air of jollity and contentment. A matter of sentiment and a soldier's claim to have seen the wolf that had frightened Red Angus's son, were topics of conversation: there was nothing graver.

Shiona, the daughter of John, had attracted the eyes and stirred the heart of a young man of decent family in Argyll's Regiment. He was known as Ian Og of the Bield, and was heir to a few acres at the southern corner of Loch Awe. There were other flirtations and light moments of affection between soldiers and girls of the glen, but this attachment was conspicuous because both parties to it were persons of some consequence, and the sentiment that bound them appeared to be earnest and conclusive. They were warned, and reproved, and threatened—by Shiona's mother, by Ian Og's commanding officer—but they were indifferent to opinion. Ian Og stood on his dignity, Shiona was defiant, and they went their own way within a cat's cradle of gossip entwining about them.

The other topic, inimical to quietude, was the wolf. The man who claimed to have seen it was one of the Lowland soldiers. He, having explained that he did not care to play shinty, said he had started to climb the mountain south of Loch Triachtan—for no better reason than a fanciful notion that the glen with its steep sides was a sort of prison, in which he felt unhappy and confined—and having lost his way on the hill, and been benighted, he was frightened by a great beast in the snow, with yellow glaring eyes. He ran from it, fell fifty feet into a heavy drift—or so he said—and blind luck brought him down to the loch again. His story was not much believed; but it woke remembrance of the tale Red Angus's son had told, and like the mutter of a coming storm a whisper of fear went to and fro among the women.

It was on the twelfth day of February that the weather changed. The wind came from the north-east, and the sky filled with the grey-blue menace of heavy snow. Two horsemen—an officer and a trooper—had come down from the ferry-landing, and for an hour the officer had walked with Glenlyon, apart and remote from others. When he had gone again, Glenlyon called his subalterns and Sergeant Barber, and gave them their instructions. Presently they went with their orders, and summoned the men to hear them. The snow was falling as they went, in a slanting, impenetrable drift of soft, wet, bog-cotton flowers. To begin with, it melted as it fell; but the air grew colder, and in a little while the floor of the glen was carpeted in white, and the still falling snow thickened on the ground. Before dark the valley and the invisible hills were all one colour, blanched beneath the dusk and gathering from the sky a weight that was scarcely palpable, and yet, by accumulation, deadening: a weight, as it curiously seemed, of silence.

In that silence, imposed by the sky, men whispered to each other and sought by murmured questions an explanation of orders they could not understand and as yet did not wholly believe. 'No quarter,' they muttered. 'Is that right? Is that what he said?' And again: 'No prisoners. It is an order from the Government, they want no prisoners.' 'They are all to be killed, and the clachan must be burnt.'

'You heard the same?'

'The very same.'

'But why—why now, after all these days?'

'In God's name, why?'

Sergeant Barber felt neither fear nor compunction. He was inured to discipline, and nothing demanded by discipline could surprise or dismay him. He knew that MacIan and his clan, regarded by authority as a tribe of robbers, had been condemned to punishment; and he was an instrument of authority, trained and dedicated. He took his pay, and was content in his service. He would, if need be, die for his meagre wage, because it was obscurely related to a loyalty which had grown from a long habit of discipline, and now enclosed his whole mind. As he set no great store on his own life—apart from the gratification of drink, and his strange pleasure, when drunk, of singing bawdy songs—he felt small respect for the lives of others. Never before had he been ordered to kill women and children, and he had no intention of doing so now; but, by his command, the private soldiers would butcher the cows and calves of the herd. He had no compunction about giving such orders, but his dignity would restrict his own activity.

The two Lindsays shared a flask of brandy, and exercising their meagre equipment of imagination, pretended to each other with beggarly excuse and threadbare equivocation that what they were commanded to do was no more than an ordinary fragment of a soldier's duty. They enjoyed the authority that went with being officers in the King's army, and darkly they suspected how insignificant they would be without their commissions. They wore a uniform that defied criticism, buttressed their importance, and commanded obedience; and by obedience they could save their title to respect.—But still they felt queasy, and wished they had more brandy to sustain their logic and fortify them in obedience. They thought of going to drink at the table of one or other of their friends in the glen; but some vague, uncertain apprehension of impropriety prevented them from that.

Like deer in a high corrie, scenting on a light, uncertain wind the pungent, but far-off odour of men, the people of the glen had caught from the red-coats the smell of their unhappiness, and moved uneasily about their houses. When Alastair, MacIan's younger son, went home before dusk, his wife told him that a child had seen one of the red-coats clapping a grey boulder on the moor—a boulder that looked like a dead and frozen stag on the dead, grey heather—and heard him say to it, 'Grey stag of the glen, get up on your feet and go. Go, go from the glen before you see what the night will bring.'

'A daft-like saying,' said Alastair. 'These men of Argyll's are as daft as children, and with a dram in them as daft as old women. There's no meaning in their words, and nothing to fear.'

A little while later he was bidden to play cards with Glenlyon and the two Lindsays and his brother John; but the party fell into dispute and broke up early, though Glenlyon was rarely ill-humoured and notoriously a late sitter. Alastair had seen the mounted officer who came to talk with Glenlyon, and with that memory in his mind, and Glenlyon's nervous loss of temper over a bad hand, he went home with troubled thoughts and lay sleepless by his wife. At midnight he rose and looked out; and from his doorway, through the falling snow, he saw a light in the cabin where the quarter-guard was housed. He put on his shoes and wrapped his plaid about him, and went to the house of his brother John. But John thought there was no cause for alarm, and Alastair went home again.

Some of the lesser folk in the glen were not so complacent, and lay all night, as if listening to the wind, but listening rather for the ill tidings that would substantiate their fear: the instinctive fear of a wild herd, lulled into security, but now scenting on a draught of intuition the familiar smell of danger.

At five o'clock in the morning the elder Lindsay, with half a dozen soldiers, demanded entry to MacIan's house. The door was opened, and the old man, warm in bed, sat up and put a leg to the ground. 'Let us have more light,' he said, with hospitality dominant in his Highland mind. 'I cannot see who my guests are, but the morning's cold, and whoever you are you will be the better of a dram.'

His wife was in her clothes. She, oppressed by the whispering and the smell of fear, had not undressed but sat all night by the fire. She went, uncertainly, to the cupboard where MacIan kept his wine, and as she fumbled in the shadows a pistol-shot, and then another, banged and bellowed under the rafters; and the great body of MacIan—shot in the head, shot in the chest—fell down upon the blankets and tumbled to the floor. Then, in a frenzy of murderous excitement, the soldiers assaulted his old, stubborn, thick-set wife, beating her with the muzzles and butts of their muskets, tearing her clothes, and ripping the rings from her fingers with wolfish teeth.

They went out to a growing clamour of flame and confusion, and the still continuing wild fall of the snow. There was a new force in the glen, for some of the forward troops from Fort William—the four hundred soldiers that Major Duncanson commanded—had found their way down the Devil's Staircase, the dangerous pass over the northern wall above Loch Triachtan; but most of them were lost and benighted, and their purpose of closing escape to the east had been defeated. Those who had crossed the mountain—their leading files had marched in a lull of the storm—looked about them, and saw strangers. But that was common to all the soldiers. The red-coats who had lived together in the glen for nearly a fortnight were now all strangers to each other.

When they were told that their duty was to destroy, utterly and without mercy, MacIan and all his people—to kill the men, women, and children with whom they had lived in kindliness—their humanity revolted against the monstrous order, but their discipline compelled mute acquiescence. Day after day they had drilled on the frozen fields, and drill had so sternly taught them the habit of obedience that now it was hardly within the compass of their thought to question an order, or doubt the inescapable necessity of obedience. But in spite of drill, and the lessons of discipline, they heard the command to murder with bewilderment and consternation; for it mocked and derided an older habit than obedience, and the kindly laws of hospitality. They had been the guests of MacIan and his clan, they had eaten their bread and drunk with them—and now to turn against their hosts was black, unmitigated treachery. In the simplicity of their hearts they had thought—they had always been told—that the bonds of hospitality were unbreakable. A host and his guest were safer company than a father and his son; or so they had believed.

But now they were commanded to break the ancient law and defile the sanctuary of old custom; and in their simplicity they saw no escape from the obedience that the voice of Sergeant Barber, day after day, had hammered into their anxious, listening ears. Obedience to that voice had been driven home like a nail, impaling thought on the blank habit of conformity. There was no way of escape but one: they must escape themselves.

In the hours of waiting, every man had gone apart, communing with himself, and striven to lose himself in the impersonation of sheer discipline that Sergeant Barber presented to them. They had pressed their hands hard against closed eyes, rubbed and fretted their cheeks to drive feeling from their flesh, and then re-moulded their features, as well as might be, to the cold, inhuman calm of discipline. They had driven sensibility out of sight, and put on, against a climate harsher than winter, thick masks of discipline. When they met again, they hardly recognised each other; but some were like grotesque and ill-drawn caricatures of Sergeant Barber.

The Sergeant himself felt no need for a mask; and Glenlyon's cracked and varnished skin was enough for him.

At Achnacon Sergeant Barber had found some eight or ten men sitting by the fire, and a volley through the door killed half of them, and wounded others. But one escaped, who asked, with a condemned man's whimsy, if he might be killed out of doors. It was the sort of jocularity that appealed to Barber, who granted him his wish. But the man who should have died threw his plaid over the heads of the soldiers about him, and took to the hill. In the nearby houses Barber and his troop found others, less alert and agile, and the bodies of those they killed, dragging them bloodily through the snow, they threw upon the cottage middens. There was a small child among them.

At Inverrigan, Glenlyon surprised nine men, and took the precaution, not trusting his marksmen, of binding them hand and foot before they were shot. But Glenlyon, whose drink-sodden mind was incapable of apprehension or remorse, was equally incapable of perseverance and application: now he grew listless, and looked about him at the flames of burning thatches that here and there strangely lighted the falling snow—that exposed, in a red and smoky glare, the drifting descent of the snow against scarlet flames and the shadow of the smoke—and turned to a rusty black the splash and smear of blood on the white carpet of the glen.

He listened with indifference—with the detachment of a man who had drunk himself into detachment—to musket-shots in the darkness, to an occasional rattle of musketry, and said to an officer who came striding towards him with purpose in his step, with intention in his carriage, 'I'll wager six to one, in groats or guineas—whichever suits your pocket—that both my doltish subalterns have made a horse's mash of their orders, and the musketry we can hear is probably the Lindsays shooting at each other.'

The officer to whom he spoke was a Captain Drummond, who, commanding the advance-guard of Duncanson's detachment from the Fort William garrison, had crossed the mountain and found the Devil's Staircase before the storm thickened. He was a man who, ruthless by nature, was susceptible, within smell of blood, to the mania of homicide; and Glenlyon's drunken indifference inflamed his temper. There was a young man nearby, in the grip of two soldiers, who stammered a plea for mercy. Drummond, with a pistol, shot him dead. A boy threw himself at Glenlyon's feet; Drummond, with his other pistol, shot him too. Glenlyon, with a sudden fit of hiccups, walked into the darkness, and Drummond, accompanied by a few soldiers whom he ordered to attend him, found a child, a woman, and an old man; and killed them.

Both Alastair and John, MacIan's sons, had escaped the slaughter; and, as Glenlyon had guessed, their escape was due, in part, to the dullard incompetence of the two young Lindsays, who had each gone to the other's objective—realised their mistake—and returning, met and wasted ten minutes in furious abuse and argument. Alastair and John, and some of their two households, had escaped the murderers, but now lay hiding under the pitiless onslaught of the sky. Nearly all the houses in the glen were aflame, and each, in the falling snow, made a core of heat in which the snow dissolved, but round which the drifting flakes were illumined in a bright and heartless prettiness. In byres and stables a few animals, caught by the fire, screamed and bellowed their pain and fear; and others, let loose, were lowing hungrily for their morning feed. Slowly the sky lightened to grey, and the burning houses were rooted to the ground in the red embers of their fallen posts and rafters.

John's daughter, Shiona, had escaped with her father, but she was late in leaving the house, having gone back to look for some trinket that her young husband had given her before he died. Her child was heavy in her arms, and she could not walk as quickly as the others. She fell farther behind, and though she knew the corrie for which they were making, she mistook her way, and presently, in a wild squall that blinded and confused her, she sank down for shelter under a stark rock that stood on the hillside like the prow of a wrecked ship. Her baby, a lusty child, began to cry with the impassioned resolution of its age, and nothing she could do or say would quieten it.

The light was coming through the winter sky, and Captain Drummond had mustered some stragglers of Argyll's Regiment—men who stood about in the warmth of burning houses with no apparent purpose or intention—to hunt fugitives and follow trails of blood. One of his little troop was Ian Og of the Bield, who, alone in Glenlyon's company, had determined to disobey his orders. He had looked for Shiona, to warn her of what was impending, and failed to find her because Shiona, a lively, gossiping girl, had been going from house to house, not so much afraid of what whispering threatened, as greedy to hear all the whispers.

Then, when Ian Og had to follow the elder Lindsay—for he dared not openly disobey—he had been led astray, and in desperation had deserted his troop; but still could not find Shiona. He had taken off his red coat and thrown it away, for a sign of rebellion, and wrapped himself in a great plaid. But now, when Drummond called to him, the dismay and wretchedness of his mind were so heavy that he followed like a bullock in a drover's herd.

They went eastward through the glen, for forty minutes or more; and Drummond, halting them, held a hand to his ear. 'What tune is that?' he asked. 'Who's playing there?'

Through the driving snow, but thin and faint and far away, came the braggart melody of a pipe-tune; and Drummond's half dozen looked at each other with secret knowledge. It was a tune they knew, for they had heard it in the glen. It was a march called *Glenlyon's Mares* that Red Angus the piper—the gifted singer of mouth-music—had composed in honour of the raid on Glenlyon's lands three years before. And now

Red Angus, in mad delight for his escape, was mocking his enemies from far up the mountain with the scorn of his wild music.

'This way,' said Drummond, cocking his ear to the tune, and led them up hill. They had gone half a mile when they heard a thinner, fretful, complaining air; and Drummond, impatient for the major quarry, said, 'There's a woman with her child not far away. Tucked in a hole somewhere. Go, you'—he pointed to Ian Og—'and let both of them sign your sword. There's no quarter given here.'

He watched Ian Og go in quest of the crying child, and led his remaining men in pursuit of the scornful piper. Ian Og climbed a ledge of rock, crossed a patch of frozen bog, and came to a slope of smooth snow at the top of which, under a great uprearing rock, he found Shiona, distracted, and the child screaming on her lap.

He knelt beside her, and took her and the child in his arms. They wept on each other's cheeks, and kissed through cold tears. The desperation of love was secondary to the desperation of their circumstance, and the passion of their tenderness quickly became urgent enquiry of their needs.—She knew, said Shiona, where her father was going. She had been bewildered by a sudden thickening of the storm, but now she knew her way and how to follow him. She complained only of the cold, and her baby's hunger.

Ian Og unwrapped his plaid and made an enclosing nest for the child. He had a day's ration of oat-bread and mutton ham, and a small flask of whisky. He gave a scrap of mutton to the child, the rest to Shiona. The child sucked the smoked meat, and was quiet. Ian Og, still on his knees, turned to Shiona, crouched under the rock, and pledged himself to meet her before summer in the house of a cousin she named, who lived by the shore in Appin. They kissed again, desperate and loving in the whiteness of the storm—but their lips parted when a snarling voice astonished them.

It was a snarl of greed, it was wild eyes flashing in a grey mask flecked with snow, and Ian Og, on his knees, reached quickly for his naked sword and swung a short cut that lopped from the leaping wolf—a wolf crazed with winter, gnawing hunger, and the warm smell of a child—his near fore-leg, and dropped him, limp and bleeding, to the snow.

With hunger more desperate than its pain, the wolf leapt again, fierce but lop-sided, and Ian Og thrust at its throat. He pricked; and the wolf crouched, snarling at him. Ian Og advanced a foot, the wolf rose on three legs—blood dripping on the snow—and Ian, back-handed, cut down and cut so hard that his sword sank from its right ear deep into the wolf's brain.

'Here is my warrant,' he said, pointing to the blood on his blade. 'I was told to kill a woman and her crying child, and I have killed a wolf instead. I do not think they will smell the difference of its blood—and a few months from now we shall meet again between Appin and the sea. But this I must preserve—it is my evidence.'

He knelt again, holding high his blood-stained sword, and kissed her closely. The child, still sucking smoked mutton, was quiet and contented in Ian's plaid on the snow.

'Do not wait,' he said, 'but go now, and I will see to it that Drummond and his men go another way.'

She took a bite or two of oat-bread and meat, a mouthful of whisky, and picked up the child. Doubly mantled, with Ian's plaid as well as her own, she went on her way, as confident now as a mountain sheep that must only hurry to regain the flock; and Ian Og, in shirt and trews, stood and waved to her. Then, light-hearted, leaping like a boy at play, ran through the snow to the path where he had left Drummond and his five soldiers when they went in pursuit of a wild piper.

He met them, returning. They had come to a cliff that seemed unscalable, and in sullen anger had withdrawn. He showed his blood-red blade and said, 'There was no trouble. No trouble at all. Two strokes and it was done.'

'I would like to have given forty strokes to that damned insolent piper,' said Drummond. 'But where is your plaid?'

'I covered their faces,' said Ian Og. 'It was only decent to do that.'

'A piece of damned Highland nonsense,' said Drummond. 'But yours is the loss, it was your plaid.' And with impatient steps led them back to the glen.

Against a background of charred and smouldering cabins, they found Glenlyon, staggering a little. 'No trophies of the chase?' he asked.

'Nothing,' said Drummond, 'but frustration and a damned urgent thirst.'

'That is the whole tale of man's endeavour,' said Glenlyon; and in the light of the low sun that now shone through a small and disparate descent of snow, his varnished face looked like an old picture, painted by a master, but dusty and cracked by neglect after many years in the attic of an abandoned house.

The soldiers, idly picking in the ruins, wandered about the burnt clachan. They, being innocent, had discarded their masks without difficulty, without consciousness of what they were doing. They had resumed their common appearance. They were again lumpy, sullen, jocular or mild, or frank and healthy. They looked themselves again. They were not to blame, and with perfect ease they had put off, and promptly forgotten, the masks they had worn for a night of alien purpose.

SIX

For a week there had been rain every day. A drizzle of rain falling from a covered sky to wet fields. The air was mild, and in woods and gardens, in hedgerow and meadow, growth was luxuriant. But the bloom of spring had gone, and now it seemed as if all the southern part of England swam in a green haze. Under a sky without colour the whole landscape was a drenched and monotonous green tumbled sea. Church towers and steeples, white cottages and castle walls, rose mournfully above the verdant flood, and soured by too much green the inhabitants of town and village were in a liverish, cantankerous, and complaining mood.

Among their rulers there were those who had greater reason for ill humour, and vented it in reprobation of misdeeds they would have condoned if their outcome had been more fortunate. There was wide-spread anger against Breadalbane and the Master of Stair for their part in the tragical affair of Glencoe: righteous anger, and anger that was self-righteous. The King was too honest to deny his own share of responsibility, but too much shaken by public opinion and the failure of their plot to conceal his anger. It was anger that grew neither from moral shame nor a hypocritical intention to exculpate himself, but from a statesman's realisation that he had been badly advised and was guilty of a grave political mistake.

The rebuilding of Kensington Palace had begun, but for the last few days, under constant rain, little had been done, and from the tall window in the Master's room William looked out, with a green reflection on his pale cheeks, at a lawn divided by raw trenches and a pile of white scaffolding under the dripping shade of exuberant elms.

Nervously, with irritable movement, he returned to his seat at the long table, where a disarray of documents was spread, and confronted the two noblemen who stood, uneasy but intransigent, to hear his judgment. They wore, all three of them, their masks of purpose: on the King the royal purpose of his singular authority, and on Breadalbane and the Master the more subtle and complex purpose of maintaining, under the King's rule, their own dominion, and of justifying themselves and all they had done.

'You have failed me,' said the King. 'You have doubly failed me, in tactics and policy. You did not, as you promised, destroy MacIan and his people, and you have not, by example of your strictness, suppressed dissension in Scotland. You have, on the contrary, infected England with doubt and disapproval of our rule. I, in my fashion—a king's fashion, who loses as much by disapproval of his policy as a Highland chief by the loss of half his men—have suffered more heavily than the Highlanders, though you killed MacIan and thirty others.'

'All military operations,' said the Master, 'are ultimately dependent on two factors, that none but God Almighty can control. The first is the weather; the second is the character and ability of the officers in command—'

'It may be true that God ordained a snowstorm lasting three days: I do not know enough of God and his Privy Council to deny that possibility,' said the King. 'But who chose the officers to execute our purpose in whatever weather might befall? You did. And with what effect? Of MacIan and his clan not more than thirty were killed, some of them children, and what was done was done so ill-advisedly that from all parts of my kingdom come murmurings and mutterings, and I am in bad odour as well as you, who deserve it more.'

'With all respect, Sir,' said Breadalbane, 'you do not know the difficulty of warfare in the Highlands—'

'This was not warfare,' said the King. 'Had it been war I would have directed it myself: to a better end! This was only the punishment—or intended punishment—of a small sect of rebels who, because by general repute they were habitual thieves and raiders as well as rebels, deserved no mercy. A small and simple operation—and still you bungled it.'

'It was a punitive measure, Sir, that required the skill and artifice of military practice,' said Breadalbane. 'And you, Sir, have never seen the Highlands. You do not know that a winter snow-storm there could defeat the plans of the greatest military genius who ever lived.'

'The greater part of MacIan's people escaped westward into Appin. The passes to Appin were not guarded. Why not?'

'It was thought that none could cross them—'

'Then your appreciation was wrong, your judgment at fault!'

The Master intervened. 'It was due to the storm, Sir, that Duncanson's detachment, from Fort William, was late in arrival. Had they been there in time—'

'Hamilton waited for twelve days before sending Duncanson into the glen. What was the reason for that delay?'

'He was waiting, Sir, until the others, who had to close the southern passes, and the passes to Rannock, should come in.'

'And who was responsible for their slowness? By God, sirs, this whole affair throws up a stink of ineptitude, with another stench that I can detect, of possible corruption—'

'No, Sir! There was no corruption, no double-dealing. All was honestly done.'

'Then stark incompetence is your only last excuse! Incompetence in the choice of men, in the handling of men, in the framing of a plan—all that piled on top of incompetence of judgment. For you told me this was the way to pacify the Highlands, and so far from that being effected, you have inflamed, not only the Highlands, but opinion here in England, and in France. Look at these letters, these journals. See what the *Gazette of Paris* has to say about it.'

'All these stories,' said Breadalbane sturdily, 'have been put about by persistent Jacobites, the rump of resistance that can't be kicked out. They seek every chance to discredit your Majesty's government and its policy.'

'And now,' said the King, 'they have found a very good chance, and are making unholy use of it. And who gave them the chance? We did. You, my lord, and you, Mr Secretary, and I who, by the displeasure of God, am your King. We are all to blame—and I am deeply to blame for my lack of judgment in taking your advice.'

Breadalbane stood in a hardihood of controlled anger that showed a surface of resistance almost metallic in its texture—as if he were a statue of himself cast roughly in bronze—and said, 'We have killed MacIan and thirty of his following. The old dog-fox is dead and his clan scattered, their houses level with the ground. So much good we have done, and every robber-clan in the Highlands now knows the strength of our intention and the weight of our hands. What I deplore—what we deplore, the Master and I—is that our purpose was not completed. And with regard to that, though I admit our officers were less competent than I had judged them, the main obstacle was the storm, for which we can only blame God, who is indifferent to our censure. But if all had gone well—'

'Yes,' said the King, 'if all had gone well, and all that pestilent clan wiped off the slate, like an old debt paid-up, we would have heard no complaint, because no one would have been left to complain; and I should not now be assailed, from England, Scotland, and France—by Jacobite dissidents, English hypocrites (always a majority) and our constant enemies abroad—for an abominable treachery that no Christian monarch can excuse, and a policy so maladroit as no government may defend!'

'Sir,' said the Master, 'such accusations are the commonplace of politics, and fall away from consistency in government as waves from a well and solidly built sea-wall. Your Government is in no danger, Sir, and can easily withstand the criticism of its natural enemies. What we did was well intended, and though it has not brought about all the good we hoped, I would do it again tomorrow. We must be patient, Sir, and yield nothing to criticism.'

'You will yield so much,' said the King, 'as to write to Colonel—what's his name, at Fort William?'

'Colonel Hill, Sir.'

'Write to him, and authorise him to receive the remnant of MacIan's clan into my peace, and reinstate them in their lands, and assure them that we have no more hostile intention against them.'

'If that is your will, Sir—'

'It is.'

'Then, Sir, it shall be done.'

'But nothing we can do,' said the King, 'will crase from the record of my reign this bloody slur you have left upon it.'

He covered his face with his hands, and his fingers moved restlessly. He kneaded the flesh of his cheeks, scrubbed his forehead, and pulled at the shape of his mouth. And apart from him Breadalbane and the Master, turning away in relief that their dreaded interview had passed without loss of office or charge of treason, were also soothing, smoothing, and obliterating (or so trying) from their features their strained and harsh expression.

They rubbed and they scrubbed, and felt beneath their fingers a horny, indurate resistance. They turned about and saw the King, from the head of the littered table, staring at them through the mask of purpose which had grown upon him. The mask of a cold, inhuman purpose that could not be removed.

And the King, staring at Breadalbane and the Master, saw them in the masks they would wear until they died: the masks of bloody intention that would forever stamp their features and shape their memory.

The Redundant Miracle

A CERTAIN PHILOSOPHER, whom his neighbours called Smoky Philip for a reason that will appear, was reduced by circumstances to a state of dire poverty. He was nobly born, and in his youth had been rich enough. But the calamities to which all men are subject—pestilence, famine, civil war, foreign invasion, the treachery of relatives and the hostility of servants—had done much to destroy his property, and when in middle life he became addicted to philosophy the remainder of his fortune was speedily dissipated.

He had two handsome daughters of marriageable age to whom the future offered little but disappointment, as their father could find for neither the dowry necessary to procure a husband. For some time, indeed, he had found it difficult to provide them with food, even of the cheapest kind. They were intelligent and vivacious girls as any to be found in the neighbourhood, and the prospect of an unwedded and scantily nourished life did not please them. One, whose name was Beta, had red hair which she braided in two glowing pigtails reaching to her waist; the other, called Dowsabell, had raven-black tresses and a very white skin. Their mother was dead.

One day, when they had eaten nothing but a crust of brown bread and an onion, Beta said to Dowsabell, 'It's high time for us to become sensible and look facts in the face. There is no money in the house, and despite our father's belief in alchemy, there is not the slightest possibility of there ever being any money—that is, unless we obtain it by our own endeavours. We are both strong and really rather nice-looking. So far as I can see there is only one thing for us to do, if we would escape this life of poverty so extreme that the danger of starvation is never absent.'

'Whatever we decide, the prospect is dreadful for girls so nobly born and delicately nurtured as ourselves,' said Dowsabell, and deeply sighed. Through the open door she could see a group of soldiers loitering. They were fine upstanding fellows, laughing loudly at some joke, and the sun shone brightly on their partial armour. 'Oh, a dreadful prospect!' said Dowsabell with another sigh.

Beta agreed with her, also looking at the soldiers. 'But I am afraid it is necessary,' she said. 'We cannot live for ever on brown bread and onions—which, incidentally, I detest.'

'That crust was the last in the house,' said Dowsabell, 'and there are very few onions left.'

'We appear to have no choice,' said Beta, moving so that she could follow with her eyes a sturdy and evidently prosperous merchant riding down the cobbled street on a little donkey.

'We have also our father to consider,' Dowsabell pointed out. 'He has had nothing to eat for several days, and after he has done so much for us it is clearly our duty to support him, if we can, in the helplessness of his age and philosophic habit of mind.'

'You're quite right,' said Beta. 'Let us go and tell him that he will have no further need to worry, because for the future we shall look after him.'

Smoky Philip was on his knees before a small fire that he blew with patient regularity. Every now and then a cloud of soot emerged and settled on his face and whiskers. As he spent many hours a day before the fire, and as he seldom remembered to wash, his whiskers, white in reality, had acquired a permanent dinginess, and his face was black as a collier's. Its lineaments, however, were still kindly, and his brow was extremely noble.

Out of a pot suspended on the fire came a smell, very disgusting, but readily accounted for by the contents of the vessel, which were eggshells, mutton-bones, old iron, frog-spawn, brimstone, horsehair, valerian, dandelions, night-shade, and certain fluids which it is unnecessary to name. Smoky Philip continued to blow at his fire.

'Father,' said Beta, 'we have come to tell you of a decision we have made. There is, as you are aware, no money in the house . . .'

'In five hours and thirteen minutes,' benignly interrupted the philosopher, 'provided that I am successful in maintaining this fire at an equable temperature, there will be in that pot a substance out of which, by fermentation, putrefaction, congolation, calcination, and other processes, I shall presently produce the *magisterium*, and with that, making projection upon base metals, deliver to you an infinite quantity of pure gold. Do not disturb yourselves about our momentary embarrassment, for in a very little time—some five months or so—I shall control the riches of the whole world.'

'We've heard that tale before,' said Dowsabell with some impatience, 'and we're still hungry. So are you, my dear father, however much you may endeavour to ignore the fact. And so, for your good as well as our own, we mean to sacrifice our delicacy, our good name, and our very selves. In a word, we propose to barter our virtue for bodily sustenance.'

'Now tell me,' exclaimed the philosopher, 'do you mean by virtue some form of conduct motivated by the sweetness and flavour discernible in absolute good; or a primarily disinterested affection whose direct object is the good of others?'

'This is no time for academic discussion,' said Beta coldly. 'In case you did not understand the significance of what my sister told you, let me explain that we intend to seek the society of men.'

'A womanly pleasure,' said her father, blowing a cloud of ashes from the fire.

Angrily Dowsabell seized and shook his arm. 'We are going to sell ourselves for bread!' she shouted.

'I shall be greatly obliged if you will also buy me some brass knobs, a packet of sulphur, and a bundle of good dry wood, all of which I require for my experiments,' said the philosopher.

'There's no use speaking to him,' said Beta furiously. 'He will never, never understand the sacrifice we are making for him! Come, Dowsabell, or it will be too late. The Count's archers are going on guard tonight.'

They turned to the door, and were astonished to see, framed in that narrow entrance, the figure of a venerable man whose face, so far as they could discern its expression in a poor light, was not only noble but full of compassion. He wore a pilgrim's grey gown and a broad-brimmed hat made heavy by many saintly images. He carried a heavy staff, and from his shoulders depended a long chain of cockle-shells. His voice, when he spoke, had a clear bell-like quality, and the air seemed to sparkle with the minute vibrations that it caused.

'I am weary,' he said, 'for I have journeyed far. I seek rest and comfort. Do I find them here, or must I travel to another door?'

'If you like cold water, you are welcome to it,' said Beta, 'but that is all we can offer you.'

'A cup of water is my heart's desire,' said the pilgrim, and seated himself upon a stool. Bending over the water he blessed it, whereupon it changed colour and exhaled a pleasant odour. He drank it and appeared considerably refreshed.

'I could not help hearing, as I stood in the door, the end of your discussion,' he said confidently, 'and I am not exaggerating when I confess that I have rarely been so distressed and shocked in the course of all my travels, which I may say have been extensive. Is it really necessary that you should make a sacrifice so painful to consider and so abhorrent to yourselves? For the manner in which you spoke of it convinced me of the loathing with which you regard this awful step. Is it, I repeat, really necessary?'

'The alternative is starvation,' said Beta, replaiting one of her splendid red pigtails.

'Starvation not only for ourselves, but for our father,' added Dowsabell, polishing her nails with an old cloth.

'Dear, dear,' said the pilgrim. 'Never have I heard anything so sad. Is your father deaf, may I ask?' For all this time the philosopher had continued to blow his fire and stir his evil-smelling pot without paying any attention to his visitor.

'No, I'm not deaf!' said Smoky Philip. 'But it's a waste of time talking to people, and this furnace needs all the breath I've got.' He blew vigorously, and the fringe of his beard caught fire. He extinguished the little frizzle of flame between his blackened hands, and continued with some irritation: 'I've told my daughters, time and time again, that if they will only have patience for a while I shall have more money than even they can spend, and I shall give them dowries big enough to buy counts or princes for their husbands. Meanwhile, of course, I admit that we suffer the embarrassment of comparative poverty, and so there's a lot to be said for their idea of going on the street. But if they consider it such a sacrifice, then surely they can endure our present discomfort for another month or two, or perhaps a little longer. Alchemy, as you know, is an exact science, and my search for the Philosopher's Stone is not only governed by reason, but assured of success provided that I remember the proper order of the thirty-seven different processes necessary for its perfection.'

'Your toil is an impious one,' said the pilgrim, 'for you are endeavouring to upset the established order of creation. Metals as well as men should abide in that calling to which they were called.'

'Nonsense,' said Smoky Philip. 'Every single thing in the world is in a state of flux, and is constantly trying to improve its condition. Lead is only lead because it hasn't had time to become gold. But I'm going to remedy that with my *magisterium*.'

'Lead is lead because it was ordained to be lead from the beginning,' said the pilgrim.

'You might as well say that eggs were ordained to be eggs, and forbid the hen to sit on them,' retorted the philosopher. 'But hens are wiser than you, and know that eggs are chickens *in potentia* . . .'

Beta, who was growing weary of this discussion, plucked at her sister's sleeve, saying, 'Come, Dowsabell, or we shall be late. The archers go on guard at sundown.'

'Stop,' said the pilgrim, and the air sparkled under the weight of his melodious voice as though a sunbeam were in the room. 'Stop!' he said. 'If there were money in the house to buy but one day's measure of bread, would not your sacrifice be averted?'

'Of course it would,' said Dowsabell. 'Nothing but dire necessity brought us even to contemplate this awful step.'

'There isn't a penny in the house,' added Beta. 'Come, Dowsabell. I'm waiting for you.'

'Look carefully about you before you go,' said the pilgrim in a kindly way.

As if by magic all eyes were turned to something that lay on the floor not far from his feet. It was a new penny, brightly shining.

'Well!' said Beta.

'I declare!' said Dowsabell.

'After I'd replaited my hair,' said Beta.

'And I polished my nails,' added Dowsabell.

'A miracle!' exclaimed the pilgrim with some complacency. 'And now you are saved from that loathsome though heroic sacrifice, for a penny is more than enough to purchase a sufficiency of bread for us all.'

'Remember to buy me some brass knobs,' said Smoky Philip with his face to the fire.

After a simple meal of bread and onions the pilgrim spread his cloak on a bench and prepared to sleep; Dowsabell and Beta retired to their garret; and the philosopher blew upon his fire with more strength than he had shown for many days.

The remainder of the bread, with another onion or two, was sufficient for their breakfast, but after that the household was no better off than it had been the previous day. The pilgrim sat on his stool, rattling his cockle-shells and telling stories of his journey from Jerusalem, and the philosopher sniffed with great interest a new smell that was emerging from his pot.

In the afternoon Dowsabell stood up and looked wistfully through the open door. In the sunshine stood a group of the Count's archers, laughing at some jest, the light gleaming on their strong brown faces and their jerkins of chain-mail. Dowsabell sighed. 'Our sacrifice,' she said, 'was only deferred, I fear. The same compulsion of poverty exists today as existed yesterday, and to save our father and our guest from the torture of starvation we must certainly subjugate our finer feelings and sell ourselves to these brutal men-at-arms. Come, poor Beta!'

'In one minute, when I've washed my face,' answered Beta.

'Look carefully before you go,' said the pilgrim. 'Perhaps there will be another miracle.'

Raising her face, still wet, from the small tin basin in which she performed her ablutions, Beta perceived immediately a bright new penny lying almost at the pilgrim's feet.

'Well!' she said.

Dowsabell stooped and picked it up.

'Oh, it's perfectly genuine,' said the pilgrim.

'What do you know about it?' she asked. 'Is it yours? Did you drop it?'

'I?' said the pilgrim. 'Oh dear no! We pilgrims never carry money. We live by faith and are justified for our belief in Providence by constant manifestations of its benevolence. Be assured that the presence of that penny constitutes a miracle.'

'Well, it looks very funny to me,' said Dowsabell.

'And to me,' said Beta suspiciously, examining the penny in her turn.

The pilgrim rubbed his hands in a contented way. 'Now you can go and buy bread for our supper without submitting to the unpleasantness for which you were so bravely prepared a few minutes ago,' he said.

While they were absent he spoke seriously to Smoky Philip, saying, 'Are you not yet convinced of the iniquity of your efforts to upset the divine discipline of things as they are? Surely you have now had conclusive evidence that the existing scheme is best for us all, and that faith in Providence is more fruitful than the impiety of works?'

'If only I had the Philosopher's Stone,' said Smoky Philip, 'I could change those pennies into gold, and then instead of bread and onions, we might sup on quails and pig's feet and wine. I'm very fond of pig's feet.'

The following day, and the day after that too, the miracle was repeated: just as Dowsabell and Beta were ready to go out and sacrifice themselves for the common good, a bright new penny appeared on the floor and made their immolation unnecessary. The pilgrim was delighted, but in the manner of Beta and Dowsabell there appeared a growing constraint.

Meanwhile the philosopher became more and more engrossed in his researches, and as the smell from his pot grew hourly richer and filthier he busied himself, in preparation for the next process of putrefaction, with the braying of horn in a mortar, the distillation of sour vinegar, and the blending of the contents of many small vials. He paid no heed to his daughters' recurring predicament, to the regular interposition of Providence, or to the entertainment of his guest. He was immersed in his art, and though the house consisted only of one room and a garret, Smoky Philip lived, as it were, alone.

On the fifth day of the pilgrim's visit, however, he was disturbed by a very loud and violent noise which, when he first became aware of it, appeared to emanate from some distant part of the town. It came gradually nearer, and finally, when Smoky Philip really gave his attention to it, was discovered to be the voices of Dowsabell, Beta, and the pilgrim mingled together in angry controversy. Inspecting them with more care, the philosopher perceived that his daughters were not only shouting at the pilgrim, but rudely buffeting, scratching, and slapping him; and had already torn out all his hair.

'What's the matter?' he asked.

'You blundering, smug, impertinent, officious nightmare of untimely piety!' shouted Dowsabell, paying no attention to her father's question.

'Snag, stopper, clog, lumbering obstruction! Beefwit, wind in the pipes, bird-brain! Robber of a poor girl's honest independence!' cried Beta.

And the pilgrim shrieked, now to one and now to the other, 'I am a saint, I tell you, and I was only doing my duty! I am St Polydore of Cappadocia, and I go all over the world performing kindly miracles.'

'Miracles!' snorted Dowsabell. 'Father, he planted those pennies himself! We caught him at it. He was hiding one in the floor when we came in, and he's got dozens more in a leather bag!'

'Dear me,' said the philosopher.

'Oh, interference! fish-bone in a cat's throat!' said Dowsabell, and thrust the pilgrim to the door.

'You needless thing, you figseed in a hollow tooth!' added Beta, and, picking up the stool on which he was used to sit, hit the pilgrim very brutally between the shoulders.

St Polydore of Cappadocia howled with pain, picked up his skirts, and ran.

Dowsabell and Beta, looking very handsome with their cheeks red and their eyes still sparkling, glared after him.

'Him and his penny miracles!' said Dowsabell.

'Wasting our time like that, to no purpose at all!' said Beta.

Dowsabell coughed. 'There was certainly no advantage in putting off the evil hour.'

'That's what I meant,' Beta explained. 'Well, shall we go now? Is my hair all right?'

'Very attractive,' said Dowsabell. 'Do you like the new way in which I've done mine?'

'My children,' said the philosopher, 'will you remember to buy me some brass knobs, a packet of sulphur, and some dry wood? And don't you think we might have pig's feet for supper tonight? I'm very tired of bread and onions.'

Escape Forever

RORY MORE had served all but forty-eight days of his sentence when, under cover of a hailstorm that came down with a roar, like a sudden white curtain, he ran from his working-party in the outer quarry. It was not an act of prudence, but Rory was not a prudent man. He was hot-tempered and impulsive; and like many Highlanders he had a long memory for slight or injustice and could nurse an injury as a young mother doting on her first child. In the two and a half years, more or less, that he had spent in prison, he had sometimes lived for days at a stretch indifferent to his surroundings, barely conscious of where he was, because his mind was obsessed by indignant memory and full, to the total exclusion of diurnal pettiness, of the black-haired, sloe-eyed, white-skinned bitch who had jilted him, and the paunchy, complacent, psalm-singing grocer whose money had tempted her away.

Morose and motionless in his cell, he would imagine himself coming suddenly upon them, and the consternation on their faces. With the luxury of deliberation he would hit her first: his knuckles, in a brusque back-hander, across her pretty, sensual mouth (her lips now trembling for fear as for a kiss) and the flat of his hand with a slap like a sail in the wind on her tender cheek—that would be enough for her—and then a chop to the jaw, a short, right-handed, down-cutting chop to her fat husband's sagging jaw, a swinging left to catch him as he staggered and jerk him up again, a couple of pile-drivers sinking deep into the short ribs . . . . So much for a start, and as he pictured himself taking so lively a revenge he would tremble in the ecstasy of his delight and wrath.

He had, indeed, already dealt with them in such a way, and done worse as well; which accounted for his prison-sentence. But once was not enough, and every few weeks the desire to punish them again—fat Lachlan the godly grocer and white-skinned Katie with her black hair growing down to a widow's peak—would waken in his mind, and isolate him in the agony of his hatred, the imagined bliss of punching his hatred home on quivering, bruised, and crying flesh.

On the day of his escape he had been thinking greedily of his release from prison, that now lay round the corner of a few weeks only, and from hour to hour his appetite for revenge grew more greedy till it possessed him entirely. No room was left for caution or common sense—at no time did they occupy much of his mind—and when the white and roaring squall blew suddenly and hid him from the warders and his fellow-convicts, he turned with the sudden impulse of a stag in rut and ran like a stag into the heart of it.

It was a day of equinoctial wrath in the wild beginning of September—the time for sudden, furious gales—and since early morning the great, gaunt prison-fortress on the cold north-eastern corner of Scotland had looked through its bleak windows at a roaring, white-wreathed sea and a sky that was sometimes vacant and ice-blue, but more often a chaos of low, fast-driving cloud and pelting showers of rain or sleet. Dawn had been bitter cold, and by ten o'clock it was arctic cold. The sleet turned to hail.

While the squall lasted Big Rory ran without check, on a straight line and hard as he could go, but when the sky began to clear he went through a bare and open landscape with a stooped and modified pace, with the cunning of experience, and one eye for cover, the other for the malignancy of chance observers. In his youth he had been a gillie—a stalker's gillie—in a great deer-forest in the western Highlands, and since then he had served, both at home and abroad, in a well-trained and hard-working commando. He knew, then, the use of ground, he had an eye for direction and a sharpened sense of where concealment lay; and, more important than any training or natural ability, that day his luck ran with him.

His course lay to windward of the prison, or a little west of windward, and if an alarm was sounded, by shot or bell, he heard nothing of it. He went fast and warily and presently came to the backward part of a roadside cottage. It was a trim and decent-looking little house, with a patch of gorse growing close behind it. He lay in the gorse, to see what movement and evidence of habitation there was in the cottage, and only a minute later a small motor-van drew up at the front door. It was new-looking, smart, and navy-blue in colour, with a trade-name on the side in discreet gold letters. A man came out, bare-headed, in a blue raincoat; whistling as he walked, cocksure, a vain little man like a dance-band leader with oiled black hair. He went to the back door of the cottage, carrying a brown-paper parcel, and a woman came out to meet him.

She was a cosy, tidy-looking creature with a plain, square face and an apron round her waist. She reached out for the parcel, but there was more to excite her than that. She showed clearly enough what was in her mind by the twittering way she talked, by the coyness with which she patted her hair and smoothed her apron, by the animation that fluttered the flatness of her face like a breeze of wind on a loose garden-gate; and the cocksure little man looked at his wrist-watch and pretended he had no time, but was eager enough for all that, and just playing to his vanity. She looked this way and that, she pretended to be modest and regretful; then smiled like sunshine in a puddle and held out her hands. He tried for a kiss and missed by half a yard. She waved at him, dismissively, and ran indoors; but didn't shut the door. He, now thwarted and desirous, followed like a ferret down a rabbit-warren; and the door, behind him, closed with a bang.

Rory, under a gorse-bush, swore blackly at them both. As if to remind him that more wickedness lay outside prison walls than ever had been confined within them, they had showed him, for his first glimpse of the larger world, the frailty and almost certainly the falsity of humankind. The frailty and falsity of woman, the vanity and lust of man, about which he had lost his Highland temper and gone to prison; so blackly he cursed them in the full scope and minute particularity of the Gaelic tongue, which was his native language; and then, with an access of common sense, ran at a crouching trot to the road where the van stood vacant and unattended. He looked inside and saw that it carried a cargo of draper's goods and haberdashery: socks and shirts, small-clothes, ribbons and jumpers, children's shoes and towels and goods of that sort. It was a small van, light enough to push, and it pointed to the way he thought he must go. He released the brake, and putting a hand to the wheel, his shoulder in the window-frame, he walked away with it. Fifty yards from the cottage he got in, started the engine, and drove off at top speed.

The road, for a start, pointed to the west, and that was where he must go. He had to cross the breadth of Scotland, from the bare and cold east coast of Buchan to the mountainous, blue-shadowed, rain-dripping west, but the road that promised so fair a beginning was delusive, and led to a tangle, a reticulation, a repeated intersection of roads, so now he turned this way, now that, but with his nose for the compass-points and his eye for the grain of the countryside he made westing wherever he could, and his luck rode with him. No one stopped or challenged him, and presently he came to a snug village with a river running through it and a wood on the rising slopes beyond; and over the bridge, where the road branched left and right, he stopped and wondered which way to turn. To his left, with its garden running steeply down to the river, was a fine square house that anyone who knew Scotland could identify at first sight as the manse; and before its front door, while Rory lingered, he had time to observe a domestic argument.

The minister and his wife and a woman who might have been their housekeeper, but perhaps was only their daily help, stood below the steps that led to the front door and moved with fretful animation, but no concerted purpose, about a very small but highly polished and well-cared-for motor-car. They were trying to find the best way of stowing, in so minute a car, three large suitcases, a hat-box, two untidy parcels, something wrapped in sacking, and a bag of golf-clubs. The minister, a tall, well-fleshed, and burly man, was impatient with the folly and ineptitude of his women-folk, but did nothing to help them; his wife fluttered like a well-meaning Rhode Island Red whose chickens were menaced by a hen-harrier; and the housekeeper (if such she was) tried unavailingly to force two suitcases and that which was wrapped in sacking into the too-exiguous boot.

For half a minute, perhaps, Rory watched them, and even his obsessed and purposive mind admitted the comedy of what he saw. But purpose dominated, instinct decided, and turning left he drove on, up hill and into the wood. Ten minutes later, however, he realised the meaning of what he had seen, its implication; he saw his chance to get a new suit of clothes. The minister and his wife were going off on holiday—housekeeper (or their daily help) had been dressed for departure too. By now the manse would be empty, and surely there would be something useful in the minister's wardrobe? He was a big man: big enough to wear clothes that would fit Rory.

Rory drove slowly on till he came to a cart-track through the wood, and for a hundred yards went up the rutted path till he came to firm ground, and then drove in among the trees and discovered a harbour for the draper's van in a copse of young firs. Before leaving it he found a collared shirt that he could wear—his neck measured seventeen inches—and underclothes, a decent tie, and socks. He took a couple of handkerchiefs and an electric torch that lay with the draper's gloves; but he left the gloves, having no use for such paltry, citified comforts. He waited in the wood till it grew dark, and then walked back to the village.

He had little trouble in entering the manse. He made a cautious reconnaissance, assured himself it was empty, and then from the washing-green pulled a handful of turf and with that broke a pane in the kitchen window. He put his arm through, undid the latch, pushed up the window, and stepped in. He used his torch discreetly, and quickly found his way upstairs to the minister's bedroom. He drew the curtains, and shone his torch more boldly. In a big, old-fashioned, mahogany wardrobe he found a pair of corduroy trousers and an old tweed jacket, patched at the elbows and the cuffs with leather, that the minister probably wore for gardening; though they were decent enough for golf.

Rory undressed, and tidily put all his prison clothes into a green, wicker-work laundry basket that stood in a corner of the corridor between the bedroom and the bathroom. He looked for a razor, and in the drawer of a dressing-table found a new Gillette in the fancy wrapping designed for Christmas presents: the minister was evidently a thrifty soul, and made no use of presents till he needed them. So Rory washed and shaved himself, in cold water, and dressed anew in the underclothes and shirt he had taken from the draper's van, and the coat and trousers he had found in the mahogany wardrobe. A boot-cupboard gave him a pair of shabby, uncleaned brogues, and in the kitchen, in a bread bin, there was the discarded half of a stale loaf. Half of that, with a tin of sardines, made his supper, and the remnant crust, with another tin, he put in his pocket. He went out through the kitchen window well-fed, decently clad, clean-chinned, and exuberantly intent on the revenge that now seemed little more than arm's length away.

He made another reconnaissance—he prowled, that is, in the darkness of the village, a darkness broken by the primrose-yellow ports of lighted rooms—and outside the schoolhouse found a lady's bicycle. The schoolmaster, a widower, had a visitor that evening: the teacher of a lesser establishment, some miles away, who at the age of thirty-two felt a growing doubt of her vocation. When she discovered that her bicycle had been stolen, she quickly realised that the hand of providence was working for her, and declared her intention of staying the night. The widower nervously consented, the lady ruthlessly exploited her advantage, and when the hand of providence put out the light, Rory, under the lesser darkness of the sky, was pedalling towards the west.

The heat of his desire gave him strength, and kept weariness at bay. But instinct that had grown up with him in the deer-forest, and been developed by service in a commando, kept him alert and wary: twenty times he stopped and lay in a ditch to avoid the lights of a motor-car, and once, near a cross-roads, he saw the car that had overtaken him stopped by policemen, and heard its driver being questioned. Carrying his bicycle he made a detour through the fields, and drove on.

When the pink and pearl of dawn were in the sky he was on the coast road that leads to Inverness, and no more than a few miles from the cluttered little town that is called the capital of the Highlands. To his right lay the silver-pointed firth, and beyond it the broken cliffs of a many-coloured, pleasant land with a background of blue mountains head-veiled in shining clouds. But Big Rory, though recognising the beauty of the scene, gave it little thought. What pleased him more was the realisation that now he was coming to familiar ground; but before he reached it he had to pass the dangers of Inverness and its close tangle of streets.

He decided, perhaps unwisely, that a lady's bicycle would make him conspicuous, so presently he threw it behind a dyke and walked into the town. He went quickly but watchfully. At that hour in the morning there were few people about, and the policeman who, having got up too early, was sauntering to his duty, could hardly help noticing him. For Rory was a tall, outstanding figure of a man, even without a lady's bicycle for decoration. The policeman stared, and Rory, turning left at the first corner, ran like a hare to the next, and there, correctly judging the policeman's reaction, ran forwards, in his direction, and turned right again to the main street. Leaning thin as a shadow against a shop-front, he peered round and saw a clear coast. He doubled across, and came into the station square. A bus was moving slowly, he sprinted and caught it, and settled down a little out of breath but comfortably aware that he could afford to buy a ticket. In the deserted manse he had found, in a kitchen cupboard, a domestic savings bank: a whisky bottle half-full of sixpences. He had transferred this useful hoard to his trouser-pockets, and felt comfortably well-off.

The bus was going north, to Beauly, Dingwall, Tain and Bonar Bridge, by the seaside road that skirts the three long, lovely land-invading firths of the eastern Highlands—the Beauly, Cromarty, and Dornoch firths—but now Rory More knew where he was, and to be going a few miles out of his way did not perturb him. His sense of purpose, indeed—his earnest mission of revenge—was stiffened by the journey, for the bus was taking him towards the country where for six long months he had toiled to make money enough to marry his false, fair-skinned, close-kissing, steep-breasted Katie with her sleek black hair . . . .

That was three years before; and he had been warned against her, as she had been warned against him. He remembered what he had been told, but remembered more clearly his first sight of her when he came home from his knockabout, wandering labour, gambling, and dissipation at the other end of the world. Mount Isa and a sheep-run at Longreach, a cattle-station on the Gulf of Carpentaria and a pearling-schooner working from Thursday Island, a rough spell as a policeman in Sydney—that was what he had gone to after three years in the army, and when he came home again, to the island,

Katie was almost the first girl he saw, and he fell in love with her as suddenly, uncontrollably, and precipitously as a boy tobogganning down a snow-clad hill.

They had warned him against her, they had warned her against him. And all their warnings had leapt off his consciousness and hers as lightly as an April storm of hail from a thick, impenetrable roof of Highland slate. Both wild, untrustworthy, unpredictable, they had foundered in a gulf of love from which, as they thought, they would never escape nor could forget the compulsion of each other's lips and hands. Marriage—the long, close imprisonment of marriage—was their only destiny, and to make their destiny viable, to give it house-money and buy furniture, he had taken employment with the Hydro-Electric Board that was harnessing, in a dozen places, the rainfall and the wild waters of the Highlands to turn rain and river, behind great dams, into power for industry; and paid high wages to the men who laboured for it.

He had gone to an encampment of labourers near the head of Glen Affric—a dozen miles from Beauly—and worked hard for half a year in the most dangerous places, in a tunnel through the hill, on the arching height of a dam, and quickly made his name as a bold and skilful man who could take command, when command was needed, and weld a gang of scruffy, indifferent, easy wage-earners into a purposive, hard-striving team. And on pay-nights he would strip them of the wages they had earned. He was an arrogant, cold gambler, and with the authority of his knowledge of far-distant places and the habits of the Antipodes, he persuaded his fellow-workers to play poker; and rooked them of their earnings. At the end of his six-months' work, after a week in which everyone had been paid extravagantly for overtime, he sat down to a game of poker that, by two o'clock in the morning, had won him £120. Then he announced, with hard assurance, his intention to stop. 'For what I've won, put on top of what I've earned and saved, is about enough to let me get married in comfort, and to get married is what I want to do, and what I'm going to do.'

But he didn't get out of the game without a fight. There were those who had lost, and they, quite naturally, were unwilling to let the winner get away with his winnings. The biggest of the losers—both in respect of what he had lost and the size of his body—was an Irishman from Donegal; and he with a dubious, shifty-eyed coterie of fellow-countrymen stood between Rory More and the door. But Rory hit him in the guts, and brought him down to chopping-level, and hooked him between the eyes and opened a cut that bled like Niagara, and the man from Donegal sank back as if he were a dying *prima ballerina* into the waiting arms of his chorus, and Rory with a backward glance of triumph and precaution went out and packed his clothes.

A man named Hamilton, whom they called the Anarchist, followed him and said, 'You might lend me a fiver.'

'Why should I?' asked Rory.

'You've plenty and I've nothing,' said the Anarchist.

'It's a poor reason,' said Rory. 'No one but a saint would listen to a reason like that.'

'It's no reason at all,' said the Anarchist. 'It's just an excuse.'

'Well,' said Rory, 'you're honest at least—'

'Then make it ten,' said the Anarchist. 'For there's damned few honest men in the world, and the rest of you can afford to pay us a living wage.'

So Rory gave him £10, and strapped his luggage to the back of the motor-bicycle he had bought, and drove away from the camp, through the long glen to the west. It was bright morning when he came to Kyle, and he should have taken the early ferry and crossed at once to the island. But in Kyle he met a man who had been his sergeant in the commando, and was now a lorry-driver working for the County Council. And the ex-sergeant said, 'Damn the County Council! Let them drive their own lorries this morning, for you and me are going to have a drink together.'

They spent the morning drinking, and talking happily about their days in the army, and at mid-day Rory said, 'It's time I went and got my breakfast.'

'Damn your breakfast,' said the sergeant, 'it's time for dinner, and God help the wife if she doesn't give us a good one.'

So Rory and the sergeant and the sergeant's wife had their dinner together, and Rory went over to the island on the ferry, and on the farther shore found a comfortable nook, where bracken grew among boulders under a couple of birches, and there lay down to sleep for an hour or two. He woke when the sun had westered beyond the mountain tops and the air was chilled by the coming of twilight, and re-mounting his motor-bicycle drove on. He went to Katie's house, whose mother was a widow, a timorous creature who was sorely taken aback to see him, and would not tell him where Katie was. She wasn't at home, and that was all her mother knew. She offered him a cup of tea, she proposed to boil him a duck-egg, or two if he wanted them, but Rory wouldn't stay. He went out, and on the village street a little dark-haired boy, with a questing nose and narrow cheek-bones, said to him, 'If it's Katie you're looking for, you'll find her with Lachlan the grocer.'

'With old Lachlan?' asked Rory.

'That's where she is,' said the boy.

To Rory, who was a true Highlander, suspicion at once became certainty, and leaving his motor-bicycle where it leaned against a dyke he walked with a furious yet furtive speed to the trim villa that housed, in a gaily windowed ground-floor front, the village's most prosperous shop. Lachlan was a warm man, a wealthy man by island standards, but an old man too. Forty-three, perhaps forty-five, and a widower whose barren wife had died a couple of years before. How could Katie see in him anything desirable? In Lachlan, who was pale, pasty, fat and pious, a psalm-singing Presbyterian whose narrow faith was a ludicrous contrast to the spacious circumference of his waist? Oh, what could Katie see in him?

Money, said Rory, whose own pockets were bulging with the thick-paper notes of the Royal Bank of Scotland, the National Bank, the Commercial Bank, the Clydeside Bank, and several others. It's his money, thought Rory, that has seduced her, and with the certainty of seduction in his mind crept carefully as an Indian scout to the back-door of Lachlan's house, and peering through the slit of carelessly drawn curtains saw, in Lachlan's sitting-room, the very evidence—or, at the least, presumption—of seduction. For there, in a capacious chair, sat white-faced, puffy Lachlan, and on his plump lap was Katie—magnolia-white to his dough-pallor—and her arms were about his neck, her beseeching mouth was on his glistening fat cheek.

With a bellow of wrath Rory ran to the door, with a buffalo-heave of his shoulder burst it in, and confronted the flagrant couple with the burning denunciation of his wrath. Katie rose with a scream, and a back-hander across her mouth, a fore-hander to the magnolia-bloom of her cheek, sent her sprawling in a corner. Lachlan, quivering like a junket in the hands of a drunken cook, rose too, and was knocked down by a fearful right-hander that—as, in due course, a surgeon testified—fractured his lower jaw two inches beyond the chin. Rory picked him up again, and punched him in the nose, with an astonishing declaration of blood. Then he pulled Katie to her feet, and very roughly took from the third finger of her left hand the engagement ring he had given her, that she still wore. She resisted him, and being a strong girl whose momentary panic had now become a pugnacious opposition, the struggle was so severe that her finger was broken before Rory succeeded in detaching the ring; though he had no intention of so maiming her.

But Katie was now very angry—it was obvious that there was no fight left in Lachlan—and with her good right hand she took a hideous and heavy china dog from the mantelpiece and threw it at Rory. She missed, and took the neighbouring dog from the other end of the mantelpiece. She missed again, but very nearly missed, and Rory, ill-advisedly, took off the top of a standard lamp—an oil lamp—and flung it at her. She nimble dodged, and the lamp, bursting against the wall, at once became the centre or core of a small but blazing fire.

'Let it burn!' said Rory, 'and I hope it will catch the black tinder of your hearts!'

With the engagement ring in his hand he went out and left them, and Katie and Lachlan, using cushions and the carpet, tried to smother the growing fire. Their fellow-villagers began to arrive, for the pinch-faced boy who had told Rory where Katie was to be found, had quickly told a dozen others that trouble could be looked for at Lachlan's house, for Rory was on his way to vengeance there; and the village had been quick to respond. More and more of them came, the fire was put out, and Donald, the village constable, a kindly man who hated trouble, said, 'We ought to be looking for Rory, or he'll be getting up to more mischief.'

Donald and a few other men went out and quickly found Rory leaning against the little wooden privy at the bottom of the small back-garden. He had become quiet and disconsolate, and there was no fight left in him. He stood there, brooding and melancholy, and when the constable said, 'If all that I've been told is true, Rory, I think I should take you into custody,' he answered, 'Just as you please, Donald. Do whatever you please.'

And then the Sheriff Court, and the silly Sheriff's utter failure to understand a man's emotion. The Sheriff taking sides with property-owners and a bitch of a girl whose finger had been broken because her finger wore a ring whose pledge she had violated. But the Sheriff stood for law and order, though the laws had been made for the protection of weaklings and the concealment of sly maleficence, and order was merely a glozing word to excuse the suppression of a good man's honest indignation. The Sheriff—a weak and disappointed, angry man—was on the nonsensical side of law and order, and moreover owed Lachlan the grocer a bill for £28, so Rory went to a long stretch of prison . . . .

That was two years ago—nearly three—and vividly he remembered it all in the jolting bus on the road to Beauly, after he had paid his fare with a few of the sixpences that he had found in a whisky-bottle savings-bank in the empty manse. As vividly as the bright-pointed firth on the one side, the trees and fields on the other, the pictures of misfortune came to mind, and mile after mile his resolution hardened to level the score.

But he watched the road, he re-mapped his memory of the country and a couple of miles short of Beauly he left the bus and following the indication of a broken sign-post took a side-road to a village with the splendid Highland name of Drumnadrochit. This road, as he well remembered, led through fat farm-land, a miniature glen of picture-book appeal, and over a bare hill-side to precipitous descent and Loch Ness. And Loch Ness lay in the Great Glen of Scotland, that led to its western shore and his island goal. But from the broken sign-post Loch Ness was sixteen miles away, and Rory had no wish to walk so far; he kept his eyes wide open, and presently saw a pair of cyclists, dressed for touring, who obligingly left their machines in a ditch and walked through a field to buy milk or eggs at a nearby cottage. He took the nearer bicycle, a racing model with low-slung handle-bars, and went on at fifteen miles an hour. He traversed the little glen, and climbing to the bare hills beyond stopped at the height of a slope to get his breath again; and looking back saw an approaching car that seemed to show official contours, the dark, unfriendly aspect of a police-car.

It was probable that he had been seen, but he could not be sure, and carrying his bicycle he ran for cover to a small copse of birches that grew on broken ground where the heather was long and grey boulders protruded. Fifty yards beyond them was a little tarn, as black as Dublin stout, and into that he threw the bicycle, then turned in the direction from which the police-car was coming, and with all the speed he could muster—but keeping low, keeping under cover—ran a course that would take him, depending always on advantage of the ground, back to the road and observation.

He came to the road round the corner of a tall patch of bracken, and looking up hill saw at the top of it the police-car, stationary. He had been seen: there was no longer any doubt of that. He rose to his knees, and near the copse of birches to which he had run he saw a policeman signalling wildly with both arms. With his right he pointed in such a way, and then with his left to a way that indicated a line of search in a different direction. His purpose was clear enough: he was instructing his fellow-officer to seek the fugitive in one sector, while he sought in another. And as both were searching, the car must be unattended.

Rory ran up hill, praying hard with all the breath he could spare that they, in the excitement of pursuit, had been careless. Whether his prayer was heard and answered, cannot be ascertained, but careless they had been, and the ignition-key was still in its socket. Rory opened the door, got in, and drove off. Though the police-officers had been neglectful in one respect, they had been punctilious in maintenance of their car, and it was a pleasure to drive it.

What gave Rory less pleasure was the realisation that the police must have picked up his trail in Inverness, and from there followed it closely. The constable, out early in the morning, had reported him, and when the bus arrived in Beauly another constable had met it and questioned the conductor; who had told him that a big man, a passenger from Inverness, had got off at the road to Drumnadrochit.—So much was obvious; but would there be more police waiting for him at Drumnadrochit, or where the minor road he was on met the main highway that ran beside Loch Ness?

Was he important enough to deserve the attention of an elaborate pincer-movement? No, no, thought Rory to himself. The police would believe that one car, close in pursuit of a mere pedestrian, would overtake and capture him without difficulty. And in that estimate of the enemy, which was justified, he drove on; but he drove at great speed, and where the road comes down to Drumnadrochit, in a fearful declivity, he narrowly escaped disaster as, with tyres screaming, he turned sharply to the left. But then he had a smart idea.

The highway, leaving the loch for a few miles, wheels inland in a tight loop, and after his initial left turn Rory should have turned right. But instead he kept straight on, for another mile or two, and left the police-car pointing back to Inverness. He took to the fields, and presently rejoined the highway not far from Castle Urquhart: a noble ruin that stands proudly, in the desolation of its decay, beside the deep waters of Loch Ness, and has in late years found a notoriety to compensate, in a small way, the loss of its ancient grandeur. It is near Castle Urquhart that those who believe in the Monster of Loch Ness have most often seen it swimming.

Now Rory's luck was in, as it had been from the start of his escape, and as he approached the highway he saw, above the Castle, a concourse of motor-cars, and down near the Castle a small horde of people. The weather was fine again, a bright September sun brought out the silver in the loch and the autumn colours in the steep hill-sides, and for tourists there was every temptation to pause and observe the many delights of a great scene of natural grandeur; and what had happened was this.—A tourist from Basingstoke (as was subsequently discovered: for the whole occasion was closely described by the newspapers) who was driving very slowly past the Castle, as most tourists did, observed in the loch a tree-trunk wrenched from its roots by the recent gale, and cried immediately, 'It's the Monster!' He stopped his car, he and his wife and his wife's mother and two children got out, and to the drivers of several other cars, coming from either direction, who were loitering in the hope of seeing the famous denizen of those haunted waters, they shouted in chorus, 'The Monster, the Monster!'

All, without hesitation or delay, ran down to the shore, and in the ecstasy of revelation perceived that their doubtful faith in the Monster was justified by the rolling, ungainly movement in the dazzling, sun-pointed water of an uprooted, seventy-foot Douglas fir. More and more tourists, coming from Inverness or Fort William, saw the deserted cars and the people gathered above the ruins of the proud old Castle, and hastened to join them; guessing immediately what they saw. And when Rory arrived there were between fifty and sixty unattended motor-cars on the road.

He, with no interest in the Monster, cast a quickly observant, analytical eye on the assembled machinery, and chose an Austin-Healey. For a dozen miles or more, on the splendid highway that commanded brightly coloured views at which he never looked, he drove at eighty miles an hour, then turned to a lesser, narrow road that led him through a wilderness of hills and moorland, and presented him with two difficulties that reduced his speed.

Within a few miles of leaving the highway he came to a vast scene of industry: the Hydro-Electric Board, for which he had worked to no good end, was building a new dam, of great majesty and huge extent, and what with the large encampment it had had to erect, and the unruly traffic on which work depended, the road for a mile or more was a broken, bumping channel of abominable discomfort and grave danger to springs. Rory, driving slowly, was exasperated by delay but more deeply perturbed when the driver of a lorry waiting to debouch from a side-road recognised and loudly hailed him. He made no response, but immediately remembered the man. It was Hamilton the Anarchist.

He drove on, and as soon as he could drove fast again. But now he was on one of those West Highland roads that are built for one-way traffic only—narrow roads, with a little swelling of their width, a plump arc, every two hundred yards or so, for a passing place—where drivers must watch closely for oncoming traffic, and nicely judge their speed and distance to avoid collision or, at the least, ugly recrimination; and fast driving on such roads is difficult and dangerous. For twenty miles and more he was lucky, but then, with a loch below him on the left-hand side and a steep drop to its edge, he tried to bluff and jump a heavy shooting-brake—a converted Rolls-Royce of 1930 vintage—whose driver, an angry, red-faced retired Colonel of Highland infantry, refused to be bluffed, and drove steadily on to meet Rory on the narrowness of the road mid-way between the two passing places; and Rory, in the wrong, had to swerve to the left.

He swerved, and his off wheels slipped from the shoulder of the road and sank in soft earth. His stolen car, before it stopped, tilted dangerously over towards the loch below it; and the intolerant shooting-brake with its arrogant driver went on and never cast a backward, pitying glance at him. Rory climbed out of his seat, and dismally considered his situation. He plucked half a hundredweight of heather and packed it under his back wheels, and got in and tried to reverse. But the tremor of the racing wheels threatened to overturn the car completely, and reluctantly he stopped the engine. He tried, with his great strength, to lift the forward end of the car on to firmer ground; but could not move it. And while he was pondering some new device a lorry drew up beside him, and its driver said, 'You've done well to get as far as this, Rory More, and if you've left tears in the pigs' eyes of the police, there's no one more pleased than me; for I've never liked them, the blue-arsed bastards.'

Rory stood scowling at the driver, who was Hamilton the Anarchist. 'You were a bloody fool,' he said, 'to shout my name as I was passing. Who heard you?'

'Not a soul,' said the Anarchist. 'I was just surprised and delighted to see you—for we'd all read about your break—but there wasn't a soul within hearing.'

'What am I to do now?' asked Rory.

The Anarchist got out, and considered the situation. 'We can't get that car on the road again,' he said, 'and in any case the police, God blister them, will probably know by now what you're driving. So it's dangerous evidence, and we'd better get rid of it. If both of us heave and lift it from this side—it's just on the poise—it'll topple over and go into the loch, and the loch is deep here. It'll disappear, and you can come on with me. You'll be making for Kyle, I suppose?'

'That's where I'm going,' said Rory, and looked regretfully at the Austin-Healey that had carried him so fast from his pursuers. But he realised that the Anarchist was right, and with him he bent and lifted the near side of the car, and turned it over, and saw it tumble into the loch with a great splash and disappear.

'You'll be a lot safer now,' said the Anarchist, and very civilly opened the door of his cab and invited Rory to step in. They drove off, and after a decent pause, to show that his curiosity was well controlled, the Anarchist asked Rory why he had broken out of prison when, to complete his sentence, he had only another forty-eight days to serve. 'It was surely a rash thing to do,' he said.

Rory told him the whole story—of how, to begin with, Katie had betrayed him, and Lachlan the holy grocer had taken advantage of her weakness, and then, in the long weeks of prison, of his recurring desire to humiliate and punish them again—and when he had finished, the Anarchist nodded his approval. He was a smallish man with a hard and solemn face, with steel-rimmed spectacles straddling a hawk's-beak nose, with short black hair and a beard-dark chin and bright red cheek-bones in between. He was an educated man, and it was said of him that he came of a good family, but was either illegitimate or had behaved so badly in his youth that he had been thrown out.

'You've been well advised,' he said, 'for violence is a very good thing—I mean purposive, deliberate, and properly directed violence—and there's far too little of it in this country, which, I fear, has become wholly decadent; as all big countries must.' Then he began the speech for which he was well known in every encampment of the Hydro-Electric Board, in which he recommended the destruction by violence of the United States of America, the Soviet Union of Russia, the British Empire (or what was left of it), France and its dependencies, the aggregations-by-force of Communist China and Mr Nehru's India, and the so-called popular democracies of Scandinavia. All of them, he said, had become too big for the humane expression of common contentment, or too bureaucratically efficient for the free development within them of the individual spirit; and therefore all merited destruction.

Rory, who had heard the speech many times before, fell asleep while the Anarchist was describing his method of liquidating the Soviet Union, and did not wake again till the Anarchist, digging him in the ribs, asked, 'And what are you going to do to that woman and the grocer?'

'Just knock them about a bit,' said Rory.

'Why not set the skies of revolution aflame with some conspicuous act of vengeance that would stagger the imagination of the world?' asked the Anarchist.

'What are you thinking of?' asked Rory.

'Why not blow them up?'

'What with?'

'With gelignite,' said the Anarchist.

'Where would I get it?' asked Rory.

'The lorry is full of it! I've two tons in the back, that I'm taking to Kyle to be shipped home to Glasgow, for it's surplus to requirements, as they say. But if you want some, you're more than welcome. Take as much as you like—and I know where to get fuse and detonators. I can fit you out for a fine, high-class explosion that'll attract attention wherever newspapers are read.'

They were, at that moment, driving along the spectacular road which, from a great height, leans above the dark and melancholy waters of Loch Duich: a scene of romantic grandeur, of superb and sorrowful association, and of conspicuous danger—for the descent to the loch was precipitous—to anyone riding in a lorry loaded with two tons of gelignite. For the first time since his escape from prison, Rory felt a weakening of his purpose.

He was not unaccustomed to the use of gelignite. When he and his fellow-labourers were cutting a tunnel through a mountain, they had exploded charges of gelignite every day. But those explosions had been carefully prepared, exactly measured, controlled by a skilled foreman, and surrounded by precautions for safety. It was wholly and entirely different to be travelling at speed, on a rough and narrow road that overhung a huge and steep descent to coal-black waters, in a lorry full of gelignite that was driven by a self-proclaimed and self-conscious anarchist who apparently took a pure-minded and aesthetic delight in explosions.

Rory grew aware of the dryness of his mouth and little draughts of fear in the warmth of his arm-pits; and because he felt that his own health and well-being were now precarious, he admitted a certain tenderness to others who might, in similar fashion, be exposed to the irruption of unexpected violence. He looked sideways at the hard composure and irrational assurance of the Anarchist's high-coloured face—straddled by those sinister, steel-rimmed spectacles—and acknowledged a fleeting sympathy with all humanity, that is forever at the mercy of men dominated by ideas. He persuaded himself, with conscious effort, that he must persist in his purpose of revenge, but not for a moment did he succumb to the temptation of blowing up Katie and Lachlan in their snug villa; but sought excuses for declining the Anarchist's generous offer.

He mumbled and stumbled over his reasons, and the Anarchist, perceiving the shallow sentimentality of his objections, grew more insistent in his assertion that a good explosion was the proper termination of Lachlan's turpitude and Katie's infidelity; and drove a little faster.

They turned a corner, and half a mile away, where the road rose steeply to a bare and narrow ridge, saw a stationary line of motor-cars, lorries, a bus, and more cars. A small and ancient Morris, towing a new and heavy caravan, had failed to climb the hill, and all the others had, perforce, come to a halt behind the holiday-makers who now stood distraught at the roadside. The typical domestic group: a defeated man, his angry wife, her bewildered mother, and two screaming children. All, and eight or ten frustrated vehicles behind them, were poised on the tall and abrupt hillside above dark Loch Duich.

The Anarchist, muttering his annoyance, approached the rearward vehicle in the stayed procession; and quickly stopped as it began to slide backwards down the hill. Its brakes had failed, and the road was greasy. It was out of control, and Rory could see the agitation of the driver and the woman beside him. He opened the near door of the cab and jumped clear before the retreating car struck them. For a moment or two he cowered in a ditch, absurdly waiting for an explosion; and when he looked up saw that the lorry now stood slantwise across the road, and the intruding car seemed firmly attached to its bonnet. He decided that his association with the Anarchist had come to a natural end, and with an inspiring feeling of relief—though Kyle was still some six or seven miles away—he left the scene of collision and stasis without the formality of saying goodbye, and resolved to walk the rest of the way.

Most of the drivers and passengers of the halted procession were now pushing and heaving at the delapidated small Morris whose failure had produced the stoppage on the hill, and no one paid much attention to Rory as he left the road and took his own line across country; with professional instinct he chose the line that offered least to observers.

He was in no hurry to reach Kyle, for he had realised from near the beginning of his escapade that it would be folly to cross over to the island by the regular ferry; he knew the ferrymen, and they knew him. His intention was to find a rowing-boat in the darkness, and be his own ferryman. And that he accomplished, for he came to Kyle, or its outskirts, after dark, and having slept for an hour or two in the lee of a haystack, went to look for a boat, and found one tied to the railway pier. He rowed across the narrow strait, and pulled the boat high up on a sandy beach so that the owner would suffer no loss except a few hours' anxiety and the trivial labour of rowing it home again. And then he set out on the last stage of his journey, the penultimate chapter in his imagined saga of revenge.

The village where Lachlan and his faithless Katie lived was still asleep when Rory reached it. The long, roadside, double line of houses stood so still and silent under the waning dark that they seemed bereft of life, a deserted hamlet in a world abandoned, by fate or its own consciousness, to the nullity of an experiment that had failed. No movement, no sound—save from an open window through which came the drone of a Glasgow holiday-maker's resounding snore—and Rory again felt some doubt of his purpose. He felt the emptiness, the fatuity, of taking revenge on a world of ghosts. But he stiffened resolution by circumspect reconnaissance of Lachlan's house, with its two ground-floor front windows displaying, in shadow, the indecent richness of a grocer's shop—the opulence of smoked hams and exotic fruits tinned in their syrup, of Oriental rice and many sorts of cheese, of oranges from Palestine and raisins from the shores of the Middle Sea—and then by wilful remembrance of Katie's milk-white beauty and her perfidy. Quietly, and with purpose renewed, he found, opposite the back door, a place where he could hide himself, and waited patiently for the house to waken.

Slowly the morning dawned, and before the sun had risen an upper window, lightly curtained, was palely illumined by the flame of an oil-lamp. A few minutes later the light momentarily vanished, to re-appear in the kitchen, of which the larger window was uncurtained; and through its glass Rory could see, in her early morning dishevelment, a scantily clad Katie, and a little while later Lachlan. He could hear, too, their voices, which were raised beyond the pitch of friendly conversation. Then Katie opened the back door, to put out the cat, and returning to the kitchen, left it open; and now Rory could hear clearly what they were saying.

They were talking in their native tongue—in Gaelic—and Gaelic, as all the world knows, is a language tuned and fashioned for the use of poets: a language of exquisite sensitivity, of tenderness and minute perception of the hundred differences in human moods and natural beauty. But what the world, in general, does not know, is that Gaelic is equally powerful in abuse and vituperation, and has at its command a vocabulary unrivalled in its lewd, rude, obscene, and scatological terminology. And the conversation that Rory overheard was not poetical, but vituperative from the beginning, and as it developed grew flowers of speech that were marvellously coarse and hardy.

It was evident that Katie was in a bad temper. She wore only her vest and petticoat—Lachlan was in shirt and trousers—and the tempest of her voice was reiterated in the wild movement of her bare arms, in the tumult of her breast. They were quarrelling very bitterly, and Katie was accusing Lachlan of every fault a husband could openly display, and of others that only the finest and most percipient imagination could discern. 'You are just the mockery of a man!' she cried. 'A miserable and puny mockery of manhood, all dressed-up in fatness and hypocrisy! You're meaner than an old ha'penny, worn thin as paper, and falser in your promises than a fart from a fat belly that boasts of richness and only expresses wind! Oh, damn your puny, misshapen little soul to everlasting hell, Lachlan, for you took me away from a good man, a fine man, a great man who would have brought me great pleasure—and all you have given me in exchange is the sight and smell of your shop that offers riches I can never handle, and there's nothing in you worth handling either!'

To all this Rory listened with surprise and deep pleasure, and his enjoyment was enlarged when Lachlan, trying vainly to defend himself, was overwhelmed by a denunciation of his weaknesses that grew ever more vehement and destructive. Katie, indeed, went too far. Her imagination and her knowledge of disappointment, in alliance with the richness of Gaelic, expressed themselves in language so intemperately abusive that Lachlan—his fat face glistening in the lamp-light, his fat stomach tremulous above his trousers—tried to silence her, not by counter-argument, but by force. He gripped her by the upper arms, to shake and reprove her. And then Katie hit him. At first with her open hands, then with her clenched fists. Lachlan, feebly defending himself, butted her in the stomach. Then Katie took a frying-pan from the kitchen-stove and with it beat him about the head and ears. She drove him from the house, out through the kitchen door, and as he ran his trousers fell, and he stumbled and halted to pull them up. Katie, unrelenting, followed with a screaming gale of abuse, and the frying-pan re-echoed from his head with the hollow desolation of a bell-buoy ringing in the trough of desperate seas.

Big Rory, with his head through the privet-hedge that divided their little back-garden, lay shouting with laughter. He felt weak and consumed by laughter, and all his rage dissolved in laughter. His long-nursed and tenderly cherished desire to punish Lachlan and humiliate his lovely Katie were blown away by the gale of her insensate wrath. He felt no emotion but a child's delight in the clowns' performance at a circus, and when Katie came back to the garden—her ruffled hair like Medusa's locks, her breasts heaving under their thin concealment of cotton, and her lovely face sharp and shining in anger—he got up and took her in his arms. She, so consumed in rage as to be incapable of much surprise, said 'What are you doing here?'

'I came,' said Rory, 'to wish you great happiness. God bless you, my dear, for you've healed a terrible sore in my heart. And now I'm going to make reparation to you of something I took from you long ago, for you've won your right to wear it again.'

She, in the aftermath of her anger—as if exhausted by it—offered no resistance, and Rory led her to the little wooden privy at the bottom of the garden, below the privet-hedge, and kneeling down wrenched out the nail with which he had fastened her engagement-ring—that had been his engagement-ring—to an inconspicuous place below the seat.

'I nailed it there,' he said, 'to show my scorn of you, and now I take it out and give it you again to show my love and admiration of you. And to thank God you're married to Lachlan, not to me!'

Katie put his ring on her finger, and began in a soothing, smoothering voice to tell him that she had always loved him, and though she had made a great mistake—but Rory interrupted her, laughing again, and with a pinch for her breast and a light kiss on her open, bewildered mouth, left her and walked up the village street till he came to the constable's house.

The constable was still in bed, but Rory knocked him up, and said, 'Donald, I have come to surrender myself. I am going back to prison, a happy man, and you will take me there.'

Donald's wife, who was a good woman, had come out too, and she said, 'You'll need your breakfast before you go.'

So they had breakfast together, of porridge and tea and fresh herring, and then the constable said to Rory, 'If I'm to take you back to prison, I'll need to have your promise that you'll come quietly.'

'No, no,' said Rory, 'that I can't give you,' and as they walked down the road together he stopped, a dozen times, to laugh; and his laughter was twice as loud as the wrath of Katie's voice and the drum-note of the frying-pan beating on Lachlan's head.

Above and behind them the great hills shed the morning mist to meet the morning sun, and the sea below them, flirting with the west wind, lifted frills of white lace. An island, hove-to under a single cloud, floated on blue water to the north, and the smoke of cottage chimneys pirouetted in the breeze. A heron stood sentry on the stony beach, a cock-grouse shouted from the heather.

'Give me a cigarette,' said Rory, 'for I won't be smoking for the next few months.'

He cupped his hands to light it, and laughed again. 'Oh, Donald,' he said, 'let us never again spend our strength in anger, or waste our time on black thoughts of revenge. No, no! We can leave that to the women. For there's no one goes unpunished who takes a woman to his house.'

God Likes Them Plain

PERDIS THE YOUNG QUEEN of Jocynthia, had often heard of the storyteller Malis. People will talk of such a one though they have never listened to his tales, and strongly disapprove matter of which they are thus ignorant. In this way it happened that Queen Perdis had an unfavourable opinion of Malis.

There was, perhaps, a small excuse for her attitude in that some of his most famous stories were flavoured with a kind of lewdness, and it was perfectly well known that these were not the historical record of things which had really happened, but mere literary concoctions. The conscientious historian who, out of pure respect for actuality, includes in his narrative a few items of human rudeness, may and indeed should be forgiven; for truth is a worthy mistress. But the man who invents such things, either from his own wanton delight in them or to amuse others whom he knows to be equally light-minded, can expect no pardon, especially from those who do not listen to his stories.

It was also true that Malis was a very ugly man, though there were many who did not object to the irregular contours, the bright colour, and the sometimes ridiculous expression of his face. These were the people who hurried eagerly and happily sat to hear him in the market-place on market-days, in a farm-kitchen or the lower end of a great hall at night, sometimes in idle weather at a cross-roads or in an orchard, and best of all at the inn of The Poor Peasant and his Cow, where Malis sometimes drank so much that he told stories without troubling to collect any fee; and these love tales, it was said, were better than all his others. Often they had to do with the disreputable friar Brother Bonamy, who, though nothing but a figment of Malis's invention, had enjoyed in fiction so many and such delightful—even if reprehensible—experiences, that Malis himself had almost come to believe in his real existence, while his audience nearly always took it for granted that he lived; and sometimes the natives of Jocynthia boasted to strangers of having met the celebrated friar, and even suffered under his roguery. Two or three impostors had also been caught unworthily exploiting the reputation that Malis had made for him.

Some of Brother Bonamy's adventures had been told to Queen

Perdis, but in a poor and illiterate manner by her nurse or in a weak and disgusting way by the ladies of her bedchamber. Hearing them in this fashion it was natural that she should dislike them and their author, for whatever its subject a story is a good story or a bad story only by virtue of the style in which it is told. The ladies of the bedchamber also insisted that Malis was so ugly that he was repulsive to look at.

One thing in particular made the Queen think ill of Malis, and that was a saying he had attributed to Brother Bonamy and which had become famous throughout Jocynthia. The saying was, 'God likes them plain', and it referred to women. Brother Bonamy was frequently busy, in a way that may be guessed, with the women of the villages and hamlets through which he wandered. With equal ardour he made love to widow, wife and maid, but though their state might be different they had always this in common, that they were pretty. And Brother Bonamy would defend his irrational prejudice for beauty with the grave assertion that it was due only to humility, since God, he said, preferred homely women to handsome ones, and a poor friar might not trespass among his Lord's most favoured servants. He must be content with those on whom God looked with an indifferent eye. That is to say, the pretty ones.

This peculiar virtue of the friar's appealed to many of those who listened to the stories that Malis made about him, and the saying was repeated every day of the week in Jocynthia by men well pleased with so plausible an excuse for visiting some light and lovely girl, when they should have been more legitimately employed with a virtuous woman who had, it may be, an obliquity in her vision, or a few black teeth. 'God likes them plain', they would say; and who, knowing the righteousness so agreeable to Heaven of uncomely women, may doubt the truth of that assertion?

But Perdis thought the saying was blasphemous.

Her first meeting with Malis was due to one of Fate's oldest and most successful tricks. A thunderstorm burst with instant silver and purple violence out of a pale calm sky while the Queen was riding, with only a few attendants, some miles from her palace. Though Perdis possessed several natural gifts other than beauty, she had only a poor seat and small understanding of equitation, so when her horse, terrified by a near flash of lightning, reared and bolted with her she very soon fell off. Her small retinue, themselves upset by the storm and now unnerved by the accident to their mistress, scattered in foolish pursuit of her horse or in a search, equally vain, for doctors and nurses. One companion only remained with the Queen, a sensible woman called Graine, who soon discovered that Perdis was unhurt, and opportunely remembered that the inn of The Poor Peasant and his Cow was no more than half a mile away. Thither, with as little delay as possible, the two women repaired, and were received with great kindness although they did not disclose their identity; for there were times when Perdis grew tired of the loud noise of loyalty. They were given an upper room in which a fire was lighted, a meal prepared, and dry clothes brought in exchange for their soaked skirts and mantles; and there they prepared to wait till someone arrived to take them home.

The storm soon passed, and the sun came out again to shine on wet roofs and small puddles, a rick of yellow straw, and a score of starlings shaking small jewels out of their draggled feathers. From the inn yard under the Queen's window rose a noise of mocking voices, and looking out Perdis saw a man, dressed rather shabbily, whom a lot of children had encircled and were teasing. He was an ugly man whose face was bright as autumn leaves with the beating of the weather upon it and the frequent drumming of wine in its veins. His nose, which was long and irregular in shape, was the brightest red of all, and his eyebrows rose in a Satanic slant towards the outer corners of his forehead. But in spite of their devilish angle his expression, at the moment, was foolish rather than wicked, for he was somewhat bewildered by the noise of the children. They were demanding that he should tell them a story, and they did not trouble to be polite to him as would older people in similar circumstances. On the contrary they assured him that his last story had been shockingly dull, and that his bald head looked more and more like a brown hen's egg every day. At this the man tried to smooth his untidy black hair over the bare dome from which it had receded, but the wind caught it and blew it out like little black wings, and the children laughed louder than ever.

But in a minute or two they grew quiet, for the man sat himself on a tub turned upside down and began to tell them a story.

'I'll tell you how the thunder and the lightning got into the sky,' he said, 'the thunder that you heard beating its drums just now, and the lightning you saw shaking its sword. But when I've told you, you must promise to keep it a dead secret, for it's valuable information I'm going to give you, and I wouldn't like to see it wasted among all the fools and common people in Jocynthia. So keep it dark, do you see?

'Well then, a long time ago, when all the animals talked the same language as men, and men would talk to the animals as often as they would to their brothers and sisters, and so learned a very great deal that we know nothing about; in those days there was once a very important feast given by the richest man in the country for the very fine reason that it is the pleasantest thing in the world to give a good dinner to the proper kind of people. And to make sure that the proper kind of people were there, the rich man invited everybody. And after the feast there was dancing. Now all the best musicians in the country were there, and the best dancers, too, and as the musicians played better and better the dancers danced higher and higher. And the higher they danced the louder the musicians played. And the louder the music the better was the dancing. And so it went on, because one good thing always breeds another, except in family matters.

'By and by the noise of the dancing reached an old man who lived far away in a wood. He had been invited to the feast, but he had not gone because when he was young he had been the best dancer in the country, and he didn't want to let people see how age had crippled him. But when he heard the pipes pealing and the drums roaring through the wood he couldn't resist the temptation to go and dance for the last time, so he put on his shoes and hurried to the feast. By the time he got there the dancers were leaping so prodigiously high that you wouldn't believe me if I told you. The old man, however, was not dismayed, but shouted loudly, "I can dance better than any of you!" and went to join them.

'But he had forgotten his sword, and it was a sword-dance they were dancing at the time. So the old man borrowed a sword from a mole, who was one of the guests, for all the animals had been invited as well as all the people, which was only fair. The mole, who had no ear for music, and wasn't much good at dancing either, was just watching, so he lent his sword very willingly to the old man.

'Then the old man began to dance, and to show them how much better the world had been when he was young—which is what the old men believe—he danced higher than anyone else. In a little while the others stopped to watch him, for no one had ever leapt so high or waved his sword so beautifully. And the drummers banged their drums still louder, and the old man danced higher and higher, and waved his sword like falling stars, and shook it in great silver patterns round his head. Then the drums all banged together, and the old man leapt right up to the roof of the sky, and the drummers were so excited they all followed him, and there, on the roof of the sky, they're still beating their drums, for when you hear thunder it's their drums you hear, and the lightning is the shaking of the old man's sword as he dances all over the roof of the sky. You can see it for yourselves, and seeing is believing.'

'But what happened to the mole?' asked one of the children.

'The mole began to build a mountain to climb into the sky and get his sword back,' said the storyteller, 'and he's still trying to build one high enough. You can see that for yourselves in the field over there, and seeing is believing.'

Now some of the children were dissatisfied with the story and said they did not believe it, but Perdis, who had listened to it all from the window, was delighted, and called to Graine, the sensible woman who had stayed with her, to ask her if she knew the storyteller's name.

Graine looked down and said in a disagreeable voice, 'Mother of God! don't tell me you've been listening to his filthy jesting?'

'Why, who is he?' asked Perdis.

'Malis,' said Graine.

'But he has just told a beautiful story about an old man who jumped into the sky,' said Perdis.

'You probably misunderstood him,' answered Graine. 'Malis's stories are all about old men jumping into other people's beds.'

Perdis, however, knew that she had not been mistaken, and that the story was both innocent and charming. It was so different from all she had been led to expect of Malis that she was puzzled, and during the next hour or two thought a great deal about him, with the natural result that she determined to see him at least once again, although he was ugly, and to hear at the very least one more of his stories, despite the evil account of them given to her by Graine.

After supper she inquired of a chambermaid whether Malis was still at the inn, and was told that he was even then telling stories in the kitchen to a company of rustics.

'There's a small gallery opening on the darkest wall of the kitchen, from which you can hear and see all that's going on without yourself being visible,' suggested the chambermaid, who had recognised Perdis's interest in the storyteller, and thought it not unreasonable.

She led the Queen to the gallery and left her there. It was hot, and a smell of late cooking rose to assail the Queen's nostrils. But the offence to her nose was forgotten in the entertainment that came to her eyes from the spectacle, smoky and blurred under a few dim candles, of some eighteen or twenty men and women, rough creatures most of them, red-faced and poorly clad, eagerly attentive to the story that Malis was telling; and now disturbing the shadows as violently they bent back on their stools, and clapped their heavy hands on their thick resounding thighs, and tossed back their heads, laughing so hugely at some happy impropriety in the narration.

For Perdis speedily found that this was a very different tale from that which he had told the children. It was indeed one of the adventures of Brother Bonamy, whose creed in love was that, as God preferred plain women, a humble friar must be content with pretty ones. And while Perdis listened to the story she grew angry with Malis, and a little angry with herself, because sometimes she felt moved to laugh with the ignorant persons below, and like them she was curiously fascinated by the wicked slant of the storyteller's eyebrows, and even by the bright knob of his irregular long nose when the candle-light gleaming on it made it shine like a cherry.

The story that Malis told had to do with the misadventures of a greedy lawyer, lured from his house at midnight by the falsehood of Brother Bonamy to visit an ugly rich old woman who, the friar said, was dying and wanted to make her will before she departed. But the old woman, so far from dying, was reading a young poet's praise of love and all its hot delight, and thinking that she herself was not yet too old to have a sweetheart. And while the lawyer was in this embarrassing situation—for the old woman soon made known her will, though it was not that will which the lawyer had contemplated—Brother Bonamy was consoling the lawyer's pretty young wife for her husband's absence.

Having discovered the nature of his consolation, Perdis thought it time to go, and returning to her room she remembered that she was Queen of Jocynthia, and had not only power over her subjects but a duty to reprove and punish them for any naughtiness in which they were discovered. So she called to her the host of the inn and ordered him to bring Malis to her room.

When the storyteller came, Perdis was sitting in a chair with a high straight back, and the yellow light of a lamp fell upon her yellow hair, and her grave sweet face, and the white hands folded in her lap.

'I am Queen Perdis,' she said, 'and I have just listened with great displeasure to your story of Brother Bonamy and the lawyer's wife.'

Malis fell on his knees, and his red face took on a foolish expression of anxiety and bewilderment.

'I also heard your tale of how thunder and lightning came into the sky,' said the Queen, 'and that I thought was interesting and even beautiful. But this other was both dull and disgusting. Why do you tell such a story, who have the gift to make lovely ones?'

'Poor men must laugh,' said Malis.

'Not at immorality,' said the Queen.

In ordinary circumstances Malis would have had much to say about such a prohibition and about the several domains of the storyteller which it threatened. But now he was silent, for he had never seen anyone so beautiful as Perdis, and the sight of much beauty often confused him. Her forehead was smooth and white, and her yellow hair tangled deliciously of its own accord, as though a tiny zephyr, caught by sweet perfume, had made there its nest and played too happily in those fair tresses ever to leave them. Her eyes were the blue of Jocynthia's April sky, and her nose was straight, her chin round as an egg. But her mouth made Malis despair, for his trade was words, and no words could ever describe its tender hue of rose petals before they have taken on the summer richness of roses, and the fine moulding of her lips, so firm in appearance but in reality so deliciously soft. Those lines, the tiny young-rose pouting of her lips, would perish at a touch, and give instead of beauty a wild and fleeting pleasure, sweet drunkenness to her lover's heart and solace afterwards as sweet. To think of her lips was madness, and Malis felt his heart grow weak and dizziness come around his head. But Perdis, waiting for an answer and receiving none, became stern, and when she tried to look stern the corners of her lips turned a little down, and her mouth seemed like a child's mouth who is puzzled and hurt by what she does not understand. Malis closed his eyes, because he did not dare look longer at the Queen's lips.

'Why do not all your tales tell of beauty?' asked the Queen sternly.

'Because till now I never knew what beauty was,' answered Malis in a low voice.

The Queen flushed red.

'In your story about the lawyer you mocked openly at God's law and man's,' she said.

'The storyteller has laws of his own,' said Malis with more boldness.

'But even you must respect divine commands, and also the wise statutes by which Jocynthia is governed and the conduct of its people ordered in decency,' said the Queen.

'Those statutes were made by rich men, among whom there is worse stupidity than among the poor,' said Malis. 'For the poor man knows he is stupid, but to the rich it seems impossible that a wealthy man should be a fool. That is why—no, that is not why, but that is an excuse for my telling stories about rich lawyers that will make my poor audience laugh. For so they are comforted in their poverty, and also truth is served.'

'Perhaps you do not approve of kings and queens either?' asked Perdis.

'Not of kings,' answered Malis.

'You are impudent,' said the Queen.

'Do you know the story of the slave-girl who slept in a king's bed?' asked Malis.

'No,' said the Queen, 'and I am not going to listen to it'

'The King was not there at the time,' Malis explained. 'He had gone hunting. And the slave-girl was in the royal bedchamber only because it was her duty to dust the furniture and turn down the royal sheets. But on this particular morning she stood for a long time gazing at the King's bed, mindless of the dust on the chairs, thinking only of the exquisite, the unimaginable luxury of lying on that yielding mountain of softness, under silken sheets, and with her head on two stuffed clouds of swansdown. Her own bed was a sack on the floor. And at last she decided that despite the danger of being discovered she must lie for just three minutes on that heavenly couch, since she knew it offered some perfect pleasure, and there was nothing in her experience of life to let her imagine its nature; for she had never even known comfort, and this was great luxury. So, faint with excitement, she climbed the five steps at the bedside, and lay on that celestial softness. And such was the comfort to her senses that she instantly fell asleep.

'But the King had changed his mind about hunting, and suddenly returned to his palace. And when he found a slave in his bed his anger was terrible, and he ordered the girl to be taken out and given a hundred lashes.

'Now when she heard this sentence the slave-girl laughed; but while she was being whipped she was silent; and after the whipping, and when cool ointments had been laid to her wounded back—for this was no barbarian court—she wept loudly. And the King was greatly struck by her conduct, and asked why she behaved in so strange a way.

'"I laughed when you ordered me to be whipped," said the slave-girl, "because then I realised how foolish it is to seek even a moment's happiness in this world. I was silent when I was being whipped because fortitude is a virtue. And after I had been whipped I wept to think that if I had suffered so for sleeping in your bed a short half-hour, how infinitely greater will be your punishment, who have slept in it for ten years!"'

While Perdis was wondering how to answer this the sensible woman Graine came in and said, 'It is time that this man went, for he has been here a long while.' So Malis, filling his eyes and his heart with a picture of the Queen, left the inn, and the next day some of Perdis's courtiers arrived and took her back to the royal palace of Jocynthia.

During the days that followed Perdis thought a great deal about Malis the storyteller, and especially about the last tale he had told. For people are always most struck with what relates to their own condition, and find therein a special virtue and significance. Perdis was not a particularly clever girl. She was quite as clever as she had any need to be—Jocynthia was really ruled by her uncle—and her face and body were so beautiful, her disposition so sweet, that no one ever dreamed of criticising her intellect. But this does not alter the fact that she was not really clever, and so she let her thoughts dwell more and more on Malis, quite forgetting his ugliness and the many undesirable things about him, and at last she commanded some of her servants to bring him to court.

Malis went with eagerness and dismay, for he, despite his wisdom, had night and day thought or dreamed of Perdis and more than anything else in the world he wanted to see her again. Yet he feared her, as a martyr glowing with God and in love with death may yet fear the flame into which he must thrust his hand.

When Malis came to court Perdis took him apart and talked to him, and after a while Malis told her an old story that he had often told in the villages, and Perdis laughed—for it was not about Brother Bonamy—and forgot to scold him as she had intended. The next day Malis returned and told her another story, and so on the day following, and the day after that, and both to Queen and storyteller that time in the day when they were together became dearer than all other hours. Yet neither Malis nor Perdis forgot that Perdis was the Queen till a day came when Malis related the masterpiece of all his stories—which has not survived—and then that fact was in some sort overlooked.

For as Malis had long since been wholly taken by the Queen's beauty, so now was the Queen captured by the magic of the storyteller's words, that lit a lamp in darkness, and opened strange rooms behind familiar doors, and wrapped in a transparent envelope of beauty some new meaning in the lives of men and women.

When Malis had told that story—which has so fortunately perished, for beside it all other stories would seem poor and trivial—and when he had finished, the Queen stayed silent for some little time and then said, 'Malis, what shall I give you in return for the pleasure you have given me? Shall I make you one of my nobles—and then you may always attend me—or shall I give you jewels, my white horses, or a sword of silver hilted with one emerald? Is there anything, Malis, that I may give you to give pleasure to you and to me also?'

Malis, heart and eyes on the Queen's mouth, said hoarsely, 'A kiss, Queen Perdis.'

Perdis flushed red, and sat, red as a rose, stilly on her throne till her colour faded and left her white as a lily. Then, saying nothing, she stood up, and Malis rose from his stool, and they met midway between the stool and the throne. The closer they came to each other the more clearly did Malis perceive the Queen's beauty, but Perdis, because she was a woman and had the wisdom of her kind without any special wisdom of her own, lost sight of the storyteller's ugliness and was not repelled by his nose and his slanting eyebrows and his foolish expression; for she had perceived his strength in the creation of beauty.

Malis took the Queen in his arms and bent to kiss her. He was trembling, but Perdis was calm. Their lips met, lightly at first as snow falling, and the Queen's lips were cool as water and sweet as wild honey, so that Malis nearly swooned with rapture, and yet was tortured by a desire to hold her more nearly and press his mouth to hers, harder and harder, till he felt through its softness the hard bone hidden underneath. So his embrace grew closer, his mouth sought fiercely for its desire, and rapture became an agony more exquisite than rapture. And suddenly the Queen put her arms about his neck, and her lips were no longer patient but passionate as his. Now she also was trembling, and they seemed to grow together like bindweed on a thorn, or like hands clasped desperately in prayer.

Then they broke apart, their hearts heavy with sweetness, and stood still and looked at each other. And as they looked their happiness failed, and their eyes filled with horror. For each was changing in the other's sight.

The Queen's face became red and coarse, her nose grew ungainly and long, and her eyebrows slanted upwards; while Malis took on a girlish beauty, his mouth turned pretty and appealing, and his hair was yellow. In a few minutes Malis recognised in the Queen a likeness of himself, and Perdis saw in the storyteller a reflection of her own beauty. Their knees weakened and their hands clutched at what would support them, lest in their terror they should fall. Then, moved by the same impulse, they ran to a mirror and saw there the transformation in themselves, and realised the calamitous interchange which had occurred.

'What can we do?' whispered the storyteller.

'Where can we hide?' cried the Queen, and stood with her back against the door. Malis stared in the mirror at the beauty which had stolen his mind.

For that is what had happened. Loosed from its hold by the surrender of his body and made volatile by the fire of his passion, Malis's soul had flown out and found a new dwelling in the Queen's breast, that in like manner had been emptied by the flight to Malis's heart of her rapt spirit. And each soul in its new habitation had rebuilt its outer walls, beauty for the Queen's soul and a lively ugliness for the storyteller's.

'Let us run away,' said Malis, and stammered so that his words became nonsense.

'We must do something,' said the Queen and tried to quiet her sobbing. But at that moment the door opened and her uncle came in with some courtiers and ladies, among whom the utmost consternation immediately spread. Malis would certainly have been assassinated had they known which Malis really was. But that was not easy to discover, until the Queen spoke in a queenly voice and said very honestly: 'This metamorphosis is not our fault, but the fault of love which suddenly assailed us. Malis must not be hurt, for I shared equally with him, and neither of us suspected this harm which has fallen. We kissed, and it must be that our minds, each set on the other, flew thither and bred in new flesh these old semblances. That is not the common sequel of kissing, but perchance we kissed too closely—Malis is not to be hurt, I say!—Now let us go to our own apartments and consider what must or may be done. See that Malis takes no hurt.'

No treaties were made, nor new laws passed in Jocynthia for the next few days, and little business was transacted at court beyond vain discussion of the fantastic catastrophe which had befallen Queen Perdis. Malis discovered to his dismay that he could no longer tell stories. He did not see things as he had been used to see them. Their points were blunted, their angels obtuse, and their colours dim. They had strangly lost significance and the shape that would fit them into a narrative. And words no longer behaved for him like balls in a juggler's hands, but fell to the ground, higgledy-piggledy, and would not even bounce when they fell. He was no longer Malis the storyteller, and his new-won beauty only recommended him to gadabout old women.

Perdis, on the contrary, saw the whole world as if some strange sun were lighting it, and what had previously been vague emotion now translated itself in apt and easy words, and she expressed her opinion in sentences both pliant and profuse. She enjoyed some novel sensations of power and comprehension. But whenever she looked in the mirror and saw her dreadful nose, those eyebrows, and that ridiculous expression, she bitterly regretted her lost beauty.

In a man's face that uncouth crimson beak was tolerable and possibly amusing, but seen above her white and lovely bosom it was horrible. 'Give me back my beauty!' cried Perdis, and lamented her loss in words that owed their cogency and coherence to Malis's wit. Malis could only gaze at the reflection of his lovely face and weakly, ineffectually, bemoan the loss of his creative mind.

All the wisest men in Jocynthia set to work to seek a way of escape from this trying situation, but as nothing of the sort had ever happened before they were hampered in their efforts by lack of experience. No useful suggestion was made until Geroin, the oldest of Jocynthia's counsellors, awoke one morning with a brilliant solution. He could scarcely wait till he had dressed, so eager was he to convey it to the Queen and so sure he felt of its efficacy.

'The beauty of my remedy,' he said, 'and almost a guarantee of its ability to cure this strange disorder of your Majesty's countenance, lies in its extreme simplicity. All the previous endeavours to rectify your Majesty's unfortunate malaise have erred on the side of undue complication, as though abundance of formulae and a gross variety of ingredients should command success by the mere weight of numbers. But that is not so. I have frequently observed . . .'

'Come to the point,' said the Queen, 'and tell us what you propose.'

Geroin mournfully shook his head to have his fine long speech thus rudely cut off, and then said: 'That you and Malis kiss each other again.'

A gasp of admiration arose from the crowded court. Geroin's remedy was indeed simple. So simple that everyone kicked himself for not having thought of it before; and the underlying theory, that what could happen once might happen again, was surely sound enough.

'Let Malis the storyteller be summoned,' said the Queen thoughtfully.

All the greedy dowagers and unsatisfied old women grinned and languished at Malis as he came in, but the men stared at him sourly.

He listened to what Geroin told him, and turned to the Queen.

'It is better for both of us that we should return to our proper selves,' she said. 'I shall always remember these weeks of knowledge when your wit has opened my eyes and taught my tongue the use of words; but I am a woman, and cleverness is not everything. Once I was beautiful, and I would be beautiful again. My looking-glass tells me a truth stronger than all your shining sentences can frame. For a woman beauty is best; strength of arm and intellect is man's good. Kiss me once again, Malis, so our minds and our countenances may be called our own.'

During the past few weeks Malis had been as unhappy as the Queen, for having lost his wits he felt, as many other young men of the time felt, that life was worthless and his own existence without meaning. So he was willing enough to re-exchange his beauty, which had brought him nothing but a few presents from the gadabout old women, for the mind that had given such happy birth to a thousand lovely or merry tales. And he went forward to kiss the Queen.

But when he came near to her he saw more clearly the slanting eyebrows, the long scarlet nose, her somewhat ridiculous expression; and he felt a strong disinclination to embrace so unattractive a woman. The Queen held out her hands to him.

'Kiss her,' said Geroin importantly.

Making an effort to overcome his distaste, Malis let his lips touch the Queen's cheek. He stood back and looked to see if her appearance should change. But nothing happened.

'Kiss her again,' cried Geroin testily. 'Kiss her closely, kiss her properly!'

With even more reluctance, and now barely concealing his dislike of the poor Queen, Malis kissed her on the other cheek, and again stood sulkily away. And still nothing happened.

The courtiers began to murmur, and Geroin shouted angrily: 'Do you not know what kissing means? Kiss her on the mouth, you fool!'

'Malis,' said the Queen, pleading, and took his hands and looked yearningly at him. 'Will you not kiss me now as once you kissed me?' And she smiled like one who seeks to please, tremulous and eager for her happiness. But when her lips parted she disclosed a broken tooth and some others that were more yellow than white. And emotion had made her nose unusually red.

'Kiss her!' commanded Geroin.

But Malis shrieked suddenly, 'No, no, no!' The poor Queen shrank back and into the stricken silence of the court the echoes of the storyteller's words horribly rebounded. Then Malis laughed, not mirthfully, but wildly as a madman laughs, and pointing his finger at Perdis screamed, 'God likes them plain! Not I, not man, but God! Let God, then, kiss her, for God likes them plain. But not I! No, no, no! Not I, not I!'

And turning, he ran swiftly out of the palace, so swiftly that before any could move to restrain him he had gone. Nor was he ever seen again, and because a swift river runs through Jocynthia people came to the conclusion that he had jumped into it and been drowned.

So Perdis was ugly for the rest of her days, and though in many ways her life was richer because of the great wit she had taken from Malis, many years passed and her hair turned white before she grew reconciled to the loss of her beauty.

Jocynthia, it is true, flourished exceedingly under her wise rule, for the storyteller's mind turned easily to the government of people whom previously it had contrived to make happy. But it is also true that the people, especially the common people, often grumbled because their life was duller than it had been, for though they all became prosperous, they no longer had the merry tales of Brother Bonamy to make them laugh.

The Three Poets

FOR KARL RAGNAR GIEROW

TRIMANDER, FOLANDER, AND TORSSANDER were all poets. They were big men, between six and seven feet tall, and whenever they stood together, or went walking together, or argued with each other in their deep voices, they made a great impression on people who observed them; which, indeed, no one ever failed to do who had the opportunity.

Trimander was the tallest—standing tiptoe with his hat on he came within a finger's breadth of seven feet—but he was hardly so robust as the others, and his long face, his dark eyes, and drooping mouth and aristocratic nose, gave him an air of distinguished melancholy.

Folander was the fattest, and Torssander the burliest. Folander was like a beautiful overgrown baby, all curves, an enormous dimpled plumpness with blue eyes and yellow hair; but in middle age his face became an angry red and his fatness was gathered into a tremendous paunch. Torssander throughout his life was an heroic figure with a chest as broad as a door and a fierce mane of reddish hair. He was also the laziest of the three, and to be recognised as such in what was often said to be the idlest trio in Sweden was a distinction indeed.

They had been students together in the University of Lund, than which there is no more humane or pleasant a seat of learning in the world. Leisure, that poor fugitive from the great cities of our time, has found a welcome home there, and is most tenderly entreated. It is no sin to waste time in Lund, for they have plenty of it and count it no more carefully than a rich man his pennies. In summer the days are long, in winter the nights: no one, therefore, need be in a hurry to go to bed, or in haste to get up. When they sit down to dine their tables are so heavily burdened, so broadly spread, so delicately garnished with all the riches of a fat green land and the populous sea which borders it, that to sit for less than two hours would be a mortal insult to the landlord and his cook, to the farmers and fishermen of Scania, to the brewers and distillers in adjacent provinces, to the *vignerons* of their dear neighbour France, and even perhaps to God Himself. There is, however, little danger of such rudeness, for the good people of Lund all know their duty, and the better sort, to show their piety, will sit for four hours or five.

Because learning has flourished there for many hundreds of years, they regard it easily, being familiar with it, and do not set to work on their books like the starving men in illiterate newly discovered countries, who fear that their imported culture may vanish overnight and therefore gobble and swallow it in huge undigested collops as quickly as they can. The art of learning has had a long life in Lund, and life itself, they have discovered there, is long enough if you are not in a hurry. Even the terms at the University are generously long, and so the students rarely trouble themselves to attend for the first week or two; and as scores of thousands of lectures have been delivered there, and thousands upon thousands are waiting to be delivered in the minds of strong men now living, and in the unpredictable minds of babes unborn, the students are not so foolish as to try and attend them all, or even to be punctual at those they do attend; for the lectures themselves are very long.

But the students do not scamp their education. They are not careless of it, or indifferent to the value of learning. On the contrary, dear reader. It is you, who at your own university spent perhaps no more than three curt years, who are more likely to have disregarded both that and other values too; for haste is the mother of many evils, the largest being vulgarity. Had you kept your terms at Lund—as now, too late, you wish you had—you might have spent nine, ten, or twelve years there, and no one been surprised.

So Trimander, Folander, and Torssander passed their youth, and in comparison with the great majority of humankind received a very good education. But because they had acquired it in the leisurely manner of Nature herself—who took at least fifty thousand years to make *us*, and we, God knows, are no more than a trial pull—because of the decent manner of their education they made no parade of it, nor set themselves up above their fellows by insisting on their superior taste and greater knowledge, but continued to live in a state of innocent wonder before Creation, and perpetual interest in the world about them. By some, indeed, they were blamed for their failure to make a commercial use of all they had learnt, and put their genius to daily work; but as it never entered their heads to do this, the continuing belief in their genius became an act of faith, and thereby a blessing to all their admirers. Each of them, during their twelve years of residence at Lund, had published a small volume of poetry, and as twenty years passed without their publishing more, their admirers had had plenty of time to get their work by heart.

Trimander's generous spirit had been fired by history, and in particular by the lives of the great and terrible kings of Sweden: by Gustavus Vasa and Gustavus Adolphus, by Charles the Tenth and Charles the Twelfth. What proud tempers they had had, what a fierce compelling energy, and demoniac ambition; and how, like a famine or the discovery of a gold-mine, they had changed the lives of all their subjects, and of many thousands of human beings far beyond their frontiers!—But what of themselves, of their own characters? What little spring, close-coiled, and powerful, had lain in their souls, and striven for release against what external pressure, to give their wars and imperial policies so great a force?

In his tomb in the great ugly church at Uppsala, Gustavus Vasa lay with a hole in his lower jaw. A hole that a peasant could stick his thick mid-finger into. He had suffered, poor king, from a rodent toothache. Year after year corroding pain had bitten deeper into the shrinking jaw, digging like an evil mole; but the distracted king had made Sweden safe from its foundations to the roof. What toothache had moved the others?

In his volume of poems, of eighty-two pages, Trimander had told four anecdotes of the kings, and written four heroic songs. Three of the songs became widely popular, and were sung wherever and whenever people felt in the mood for such noble themes.

Folander, fat Folander, found a different inspiration.

The opening leaves of a beech tree moved him more deeply than memories of a mortal king, and the nimble yet prudent balance of a fish in a pool seemed to him more delicately to express the miraculous ability of living things than the headlong career of famous Generals and their sweaty squadrons. Dragonflies would perch upon his plump hand while he memorised their hues, and he knew all the tunes of the smaller birds. His observation was acute, his understanding born of a lively unpretentious sympathy, and his language mellifluous. His book of poems was slightly larger than Trimander's, and every well-brought-up girl in Sweden could recite at least a dozen of them.

Some of Torssander's more superficial friends used to wonder why he, like Trimander, had not been attracted to the heroic past. His broad chest, his thews, and his stature all suggested an affinity with the warrior ages, and his mind was no less powerful than his muscles. But Torssander bent all his strength to the confection of wit. He spent the power of his understanding on the analysis of human motives and the disentanglement of human situations; and then his heroic lungs produced a great wind of laughter, while his literary talent compressed his findings into the smallest possible number of lines. His laughter was kind, however, and in the resolution of the problems he considered, his wit discovered a dry benignity. By his poems unhappy lovers were reconciled to disappointment, husbands compared their betrayal with the notorious horns of the great philosophers, philanthropists perceived that ingratitude is native to man, and romantic girls with narrow ribs and imperceptible small breasts realised that living men did not behave like the figments of a birthday dream. His book had wider margins, far deeper spaces under the last lines, than Trimander's or Folander's, and some of his poems, that occupied a whole page, were merely impudent and quite unanswerable riddles. But he had one irreverent song that everybody learnt, and in single lines or couplets he was quoted even more often than the others.

And now, most patient reader, you are in a mood to ask me this question: How, if they were all so idle, how did they live?

There is nowadays, perhaps, too much interest in the mechanics of existence. I have said before, and I shall probably repeat it, that the *how* of life is of little consequence in comparison with the *why*.—But you are not to be blamed, sir, for your curiosity, and I, like you, am more commonly concerned with the flavour of a shoulder of mutton than the philosophical justification for keeping sheep, and so, without too much detail, I shall answer your question.

Trimander was subsidised by the nobility. They, the simplest and most trustful of humankind, all firmly believed that in his forthcoming exegesis of history he would, by mere truth's compulsion, exalt the heroic deeds and accomplishments of their ancestors; and so they used to make him their guest for six months or a year, with a free run of their archives and the picture gallery, or in town would tactfully leave upon his table a cheque for two thousand crowns. He, being single-minded, was no spender except upon books and writing-paper, and lived easily enough.

Folander married a widow with some property of her own, in Dalecarlia, and the bequest of her late husband's shares in the steel-works at Sandviken. Folander had no cause to worry.

Torssander, on the death of his parents, inherited a little money, and spending it freely while it lasted, established for himself the abiding reputation of being well-to-do. As a consequence of this wise investment, casual friends used to invite him to stay with them, who would never have embarrassed themselves with hospitality to a poor man who might have shown unseemly gratitude. Publishers, aware of his independence, begged his opinion of difficult manuscripts, and paid him handsomely. Three of them, at different times, offered him substantial advances on his autobiography, which he had no intention of writing, and he accepted their money with a kindly thought of composing, in the indeterminate future, some genial fictions that would satisfy them and please their public. Editors bribed him to write reviews, which he did with a just appraisal, but always six months late. Torssander's receipt of money was irregular, but he lived; and on the whole lived well.

A further question may be asked, and since it is prompted by simple ignorance, mere courtesy compels an answer to it. How, comes the new demand, did Trimander Folander, and Torssander not only maintain their poetical reputation—but, in point of fact, enhance it—if for twenty years after leaving Lund they wrote nothing to substantiate it?

The answer to that lies buried—but buried quite comfortably alive—in the character of Sweden and the nature of the Swedish people.

Sweden is both large and little. Geographically measured, it is so long as to stretch from Copenhagen to Naples if it could be unhooked and hung as a pendicle from a suitable place; but socially it is small and fairly compact. People in one part of it are well aware of what people in another part are doing, and of the thoughts that promote their actions. Everyone, for example, knows that the people of Småland are deplorably like the Scotch, and though the southerners of Malmö pretend to believe that the northern suburbs of Stockholm are infested by Lapps, they and everyone else in Scania have rich uncles there who are doing very well for themselves. Nor is anyone in the southern half of the country in any doubt about the shocking morality, especially in winter-time, of everyone in northern parts. Stockholm itself is such a lordly capital that hardly can Europe match it, save perhaps with Venice, yet even in Stockholm there is something small and familiar such as more often exists in a little prosperous market town.

There is another notable contradiction—that somehow is quite happily resolved—in the national aptitude for engineering and the popular addiction to poetry. The foreign visitor, looking at pylons, dams, steel-works, bridges, acqueducts, roads, hydro-electric installations, and smoothly running railways, inevitably remarks, 'What engineers they are!' But the sensitive native, bombarded by the lyrical composition of innumerable friends, encircled by poetry-readers in the cultural associations that on all sides abound, and melodiously deafened by epic dramas in every theatre, exclaims with a melancholy pride, 'What poets we are!'

And both are right. Poetry luxuriates in the comfort that engineers have built, and the engineers continually recreate themselves for fresh tasks with lyrics written upon the streams which they have dammed. If many of the songs are sentimental, that is explained by the climate; for snow lies deeply upon Sweden for many months in the year, and because most of the population is still rural and scattered, every red-walled house is a lonely outpost—warm but precarious, a sweet and perilous achievement—against the enormous wild enmity of winter. Now the songs that are sung everywhere in the outer garrisons of the world, in lonely outposts, are sentimental songs; for cynicism and the shallow wit of irony flourish only in great crowded cities where everyone is a stranger and nobody can be trusted. Smother mankind in snow, divide house from house by a mile of woodland or undulating blanched fields, and everyone will sing sweetly, a little sadly, and with a prevailing sentiment. In such circumstances it is an achievement to survive, a triumph to be comfortable; and gratitude is proper, tears are not amiss.

It was, then, in this comfortable domestication of a long, wild, lovely land that the names of Trimander, Folander, and Torssander were so easily remembered, and confidence remained in their intrinsic virtue and persisting promise. Nor was their promise denied.

Twenty years went by, and each of them, each within a few months of the other, produced a new book. But what a change there was, in every case, between the first and second volumes!

Trimander had found a new king. As he grew older, and thought more deeply of the proud and purposeful monarchs, he became uneasy in their remembered company. Their power had been absolute, their most trivial motives had compelled fearful events, and under the canopy of their thrones triumph and catastrophe had balanced on a private whim. He no longer felt safe or comfortable with them, and their great nobles were no better, for though their power had been less, its quality was the same and its exercise had been unpredictable. So he who had gloried in it, grew afraid of the heroic past. Now in his mind it was full of inhuman harsh-spoken men in black armour, who broke each other's limbs like lobsters' claws, lived in a dark conspiracy with their fingers on the hilt of a dagger, and died stark mad with frogs and newts in the dungeon beneath a cousin's moat.—How glad he was, after a long day's reading, to go down to dinner with the civilised descendants of these grim Counts! In a world that does not all grow better, he often told himself, the nobility is vastly improved. Now that they have lost their power, their manners are delightful.

So Trimander, by a natural process of sympathy, found his thoughts dwelling more and more fondly upon that king of Sweden who himself was frightened of his nobles, and to ensure a little honest friendly company on the throne married a Corporal's daughter. Trimander was living with an aristocratic patron in the south of Sweden when finally he transferred his allegiance to Eric the Fourteenth, and he made his decision immediately after a visit to the ancient castle of Kalmar.

With sombre dignity and walls of a prodigious thickness the castle stands by the sea-shore. It was near Christmas when Trimander went there, and the shallows of the sea were frozen, snow lay deep on the fields, and black-purple clouds to the east threatened a new storm. On that dark and melancholy day two rooms only in the castle were so intrinsically cheerful as to expel from his mind the shadows of outer gloom, and make him forget how cold were his hands and feet and nose. One was called the King's Room, the other the Queen's. Both were panelled with a light wood inlaid, so as to make charming pictures or patterns, with strips, cantles, and divers shapes of other wood stained in gentle colours. In the King's Room, so confected, were two rural landscapes, and in the Queen's some ingenious cubist designs.

Trimander was delighted, and quite enraptured when the Custodian of the castle told him that the pictures were certainly contemporary with King Eric, and more than possibly—even probably—his own work. But the King had lived in the middle of the sixteenth century, said Trimander, and landscape painting was unknown in northern Europe till very much later than that, while cubist theories of art had had to wait for Picasso.—He was before his time, he was a genius, said the Custodian calmly.

Then, seeing how warm was Trimander's appreciation of the Monarch's work, he pressed with his hands upon one of the inlaid panels, and opened a little door. Behind it—oh, impossible!

He was civilised, said Trimander, his voice trembling with emotion. He in himself was both parts of our dear country. He was engineer and artist too.

He was a great man, the Custodian agreed.

Trimander stepped into the little room disclosed by the opening of the secret door, and looked reverently at the water-closet which the King had designed for his comfort.

They called him mad, he said, his voice hollow with alternate scorn and reverence and the echo from the closet. Mad indeed! He alone, in that barbarous age, saw the possibility of beauty and convenience living together to the benefit of both. Mad, my God! It was *they* were mad, and he alone was sane.

Trimander's second book, therefore, was all in praise of the most gifted but unfortunate of kings, poor Eric the Fourteenth. It included a poem called *The Nobles*, in which he laid bare the Monarch's most reasonable fear of men in armour; and the second, entitled *Karin's Wooing*, was an idyllic conversation, an eclogue swift and dainty as anything Theocritus wrote, about the wedding night of King Eric and the Corporal's daughter. The third of the poems, which celebrated the more fruitful Swedish marriage of beauty and convenience, was *The King's Room*. The book, with seventy-eight pages between its covers, was rather smaller than his first, but its success was much larger. The critics praised it, the public bought it.

Folander, fat Folander, published his second volume two months later, and a few of the critics were scornful, while some, frankly puzzled, honestly withheld their opinion. But everybody else bought, borrowed, or stole a copy as quickly as possible, for Folander's lyrical pleasure in life had with the years matured, and in enchanting verses he now celebrated certain forms of still life. He had written a poem called *My Birthday Dinner*.

The development of his mind was clear and logical to all his ordinary readers; only the more academic critics were angered by it, or doubtful of its propriety.—The turning edge of a young leaf, he had said in his youth, is beautiful. The flight of a bird in the pale bright air of spring, and the muscular balance of a trout in a quick green stream, are symptoms of the ecstasy that attended Creation, and that we have lost or forgotten as the heresy fastened upon the world that life was labour.—But youth's melancholy sweet perception had now become, with no loss of verbal dexterity or mellifluous phrase, the sapience of middle age, and instead of his exquisite appreciation of Nature in her May, there was a full-grown delight in *nature morte*.

Look at the curled flesh of a fat eel upon my plate, he said, and drink from my glass this pale yet burly distillate of the Ostrogothic corn! Here is Nature in her ripeness, and we who loved Nature with our eyes and hands, now love her also upon the tongue and in the warm caverns of our body!

On the subject of herring he was truly profound, and touched deeper notes than any he had struck in his early poems. He was most nobly moved by smoked salmon, and in the verses in which he slipped a delicate sharp knife into the fat breast of a well-roasted blackcock, and saw the tenderness within, his voice cried like Queen Dido when Aeneas sailed away, for at that moment he beheld the transience of life that makes it so dear and dreadful. But fortunately in his glass there was a Burgundy of the most generous heart and soft perfection, and the following stanzas became more cheerful. He taught many too thoughtful connoisseurs that reverence of a great wine need not inspire timidity.

For sheer brilliance, however, there was nothing to equal his pages that described the smörgåsbord. Here was such a felicity of word and phrase, of rhyme and arrangement, that his vision of the elegant and richly varied table—the bright armoury of fishes, the patina of reindeer meat—that his stanzas reminded many of his more widely travelled readers of the glittering mosaics of St Mark's in Venice. Nature-lovers, said one of his later and more enthusiastic critics, have hitherto pursued their study and chanted her praise in woods and meadows. But now, taught by Folander to know better, they come to the dining-room.

Hard upon the heels of *My Birthday Dinner* came Torssander's volume. He, like the others, had weathered a crisis. He had discovered that the human estate was more closely limited than at first he had supposed. He had learnt that minor situations have a habit of recurring, that love merely goes in and out like the tide, that to explain man too deeply is to explain him away—and he had come to the conclusion that if he should continue to be witty at man's expense, he would either become repetitious and a bore, or nihilistic and a nuisance. It is clearly better, he said to himself, to do nothing from the beginning than to work so laboriously that you come to nothing in the end; and in this belief he had for some years led a very easy life indeed.

He played chess with various friends some five or six evenings a week, and presently, as the fascination of the game more strongly held him, he took to playing in the afternoons as well. Then he must play in the morning too, but now he encountered difficulty, for not many of his friends lived so idly as he, and even the idlest, he found, had no inclination to play chess after breakfast. So Torssander learnt to play against himself.

This involved a mental discipline of the most stringent sort, and required unlimited leisure. He found that he could play this internecine game most conveniently by setting the board upon the floor and lying prone—first on the one side, then on the other—to study the position and make his moves. He was cared for, at this time, by a devoted housekeeper, a widow with a son of eight or nine years old, and Torssander trained the boy to bring him in, silently and without comment, a pint of beer every forty minutes. So reinforced, his games were often arduous and long, and he had better opportunity than most players to muse upon the accidents of play and the delicate relation of the pieces. He perceived in time that the application of a set of unbreakable rules to pieces of various but predetermined functions—some straightforward and humble, some strong and capricious—produced many situations which, under the finest analysis, were *witty* expressions of the Whites' perplexity or the Reds' advantage. Here were contests that broke no bones, that deployed intelligence without emotion, that came to a decent conclusion and could be started again, and proved—as he had always suspected—that the art of action, perhaps of life in its entirety if it were not so obscured by gross humours, was *wit*. And so his second volume was entitled *A Game of Chess*.

The public, to begin with, was dubious, but the critics were delighted. Swedish literary critics, having been soundly educated in twelve years' residence at Uppsala or Lund, are widely conversant with the literature of all Europe, know English, Russian, French, German, and Italian as well as their own, and so they had no difficulty in perceiving that Torssander's technical model had been Pope's *Rape of the Lock*. To state this, with authority, gave them their initial pleasure, and most of them by judicious example found Torssander's skill in the nicely engineered couplet no whit inferior to his example. But their second and greater joy came from their analysis and tracking-down of Torssander's metaphysics. Torssander's *Game of Chess* had been played against himself, and so exhibited the eternal dualism of man.

Here, then, was a fine quarry for the critics. Some, it is true, the more popular and superficial, perceived in this battle of the divided self no more than a struggle between Conservative and Modern, and a few Freudians went far astray with a laborious explication of the Ego and the Id. Half a dozen elderly gentlemen were so bold as to see in its microcosm the struggle between God and Mammon, and eighteen or twenty worthy but somewhat conventional reviewers hailed the poem as the latest demonstration of the never-ending battle between the Classical and the Romantic schools of thought. To their enduring fame, however, the two senior critics in Sweden concurred in a masterly interpretation of it as an amicable duel between the Confucian attitude to life and the antithetical laxity of Lao-Tze. One of these erudite gentlemen, moreover, proved to the satisfaction of his readers that Sweden itself exhibited the Celestial antithesis: Our engineers, he said, are the modern Confucians, our poets the Taoist followers of Lao-Tze—and Torssander's poem is therefore a work of analytical but devoted patriotism.

This huge dispute, sprawling over hundreds of columns in the daily papers, made *A Game of Chess* not merely a poem, but news; and the general populace, though still perplexed, bought it by the thousand.

Now Trimander, Folander, and Torssander became national figures indeed, and for a year or so lived such a public life as only politicians and actresses are normally accustomed to. They lunched in public, they dined in public, and in the daily papers the public read with whom at night they lodged. For several months Trimander and Folander and Torssander enjoyed their fame, for it brought them together more often than the preceding years had done, and in despite of their altered philosophies they found in each other's company a source of gaiety like that of their youth at Lund, and their quips and epigrams, their puns and profundities, were widely quoted and swiftly spread from Trälleborg in the South to Haparanda in the arctic North. But fame brought satiety more quickly than leisure, and within eighteen months of the publication of their second volumes each had retired to the quietness of his earlier residence: Trimander to a nobleman's castle in Scania, Folander to his wife's property in Dalecarlia, and Torssander to his lodging near Stockholm.

Again the years passed, for there was nothing to stop them, and from Haparanda to Trälleborg people said to each other, 'See what Trimander and Folander and Torssander will do next! Oh, what poets they are, and when next they write we shall not only see more clearly the beauty of the world, which so far is its only reality, save hunger and death and such-like fatalities, that we can put our hands to; but also, perhaps, something of the inner and coherent meaning of it all.'—For these simple people knew perfectly well that life was a trap for them, and that the function of poetry was to show their way out of it.

But year followed year, with the smoothness of water bending and falling over invisible rocky steps in a deep stream, and neither Trimander nor Folander nor Torssander published another verse. The result, however, Sweden being what it is, and the people having time to get by heart the contents of their second volumes, was not an obscuring of their fame, but its enlargement yet again by the most powerful and persistent of all agencies: by the aggravating warmth, that is, of pure faith.

Twenty years went by, and none of them wrote another line, but when they were all near seventy years old the general confidence in them was deeper than ever before, and there was a momentary expectation of their publishing, severally or together, something that should be like a mixture of the *Iliad* and Blake's *Songs of Innocence*; of Heine and the *Laxdale Saga*; of *Tartuffe* and *Fredmans Sånger*—an expectation of God's plenty in swift yet pregnant, bold but graceful phrases. But Trimander and Folander and Torssander chose differently. They chose instead to die.

Folander was the first to go. He was invited to a crayfish feast, and died of a surfeit. Now, in any less civilised or sensitive a country than Sweden, such a death would have been contemned and poor Folander denounced for vulgar greed. But in Sweden they perceived the truth of the matter, and knew that he had died, not of gluttony, but of romantic devotion to an idea, to a ritual, and a faith. For the dainty little crayfish are caught beneath a summer's moon, they are summer's river-fruit, and when they are piled like coral in a crystal dish everyone sees in them the token of summer's triumph over the prison gates that winter had closed upon the running streams for so many weary months; and so eats as many as he can to share the triumph as fully as he may.

Folander had eaten a prodigious number—but exactly how many is still a matter of dispute—when, reaching slowly forward for yet another, his companions saw his rosy face turn suddenly a darker red, as when the westering sun has touched the horizon, and with a shudder he clutched the tablecloth, his glass of schnapps fell with a little crash to the floor, and Folander sank backward into his chair. The sun had set.

Trimander was living in a castle on Lake Mälaren at that time. He cried openly when he heard the news, and sobbing still, retired to his room. He did not come down to dinner, and a servant said that he had gone for a walk. It was raining heavily. His host grew anxious, and sent out some young men to look for him. But it was after midnight before they found him, soaked to the skin, and brought him home. He died of pneumonia three days later, and in the stove in his bedroom they found a little heap of ashes. Whatever he had written in the last few years of his life he had taken with him to the grave, like helmet and sword and shield in a Viking's burial.

Torssander was found dead a week later. His chessboard was on the floor, and on either side the pieces were so disposed that a single false move would open their array to rout and dissolution. The board, as it stood, was taken with pious care to Skansen, where it still provokes endless discussion among devotees of the game.—Had Torssander, they ask, simply demonstrated his witty understanding of chess by arranging his men in such a way that a mere touch would undo them all? Or had he, in his last contest, brought by serious play and the deployment of equal forces, both sides to an abyss; and read the parable?

For Torssander, dead, sat at his table with an unfinished poem before him.—He had come, so he wrote, to a house that seemed empty, but the plate on the door was well polished and its old lettering, almost rubbed away by time, spelt the name he looked for: *Death*. Here, to this house, his friends had come, and he must learn for himself what their welcome had been. He knocked, but no one came. The house indeed looked empty, but on a window a curtain moved. He knocked again, more loudly. Still no one came. He knocked a third time . . . .

There the poem ended, and Torssander's pen lay broken between his hands.

No work of literature could have pushed their fame to such a height as this common work of death. Now, having shed their mortal parts, they scared above Sweden like the three crowns of the kingdom that gleam over Stockholm in the sky; and they and their poems, as if under a great light, became visible to all. Death had established their immortality.

It did more, indeed, for in a curious way it brought the poets closer to the simple people who admired them. Resolved by death, their genius at once became part of the soil and history of Sweden, of which quite ordinary people such as clerks and sailors and village shopkeepers, were equal heirs with Counts and professors and fashionable ladies; and the greatness of Trimander, Folander, and Torssander, which in their time upon earth had held them at a little distance from their readers, now entered their readers' minds as a morsel of their natural heritage. By their solemn act of dying, the poets presently became one flesh with all their fellow-countrymen.

The Wrong Story

'ON YOUR RIGHT is the largest and most beautiful cemetery in Noo Orleans. Now owing to the marshy nature of the ground more people are buried in tombs on top of the earth than in graves dug into the earth, and that broad white wall represents the latest way of disposing of the dear departed. It consists of compartments in three layers. Those on the bottom shelf cost sixty dollars, the middle ones seventy-five, and the top ones ninety dollars. You buy a compartment, you slide in the casket, you lock the door, and put the key carefully away with the deceas' photograph and the mortgage on your Chevrolet.'

The guide put down his small cardboard megaphone and smiled roguishly, benignly, at the twenty people in the motor coach, whose faces were always at different levels as they bumped up and down or looked here and there. Nineteen of them turned their heads half-right, and stared with respectful curiosity at the white chaos of tombs and statuary, of angels, crosses, broken columns, temples and little mausoleums. The meaningless names of many totally forgotten people were handsomely preserved. But modern economy or the American belief in concentration had prescribed for many more only a cell in the broad honeycombed wall to which the guide had called particular attention. The nineteen tourists, most of whom already lived in apartment houses, were apparently impressed by this homely and sensible innovation.

But the twentieth scarcely glanced at the cemetery. She was a plump woman of rather more than thirty-five, and she sat in the front seat. She had black hair, a wide mouth, and thick white skin. The guide's genial appearance seemed to attract her more than marble crosses.

The cemetery was left behind, and with a slight switchback movement the motor coach crossed a broad transverse street. The guide slipped the megaphone over his mouth again.

'That bump which you felt just now,' he explained, 'was due to crossing one of the main canals of the Noo Orleans drainage system. It is now the broadest covered drainage canal in the world, and as you could see it runs under one of our busiest streets. Formerly if a lady wanted to cross the street she had to take her shoes in her hand.

Now as soon as she steps off the sidewalk she takes her life in her hands.'

All the tourists showed some appreciation of the joke. Some, simply pleased, honestly chuckled. Some nodded as if to say, 'How true!' And others displayed the sophisticated tooth of social mirth.

The dark-haired woman in the front seat, however, threw back her head and laughed outright, showing large handsome teeth that appeared rather yellow against her carmined lips. The guide, from his slightly higher seat, glanced down at her and smiled.

He was a jovial-looking man with little twinkling eyes and a red shiny face. His skin seemed tough, as if it had been exposed to extreme conditions of weather and would grow an abundant beard. When he took off his peaked official cap, to mop his warm head, a white line showed about an inch above his eyebrows, and his high round forehead (he was half-bald) looked astonishingly pale. It gave him a particoloured appearance that almost suggested a circus. From his nose to his mouth ran deep outward-curving lines that puckered his face into a lasting smile, and the corners of his mouth turned upwards to meet these lines and so increase their jovial effect. He wore, in fact, a smile that would not come off.

The tourists settled down to a period of cautious indifference as the guide began to recommend other excursions, and to suggest that those who intended to see the farther environs of New Orleans might as well buy their tickets from him.

'This is how we make our living, ladies and gentleman,' he explained. 'The driver and I get a small percentage on the tickets we sell, and if you care to do us a favour and at the same time profit by the new and varied experience you gain on these marvellous sightseeing tours . . . Leaving at two-thirty this afternoon, ma'am, and we call for you at your hotel.'

The woman in the front seat took a ticket, and led away from prudence by her example several other passengers engaged themselves to join the afternoon tour. The guide was pleased by his success, and while he distributed tickets he made little jokes and flattered his charges in a knowing voice.

'. . . as nice a lot of folk as we've had this year. That's what I told Ed there'—he jerked a thumb at the driver—'as soon as I saw you. I knew I wouldn't have to use much persuasion to intelligent folk like you.' His grin deepened and he looked down at the woman in the front seat in a familiar way. 'I'm a thought-reader,' he said, and winked at her. She laughed, vaguely flattered, and pulled her skirt farther over her knees.

The coach went on its way, through the City Park where the guide made a story of the Duelling Oaks and the wild young men, or angry old men, who had fought beneath them for various causes, some of which were the complications of love. The woman in the front seat stared at the trees with morbid curiosity.

The route then led down St Charles Avenue, and the guide pointed to the millionaires' houses with their handsome gardens, and mentioned their owners' wealth with a rich and easy familiarity.

When the morning's trip was over he said cheerfully, 'Well, I'll be seeing most of you again in a couple of hours' time, so we needn't say good-bye. See that you all get a good dinner, but don't eat so much that you want to go to sleep after it, or you'll miss a mighty fine tour.'

Most of the travellers were pleased with their morning's outing and made complimentary remarks to the guide as he helped them out of the narrow door of the coach. Some, however, were blasé, and said how stiff they felt after sitting so long in a crowded vehicle. The guide behaved to all alike, showing the same genial face, the same smile of unchanging good humour, to crabbed customers and contented ones; but as the last was stepping out he muttered to the driver, still without changing his expression, 'For Christ's sake, Ed! They get dumber and dumber every day.'

The driver answered, 'That dame sitting in front seems to have taken a fancy to you, Al.'

'The bigger they are the harder they fall,' said the guide with his jovial look.

It was I, sightseeing in this unenterprising way, who left the coach last and so overheard this small conversation. I had bought no more tickets, and my normal appearance of diffident inconsequence was exaggerated by the oppressive heat. Obviously the guide had no reason to respect my feelings, and I was not insulted by his somewhat contemptuous indifference to my person and power of hearing. I was interested, however, by the contrast between his happy smile and the cynical boredom of his voice. His facial expression was apparently fixed as firmly as that of Ozymandias's statue in the sand, and bore no relation to his real feelings. It was a grinning mask, ingrown and permanent.

I lunched alone, in a Creole restaurant to which I had been recommended, but it was too hot to enjoy anything more solid than iced melon, and the admirably cooked, ingeniously seasoned chicken was almost wasted. It was foolish, perhaps, to have gone to New Orleans in June, but as I had no other opportunity of seeing that charming city I had determined to endure the unpleasantness of its summer climate for the sake of its other attractions. But I was beginning to regret my enthusiasm, for I had arranged to meet a friend there with whom I was to travel across the continent to Los Angeles, and that morning I had received a telegram saying he had been delayed and would not arrive for another forty-eight hours. I was not made happier by the prospect of two more days and two more nights in windless air so excessively charged with hot moisture.

Because it was too hot to walk about, and because I could think of nothing else to do, I decided to go on the second sightseeing tour, for which, a little earlier, I had resolutely refused to buy a ticket. The thought of the guide's Ozymandias-grin had become rather entertaining.

When I arrived at the starting-terminus the woman who had occupied the front seat on the morning tour was already in her former place. She had taken the opportunity to paint her lips more brightly, with a bolder and more provocative line, and to buy some flowers for the front of her dress.

We drove for a considerable distance out of the city, and for some time passed nothing which Al, the guide, thought worth describing. He talked instead to the woman in front of him, and I was close enough to hear him asking her how long she had been in New Orleans, and whether she liked it.

'Two days,' she answered. 'It's a swell place, isn't it? Kind of romantic, don't you think?'

'Sure,' he said. 'It's the most romantic city in America.'

'I wish I knew half as much about it as you do.'

'Then you wouldn't want to come on any sightseeing trips,' he said, laughing.

'That's so,' she confessed. 'I hadn't thought of that.' And laughed too.

When we reached an old plantation house the guide began to talk with his usual felicity, and the tourists turned from one side to the other as he bade them; peered out of windows; and pointed out objects of interest to their friends. The guide's patter was unfailing, and his smile made everything he said seem very agreeable.

We passed a broad field, tree-guarded, in which cows were grazing. 'See those cows?' he said. 'They're what provide Noo Orleans with all its milk and butter and eggs.'

There was a shout of laughter as the tourists detected this happy blunder. Al pretended to be puzzled by their mirth, and asked what was the matter. When his error was explained to him he pushed back his cap, scratched his pale broad forehead in a rueful way that his smile belied, and said in a tone of mock penitence, 'Well, you can't expect one man to know everything, can you?'

Long after the others had exhausted their mirth the woman in the front seat continued to be merry about Al's *gaffe*. At first she laughed outright, so heartily that she found occasion to dab her eyes with a small slightly-soiled handkerchief. Then, overcoming the more boisterous part of her emotion, she bent her head and giggled quietly, as if there were some specially titillating feature of the joke, invisible to others, that she was privately enjoying. She glanced upward at the guide, with a tentative intimacy in her look, as though she were offering to share this secret with him, or at least to show how much she appreciated it.

Al met her obscure glance of understanding with his jovial unchanging smile.

On the following morning I went to look once again at the old French Market. I had already been there two or three times, but its fascination was not easily exhausted. The market gardeners who brought produce there were descendants of the long-since evicted settlers of Acadia, and their language, as they argued, expostulated, gossiped, was a mutilated and antique French.

Their shabby motor-trucks and old unpainted horsewagons, loaded with beans, potatoes, and water-melons, stood in lines at right angles to the pavement. Most of the horses wore peaked straw hats through which their ears protruded. The broad pavement was shaded by awnings, between which came hot bars of sun. The merchants were a curious mixture. They were olive-skinned, they were dark and Mediterranean-seeming.

There were negroes and mulattoes, there were old women in sun-bonnets, fat French-looking women, lazy men half-sleeping in the shadow of their wagons, and here a couple of men playing cards on a packing-case table. Behind the baskets and sacks of potatoes piled along the pavement were dark little shops in which men, their hats tilted back, sat to eat and drink. Some of the shops were curiously lit as if by an overflow of reflected light.

The baskets loaded with potatoes, the brown knobbly sacks so tightly filled with them, gave off an earthy smell, and next door to that dusty savour would be the sweet odour of pineapples. There were baskets of long bright green beans, and glossy purple egg-plant. There were hundreds of huge green water-melons, with here and there a triangular wedge cut from the side of one to show its fresh, pink, loosely-seeded flesh.

There were cantaloupes with grey mottling on their taut dull hides, lemons from California wrapped neatly in yellow tissue paper, golden plums, and glaring red tomatoes. There were cabbages, lettuces in great leafy stacks, and strange green twisted growths like vegetable snakes or eels. There were sacks of coco-nuts.

While I walked about and observed with great delight this rich variety of fruits and men, I noticed, some little distance from me in the half-crowd, a familiar female figure. It was the woman who, on the previous day, had sat on the front seat of the motor coach. She was now moving vaguely from stall to stall, considering the profusion with sometimes a kind of bewilderment, sometimes an obvious greed. She would stop to finger the smooth tomatoes, the rough cantaloupes, and voluble men would shout to her how good and cheap they were.

She listened, not understanding what they said, and, as if frightened of being swindled, walked on reluctantly. By-and-by she looked at her watch, and, having seen the time, quickened her steps. Yielding without shame to curiosity, I followed her. She took from the bag she carried a little round case, the size of half-a-crown but thicker, that held a mirror, a puff, and a cake of solidified powder; as she walked she dabbed and rubbed her nose, that the heat had made shiny.

She turned a corner or two and came to a square in which three or four motor coaches stood empty except for their drivers. The tourists they had carried were in the Cabildo museum and other near-by buildings of a social or historical interest, where their guides elucidated for them the significance—a morsel of the significance—of such things as slave blocks, monuments, and altar-pieces, or talked glibly of Louis Philippe and the pirate Pierre Lafitte.

The woman went into the Cabildo, where Al was entertaining a party with his jocular descriptions and his smile. She joined his audience and quietly but determinedly forced her way to the front of it. Al was discussing, with ready gaiety, some leg-irons saved from the old traffic in slaves.

He recognised the woman, and when he had finished his discourse—I was looking at a case of miniatures not far away—said to her, 'Well! Still interested in Noo Orleans?'

'I'll say,' she answered. 'It's awful interesting, isn't it? I've been to the French Market, and then I found myself outside of here, and remembered what you said about it yesterday. So I thought I'd come in and have a look at it. It's kind of interesting, isn't it? I didn't expect to find you here though.'

The tourists had left. Al and the woman followed them slowly, talking together. I stayed in the museum the rest of the morning because it was many degrees cooler than the streets.

That night the heat was abominable, and though I turned my ceiling-fan to full speed I couldn't sleep. It did nothing to cool the room, but only disturbed the stale damp air from its corners, churned the moist air that drifted sluggishly through the window, and sent it down on me in hot waves. As sleep was impossible I tried to entertain myself with some light and easy forms of thought. I considered the curious morality of a talking-picture I had lately seen; dissected the appalling stupidity of a remark I had recently made, and the embarrassment I had suffered; tried to remember Hilaire Belloc's poem about Peter Wanderwide; rehearsed a possible conversation with the friend whose failure to keep an appointment was causing me this discomfort; reviewed the French Market, some wrought-iron gates and half-hidden courtyards in New Orleans, and suddenly came to a remarkably vivid picture of Al with his unchanging smile, and the fat woman of the motor coach.

I began to speculate about her. She had been fairly good-looking a few years before; she was married, or had been; she was on holiday, her clothes were new, and she was alone; her attitude in the Market, her dependence on organised sightseeing, hinted that she was not accustomed to travelling far from home; despite her heavy and sometimes sullen look there was in her bearing an eagerness, a clumsy desire to enjoy herself, a greed that probably came from long repression; and her voice suggested a Middle-Western origin.

This combination of repression and the Middle West immediately suggested a story, for I had read at least a dozen novels about the spiritual indigence of life in the small towns of Ohio, Indiana, and Minnesota, and I knew, on their authority, a lot about the tragic possibilities of emotional starvation. Women like diminished shades of Emma Bovary lived on every second street, and in their questing imprisoned souls grew dreadful havoc.

There was a writing-table in my room, and plenty of notepaper. I got up, turned on the light, and began my story with a description of sightseers pausing to admire the curious burial system of New Orleans. One of the sightseers was the woman with the thick white skin, and by fixing her attention—and the reader's—on that huge gruesome apartment-house tomb, I hoped to secure an introductory suggestion of grimness, tinctured with a certain levity that, to the understanding mind, made it grimmer still. I described the genial smiling guide, and showed the beginning of the woman's attraction to him.

It was his jovial appearance that fascinated her, because it implied happiness and generosity very different from anything she had known in her unfortunate married life. She came from a small town in Indiana. At twenty-two she had married a man double her age, stupidly attracted by his prosperous condition and an appearance of virility that he wore as falsely as a wig. He had roused her passion—it was all ready to be roused—and then his own had dwindled and died like a stream in summer; and with its disappearance had come a sleepless jealousy that made him nag and bully her, and keep her short of money lest she should buy new clothes to attract better men than himself. She was frightened of him, and clung in a dull and timid way to such comfort as he still provided—shelter and enough to eat—though his specific failure as a husband often made her nearly frantic with a kind of snivelling indignation.

At twenty-eight she was hysterical and thin, and often dreamt that she was going mad. She was terrified at the mere thought of leaving her husband, however, and too stupid to deceive him with any of the young men she knew. But at thirty-three she had grown resigned, in a sulky way, to the disabilities of her life, and was beginning to put on weight.

When her husband snarled at her she would answer in a voice as rough as his own, and taunt him with his insolvent physique. But he knew by this time her cowardly and shiftless nature, and he set no more than their proper value on her taunts, though they never failed to anger him. They were largely the admission of her helplessness. She dared not leave him and she wasn't clever enough to have a lover.

At thirty-five she was so fat that she considered dieting, though she did not practise it very much, and her fits of hysteria had given way to a recurrent bored inertia. She smoked cigarettes till her tongue was sore, and spent hours of sluggish wonder over magazines that published photographs of film-stars and gossip about Hollywood. Then her husband died of some sort of gastric trouble, and she found herself free and independent, for he had left her 8,000 dollars' worth of bonds, life insurance policies for 10,000 dollars, a two-year-old motor-car, and some indifferent furniture.

Several weeks passed before she properly realised her freedom and discovered sufficient energy and independence to enjoy it. But when three or four men began to pay her attention—everyone in town knew the extent of her fortune—she felt a sudden access of pride and vitality, and determined to forget her wasted years in prompt enjoyment. She resolved to travel, and through ignorance and ill-luck (not knowing how unpleasant was the summer heat) chose to visit New Orleans first.

Her relations with Al pursued a normal course—normal in such circumstances, that is—to the goal of a joint habitation. She was completely fascinated by the robust ever-smiling guide, and he, though not very much attracted at first, was sensibly influenced when he discovered how much money she had. They were married a fortnight after their first meeting.

She told Al, in great and ever-recurrent detail, about her life in Indiana, and for some time he found her stories interesting. He made jokes about her dead husband that the richness of his smile greatly enlivened, and they laughed very happily together about the poor man's shortcomings. The woman, for a little while, was vastly pleased by her new life, laughed with clumsy gaiety, and was proud of her enterprise in going to New Orleans. She acknowledged its appeal.

She vaguely apprehended in the unfamiliar southern city a life richer and more satisfying than the life in northern towns, and in the French Market, to which she returned again and again, she found a symbol of its natural wealth. She was enraptured by the multitude of fruits, their colours and their smells, and to hear the incomprehensible accent of the Acadian farmers satisfied her vestigial feeling for romance.

Not for several weeks did she realise that Al had married her for her money. At first she was liberal with it, but as his demands grew heavier and more frequent—he was unlucky as a gambler, and misfortune made him reckless—she began to grumble, grow fretful, and was disinclined to subsidise his unprofitable interest in poker and craps. They quarrelled with increasing frequency, and the woman was sometimes frightened, sometimes angry, to see that, however violent were Al's words, however fierce his voice, a smile of apparent geniality invariably accompanied them. In the heat of his wrath it twisted and curved his face into a semblance of gay good humour, and his high bald forehead gave him the parti-coloured look of a circus clown, so that his whole appearance suggested a brutal mockery.

His demands for money were always successful in the end. He either frightened her into giving it, or cajoled her. If he had had a few drinks he found it easy to woo her, and to flavour his wooing with the winning jocularity of their early acquaintance; but when he was quite sober he usually bullied her into giving him what he wanted. She grew sullen again, whimpered and nagged in a querulous way, and developed a protective taste for gin.

After a year of marriage her money had nearly gone, and Al was eager to get rid of her. She clung to him with tenacity and cunning, however. The desperate fear of being cast off, and left alone, quickened her wits and enabled her to see through all his attempted schemes and devices. She threatened to become as immovable as his smile.

They hated each other very thoroughly. Her fatness, her limpet-hold of him, her shiftlessness, her querulous voice that constantly reproached him with wasting her fortune, quickened Al's hatred for her; while she hated him for robbing her of wealth, for mocking her, for making her dependent on him, and for the inhuman fixity of his meaningless smile.

Their quarrels became more and more violent, and the woman lived in a state of fear that was presently justified. For one night Al struck her with a poker, and the sight of her sprawling on the floor, with blood on her face, roused in him the lust to kill. He hit her again and again, with increasing savagery. Her screams faded into moaning, and still, with desperate hands, she tried to ward off his blows. Through the branching guard of her arms, her stretched and despairing fingers—through the darkening mist of unconsciousness, she saw his inhuman smile as the mask of murder.

That was the story I made. When it was done—I had left *lacunae* to be filled in later with description and some conversation, but the whole frame was complete—I returned to bed with a pleasant feeling of accomplishment soothing my brain, and slept for the few remaining hours of darkness.

I woke to the whirring of the ceiling-fan. It was still hot, and through my window, that was higher than any neighbouring building, I looked out at the great arc of the Mississippi, walled in with wharves and warehouses, overhung with a huge dense canopy of lustrous mist. I rang for some tea, and when it came I read the story I had written.

My pleasant feeling of accomplishment quickly vanished, for it seemed very bad. The hour of conception is seldom critical, but in the light of morning I discovered the situation to be trite, the psychology superficial, and the device of the unchanging smile—founded though it was on actual observation—appeared unnecessarily melodramatic. I admitted then that I knew very little, except from novels, about middle-aged women who lived in such states as Indiana and Ohio, and suffered from repression of their spiritual, emotional, or physical requirements.

I knew little of them in fact, and I had never found the idea of them sufficiently interesting to build up inductive theories that might present an appearance of persuasive actuality. Except for the soporific effect of its composition the story was a failure. At any rate I was neither interested nor convinced when I re-read it, and without hesitation or regret I tore it up and threw the fragments into a wastepaper-basket.

My friend arrived about midday, and we left that afternoon on our long journey across the continent. I thought no more about Al and the woman from Indiana—my exercise in fiction had clouded their reality for me—until, months later, a newspaper brought home to me, with considerable emphasis, their actual existence.

I was living in San Francisco at the time, and among the few unworthy things in that magnificent city are its newspapers. They are vulgar, sensational, and except for their criminal reports quite untrustworthy. But they handle crime with circumstance and authority. My attention was attracted by a headline that read 'New Orleans Hatchet Murder'. The story was illustrated with a couple of photographs, one of which I immediately recognised by a large and seemingly jovial smile. The other was hardly so distinctive, for the woman's expression was unfamiliar and a little unexpected.

I read the account of the murder with some excitement, for, in spite of the dislike I had conceived for my story, and the lack of conviction I found in it, several of my surmises had been correct. The woman had been a widow. After an unhappy married life she had gone to New Orleans on holiday and speedily fallen in love with the smiling guide. Al had married her for her money. He was a confirmed gambler. As soon as her fortune was spent their relations had become unfriendly, and on several occasions the neighbours had been alarmed by the violence of their quarrels.

So far I had been right, and yet I was glad that I had destroyed my version, my prophecy, of their tragic story; for now it became more obvious than ever that I knew little—that I knew nothing indeed—about women who had been thwarted, repressed, and emotionally starved in small mid-western towns. My ignorance was here made manifest, my main induction brutally demolished.

For Al had not murdered the woman. She had murdered him.

The Crusader's Key

BERTRAN DE SALARS, lord of Caraman and Salars, a Poor Knight of Christ and of the Temple of Solomon, said to his wife Jehane, 'There is in my mind no smallest doubt of your honesty, nor must you think that what I am now about to do can ever be regarded as an insult to you, as a reflection on your character, or an indication of my lessening esteem. I am afraid it will be necessary for you to take off all your clothes.'

With some bitterness in her voice the Lady Jehane answered, 'If you do not doubt my honesty I cannot see why you should take such precautions to keep me honest as make it seem that good behaviour is contrary to my intentions.'

'You are a woman,' said Bertran mildly.

'It is late in the day to reproach me with that,' said Jehane. 'I think you have been glad of it once or twice, and now to blame me for what was God's will and has been your pleasure is mere petulance, and not worthy of a knight who proposes to venture his body for the rescue of God's holy city from the Saracens, since God in His wisdom made Eve as well as Adam, and said no word to Adam whereby he should think it right to reproach her with the nature and condition established in her to further His purpose of comforting Adam with an helpmeet and a lover. Still less did He give man warrant, in that garden where warrant was given for so much, to load a woman with chains and put padlocks on her when he went abroad on errands of his own choosing.'

'You are overwrought,' said Bertran, 'and so you fall into a torrent of words without perceiving to what shoal of fallacy they bear you. For it was not God but the Serpent who gave to Eve that part of her nature which, in these wicked and degenerate times, appears to dominate all the rest. Nor do I believe that even the Serpent would so have worked upon her had he properly foreseen the future. In Eden there was no other man save Adam, but now there are men walking in every field. And since it is woman's part, as you have said, to be a helpmeet and a lover, man must of his own wit—that God gave him—devise means whereby his wife shall love and help him only, and not squander her mercies on all the world.—You must take off your shift as well, my dear.'

'There then!' said Lady Jehane, and passionately threw the garment from her. Her cheeks were bright red, from modesty a little and from indignation a great deal, and so hot was her blood that the March wind, blowing lustily through the tower window, chilled her not at all but merely tempered her anger.

'You are very beautiful,' said Bertran.

'Keep your mind on the Sepulchre,' said Lady Jehane.

'My thought is fixed on it and my heart is ever grieved for its present unhappy state,' said Bertran. 'I do not think you will find the chain uncomfortable, and the links are so smoothly worked that they cannot chafe you. The padlock, I admit, is somewhat heavy, but were it lightly made it could not be secure.'

'My heart was light, yet my love for you lay safely in it,' said Lady Jehane.

'I shall be gone three years,' said Bertran, 'and every month of those years the temptation of benevolence will assail you, pricking of the flesh will stir your woman's wish to give, and voices in your blood will call as dry earth calls loudly for the piercing rain . . .'

'No, no!' cried Jehane. 'I am your wife, faithful to you and desirous of no other man.'

'You are a woman,' said Bertran, 'and I shall be gone three years.'

Then he put round her waist the girdle that was called the Crusader's Belt—since many knights and noblemen so guarded their wives from shame and even, they hoped, imprudent thoughts while they, far off, battled with the infidel for Christ's tomb and captured city—and when he had adjusted the chain so that it lay close to her side, and yet not so close as to cause discomfort, he fastened it with a heavy padlock, locking that with a key, and tied the key to a cord that he put about his neck.

'This I shall call your heart's key,' said Bertran, 'and it shall lie against the beating of my own heart.'

But Jehane made no answer. She put on her clothes again with abrupt and trembling movements, and in her bearing was a muted wildness. She stood by the narrow window, high in the round grey wall of the tower, and looked at the liberty of earth beyond her. Clouds rolled or swam in open sky; the wind leapt freely through black branches flushed green at their myriad tips with buds half-opened; a hawk poised, trod empty space, and stooped; lambs leapt with ungainly joy in tilted fields—but Lady Jehane, hands pressed to waist, felt under her fingers the hard steel chain, and her body shrank within its hold, and beneath its weight her strength grew weak. She breathed harshly through open mouth, and heard only as some unmeaning noise the farewell her lord was speaking.

She gave him her hand to kiss, but her hand was cold, her head averted.

'I shall not be happy till Jerusalem is girt with Christian steel as you are girt,' said Bertran.

'Ah, poor city!' cried Jehane.

'Poor city indeed,' said Bertran, 'and that is why we must ride to its relief.'

From her window Jehane looked down and saw the horsemen stiffen to obedience when her lord came out to them. At his word they mounted and rode from the courtyard. Women followed, clamorous at their horses' heels, children shrilly whooped, and those with a better understanding as noisily wept. When the Crusaders had forded the river, splashing through bright shallow water, they turned southwards and rode in file. Bertran waited by the ford till they had crossed. Then he turned to his castle and saluted Lady Jehane—though he could no longer see her, because she had turned away from her window to sit on a little stool and crouch there like an old woman, thinking nothing whatever about the perils and discomfort to which her lord was riding, but very bitterly concerned with her own misery.

The lord of Caraman and Salars sighed and shook his head in a wistful movement that consorted badly with his military appearance, with the short manly beard he wore in compliance with Templar custom, and indeed with the Templar tradition to waste no time on topics of sentiment. But though he knew Jehane to be unhappy, and though the knowledge grieved him, he comforted himself with the assurance that he had acted wisely and for the ultimate benefit of both himself and his wife. He patted his brown surcoat, with the great red cross on it, and felt beneath it her heart's key. 'She is safe,' he thought, and putting spurs to his horse cantered to overtake his troop.

For a week of tedious days the Lady Jehane maintained a demeanour that to her household appeared the perfection of widowed grief. She was listless, she would not eat, her cheeks were pale and her eyes were red, she was irritable when spoken to, and would burst into tears to atone for her unkindness. 'Ah!' said her servants and her friends, 'what desire she has for that Bertran with his Templar's beard, his heavy speech, and his concern for this matter of the Sepulchre! Who would have thought that such a man could blow love's flame so hot, and leave so desolate a hearth behind him?'

But the truth was that Jehane never gave a thought to her lord except in the way of anger against his stupidity. Under a seeming gaiety and lightness of manner she was in reality extremely virtuous, and though she delighted in the society of troubadours and others who spoke much about the art of love, she had never felt the slightest inclination to abandon herself to its illicit practice. To be loved by Bertran was rather different, of course, though even his embraces, despite the favouring circumstance of the Church's blessing, had really given her very little pleasure. And love unconsecrated was mere bestiality.

That Bertran could think of her yielding to brutish heat like a heifer in the fields or some gap-toothed peasant in a barn! That was pride-shattering, that broke her heart as though her heart had been herself in a mirror broken by a stone. And then there was the intolerable burden of the chain, ever present, printing her side with its abominable links, and by its presence fixing her mind on the lewdness it prohibited. She had no wish to think of evil, but the chain held her to thoughts of evil as surely as it bound her to continence. 'It makes me a slave, it makes me an animal,' she thought. It was moreover extremely uncomfortable.

And then one morning Jehane was wakened by the amorous voice of the troubadour Simon Vidal singing an alba, or morning song, to her sister Maulfry, a laughing handsome girl to whom such flattery was often paid. The alba was a passionate complaint against the intrusive sun, that drove back the friendly dark and with cruel fingers tore lovers from their lovers' arms.

So coldly blows the wind of dawn
Upon a naked heart,

sang the troubadour.

'It sounds quite sincere and convincing,' thought Jehane. 'Someone who knew nothing of our customs might well believe that he had really spent the night in Maulfry's arms and was singing out of uncontrollable grief at parting from her. But he has probably given several days to the composition of so charming a lyric, and was wakened by his servant just in time to get up and sing it so that the sun might rise on its last notes.'

Vidal sang another verse. Though shrill with pain his voice retained the loveliness of conscious art, and the melody was plucked with proficient yearning from the strings of his lute:

I flee before the sharp-edged light
Towards another dark;
How cold becomes the world at dawn—
Cover your naked heart!

'I wonder!' thought Jehane. 'That last verse seems to have a more personal note than is usual, though of course many troubadours make their songs provocative enough, and try to give the impression that even more has happened than they are willing to tell. But nobody really believes them when they are like that, and it would be a pity indeed if people did believe them, and so forced them to speak the truth, for you can't make much poetry out of truth alone or compose a song by merely saying what actually occurred. And yet I feel rather anxious about Maulfry, for there was certainly a lot of feeling in Vidal's alba, and she is brave enough for anything. Perhaps he did spend the night in her room!'

Then—'Why,' thought Lady Jehane, 'now I am getting like poor Bertran, who always thinks the worst has happened or is going to happen. Were it not for this wretched chain I should never have suspected anything, but under its influence I am ready to believe in all manner of impropriety. People really do seem wickeder than I used to think them, but then formerly I was so innocent that I could rarely imagine how evil occurred, and had to take the world's lewdness on trust. Which was, perhaps, a little dull on the whole. But now I have no difficulty whatever in picturing the vicious state into which society has fallen.'

And a little later she exclaimed, 'It is Bertran's fault, and he has only himself to blame! It is due solely to his action that henceforth I shall not only take pleasure in believing the worst about people, but also in behaving myself with all the impropriety of which I am capable. It is true that I am not capable of much, owing to this miserable chain, but I shall do what I can to justify Bertran's belief that it was necessary!'

Lady Jehane was now happier than she had been since her lord first announced his intention of girdling her to compulsory chastity. From that morning when she heard Vidal singing, her demeanour changed, and the castle of Caraman, that had shared her gloom, now participated in her gaiety. Under the quickening influence of spring, troubadours were rivalling the mating birds in the profusion of their melodies—while far excelling the simple lark and the untutored willow-wren in fertility of invention—and some of the most accomplished paid visits to the castle of Caraman when they heard that not only the Lady Maulfry but also the Lady Jehane was in a mood to welcome their art and themselves.

Vidal, hopelessly enslaved by the beauty and gaiety of Maulfry, had become rather one of the household than a passing guest. Under the soporific influence of a permanent interest and a settled domicile his songs had acquired a certain monotony—though that which awakened Jehane had been brilliantly individual—but now, when other minstrels sang in his hearing their delight in Jehane's fair beauty, his wit was stirred afresh and his jealous pride in Maulfry found expression in ever new and more daring felicities. This championship of dark Maulfry, vaunting her eyes in a brave conceit and her lips in the most exquisite of tunes, inspired in its turn the visiting troubadours to novelties in compliment and rare device in melody when their opportunity came to hymn the golden loveliness of Jehane. For if Maulfry was starlight on the velvet breast of night, Jehane—as one of them remarked—was dawn lifting its small clouds of white and rose from a pale gold field of barley. Maulfry, to put it shortly, was dark and slender, while Jehane was very fair and somewhat inclined to plumpness.

So timing his arrival that he could bear with him the first spray of almond-blossom, Gilles de Mercadet came one morning to the castle. When his name was announced a flutter of anticipation passed over the ladies of the castle like a breeze that comes roughly into a flower-garden, and those of the gentlemen present who were interested in poetry turned with the liveliest expectancy to see him whose fame as a troubadour outstripped even his reputation as a lover.

Gilles de Mercadet was tall and excessively handsome. His legs were long, his brow was broad and white, his hair had the sombre brilliance of a raven's wing. His chin was determined, his nose severe, and his eyes were dark and lustrous under melancholy lids. His hands were shapely and a nervous passion animated his fingers. He came into the hall with his joglar behind him—a little man, ugly and red-faced—and fell on his knees before Lady Jehane. She welcomed him gladly, and took the almond-blossom from him, and put it to her lips.

After the interchange of some courtesies Jehane said, 'You have travelled far, sir, I think, for had you been living in this neighbourhood, I would have heard of it.'

'I have come from Perpignan,' said Gilles.

'That is far enough,' said Jehane, 'and I am glad you have had so long a journey, since now you will be tired of travel and content to stay here.'

'Does any man who has once seen you ever go farther or fare home again?'

'My husband has gone to the Holy Land,' said Jehane.

'Marriage, that gives a man rights, ever robs him of reason,' said Gilles.

After a little while Maulfry asked, 'Did you not find the air of Perpignan to your liking, sir?'

'The air was good enough,' said Gilles, 'but those who used it were less to my fancy.'

'I have heard the ladies there are most beautiful,' said Jehane.

'Even were they as beautiful as they esteem themselves, that would not excuse their demand for admiration,' said Gilles.

'We are modest people here,' said Jehane.

'Then your virtue must exceed your judgment,' answered the troubadour.

On the following morning de Mercadet looked white and weary. His eyes were more profoundly dark, hooded more deeply by their melancholy lids, and his cheeks were pale with the transparent pallor of suffering.

With the anxiety of a hostess and a woman's pity for the pain of a young man so handsome, Lady Jehane asked if he had not slept well.

'I was visited by something more importunate than sleep,' he said. 'An inspiration, a thought, a vision,' he explained, seeing Jehane looked questioningly from one to another of her ladies.

'Perhaps your room was not comfortable,' she suggested.

'It has a window,' said Gilles. Then he took his lute from the joglar, and after striking two or three preliminary chords to arrest the general attention—which he did very easily—he sang the following lines to a tune of surpassing merit:

I looked through my window and caught my heart with a cry
To see the late moon and the dawn sharing the sky.

I saw the slim gold crescent of the old moon lean
Over the hill in a vapour of gull's-egg-green;

While a span to the north another day began
As the sun's bright fingers opened an apricot fan—

Faced with the loveliness of those lovely two,
Lady Jehane, how could I help thinking of you?

To all but one of the many compliments evoked by this charming song de Mercadet seemed indifferent. Even to Jehane, who thanked him in words as pretty as the song, he seemed more concerned with some secret thought of his own than with the expression of hers, though that might have gratified any poet on earth with its politeness. But when Simon Vidal, his fellow troubadour, said with all the enthusiasm of his generous nature how greatly he admired the contrast between the level pacing of the verse rhythm and the urgent fire of the accompaniment, why then de Mercadet was roused, grew talkative, excited even, and played again to show how the heavy words reined back the sweet impatience of the melody. Talking still, of sirventes and tenson, of alba, serena, and planh, the two poets went off together, leaving their audience somewhat astonished and rather at a loss for further amusement.

But Jehane, sitting alone, was well pleased with de Mercadet's strange behaviour, for she thought it meant—despite his reputation for gallantry—that he was a poet enthusiastic only for his art, and so not likely to embarrass her with the attentions of a lover. For though she had resolved to fling propriety to the winds she found this to be more difficult than she had expected, and much less pleasant. Adventures even upon the outermost fringes of love's play made her strangely uncomfortable. Her daughter, a child some two or three years old, was a plain little girl with a strong resemblance to her father in her small blunt nose and square chin; and whenever a courtier became gallant Jehane would unfortunately remember the little Aélis and foolishly experience a sensation of guilt. Her belief that de Mercadet would be content to sing of love, without endeavouring to practise it, was therefore most comforting.

For some days his behaviour was all she could desire. His demeanour was that of a man ravaged by passion, his pale cheeks were apparently the emblem of a lover's pain, and his black hair suggested the ensign of a dying heart. But he appeared satisfied with the composition of several charming songs, ardent indeed, but with a kind of impersonal poetic ardour rather than a lover's heat; and in a tenson with Simon Vidal he raked the visible universe for symbols and similes with which to praise his mistress, but so contrived his flattery that it had an air of detached criticism wholly devoid of any insinuation that the flatterer might be entitled to a reward for his discernment.

So completely lulled were Jehane's suspicions that one evening, some weeks after de Mercadet's arrival at the castle, she walked with him alone in a garden by the river and watched with him the moon's image in the wrinkled water, and saw it run in silver slippers to the still obscurity of the farther bank. The air was full of summer perfumes. A nightingale sang, its voice choking with sweetness, and stopped on a broken note. Then de Mercadet turned to Jehane, and with a passion in his voice that he no longer troubled to conceal, sang softly:

Silent sits the nightingale
To hear the passion of my cry;
Paler grows the moon so pale
To see how pale am I—
Pity me, Lady Jehane,
Pity me, else I die!

Jehane was seriously perturbed by this sudden attack. She was immediately conscious of opposing forces that tore her soul, and between the soft importunacy of her senses—stirred by music, the scented night, and the pandering moon—and the strong restraint of her moral nature—aggravated by fear of her impetuous lover—she was in a truly pitiable state. Her heart was touched by desire but her knees were trembling in their fright before a lover. The fleering moon cried 'Yes!' but a memory of her snub-nosed daughter clutched her skirts and holloa'd 'No!'

With a plea for gentleness and a promise for tomorrow she won respite from de Mercadet, and returned to the castle in a greater flutter than she had known since, at the age of thirteen, her sleep was spoiled by a vision of St Michael bearing an outrageously destructive sword. Not till she was alone in her room did she remember, with a sense of anti-climax, her protective girdle and the key that hung round the lord of Caraman's neck in Acre or Cyprus or some such distant place.

Now de Mercadet laid siege in earnest, and as the constant state of excitement in which she lived notably increased Jehane's beauty, so the troubadour's ardour was maintained not only by resistance but by the steady growth of her charm. She also acquired, without knowing it, the pricking art of the coquette, and so for a week she would be coldly virtuous, for a day she would be fond and warm, kissing even, once even clinging and on the point, so it seemed, of yielding utterly. De Mercadet's manner was variable as hers, for in the morning he often behaved with the insolence of a dictator, and in the evening as frequently threw himself at Jehane's feet in the attitude of a slave. He made a certain number of songs in her honour, but it was generally remarked that they were far inferior to his earlier compositions. He added new verses to that which bore the refrain:

Pity me, Lady Jehane,
Pity me, else I die!

—and those best qualified to estimate the merit of such things declared that no part of it was worthy of a troubadour of his reputation. But if de

Mercadet's creative power declined, so did Jehane's critical ability, for in time she grew to think that refrain the most exquisite and moving verse she had ever heard.

It was on a day in autumn that de Mercadet drove her to her last defence, and she had to confess that she wore a chain binding her to impenetrable chastity. On other occasions when the troubadour's wooing pressed her hard she had sometimes conveniently forgotten the belt, sometimes most opportunely remembered it—but she had never mentioned it. It was her last rampart, her ultimate winning card, and now when de Mercadet had at last stormed all other opposition, and treachery in her own breast cried her to surrender, she told him, in a mood between triumph and despair, of the proscriptive chain, the inviolable lock.

For a little while de Mercadet was nonplussed. His attitude proclaimed defeat. He stood by an open window and let the wind blow coldly on his tears. Then, turning the situation upside down, he saw suddenly both comfort and hope in the steely prohibition of the Crusader's belt.

He cried excitedly, 'This, then, is the reason you have so long refused me! This paltry chain is the only bar to our felicity! I had thought you lacked love to meet my love, and that was why you turned from me so often and so coldly, and thinking that I came near to despair. But now I know that nothing but a few steel links have kept you from my arms . . . .'

'No, no!' cried Jehane.

'Now I am assured of that I grow happy indeed. For steel can be cut, links broken, or padlocks picked. I will get keys, Jehane, a sharp biting file, and loose you from these trifling shackles within the hour.'

Indignant and queenly tall, Jehane said furiously, 'Do you expect me to strip and stand naked while you do your tinkerwork? You are mad indeed if that is what you hope.'

'Then I will find a smith,' exclaimed the troubadour, 'some old and shrivelled smith, and pay him well for his work, and then put out his eyes for daring to see the glory of your waist.'

But Jehane grew angrier still and cried, 'Am I a horse that I should be taken to the smithy, or do you think me a monster that I should scratch men blind?'

De Mercadet had some difficulty in pacifying her, but presently she grew more calm, and then he left her, saying he would think of other means to get rid of the obstructive belt, and bade her be of good cheer in expectation of success.

The following day, when chance left them alone together, he said with great eagerness, 'Lady Jehane, the most difficult problems often have very simple answers. Now this is the truth, that you are the most beautiful woman I have ever seen, but you are far from being the slenderest.'

'So!' said Jehane, 'you call me fat now. Well, that is a change from your compliments.'

Patiently de Mercadet explained that he had said nothing of the sort. He had never mentioned fatness. 'Is Juno fat because her beauty is more amply drawn than Diana's?' he asked. 'Has not a flowing curve, an arc, more beauty than a poor straight line? What is there to see or commend in a green stick of girlhood? But every contour of your perfect womanhood is Cupid's bow bent to kill.'

'Is there any point to all this?' asked Jehane.

De Mercadet hesitated. 'It might be possible,' he said, 'to reduce the fullness of your beauty without impairing its essential quality. And if by chance you grew more slim—if Love's bow were here and there unbent . . . .'

'The chain would fall off as from a green stick of girlhood?'

De Mercadet bowed. 'Will you not spare a penny or two of your beauty's opulence to buy love itself?'

'And how am I to do that?' asked Jehane.

'There are various ways. Some strenuous exercise, for example . . .'

'What,' said Jehane, 'shall I kick and prance, turn flesh to dew, and wipe it off? You must think of some easier way than that, good Gilles.'

Again the troubadour spoke with a diffidence unusual in him. 'Hermits and other ascetic people grow thin by living on a meagre diet of roots and herbs.'

'So you would have me starve for love's sake?' said Jehane. 'But such a plan appeals to me no more than jumping does, and I shall neither run to make me lean as a hunting dog, nor starve to grow thin as an anchorite, since the sole benefit from either would be yours in possessing me.'

Because the Lady Jehane was in so difficult a mood de Mercadet made no attempt to expose the fallacy in her last statement, nor indeed to recommend further the courses he had already suggested. But with an air of melancholy arrogance he begged leave to go, and left her. Nor did he leave her for the moment only, but for a space of several days. Servants saw him in the early morning, when the river mist accentuated his pallor, as he walked solitary in the gardens; and in the evening twilight one might observe him by the edge of a wood, dark against its darkness, and staring into the sky as though impatient for the coming obscurity of night. But except for these crepuscular glimpses he was rarely visible, and he spoke to no one. The reason for his strange conduct was widely canvassed and gave ground for much conversation. The friends and servants of Lady Jehane were inclined to be proud of their supposition that she had broken his heart, for they would in a sense share in her prestige if this were so.

But Jehane herself was scarcely so happy. In de Mercadet's absence she felt more drawn to him than had been usual while he sat beside her, and she thought about love, even illicit love, with a broader mind when its exponent was no longer at hand to put her tolerance to the test. Since there was now no one to speak to her of love—for all others had retired before de Mercadet's wooing—she thought she would like to be loved. She remembered the troubadour's suggestion that she might grow slimmer, and so rid herself of the belt, by attention to her diet. She considered her image in several mirrors and discovered with some reluctance that her beauty might even be enhanced by judicious decrement of its superfluity. And so for an unhappy meal or two she pushed the cream-jug away from her, tortured her appetite with lettuce and a biscuit, and when her friends proffered sweetmeats turned with a shudder in the opposite direction.

This asceticism was of brief duration, however. Jehane's loss of appetite was reported in the kitchens, and her cook, a loyal and loving servant, set his mind to the confection of a pie that would restore her to health by its irresistible awakening of hunger. In this he most happily succeeded.

As ambergris will proclaim its virtue from afar, so did the pie. An odour of richness came out of it, not in a great vulgar gust, but in subtle streams and airs that took the nose with sweetness and brought moisture to the tongue. When Lady Jehane smelt this enchanting smell her thought was, 'How poor and frail a thing is love compared with table joys!' The idea of starving herself for such a trifling pleasure as de Mercadet's embraces appeared, in view of this magnificent pie, so wild an absurdity that she laughed aloud, and covered the amazement that her laughter produced by calling to her sewer, 'Cut quickly, man! Must our hunger wait for your convenience?'

Thereupon he sewer invaded the pie with a great knife, and cutting a thick wedge of crumbling pastry discovered beneath it a store of larks, leverets, quails, pigeons and other small fowl. 'Love!' thought Lady Jehane scornfully as she filled her mouth with this succulent variety, 'what man's love is worth a lark and leveret pie?' And as she pushed her manchet of bread into the hot dark gravy she was vastly amused to think of anyone forsaking the joy of eating to take a lover or find beauty in slimness. 'Green sticks of girlhood!' she muttered. 'Boy,' she said to her page, 'bring me more pie!' And patted her plumpness with a sigh of content.

She was eating sugar plums when de Mercadet found her that afternoon. She felt a little pang of remorse when she saw how pale and handsome he was, but hardening her heart she said, 'Well, good Gilles, have you found new arguments to persuade me into starvation?'

But de Mercadet said eagerly, 'There will be no need of that now, I think, for I have thought of someone who may help us by simpler means.'

'Do not suggest a smithy again,' said Jehane.

'When I was in Perpignan I taught something of my art to young Charles de Gaucelm, in whose father's house I lived for a certain time. I taught him to make an alba, to hold his own in a tenson, and how to improve his playing on the lute. For this he was grateful, as you may well imagine, and since he was adored by all that household, all that household competed with him in gratitude and still would be willing to do much for me—It was none of their fault that I left Perpignan.—Now there is in the house an old nurse whose wisdom in leechcraft and skill in herbs are indeed remarkable. She was born in Brittany, and she learnt her secrets there. Among her most notable cures was that of a certain dowager countess whose breath grew insufficient on account of her fatness.'

'What has this to do with me?' said Jehane. 'I can breathe well enough.'

'The old nurse paid no attention to the countess's breath,' said de Mercadet, 'but she gave her a certain medicine which removed her fat.'

'Oh,' said Jehane.

'In three or four weeks the countess was slender as a girl, and this without inconvenience to herself.'

'She was not forbidden to eat?'

'Her appetite grew better and she ate more heartily every day,' said de Mercadet.

Jehane took another sugar plum. 'You are going to see the old woman, to buy her medicine?'

'It will be neither pleasant nor safe for me to return to Perpignan,' said de Mercadet, 'but I count it a small adventure when your love awaits for my return. Ah, Jehane, when your belt falls, how will our sadness fall! What joy will be loosed when your chain is loosed, and rapture, not steel, may gird you!'

Jehane said little to that. She was rather thoughtful, and as usual not quite sure where her thoughts tended. But she gave de Mercadet permission to leave the castle on his errand, and before he went kissed him on the mouth. The troubadour's soul was exalted by this warm and freely-given kiss, but in truth it meant little. It simply concealed the fact that she did not know what to say to him.

It was October when de Mercadet rode with his joglar from the castle of Caraman. Christmas came, and he did not return. Winter passed, and there was no news of him. Jehane thought less about him now, though with increasing frequency she thought about his errand, and the Breton medicine appeared infinitely desirable, for the coldness of winter had sharpened her appetite and the chain, in consequence, had grown somewhat tight about her waist. She desired most fervently to be rid of it, and that without any thought of love as a sequel to freedom.

Spring was ripening into summer before de Mercadet came back to Caraman. He rode in one evening, travel-stained and weary. But though the vagaries of the weather had taken the colour out of his clothes, they had put colour in his cheeks, and he looked both strong and well-contented with what he had done. He walked with a jaunty air and spoke in a ringing tone. Jehane grew uneasy when she saw his confidence, but very soon she asked if he had the medicine with him. 'And why have you been so long on your journey?' she said. 'Perpignan is not so far that a man needs half a year to go there and come back.'

De Mercadet laughed. 'I have the medicine,' he said, 'and I've been to Brittany for it. I lived there in a fisherman's house, breathing the smell of fish and living on haddock and black bread, till winter passed and the roads were fit to ride on again. Would you do so much for me, Madame Jehane? No? Wait till you have heard the songs I made riding south in the rain and sun to see you, and when you hear the least of them you will be fast in love and ready to say yes to anything I ask.'

'Let me see the medicine,' said Jehane.

'Hear my songs first,' said Gilles. And he sang, till midnight came, the loveliest songs he had ever made, and all the ladies were ready to die for him, and the gentlemen would not let him stop, and at every door were servants, hoarsely breathing, thrusting in their heads to hear this wealth of verse and melody. But Jehane, feeling the belt tight round her waist, thought crossly that he might have given her the medicine first.

She got it on the following day. 'What is it, and how is it made?' she asked.

'It is prepared from a certain kind of seaweed that grows in Brittany,' said Gilles. 'They burn it in pits on the shore, and from the ash it is possible to extract this medicine, though the secret is known to few. But the old nurse at Perpignan, whose own store had all been used, sent me to a sister who shares her cunning, and she gave me this flask.'

'It will do me no harm?' asked Jehane.

'None,' said Gilles.

Then Jehane took her first dose, and made a wry face after it, but filled her mouth with a sugar plum to take away the bitterness. In two weeks' time she was slimmer than she had been for months, and after another week the chain hung loosely down on her hips. She was greatly pleased by this, but less contented to observe de Mercadet's growing exultation, and to hear each evening a serena inspired by the pleasures which he anticipated with increasing confidence. She preferred his old mood of melancholy, and a year of continence had made her so used to it that she felt an extreme reluctance to bother herself with the untidiness of love, the heat and proximity of a lover.

The morning came when the diminished ambit of her hips was no more than an inch or two greater than the circumference of the confining belt. In great excitement she wriggled and twisted and thrust down the links. They were slow to overpass her hinder plumpness, but after some more squeezing, kneading, and pushing, they fell clear, with a rattle and chink, and lay loosely about her ankles. With a cry of delight Jehane leapt over them, threw out her arms, capered and bent and shook herself in the ecstasy of release. Truly light-hearted, she became almost light-headed with joy. She was sobered only by the obtrusive thought of her obligation to de Mercadet. She grew resentful then, to think that the perfection of her happiness should be so impaired. She sulked, she looked out of the window, frowning. She was, it happened, in the tower room where she had said good-bye to her husband. By leaning far out of the window—it was just broad enough to let her shoulders go through—she could almost see her image in the green moat beneath her. But she was not dressed for leaning out of windows, and hurriedly she withdrew her head.

There was a mirror in the room, and she saw that slimness truly suited her. She had not looked so lovely for years. She turned this way and that, and with shame for her meagre gratitude admitted what she owed to de Mercadet. He had restored her freedom and renewed her beauty. What a pity that he wanted a reward. And how deplorably his manner had changed from that attractive melancholy air. Ah, if only she desired to love! If love were not so rude and overwhelming!

And yet he deserved reward, and generosity would suit her best in bestowing it.

But he must give her time. He must be content with seeing her and singing to her. He must not be roughly importunate. She would talk to him and tell him so, and promise her love for some day next year, or the year after. She herself was not impatient for embraces, so why should he be in a hurry?

Having come to this decision Jehane dressed herself, called for a page, and bade him find the troubadour and request his presence in the tower room.

She awaited him calmly. But Gilles came in with exultant laughter, saw the discarded chain immediately, and bearing down her protesting hands caught her in his arms and hugged her with alarming vigour. He was in a rollicking mood and it seemed to Jehane as though he meant to claim his reward on the spot.

She was extremely irritated by his jocular manner, and repulsed him sharply. Had he wept, had he fallen to his knees, had he sought her with a melancholy hope and humble passion, it would have been easy to be kind—kind and yet firm. But that he should canvass her love with hilarity was abominable. 'Let go, Gilles! Take your hands away! Stand back from me!' she cried.

'Ah, little prude,' he said. 'Have I not waited long enough? What hinders now?'

'Don't come near me,' cried Jehane.

'Little prude!' he cried. 'Bed is the place for little prudes, and the place for me. Come, sweeting, to bed, to bed!'

Jehane was horrified. Hands out to ward him off, she backed away from him, round the room and round again, and Gilles followed close, laughing loudly, calling her miser's money, wild bees' honey, and little prude. Round the room they went again, but as Jehane re-passed the window she stopped suddenly with a cry different from her protesting cries. She forgot de Mercadet, she stood motionless, and stared in a white silence at what she saw. His exuberance dulled, de Mercadet came quietly behind her and looked over her shoulder. He saw two men crossing the river at the ford, a few hundred paces from the castle gates. One wore the white surcoat of the Temple, but the red cross on it was faded to a dull and lifeless hue. They drew nearer, and rode in across the lowered drawbridge. Jehane ran to the opposite window that looked into the courtyard. It filled with clamour as the horsemen rode in and were surrounded by twenty, thirty, forty people shouting and begging for news.

'Do you know these men?' asked Gilles.

'One is my husband's squire,' she said, and spoke in a queer breathless voice. They waited uncomfortably, saying nothing, and heard him climbing the tower stairs. He came in. He was a boy in years, but older than his years, brown-faced, and with a certain grimness stamped on his youth.

'Where is he, Piers?' asked Jehane. 'My lord, I mean. Your lord and mine, Piers?'

'Have courage, madame,' he answered. 'The Knights Templar never showed more gloriously. It was at Damietta. We were the first to attack and the last to retreat. But for us the Christian army had been destroyed.'

'He is dead?'

'Yes, madame.'

'Ah, God, God!' she cried, and for a little while stood blank of face while the grim young squire told his story. Then she said, 'Tell me again, for I did not hear you.

When he had told the whole tale again he fumbled in a pouch, found a key tied to a cord, and gave it to Jehane. 'My lord took that from his neck a little time before he died,' he said, 'and bade me bring it home to you.'

Jehane took the key and wept, wildly at first and with great sobs. The squire left her then, being given leave, and de Mercadet stood silent. But after a while he said softly, 'Love lives though many die.'

Jehane looked at the key. 'Go now' she said, 'and leave me alone. I must be alone,' she repeated, and thrust de Mercadet to the door.

'I also will say a prayer,' he said.

Jehane sat for a long time, holding the key in her hand, and many thoughts came into her head, but into her heart came slowly a feeling that, she was horrified to find, seemed very like relief. Shocked by this discovery she conjured up a picture of Bertran on their wedding day, another of Bertran bleeding to death at Damietta, and contrived to squeeze out a few more tears. But they came reluctantly. Only under the shock of foreign news, the sudden wound made by the word of death, had the fountain of misery truly opened, and now its small store was shed. For though she had loved Bertran once, her love had not flourished since he tried to make it prisoner and lock it up; and so she thought of his death coolly enough when the shock of its announcement had passed. But she did not like to admit this, even to herself, and preferred to think she was truly grief-stricken and most tragically bereaved. And now came creeping a cunning thought, a sly round-the-corner thought, that here, in new widowhood, was an excuse for getting rid of de Mercadet, 'How dare he talk of love at such a time as this,' she thought. 'Grief for poor Bertran is my only interest now, and little Aélis orphaned now!' She sniffed and sighed, and three small tears fell slowly. The key was pressed between her hands. 'To send it back was a kind and noble thought,' she cried, 'but how lonely and insecure it makes me feel to have it.' And then she thought, 'It is my duty to requite that last kindness, and if I sacrifice my liberty again it will be well requited—I can be as noble as you, Bertran—and also I should feel secure again, and Gilles can fret and plead as he pleases then. But that is not why I shall do it. I shall do it to show my grief for Bertran's death, and because I am widowed now, cut off from joy.—And Gilles can think what he likes.'

The next day de Mercadet came to talk with her in the room in the tower. She said, 'You have served me well in your love for me, Gilles, and I had not meant to leave you unrewarded. But now this news has come that drives love from my heart, and all joy from this castle, and our love is no longer possible. Bertran's death made it impossible, and I have made it doubly impossible.'

'What have you done?' he asked.

'My lord sent me a key to unlock the belt he clasped me with. As things have come about there was no need for that. And yet I have made use of the key.'

'You have put on the belt again?'

'I put it on again, and pulled it tight, and locked it,' said Jehane, 'and now I have no more need of the key.'

She went to that window that overlooked the moat, and threw it out. They heard the tiny splash it made as it struck the water.

'You did that because of the great love you had for your husband? You did it in sorrow, renouncing the joys of this world?' asked the troubadour.

'Yes,' said Jehane.

De Mercadet laughed. 'Little liar! Little prude!' he said. 'Yes, weep if you like, for your tears mean little enough to you and nothing at all to me. Yet I do not bear you ill will. Not now. Were I as other men I might, but I am not like other men. For I am a poet. Other men would complain at spending a barren year in your service, but my year has not been barren, for I have made some good songs. It often happens that the women for whom one writes the best poetry do least to deserve it—but what does that matter? The poems are there, and will serve to praise and thank less prudent ladies, whose kindness comes so quickly there is no time to write well in their honour. Were it not for prudes like you, little prude, the generous ones would scarce get a verse at all to praise their sweet lips and lovely eyes. This most wise thought came suddenly to me in the night—for I guessed what you might be doing—and so I bear you no ill will, for you have done me no wrong. But neither do I love you, Jehane. My love was put away in the cupboard for too long, and when you cracked it I found it was like a rotten nut. There was nothing in it, Jehane. So do not eat too much, for the old woman's medicine is done and I shall not be at your service another year to ride to Brittany.'

Having uttered this rude and abominable speech de Mercadet took leave of Jehane and went to his own chamber. With no sign of sorrow or distress he made speedy preparations for departure, and a little after noon rode out of the castle, singing as he went, to the scandalising and horror of all who heard him. Nor did Jehane ever see him again, though for the rest of that year he lived in the castle of Hauterive, that was no more than forty miles away. And there he sang again the songs he had made for Jehane, and had by them great honour, and also, it is said, the favour of the Lady Saill, who dwelt there.

And one day de Mercadet was talking to a soldier on guard at the gate when a bowman, a mercenary from Italy, came and asked if he could find employment there, for he had just been thrown out of the castle of Caraman for drunkenness—though he had not been so much drunk as smitten with a sudden fever, he explained. De Mercadet asked him what news he had from Caraman.

'The Lady Jehane has been out of sorts this last week or two,' said the archer. 'She is a lady who likes to eat well—and who shall blame her for that?—and now whenever she takes a heavy meal she experiences, it is said, a feeling of pressure round her middle. And for that reason she is looking somewhat unhappy. Nor is that all, for she says that she suffered a loss one day while walking by the moat. And the moat has been drained and everybody is paddling in the mud seeking what she let fall there.'

'And what was that?' asked de Mercadet.

'A key; a key tied to a piece of cord,' said the archer.

Wineland

ONE. THE FINDERS

THERE WAS A MAN called Bearne, who was more fond of his father than is commonly the case with young men. He sailed out of Norway one summer with the intention of spending the winter at home, in Iceland, but found when he came there that his father had gone to Greenland. Bearne at once said he would go there too, and made his crew agree to sail with him, though neither he nor any of his men had ever been in the Greenland sea. They ran into bad weather, fog and north winds, and were carried out of their course. They drifted about for many days, and were wholly lost. Then, far to the west, they saw land. It was new land, that no one had ever heard of before, and the men wanted to go ashore. But Bearne would not let them, saying he meant to go to Greenland and nowhere else. They saw more unknown land, and turned away from it. Then they had a favourable wind and ran eastwards, and came at last to the south part of Greenland, where Bearne spent the winter with his father as he had intended.

There was a lot of talk about his lack of interest in the new country he had found, and no one thought any the better of him for not having gone ashore to see what it was like and what people lived there. The unknown land was much spoken of, and many thought hopefully of sailing westwards to seek it out either for gain or to show themselves men of mark. But the Norsemen who were settled in Greenland were few in number and not great in wealth, nor were there many ships there large or seaworthy enough to make the voyage, so for some time nothing was done, though the talking went on.

But Eric the Red, who was the man of most note in Greenland, had a son called Leif, who was afterwards called Leif the Lucky. He was a tall man, stronger than others, but gentle in his behaviour, wise in counsel and noble in appearance. He went to see Bearne and asked if he would sell him his ship. Bearne said he would if he got a proper price, and Leif did not haggle with him. Then Leif gathered a crew and chose good handy men, well used to seafaring, though not famous for weapon-skill or great deeds. They were thirty-five in number.

There was a southern man called Dirk, who had been for many

years with Eric the Red, and had fostered Leif. He was too old for such a voyage, but he was so fond of Leif that he would not willingly let him go out of his sight, and he had grown tired of living in Greenland. He told Leif, 'I am coming with you on this voyage, and that for two reasons. You're not to be trusted by yourself, and I'm not going to put up with living in this dreary country any longer. There's nothing here but the sea at your doorstep and snow-mountains over your roof. There's neither wood nor warmth in the whole land, and before I die I want to see something better than fields not big enough to patch my breeches and trees not thick enough to shelter me when I take them down. In my own country there is everything a man needs to make him happy, and why I ever left I can't think, except that I was young at the time, and being young was a fool. But that's an old story now, and what I want to say is that no land can be worse to live in than Greenland—my belly is dried up with eating salt fish and bad cheese, and I would give all I own for a horn or two of wine—so I am coming with you, to look after you and because these new lands, if we ever get to them, cannot fail to be better than this.'

Leif let him have his way, and Dirk gathered his goods together and brought them on board. He was a High German from the Rhine, and while he had been in Iceland with Eric he had grumbled a good deal about the poorness of life there. But when Eric went to Greenland Dirk grumbled more and more, because barley would not grow there, and the cattle were thin, and there was nothing to drink. On the Rhine, said Dirk, every man had his own vineyard, and made his own wine and plenty of it. 'And we drank it too,' he would say, 'and that was a proper return for our labour. But here a man might as well be a horse for all the good he gets out of his work.'

Now Leif got his ship ready, and put to sea when they were bound, and had good weather. They first found the land that Bearne had found last, an island with high mountains and snowfields on them, and went ashore there. But they did not stay long, for it was barren. Leif called it Slate-land.

They set sail again, and came next to low-lying country, with bushes growing, and long white beaches. Leif called it Markland, but said they must go farther yet. So they put to sea again, with a strong north-east wind behind them, and after some days they saw land, and to the north of it an island. They went ashore there, and looked about them. The weather was fine, and there was dew on the grass. They put their hands to the dew and tasted it, and it was sweeter than they had ever tasted before.

Now they sailed a little south of the island, and rounding a ness they came into a firth, and ran aground there. They were so eager to go ashore that they did not wait for the tide to turn and float the ship, but put off in their small boat. Then they came back, at high water, and towed the ship into the river, and up the river to a lake, and anchored it there. They took their hammocks out, and slept ashore. It was a good land they had come to, green to the eye, and warm and comfortable.

They made up their minds to spend the winter there, and built a large house with a stockade round it. There was self-sown wheat, and such good pasture that cattle might graze all through the year. There were tall trees, and salmon in the river and the lake bigger than they had ever seen before. The day and the night were more equal than in Greenland.

When they had closed the house all round with a stockade, Leif said to his crew, 'Now I am going to divide you into two watches, one to stay at home, and the other to search out the land and see what it holds. The homeward watch will fish or do work within the stockade, and the outward watch will go as far as they can by daylight, now in one direction, now in another. But the outward watch must be home before darkness, and they must keep together.'

The watches were chosen, and the work began of exploring all the country near by. But one evening the outward watch came home, and there was a man missing. This was Dirk, the Rhinelander. Leif was more angry than any had seen him before, and spoke so harshly to his crew that they were taken aback, for he had always been mild in his ways, though firm enough when it was needed. But Dirk, he said, had been his foster-father, and he valued him more than any man there. He was moreover so clever with his hands, and skilled in all kinds of wood work, that he had been the most useful of them all in building the house and the stockade. So Leif said they must go and look for him, though darkness had fallen, and he took twelve men and set out from the house.

But a little way from the stockade they saw Dirk walking towards them, and Leif shouted to him gladly. But Dirk did not reply, though he was muttering to himself and laughing. They took him into the house, and torches were lighted, but still he would not speak in any tongue they could understand.

Now Dirk was a little man, rather miserable to look at, with a very small narrow face and big rolling eyes. Leif said to him, 'Why are you so late, and how did you get left behind by the rest of the men?'

Dirk laughed, and mopped his face with his hands, for he was sweating. His eyes were rolling this way and that, and he was talking very quickly in High Dutch. But no one understood him. Leif said again, 'Why are you so late, and where have you been?'

Dirk rolled his eyes, and made faces, and spoke more quickly than before, but still in Dutch. Then he stopped short, and rubbed his face, for he could not think of the proper words. But at last he spoke in the Northern tongue.

'Vines,' he shouted. 'I went a little farther and I found vines and grapes, I tell you!'

He tore open the front of his shirt and pulled out little bunches of grapes. He had filled his shirt with them, and many had been crushed, so his belly was stained red with their juice.

'Now we can make wine,' he said, 'as we used to in the Rhineland. O Leif, my son, this is a fine place you have brought us to!'

TWO. THE SETTLERS

Early in the next year Leif made ready for sea and sailed out of Wineland, as they now called it, to go home. Off the south-west coast of Greenland he rescued, from a ship that had gone ashore on a reef there, a man called Thore and Gudrid his wife. Thore died soon after they came to Greenland, but Gudrid stayed with Eric the Red at Brentlithe. Eric had three sons, the eldest of whom was Leif, and a daughter called Freydis.

Thorwald, his second son, made a voyage to Wineland. He went farther north than Leif had been, and was killed by Eskimos, whom the Norsemen called Scraelings. Then Thorstan, Eric's third son, set out. He had married Gudrid, Thore's widow, and took her with him.

But they did not get far, for they were wrecked on the west shore of Greenland and spent the winter there. There was sickness in that settlement, and Thorstan died of it. But Gudrid went back to Brentlithe.

The next summer a man called Thorfinn Carlsemne came out from Iceland. He was a trader, wealthy both in money and stock, and Eric asked him and his partner Snorre to spend the winter with him. He entertained them so lavishly that before Yule came there was a shortage of food in the house. But Thorfinn gave Eric all that he wanted of malt and meal, from the store he had brought in his ship, and the Yule feast was made with great splendour.

Now Thorfinn was much taken with Gudrid, for she was the handsomest of women, and she knew how to behave well with strangers. But when Thorfinn asked her to marry him she said that Eric must decide that. So Thorfinn took his suit to him, and Eric heard it favourably and said, 'It seems likely she will only be following her fate if she marries you.'—For prophecies had been made about Gudrid, that she would not marry another Greenlander, that she would be wealthy and travel far.—So the match was made and the Yule feast was lengthened and became a bridal feast.

There was always a lot of talk going on about Wineland, and now it came to be thought that Thorfinn was the proper man to take command of a voyage there, since Leif was married and settled down, and his wife was unwilling for him to leave home. But Thorfinn was wealthy, he had a good ship and a good crew, and he seemed the man to lead an expedition. Many pressed him to make the voyage, and Gudrid was always urgent that he should go and take her with him. So when spring came he and his partner Snorre fitted out their ship, a second ship was made ready, and then Freydis, Eric's daughter, said that she and her husband were also going.

Freydis was a big woman, as tall as her brother Leif, and forbidding to look at. She had a violent temper, and little control of it, and she was ruthless when she could not get what she wanted. Her husband's name was Thorward. She had married him for his money, for he was base-born though rich, and a man of no account except for his wealth.

The three ships left Brentlithe together, Thorfinn and Gudrid in one, Freydis and her husband in another, and the third belonged to two brothers called Helge and Finbow. There were about thirty men in each ship, and five other women besides Freydis and Gudrid. They took cattle with them, and goods of every kind to make a new colony. Two days out from Greenland they ran into fog, and Thorfinn's ship was separated from the others. He held his course, and the landfall he made was an island in a broad firth, where the seabirds laid so thickly that a man could not walk without treading on their eggs. Thorfinn sailed far up the firth and unloaded his cargo and settled down for the winter. But this place was well to the north of Leif's settlement.

The other ships came to the house that Leif had built, and Freydis and her crew were the first ashore. When Finbow and Helge followed they found she had taken all her goods into the house, and left no room for them, though they had all agreed to share alike and have equal rights and profit in what they found. But now Freydis said that she had the greatest right to the house, since it had belonged to Leif her brother, and the others could build one of their own. So they had no sooner landed than there was ill-feeling between them.

Thorfinn and Gudrid and their crew had a hard winter. They had cut no hay for the cattle they brought, and both hunting and fishing failed them. They killed a whale that came ashore in the firth, and cut it up and boiled the pieces, but they were all sickened by it. Then the weather changed, and they got fair winds for fishing, in time to save them from hunger. Gudrid bore a child there, and he was the first of the Greenland people to be born in Wineland.

In spring they loaded the ship again and sailed southwards, and came to the other settlement. Freydis was living in the house that Leif had built. She said, 'Now there will be trouble when so many people come to live in the same place.'

Thorfinn and Gudrid thought they would share Leif's house with her, but Freydis said, 'There is no room for all of us, and Thorward will show you a good place to build a house of your own.'

Her husband grinned and scratched his head, but said nothing. Gudrid said, 'It was our agreement, before we came here, that we would share everything alike.'

Freydis said hardily, 'It takes two to make an agreement, but one can break it.'

'It is foolish to offend those for whom good luck is foretold,' said Gudrid. She never forgot that wealth and a high position had been promised her, and it was thought she spoke of this prophecy too often. Her voice, when she talked about it, was always calm and her manner a little proud.

Freydis grew angry. 'Better bad luck of my own than a share in your good luck,' she said, 'and better bad luck than a bad neighbour.'

Then she went indoors, and Thorward took Thorfinn and Gudrid to show them where they might build their house. But till it was built they had to sleep in their hammocks.

There was no fault to be found with the country they had come to. Self-sown wheat grew in the hollow land, and on the hill-slopes there were vines. Every brook was full of fishes, and when they dug trenches down to the sea, the flood-tide filled them with sea-fish. There were deer in the woods, and abundant pasture for their cattle. But there was little friendship or good-will among the settlers, for Gudrid thought that she and Thorfinn should hold the first place in people's esteem, but Freydis mocked her and made mischief with everything she said. There was also much jealousy of those men who had brought their wives with them, and the married men were none too easy in their minds about what was going on.

Early one morning some of Thorfinn's crew saw nine hide-boats with men in them. They took a white shield as a token of peace and rowed towards them. The men in the hide-boats were small and ill-favoured, their hair grew long and ugly, they had big eyes and broad flat cheeks. These were the Scraelings. They were very astonished to see Thorfinn's people, but they waited till the Norsemen came near. Then they turned and rowed away down the firth.

No more Scraelings were seen till that winter was over. Then one morning a great fleet of hide-boats came up the firth, so many that the whole breadth of it was covered, and the Scraelings came ashore with bundles of pelts, and fine grey furs, and wanted to sell them. So the Norsemen set up a market, and what the Scraelings chiefly wanted to buy was red cloth and weapons. But Thorfinn would not let them have either swords or spears, and when the red cloth was nearly done he cut it into finger-breadths, and the Scraelings gave as many skins for a finger-breadth as they had for a large piece of it.

While the market was still going on, one of the Scraelings picked up an axe and ran away with it. But some of Helge's men saw him and followed, and killed him. Then the Scraelings all drew together, and howled at the Norsemen, and shook their weapons, which were jointed sticks like flails. But before there was any fighting Thorfinn's bull came out of a thicket, and pawed the ground, and bellowed loudly. Then the Scraelings took fright, and ran to their boats, and rowed away.

But three weeks later they came back, a whole multitude of them, and the Norsemen met them some way down the firth. The Scraelings had war-slings, and hailed stones on the Norsemen, who fell back before them till they came to their settlement, and there was hard fighting there. The Scraelings had an engine that threw stones as big as a sheep's stomach, and the Norsemen were getting the worst of the battle.

Then Freydis came out and taunted them. 'This is a pretty sight,' she shouted, 'to see fine fellows like you running away from a pack of dirty little runts! I'd do better myself if I had weapons!'

Freydis was pregnant, very near to her time, and slow on her feet. Some of the Scraelings made at her, and she could not get away from them. There was a dead man before her, Thorbrand Snorreson, with a slate-stone stuck fast in his forehead. Freydis bent and took up his sword, and made ready to defend herself. The Scraelings ran at her, and Freydis took her breasts out of her shift and slapped them with the sword and shouted. She was a big woman made bigger by her pregnancy. The Scraelings stopped short. Freydis slapped her sword on her huge breasts and roared again. Then the Scraelings took fright, the whole multitude of them, and ran without stopping to their boats and fled down the firth.

Thorfinn and the other men came up to Freydis and praised her greatly for her courage and gallant behaviour. But Gudrid said, and many heard her, that the Scraelings had previously been frightened of Thorfinn's bull. 'It is clear,' she said, 'that they are not used to cattle of any kind.'

THREE. WOMEN'S COUNSEL

The prophecy that was made of Gudrid's wealth came about in this way. When she and her second husband, Thorstan Ericsson, were wrecked in West Greenland, they went to live with a man called Thorstan the Black, and it was in his house that Thorstan Ericsson died. Thorstan the Black's wife had also died of the sickness that was there. Her body lay in the same room with Thorstan when he was dying, and it seemed to him as though she were trying to creep out from under the bedclothes and come on to his bed. He struck at her with an axe, and cried out to Thorstan the Black to come and take her body away.

Then Thorstan Ericsson died, and after he was dead he sat up and called for Gudrid to come to him. She went, though not willingly, and Thorstan said that he greatly wished to foretell her fate, so that she might bear his death more easily. She would marry an Icelander, he said, and settle down in Iceland. But first she would go south over sea, and she and her husband would live long together and prosper greatly. Their children would be a noble family, of good report, flourishing in all ways, but Gudrid would outlive her husband. And in her last days, said Thorstan, she would build a church, and take a nun's consecration, and die in holiness.

Now it seemed to Gudrid that if this prophecy were to come true, she and Thorfinn had better not stay too long in Wineland, for it was too dangerous. So she began to urge Thorfinn to gather his goods together, and sail for home.

Thorfinn was not willing to go so soon, and he prevailed on the others to join with him in sending out parties to explore some other parts of the land, to see if they might find a place that no Scraelings came to. Then they made coastwise voyages, both north and south, but wherever they went they saw hide-boats in the firths, or found other traces of the Scraelings. Then they came back and said the Scraelings had set spies on them, and would follow them no matter where they settled.

Gudrid talked more and more about going home, and Thorfinn began to listen to her. He was a good trader, a clever man, but not warlike in his ways, and he also had grown somewhat frightened.

But Freydis had no fear, and thought more of making mischief than of any danger. She had been told what Gudrid said of her after she had driven off the Scraelings in the battle at the market-place, and she was eager to score off her in some way. When she heard that Gudrid wanted to leave Wineland, she thought of a plan to stop her.

She woke early one morning, when winter was nearly over, and got out of bed and put on some clothes. She took her husband's cloak, and went out of doors. A heavy dew had fallen, and Freydis was barefooted. She went to the house that Finbow and Helge had built, and found the door ajar, for a man had gone out a little while before. She stood in the doorway, and Finbow, who slept farthest up the hall, woke and asked her what she wanted.

'I want you to get up and come out,' she said, 'for there is something that you and I should talk about.'

Finbow came out, and they went to a tree that grew against the hall, and sat on a bench beneath it.

'This is a good land,' said Freydis.

'It is fruitful, and I like it well enough,' said Finbow. 'But I don't like the ill-feeling that has grown among us here.'

'Gudrid is making that worse by her talk of going home, and so splitting our company.'

'That is true,' said Finbow, 'for if we were all friendly together, and made common cause, we would have nothing to fear from the Scraelings. But Thorfinn is a trader, and no fighter, while Gudrid has only one thought, and that is to get away from here.'

'Then let us put a stop to that,' said Freydis, 'by killing her and Thorfinn, and taking their ship for our own. It is bigger than yours and a better ship than mine, and would be useful to us both.'

But Finbow would not agree to that, so Freydis left him and went home in a great passion. She got into bed with cold feet, and so wakened Thorward. He asked why she was so cold and wet.

'I went to see Finbow and Helge,' she said, 'and asked them to sell me certain goods that we need. But they would not listen, and one struck me on the face. So now will you get up and avenge me, and kill Finbow for what he has done? For I tell you I so hate him that if you let him live I shall no longer live with you.'

It was always the way with Freydis that she would wholly lose her temper when she did not get what she wanted, and now she was mad with rage against Finbow because he would not help her take revenge on Gudrid. But Thorward was not to be moved, and turned away from her and made out that he was sleeping.

'It is easy to see I am not at home in Greenland, where you would be quick enough to avenge me, lest Eric and Leif should hear how chicken-hearted you were,' said Freydis bitterly.

Now it began to be spoken of that Freydis was plotting against Gudrid, and when Thorfinn heard that he called a meeting of all the men, and said, 'There has been ill-feeling and dissension among us ever since we came here, and now it seems too late to hope for betterment in our relations. There is moreover a constant danger from the Scraelings, who are too many for us, and so, though the land is fruitful and good, I have made up my mind to go home to Iceland. But if any of my own crew should wish to stay here, they can do so, and if any of the others want to come with me, who are free to come, I shall take as many as I have room for.'

Then there was much talk and argument, and the end of it was that Thorfinn and Gudrid set sail for Iceland, with some of Finbow's men as well as their own, and came there safely and settled in Rowanness. But the others stayed where they were, and all the married men stayed, for their wives were unwilling to make the voyage.

For a little while it seemed as though there was a better feeling among the settlers, but Freydis was nursing her grudge against Finbow and soon she began to spread lies about him and his brother Helge. She said they were making ready to go elsewhere in Wineland, and would betray them to the Scraelings. Then she hid certain jewels and loose goods, and said the brothers had stolen them. She worked on Thorward and his men for a long time, till they were ready to believe anything, and one night she said she had heard Finbow and Helge plotting to set fire to their house, that Leif had built. So the next morning they rose early, taking their weapons, and went to the brothers' hall and fell on the men there before they were awake. Finbow and some of his men fought well, but they had little chance, being naked, and they were all killed. Freydis herself killed the women who were there.

Now Thorward and those men who were left said they would stay in Wineland no longer, for clearly there was no luck there and no one cared to live beside the graves of so many men they had murdered. But Freydis said, 'If we go back to Greenland I shall be the death of anyone who tells what happened here. We can say that Helge and Finbow chose to stay in Wineland, and so we left them.'

They launched their ship, then, and loaded it and went aboard. They lay for a little while in the middle of the firth, and watched a party of Scraelings come into the settlement to see if anything had been left behind. One of the Scraelings, bigger than the rest, found an axe under Finbow's hall. He took it up and looked at it for a long time, for they had no steel and did not know what it was. He turned to a man who stood near and struck at him, and he fell down dead at once.

The big man looked at the axe again, staring awhile at it, and then he threw it into the sea as far as he could. After that the Scraelings left the settlement.

Freydis and the others came safely to Greenland, but though she gave handsome gifts to her crew, to make them hold their tongues, the story got about that she had murdered Helge and Finbow. Leif would not punish her as she deserved, because she was his sister, but she and her husband were avoided thereafter, and they did not thrive. As time went on they were considered good for nothing except what was bad.

The Abominable Imprecation

Unlike so many musicians, Perigot was handsome. His eyes were blue and his hair was black. A lock of it fell with engaging disorder over his broad forehead. Even while he played upon his pipe, his upper lip, pursed for its melodious task, retained a whimsical fascination, and when he put down his reed and yawned, he showed white teeth that looked the whiter for his brown skin, and the arms he stretched were long and muscular.

The river-nymph, Cleophantis, hiding in a clump of yellow irises, felt her natural shyness conquered by a much stronger force, and first cutting, with a silver sickle she carried, a few of the tall flowers to supplement her exiguous costume, emerged from her shelter and walked towards him. Her voice was a little uncertain with mingled excitement and shame, and as she spoke a blush played prettily on her pale cheeks.

'I don't want you to think that I am one of those impressionable creatures who lose their heads on every possible occasion,' she said, 'but really, I've never heard anything so lovely as that last little dancing tune. Of course it's impertinent of me to speak like this to an utter stranger, and quite unforgivable to ask him a favour, but you would make me so happy if you were to play it again!'

Perigot, at first, was amused rather than surprised by her appearance and ingenuous request; for his playing had often attracted, from their river-homes or dark-blossoming corners of the wood, nymphs and dryads whose fervent admiration of his skill upon the pipe had invariably been succeeded by a declaration of their tenderness towards himself. To begin with he had been flattered by their addresses, but after some dozen encounters he had discovered an unsubstantial airy monotony in their company. They were agreeable to look at, they pattered a few pretty sentences, but they had no personality and their charm was vapid and standardised; so Perigot had long since ceased to be impressed by the undines, sylphs, and hamadryads, errant glimpses of whom threw so many of his contemporaries, less gifted than himself, into a perfect fever of desire. Now, thinking that here was only another of that kind, he was not very interested by the nymph's appearance, but before she had finished speaking he perceived in her something different, a quality that made her far superior to the trivial sprites of his previous acquaintance, and hurriedly rising he led her, with pleasant words of welcome, to a cushion of comfortable green turf.

Putting down her silver sickle and discreetly arranging her bunch of flags and yellow irises, she smiled and said, 'My name is Cleophantis, and I am, so far as we know, the youngest daughter of the Moon King.'

Perigot played his dancing tune, and all the birds within hearing flew near to listen, while a brock came out of the wood with a small deer following it, and from the river-bank tumbled a sleek family of otters.

'That was beautiful,' said Cleophantis when he had finished. 'Oh, so beautiful! I could sit and listen to you for ever.'

Her voice and eyes, however, betrayed a regard for Perigot greater than that for his music, which Perigot quite clearly recognised; for though he was not conceited he was intelligent. Generally, when he noticed this transference of interest in his audience, he was displeased and bored, for he knew how readily a nymph was taken by mere outward appearance, and as an artist he was depressed to find that his music had never more than a minor appeal for women. But now he was delighted to see the brightness of Cleophantis's eyes, their bashful veiling by long lashes, and to note the tremor in her voice. He sat down beside her.

'Your father won't be up for hours yet,' he said, and kissed her with a warmth of which she, in the coolness of her river, had never dreamed.

She sprang from him, dropping her flags and flowers, red as a lily-pool at sunset, and Perigot, laughing and eager, pursued her. He caught her easily, but when he found her shyness was real, and not assumed, he became gentle and courteous with her, though her beauty, of which he became ever more sensible, constantly tempted him into little sallies of ardour. These Cleophantis rebuked with increasing distress, for she had fallen deeply in love with the handsome shepherd, and only her early training in the chaste schoolroom of the osier beds prevented her from yielding to the persuasion which intermittently escaped his disciplined politeness. At last she said she would have to go, and nothing Perigot could say would make her tarry longer, for she was afraid of the awful lengths to which love might lead her.

'But you will come back?' said Perigot, pleading.

'Perhaps,' said Cleophantis, and meant, 'You know I will!'

'And you will not always keep me at arm's length, or even a finger-breadth away?'

'I am going to speak to my elder sister about you,' answered Cleophantis, and though Perigot groaned, for he thought this was an ill omen for love, Cleophantis continued, 'She is extraordinarily wise, and I have the greatest respect for her opinion. It is true that she has never had a lover, but in spite of that she is very broadminded. Oh, Perigot, if she says we are right to love, how happy I shall be!'

'You will come tomorrow?' said Perigot.

'At noon,' said Cleophantis, 'and for a pledge that I shall return, keep this sickle. Its blade is silver from the Mountains of the Moon, forged with the last heat of the moon, and tempered in its coldest stream. No man or beast can resist its edge, and the handle is an emerald that will keep its owner always in health.'

While Perigot was examining the sickle, Cleophantis, fearing her resolution would fail, ran to the edge of the nearby stream. She stood for a moment on the bank, looked back, and whispered 'Perigot, my heart!' But Perigot's head was still bent over the flashing blade, and so she stepped unseen into the welcoming river. When Perigot looked up she had gone.

The sun was low and he realised that it was time to go home, so he whistled to the sheep-dogs that were lying far afield, guarding the fringes of the flock, and they gathered the sheep before them while Perigot, thrusting the sickle under his belt, played on his pipe the merriest song the meadows had ever heard, and strode briskly towards the hill on the far side of which stood his father's house. It seemed to him that the quicker he walked the sooner tomorrow would come, and with it Cleophantis—if her sister let her; and his tune grew so glad and so exciting that the lambs capered madly, and the old ewes were puzzled, and the half-grown rams leapt like mountain goats as they followed him over the hill.

Perigot's mother sighed when he came in to supper, for she at once perceived he was in love again, and she was always nervous when her sons were in that state of mind; but his father, a heartless and wealthy man who owned several thousand sheep, two rich valleys, and much hill-land, asked in a gruff voice if the flock was safe, and finding it was, told Perigot to keep quiet while he ate, for only children or idiots, he said, must sing with their mouths full of porridge.

In the morning Perigot rose early and was about to lead his flock back to the river-pasture when a man who looked like a Saracen or an Indian, and who had been lounging by the sheep-fold, stopped him and said, 'I've heard tell you know a good fighting-cock when you see one, sir?'

Now Perigot was a sportsman, and though till that moment his thoughts had all been of Cleophantis, as soon as the Indian spoke of fighting-cocks a picture rushed into his mind of brave birds tussling in the air—bronze feathers gleaming, spurs clashing—and eagerly he asked, 'Have you any to sell or match with mine?'

'Better birds than any in your country,' said the Indian.

'I doubt that,' answered Perigot, 'but I'll have a look at them.' And he called Thenot, his younger brother, a freckled boy with a snub nose, and told him to take the sheep to the river-field, and he would follow by and by.

So fine were the Indian's birds, and such a heroic main was fought, that the sun was overhead before Perigot remembered his tryst with Cleophantis. Then, in a kind of panic, he threw some silver coins to the Indian and began to run, as fast as he could, up the steep path that led over the hill to the riverside grazing. He knew that he would be late, and though he tried to comfort himself with the thought that a little waiting never did any girl harm, he could not convince himself, for Cleophantis was the Moon King's daughter, and very different from any other nymph or forest-girl he had ever seen.

It was a full hour past noon when he reached the flock, and immediately his young brother called to him in a strange sobbing voice. Thenot's freckled face was tear-stained, and in great distress he gasped, 'She's dead, Perigot, she's dead! Oh, why didn't you come in time? She waited for you a little while, walking to and fro, and then she sat down, for she felt weak, and still you did not come, and presently she fainted. I rubbed her hands, but they were so delicate I could not rub them hard. Once she opened her eyes and asked, "Do you see him coming?" And then she said, "My heart is breaking", and she died. Oh, Perigot, she was lovely! Why did you not come in time?'

Perigot, numb with remorse, looked down at her where she lay like a plucked lily on the grass. He could not speak, and his brain was too cold even to frame a proper thought. He just stood and looked at her, and knew that he had never seen such loveliness alive. Suddenly Thenot gave a frightened cry and ran away. Perigot looked up and saw, coming to him from the stream, a tall and dreadful nymph with a black river-squall blowing about her, bending the grass and flowers and chilling the summer air.

'Murderer!' she said. 'Killer of my sister!' She raised a wet arm round which a water-snake was twisted. The river-squall howled at her back, and Perigot, shivering with cold, fell to his knees beside the dead girl.

'I never dreamt that such a thing could happen,' he cried. 'Truly I loved her, and truly I hurried to be in time!'

'Murderer and liar!' said the elder sister in a terrible voice. 'An unkind thought could bruise her skin, you must have known that such neglect as yours would kill her. But I'm not easily hurt, and I'm not easily swayed by a handsome face and soft words. Be quiet, murderer, and hear your punishment. Oh, my sister, he who killed you will suffer more than you and ten thousand times as long!'

For a moment the squall was silent, and the dreadful nymph, whose face seemed to Perigot like broken water in its darkness, said in a clear hard voice, 'The curse of Shepherd Alken be on you!'

Then the storm howled again, and under its wings the nymph took up her dead sister and carried her, over the broken flowers and bent grasses, back to the dark and sullen stream.

For more than a week Perigot lived in utter misery. His pipe was silent and his flock untended. Wolves stole a lamb or two, and he never heard the woeful bleating of the ewes. But his father, counting the sheep and finding several missing, rated his son with harsh and brutal words.

'You're the fool of the family,' he shouted. 'You've wasted your time cock-fighting and playing that idiot pipe of yours, and now you blubber for a week because a worthless undine jilts you. I'm ashamed and sick of the sight of you!'

'Then let me go away from here,' said Perigot. 'I'm tired of keeping your silly sheep. I must do something braver than that, something dangerous and great, to justify my wretched life and perhaps forget, in peril of my own death, the death of Cleophantis.'

'H'mph!' said his father. 'If you mean what you say—but I doubt it—you'd better go to Gargaphie. The King's in a pretty pickle, and shouting east and west for help.'

'No, no!' cried Perigot's mother, 'not there, he'd be killed as all the other young men have been killed, and to no purpose at all. You mustn't go there, Perigot!'

'Tell me what is happening in Gargaphie,' said Perigot.

'Oh, the usual thing,' said his father, that heartless man. 'A dragon has gone off with the King's daughter, and killed a dozen young fools who've tried to rescue her. Do you fancy dragon-baiting? She's a well-made girl, I believe, and I suppose you could marry her if you got her away. That's the orthodox reward, isn't it?'

'I shall never marry,' said Perigot bitterly. But the thought of so desperate an adventure made him resolute to go to Gargaphie, and when he remembered the sickle that Cleophantis had given him he felt confident of his ability to slay the monster who had stolen the

King's daughter; though so far he had never seen a dragon and had only a very vague idea of what one looked like.

His mother wept when he told her of his determination, but finding his intention fixed she made such preparation for his journey as seemed suitable. Perigot polished his magic sickle with a woollen cloth and felt happier than he had been since Cleophantis died. Only the memory of her sister's curse hung like a little cloud over his mind. He had told no one about it. He had, indeed, tried to forget it, and in his preoccupation with grief almost succeeded. But now, for the first time admitting his anxiety, he thought it advisable to discover all he could about the malediction with which he had been saddled.

His old nurse Dorcas was an aged woman with a great reputation for wisdom, and Perigot, on the evening before his journey to Gargaphie, went to the fireside-corner where she sat spinning, and said in a conversational way, 'Tell me, Dorcas, have you ever heard of a shepherd called Alken?'

'Indeed and I have, Master Perigot,' she answered, very glad of the opportunity to talk and show off her knowledge. 'And a wicked old man he was, and hated everybody, and what with sitting by himself for days on end, and talking to serpents and owls and mandrakes, he invented the most horrible curse in the world, partly to punish his poor wife, who was almost as nasty as he was, and partly out of pure spite against all humanity.'

'What was the curse?' asked Perigot.

'Well, it was like this,' said Dorcas, putting aside her wheel and sucking her old gums. 'Shepherd Alken used to think a lot about the misery of his life, and indeed he'd hardships enough, what with sitting all day in the hot sun, and little to drink, while he watched his sheep; and lambing them while the snow was on the ground, and that's hard work; and always the danger of wolves; and knowing he'd be poor to the end of his days. But all he thought about his misery was little to what his wife said about hers, for she'd had eleven children, and those who didn't die brought shame and disgrace to her; and to keep her house clean was heart-breaking, for the fire smoked and the roof leaked and the hens came in through the broken door, so to tell the truth she had something to talk about. But the shepherd hated her for it, and thought his own life was far, far worse. So he made up a curse that turned her into a man, and he sent her out to keep the sheep while he sat at home. And he had the satisfaction of hearing her grumble louder than ever, for she could stand neither the heat nor the cold, and she was terribly frightened of wolves. But though it pleased him to hear her complaining so, he wasn't comfortable at all, for there was no one to cook his supper, and the hens made the floor like a midden, and if there was no smoke in the house that was because the fire was always out. So he thought he would use another kind of curse on himself, and turn himself into a woman, and then housework would come easy and natural to him. Well, he spoke the words, and the very next morning he was a woman. But somehow he didn't like it, and every day he liked it less, and when, old though he was, he found himself in the family way, as they call it, he nearly went off his head altogether. So it seemed to him that if there was one thing harder than being a man it was being a woman; and the way his wife grumbled showed him that the only thing worse than a woman's life was a man's life. And then he thought that if he could put two curses into one handy-like little sentence he could do a lot of harm in the world with it, and that's what he wanted. Well, he talked to his friends the Owl and the Serpent and the Mandrake, and they helped him, and by and by he had it, and the first use he made of it was in his own house, and he and his wife changed places once again, and she bore her twelfth child and died of it. But the curse became famous, and wicked folk who know the way of it use it a lot, just saying "The curse of Shepherd Alken be on you", and that signifies "If you're a man, become a woman. If you're a woman, become a man". And that's enough to spread misery wherever it goes, as you'll learn, Master Perigot, when you're a little older—though there's nothing but good fortune I wish you, as you know.'

Perigot listened to this story with growing consternation, for he remembered that lately his voice had assumed, once or twice, a curious treble tone, and before he went to bed that night he examined himself anxiously to see if there were any further signs that the malediction was working. He discovered nothing, however, except a little plumpness about his chest, and even that he was not very sure of. The next morning he set off for Gargaphie.

He travelled for a week, and came by degrees to country more mountainous and savage than any he had seen before. In Gargaphie itself there were everywhere signs of grief and mourning faces, for the Princess Amoret had been popular as well as beautiful, and the thought of her durance in the dragon's cave caused great distress to young and old. As soon as Perigot made known his mission he was taken to the King, whose gloom visibly lightened when he heard Perigot's stout assertion of his intention to slay the monster and rescue its poor prisoner. But he was a fair-minded man, and he thought it his duty to warn Perigot of the danger he was about to face.

'That wretched dragon has already killed twelve brave young men, all apt in war,' he said.

'I am not afraid,' answered Perigot, and the King, seeing his bold attitude, his broad shoulders, and the stern light in his blue eyes, felt there was at least a possibility of his success.

'I have promised my daughter's hand to her rescuer,' he said, 'and though of course I speak with a father's partiality, I think I may say without fear of contradiction that she is the most beautiful girl in all Gargaphie.'

'I shall never marry,' said Perigot in a grim way, 'and I undertake this adventure without any hope of personal gain.'

'I can show you a picture of her, if you don't believe me,' said the King, a little testily; but the Queen interrupted him, and said to Perigot, 'Your attitude, sir, is a noble example to us all', while to the King she whispered rapidly, 'Don't argue! Can't you see that he has had an unfortunate love affair, and will fight all the better for it, being careless of his life?' So the King, who appreciated his wife's good sense, said nothing more except to call very loudly for dinner, which had been put back because of Perigot's arrival.

In the morning the King and his courtiers led Perigot to a high rock from which he could see the dragon's den, and there they waited while he went forward alone, for such fear had the monster spread that none dared go within a mile of the waterfall behind which it lived. But Perigot, feeling perfectly confident, climbed down to the torrent-bed, and thence by a narrow path got to the dragon's lair. Lightly he sprang to a rock that the waterfall sprinkled with its high white splashing, and there, first easing the sickle in his belt, he sat down and began to play upon his pipe. First, in a whimsical mood, he played a serenade, but that had no effect, so he began a little taunting air, full of gay defiance, with shrill notes in it that suggested a small boy being impudent to his elder brother. And presently, through the rushing veil of the waterfall, Perigot saw two huge and shining eyes.

The dragon poked its head out, and when it snorted the waterfall divided and was blown to left and right in large white fans of mist. Perigot now played an inviting tune called *Tumble in the Hay*, and the dragon, amazed by his fearlessness and somewhat attracted by the melody, pushed farther through the waterfall, that now spread like a snowy cape about its shoulders. Its colour was a changing green, on which the sun glittered wildly, and its eyes were like enormous emeralds. Perigot was dazzled by them, and had he not been aware how exceptionally well he was playing, he would have been frightened. As it was, he changed his tune again, with a flourish of sharp leaping notes, and what he played now was an irresistible ribald air called *Down, Wantons, Down.*

The dragon, surprised, then tickled, then captured by delight, opened its enormous mouth and roared with joy. It plunged into the pool in front of the waterfall, and Perigot was soaked to the skin with the splash it made. But he continued to play, and the dragon rolled and floundered in its bath, and what with the sunlight on the waterfall, and the sun shining on its glimmering hide, it seemed as though someone were throwing great handfuls of diamonds, emeralds, and opals into the pool.

Perigot finished the ribald song and slid cunningly into a tune so honey-sweet, so whispering of drowsy passion, that one thought of nightingales, and white roses heavy with dew, and young love breathless and faint for love. The dragon stopped its whale-like gambols, and sighed luxuriously. It rolled over on to its back, and a dreamy look clouded its emerald eyes. It sighed again, like far-off thunder, and came closer to the rock on which Perigot sat. His pipe sang more sweetly still. A kind of foolish smile twisted the dragon's horrible mouth, and its eyes half-closed. Its head was touching the rock.

Sudden as lightning Perigot drew his moon-made sickle, and slashed fiercely at the monster's thick green throat. The blade went through its tough hide, through muscle and bone, as easily as an ordinary sickle goes through grass; and torrents of black blood stained the pool that the dragon's death-struggle made stormier than a tempest-twisted sea. When the headless body at last was still, and blackness lay like a film on the water, Perigot, first cleaning his sickle, climbed by a way he had discovered through the waterfall and into the cave behind it. There he found the Princess Amoret, tied to a rock but apparently unharmed.

He cut her loose and helped her out of the greenish cave that was full of the noise of falling water. She looked at the dead monster, turned away with a shudder, and still for a minute or two did not speak.

Then she said, 'How can I express my gratitude? For words are such little things, mere symbols of conventional emotion that time has defaced. I need new words to thank you, but, alas, I am not a poet and can make none. You are an artist, though—I heard your music—and know how I feel.'

'I am only too happy to have been of service to you,' said Perigot a little stiffly.

The Princess suddenly knelt and embraced his knees. 'You have rid me of the most horrible fear in the world,' she said, and when she looked up her eyes were clouded with tears, and her face was radiant with happiness because her life had been saved, and because her rescuer was so handsome, and so gifted a musician.

The path was narrow, and as the Princess was weary from long restraint, and as Perigot found that he could talk to her more easily and with more pleasure than to any girl he had ever met before, they took a long time to return to the rock on which the King and his courtiers waited so anxiously—for at that great distance they had been unable to perceive how the battle went. The King's joy at seeing his daughter again was overwhelming, but when he had satisfied himself that she was unhurt, and embraced her a score of times, and blessed all heaven for her deliverance, he remembered the necessity of thanking her rescuer, and did so very heartily.

'And you thought you wouldn't want to marry her, eh?' he said. 'Well, haven't you changed your mind by this time?'

As it happened, Perigot had; and no one who realised the excitement of his battle with the dragon, or observed the beauty of Princess Amoret, accused him of undue fickleness for so quickly forgetting his determination to respect in lifelong celibacy the memory of poor Cleophantis. Nor was he embarrassed by the reminder of what he had said, on the previous evening, about his views on marriage. He merely remarked with some dignity, 'I had no wish to force my attentions on the Princess until I had ascertained the possibility of their welcome.'

The courtiers were all impressed by this evidence of a noble temper, and Amoret immediately cried, 'Father, let there be no hesitation or pretence about this. We love each other, and we were made for each other!'

'That's the way to speak!' said the King. 'There's nothing like honesty, and we'll have a wedding after all. I like weddings.'

The Queen, a tolerant and kindly woman, was made so happy by Amoret's return that she hardly cared whom her daughter married, if the match were dictated by love; and thereupon the King, in great spirits, declared that Perigot should wed her that night—'If it's quite convenient for you, my dear?' he added.

'Quite convenient,' said Amoret, 'and, indeed, just what I wish myself.'

Preparations for a feast were speedily made, and with much ceremony the marriage took place. At a late hour Perigot and his bride retired to their chamber.

For an hour or two Perigot had been feeling his clothes uncommonly tight about his chest and hips, but he imagined the discomfort was due to somewhat excessive eating and drinking. When he undressed, however, he discovered to his horror that the nymph's curse had taken effect, and he had become, for all practical purposes, a woman.

The shock almost unnerved him, but with a great effort he retained his self-control. His predicament was appalling. Not only was he madly in love with Amoret, but Amoret was madly in love with him. She approached him with endearing words, and when Perigot offered her a slight and distant embrace, which was all he dared to offer for fear of revealing his shameful secret, she accepted it with really pitiful disappointment. He stood for a long time looking out of the window, while Amoret sat on the edge of her bed and wondered why Perigot had turned so cold or if this was all that marriage meant. She could not believe that its mystery cloaked precisely nothing.

After an agonised vigil of the dark sky, Perigot remembered his pipe. He took it from the chimney-piece where he had laid it, and played a gentle phrase or two.

'You must be tired, my dear,' he said. 'Let me play you to sleep.'

Amoret turned her face from him, and wept quietly into her pillow. In a little while, however, Perigot's sweet and mournful lullaby soothed her brain, and drove consciousness away, and presently she slept. Perigot lay awake till morning, so bitter were all his thoughts, and before the sun was up he dressed himself and went out, and left Amoret still dreaming.

The day was embarrassing to them both, for in Gargaphie weddings occasioned a certain jocularity that often made ordinary brides and bridegrooms feel uncomfortable. But no wedded couple had ever been in the curious plight of Amoret and Perigot, and their distress at the customary witticisms was so marked as to make even the wits doubtful of their taste. And the day's embarrassments naturally increased as darkness fell, for Amoret was full of doubt and more affectionate than ever, and Perigot was doubly miserable. That night it took him at least an hour, and he needed every bit of his skill upon the pipe, to play his bride asleep.

This wretched state of affairs continued for several days, until the Queen, seeing how unhappy and even ill her daughter looked, talked seriously to her for a long time, and at last elicited some part of the facts.

'But my poor dear!' she said in amazement.

'I assure you that what I say is true,' sobbed Amoret. 'Every night he plays his pipe until I fall asleep. Sometimes I wonder if he is a man at all.'

'The King must be told immediately,' said the Queen with decision, and straightaway went to look for her husband, in spite of Amoret's protests, who still loved Perigot dearly and feared that her father would do him harm.

The King, though normally a genial man, lost his temper completely when he heard what the Queen had to say.

'I suspected something of the sort!' he roared. 'Did you hear his voice last night? Squeaking like a girl! The insolent impostor! I'll wring his neck with my own hands, I'll drop him over the battlements, I'll hound him out of Gargaphie!'

'There must be no scandal,' said the Queen, quietly but firmly. 'Not for Perigot's sake, but for Amoret's. The girl has suffered enough without being made the subject of national gossip. I admit it would be a good thing to get rid of Perigot, but it must be done discreetly. I'm sure that you can think of some clever plan to remove him quietly and without fear of unpleasant comment.'

'There's something in what you say,' admitted the King, 'and as for plans, my head is full of them. It always is, and that's why Gargaphie is a happy and prosperous country. Now what about sending Perigot off to retrieve the golden apples that my great-grandfather lost? He'd never come back from that errand alive.'

'You'll never persuade him to start on it,' objected the Queen.

'Nonsense,' said the King. 'All that's needed is a little tact and diplomacy. Just you see.'

As soon as the Queen had gone he sent his personal herald to look for Perigot, and when the young man appeared, greeted him in a serious and friendly way.

'Perigot,' he said, 'there is a stain on the escutcheon of my house which I think you are the very man to erase. In my great-grandfather's time we had, among our family treasures, three golden apples that were said to confer upon their owners health, wealth, and happiness. Whether or not that was so, they were at least intrinsically valuable, and as objects of art, I believe, incomparable. Unhappily, in an affair that did credit to neither side, they were stolen by the Cloud King and taken by him to his favourite castle, which, as probably you are aware, is seven days' march to the north of Gargaphie. On several occasions enterprising young men have endeavoured to retrieve these apples, but every one of them, I am sorry to say, has perished at the hands, or in the teeth, of a curious monster, half-human and half-dog, that the Cloud King retains as a kind of seneschal or warder. You, however, who kill dragons with such ease, would probably make short work of the Hound-man, and if you can bring back those apples I shall seriously consider making you my heir. I don't want to press you, of course . . .'

'There's no need to,' said Perigot, 'for I'll go very willingly. When can I start?'

The King was a little astonished by his eagerness to undertake so perilous an expedition, but as he did not want to give Perigot an opportunity to change his mind, he said, as though thinking about it very carefully, 'Well, there's a full moon tonight, and if you're really in a hurry you could start at once. I'll give you a guide for the first part of your journey, and after that anyone will tell you your way.'

So Perigot said good-bye to Amoret and set out on his desperate enterprise. His hope was partly to forget in danger the embarrassment of his married life, and partly to give healing time a chance to restore him to his normal shape. For the curse, he thought, might be a passing or impermanent one.

For seven days he marched through wild and desolate country, where the clouds hung ever closer on towering black mountains, and the crying of eagles came hoarsely through the mist. It was a cold and friendless land, and no sign of his returning manhood, except his intrepid spirit, came to comfort him. On the eighth day he reached the Cloud King's castle, and over it, to his surprise, the sky was clear. The castle was empty and deserted except for the great grey Hound-man lying at the gate.

When Perigot appeared the Hound-man rose and growled, and the brindled hair on its neck bristled terribly. Perigot took out his pipe and began to play the first tune that came into his mind. The Hound-man lifted his head and howled most dismally. Perigot played something else, and the Hound-man bayed like a pack of hunting-dogs. Clearly music would have no effect on him. So Perigot, putting away his pipe, drew his moon-made sickle and warily advanced.

Showing great fangs like icicles, the Hound-man leapt to kill him, but Perigot neatly evaded its rush and cut off its right arm. Foaming at the mouth the brute again attacked him, but this time Perigot with great skill lopped off both its legs, and the Hound-man fell to the ground and lay dying. Its eyes began to glaze, but the wickedness in its heart still lived, and out of its great throat came a growling voice that said, 'The curse of Shepherd Alken be on you!'

'What did you say?' demanded Perigot excitedly.

'The curse of Shepherd Alken on you!' repeated the Hound-man. 'If you are a man become a woman, if you are a woman become a man!' And died in that instant.

Perigot was so excited that he almost forgot his errand, but just as he was turning back to Gargaphie he remembered that he had come to look for some golden apples, and breaking into the castle speedily found them in the Cloud King's bedroom. He put them into a satchel he had brought for the purpose, and then, wasting no more time, he began to run southwards down the path he had lately climbed so grimly. He made such speed—for his clothes no longer felt tight about his chest—that he reached Gargaphie on the evening of the fourth day, just at the time when everybody was getting ready for bed.

The King was astounded to see him, and despite his pleasure in regaining the golden apples that his great-grandfather had lost, found it difficult to infuse his welcome with any cordiality. But Perigot paid little attention to the King. Amoret, he was told, had taken her candle a few minutes earlier and already retired to her chamber.

She, poor girl, was delighted by his return, for she loved him though he had deceived her, and she had feared he was dead. But after they had embraced each other once or twice she remembered her former disappointment, and a little bitterly she said, 'Where is your pipe, Perigot? Aren't you going to play me to sleep?'

'That for my pipe!' said Perigot, and threw it out of the window.

'Perigot!' she said.

'Amoret!' he answered, in a deep manly voice that made her heart flutter strangely.

The following morning it was Amoret who rose first, and left Perigot sleeping. At her chamber door the King and Queen were waiting for her.

'Well, my dear,' said the King, 'I'm afraid that my attempt to get rid of your so-called husband has failed, well-thought-out though it was. But don't worry. I've plenty more plans in my head, and when he's out of the way we'll get you a proper man.'

'A proper man!' said Amoret, laughing happily. 'Oh, my dear father and my very dear mother, he's the most wonderful man in the whole wide world. I wouldn't change him for all the husbands in Gargaphie.'

Pathans

A PATHAN'S HATRED is like a dung fire. It may smoulder unnoticed for a long time, and then leap suddenly into flame that devours both fire and what it touches. It is said, moreover, on the Prophet's authority, that God loves sneezing and hates yawning; for when a man yawns, Satan laughs at him.

It was foolish therefore, and perhaps doubly foolish, of Sikander Shah to yawn so openly at Shamsi Mia Syed's request. But he was tired, for he had heard the request so many times that night, and he had no intention of yielding.

'Give me another week,' said Shamsi Mia Syed, 'and by God, I will pay you the money in full. One week only, and I will have the whole sum, with old interest and new interest, and perhaps a present of some kind as well.'

But Sikander Shah put back his head and yawned widely, so that his mouth looked like a black hole above the hairy darkness of his beard. The yellow light of two brass lamps swung gently to and fro, as they swayed in the soft wind, and threw alternately pallor and inky shadows on the faces of the disputants. There were five of them, four Pathans and a Punjabi, sitting outside a tea-seller's hut on the Mahim Road that leads northward out of Bombay. It was late; nearly midnight. But Sikander Shah and the Punjabi, Gulab Singh, were watchmen over two half-built houses near by, and the others were nightbirds by choice and habit.

The wind washed through the palm trees, with a sound like the falling of little waves on soft sand, and from far away came the steady rhythm of drums beaten for a wedding feast. The road through the trees was hidden in darkness, but the feathery tops of the palms were visible against a faintly starlit sky. Here and there the lower darkness was blurred with yellow moons where tea-sellers' stalls and a toddy shop still catered for a few late customers.

'Not another day beyond tomorrow,' said Sikander, recovering from his yawn. 'Either I get eighty-four rupees by tomorrow night, or word goes to my brother in Peshawar, and the girl you know of . . .'

'What about her?'

'She will be sent where she can redeem the debt, and perhaps even make up for the gift you promised me.'

Shamsi Mia Syed snarled like a dog. His cousin, Daud Khan, said hoarsely, 'Give him a week's grace, and be done with this talk.' He was younger than the others, a sulky-looking man with fat cheeks. He wore a new light-blue pagri and a heavily embroidered waistcoat that he had stolen, by daylight, in a crowded bazaar.

'Why shouldn't he pay me tomorrow?' retorted Sikander. 'He has the money, and more than the money, and you all know it.'

'That's a lie,' shouted Syed. 'I've no money!'

'Then you've given it to the Kashmiri girl, the harlot who lives . . .'

'What does it matter to you where she lives?'

'Ho, ho!' laughed Gulab Singh, the Punjabi. 'A harlot here and a virgin waiting in Peshawar! *Hath sukha Pathan bukha!*'

The proverb means a Pathan is so greedy that he will be hungry again as soon as he has washed his hands after meat.

'If a Hindki can't hurt you he'll make a bad smell,' sneered Daud Khan, glaring at the Punjabi and calling him by the name he would like least.

Gulab Singh's face darkened as his slow wits searched for a proper reply. But before he could find one, Mahomed Khan, who had sat silent through most of the discussion, said roughly they had argued long enough, and there was no sense in looking for new quarrels now.

'By tomorrow night, then,' said Sikander Shah, and reached for his lathi, the five-foot iron-shod bamboo that was either a staff or a weapon.

'In the name of God!' jeered Daud Khan, but Syed, staring sullenly, said nothing.

Sikander Shah stood up and prepared to go. 'What's the good of the Kashmiri girl if she can't find eighty-four rupees for you?' he asked, grinning in the lamplight so that his teeth shone and shadows darkened the harsh lines of his face.

But Shamsi Mia Syed was still silent, and the two nightwatchmen went off to the half-built houses near by, their lathis ringing once or twice on loose stones as they moved through the darkness.

The three others sat where they were. Daud Khan, with a kind of sullen inquiry, looked at Syed, who avoided his eyes, while Mahomed Khan impassively sucked the smoke of a cigarette through his clenched fist.

'He has two hundred rupees at the very least,' said Mahomed Khan quietly. 'He offered to lend so much to the Parsi who has the toddy shop, and showed him the money.'

Syed looked up and caught the eyes of Daud Khan. A grin spread over the younger man's face. Syed's mouth was twitching. 'Come,' he said, and stood up. The three of them went down the road in the opposite direction to that taken by the nightwatchmen.

It was about three o'clock in the morning when Sakharan Ragu, a cart-driver, stirred in his sleep, woke, and rose from his charpoy coughing in the chilly darkness. He lived in a grass-roofed shed between the teashop and the two new houses over which the Punjabi and Sikander Shah kept watch; and across the road, in another draughty hut, slept the two bullocks he looked after. Grumbling and half-asleep he pulled a red shawl round his head and went to feed his beasts. The great humped cattle were warmer than he was. They had filled their shed with an odorous heat, and when Sakharan came out of their stable he shivered and coughed again. His throat was dry and sticky from the pan-leaves he had chewed the night before, and he went to a near-by water-tap to drink and clean his mouth. But he heard the water running before he could see the tap, and he approached cautiously to see who was there.

Three men were washing their hands. They were tall and burly, and Sakharan Ragu was neither big nor bold. He drew into deeper shadow and watched them. By the shape of their pagris, by their full flowing trousers, and by their size he knew they were Pathans, and Sakharan stood very still. It would be unwise, he thought, to intrude unnecessarily on their society in the darkness and loneliness of night. The stars were bright enough for him to see what they were doing. They were washing their hands and arms and feet, and one was scrubbing something that he put, after cleaning, into his pocket. None of them spoke, and in a little while they went off together down the road towards Bombay.

Sakharan went to the tap—the Pathans had left the water running—and cupping his hands, rinsed his mouth and drank. Those Pathans were devils, he thought, walking mysteriously at night. It was lucky they had not seen him, or what might they have done to him? Robbed him if he had any money—which he had not—or murdered him for spite at his poverty. Sakharan Ragu went back to his grass-roofed hut and thankfully fell asleep again.

It was a little nearer morning when Police Sepoy Ramchandra Krishna, standing at the mouth of a dark lane on the outskirts of Bombay, saw three Pathans walking swiftly under the light of a street lamp. He was a zealous young man, and Pathans, when walking abroad at such an hour, were a suspect people. He saw moreover that the tallest man of the three was holding one hand in the other, as though it had been hurt. Ramchandra Krishna called softly to another policeman, who was smoking a cigarette in the deeper darkness of the lane, and together they followed the Pathans. After doubling down a lane, along another street, and back to the main road by a dark alley, they confronted the suspects at a well-lighted corner.

'It's late to be out,' said Ramchandra. 'Where are you going?'

'What's that got to do with you?' growled the tallest man. The Pathans looked stupid at the sudden encounter. They might have been dazed with drink, or heavy from lack of sleep.

'What have you been doing?' asked the sepoy.

'By God and by very God,' said the tall one explosively, and stopped, having no more to say.

'We were at the house of my father's cousin, who lives in Bandra,' said another, 'and now we are going back to our lodging to sleep.'

'Was there any fighting in Bandra?' said Ramchandra, and he touched the hand of the tallest one that was tied in a rough bandage. The Pathan drew back and made, half-heartedly, a threatening movement with his lathi.

'So that's your game,' said the sepoy, drawing his truncheon. 'You'll come to the Police Station, then, and tell your story to the Inspector.'

The other sepoy shrilly blew his whistle as the Pathans backed against the wall, and in a few seconds two more policemen ran up, their round yellow caps like little haloes in the dark.

'Come,' said Sepoy Ramchandra Krishna, and marched off his captives. The Pathans offered no resistance. The tall one's little show of defiance seemed to have exhausted him. They were listless and dumb, as though only half-awake, or too weary to care what happened. They showed no wish to escape, till, at the door of the police station, the youngest of the three, who wore a richly embroidered waistcoat, suddenly turned and kicked the bare shins of the sepoy beside him and made an effort to bolt. But the sepoy jumped and clung to him like a terrier, and another struck the Pathan heavily with his truncheon; the blow was softened by the smart blue pagri it fell on, but it was heavy enough to sober him. The three were pushed into the station and the door banged behind them.

They were searched. They all carried fairly large clasp-knives, in the joints of which were little packings of damp mud, as though they had been cleaned in the ground and washed in water. The tall one had a cotton bag in his shirt which held, in small notes and coins, a hundred and sixty rupees.

'It is money I have saved,' he said, and looked greedily at the dirty notes.

The Sub-Inspector who questioned them got no satisfaction. The oldest of the three, who had said they were coming from Bandra, repeated his story, but as if worn out by so much invention he could not find a name for his father's cousin whom they had been visiting.

'Were you drinking there?' asked the Sub-Inspector.

The oldest one thought awhile. 'Yes,' he said.

'No, we drank nothing!' shouted the tallest one, and glared angrily at his friend. He had once got into serious trouble for beating a man when he was drunk.

'How did you hurt your hand?' asked the policeman.

'I fell,' mumbled the Pathan.

'Take that rag off, and we'll see what you fell on. A knife, wasn't it?'

The bandage was stuck in a clot to the back of the hand, and when a sepoy ripped it off, a long cut, running from the knuckles over the wrist on to the outer forearm, began to bleed again.

'Lock them up,' said the Sub-Inspector, and telephoned to police headquarters. He described the three Pathans, and asked if there were news of any violent misbehaviour in which they might have been concerned. But so far as police headquarters knew, the night had been peaceful.

An hour after dawn two children and a pariah dog found the evidence the Sub-Inspector wanted. Bhana, the four-year-old son of a toddy-drawer who lived some distance from the half-built houses where Sikander Shah and Gulab Singh had been employed, wandered from their hut among the trees in pursuit of a pariah puppy. His sister was with him—she was a year younger than he—and they were ineffectually pelting the puppy with small stones. The puppy, yelping thinly, ran through the undergrowth to the compound enclosing the houses, and entered through a gap in the unfinished wall. It stopped beside a broken charpoy, and sniffed curiously at what lay on the ground. Then it threw up its head and tried to howl. But unhappy squealing was the best that its puppy voice could do.

Led by the uneasy notes the children came into the compound and trotted up to the broken charpoy. They stood silent for nearly a minute, eyes wide and mouths open, staring at the ugliness that lay in the calm blue sight of the morning. It was maimed and red. And then, together and without speaking, Bhana and his sister ran back to their friendly hut, to their father and mother and their father's mother who lived in it.

Wide-eyed still, Bhana gasped and pointed to the compound, and said something about a man and blood. His sister, who had tripped and fallen in the undergrowth, lay howling twenty yards away, unregarded. The toddy-drawer called to a neighbour, and, a little frightened, went to see what was wrong.

A dead man lay beside the wreckage of a string-bed. His throat was cut and a gash on his right cheek ran down into his beard. The face, drained of blood, was yellow, and the eyes were wide open.

'It's Sikander Shah, the nightwatchman,' said the toddy-drawer to his neighbour.

'And there, in the grass . . .' said the other man.

The pariah dog had found something else, half-hidden in a tangle of long grass and rank creepers; another body, bruised and bloody about the head, and gralloched as though it had been a stag.

'The Punjabi,' said the toddy-drawer, fascinated by the horrid sight.

'This is murder, undoubtedly,' said his neighbour solemnly. 'We must call Sithiram, the policeman.' And he ran off to the road.

Moved by the inquisitive sympathy that violent death excites, a little crowd gathered quickly round the bodies. Toddy-drawers, coolies, a few shopkeepers, and a dozen curious children stood enthralled by horror.

'The Pathans!' cried Sakharan Ragu, suddenly breaking the silence. 'There were three Pathans here in the night. I saw them washing their hands at the tap!'

A murmur went through the crowd. 'Pathans!' they whispered.

'Indeed, that is Pathans' work,' said an old man, pointing to the watchman who had been ripped open.

'He was drinking tea in my shop last night,' said Haji Miadad, who kept the tea-stall down the road.

'Even your tea shouldn't do that to a man's guts, Hajiji,' said a tall coolie, grinning. But Haji Miadad did not rise to the insult.

'These two, and three others whom I did not know, sat and talked together for an hour, or maybe two hours,' he said. 'Then they went away, and what they did afterwards, God knows.'

A voice of authority announced the arrival of Sithiram the policeman. 'Let everyone stand back,' said Sithiram. And everyone crowded a little closer to watch him while he examined the bodies. He picked up a small pocket-knife that hung from a chain fastened to Sikander Shah's belt. The knife, open and bloodstained, had been hidden under the broken charpoy.

'Has anyone touched these bodies?' asked the policeman.

'No, no!' Hurriedly the crowd assured him. 'That is just how they were found.'

'It was thus that my son said they were lying . . .'

'Who found them?' interrupted Sithiram.

'I and my son,' said Bhana's father. 'He came running, saying this one was lying with blood on his face . . .'

'I saw them too,' piped Bhana's sister.

'They are both clever children,' said the toddy-drawer, looking down at them where they squatted naked at his feet. 'Once I remember . . .'

But his reminiscences were spoilt by the cart-driver, Sakharan Ragu, who was eager to share the publicity.

'And it was I,' shouted Sakharan Ragu, 'who saw the Pathans in the middle of the night. While I was drinking at the tap there, having fed my bullocks. . . .'

'*Chūp,*' said the policeman. 'Let all others be silent. Now what is this talk about Pathans?'

'Am I not telling you? While I was drinking at the tap, about two hours before dawn, or perhaps three, or even a little more, I heard a noise, and turning round saw three men, Pathans, on the road near by. They stayed where they were till I had finished drinking, doubtless being frightened to interfere . . .'

'Be quiet!' said the policeman again, as the crowd laughed derisively at the cart-driver's claim to have struck fear into the heart of a Pathan.

'Then,' Sakharan continued, a little sulkily, 'then they went to the tap themselves, and washed their hands and feet.'

'There were three Pathans who sat with these two drinking tea last night,' said Haji Miadad.

'You would know them if you saw them again?'

'Without any doubt,' said Haji Miadad.

'And you?'

Sakharan Ragu hesitated. 'Two perhaps. But the third I didn't see very clearly.'

'Being very frightened, perhaps he kept his face hidden from you,' suggested Sithiram unkindly, and the crowd laughed again. 'You and you and you,' he continued—pointing to Haji Miadad, Sakharan, and the father of Bhana—'will likely be wanted as witnesses. So do not go far away from your houses. And now let someone run and tell my sergeant what I have found, and ask him to come quickly.'

Two children ran off, shouting excitedly for the importance of their duty, and Policeman Sithiram squatted on his heels inside the circle of spectators who still gazed, but no longer in silence, at the dead bodies.

On the following morning, when the inquiry into the double murder was opened, the coroner's court was crowded. There were many Pathans there, some of whom were friends of the prisoners. The police had been busy, and the three men, arrested on suspicion by the alert Ramchandra Krishna, had been identified, satisfactorily by Haji Miadad and not so satisfactorily by Sakharan Ragu, as the three who had sat with the murdered men and later washed their hands and feet of bloodstains at the roadside tap. It was proved that Shamsi Mia Syed owed money to the dead watchman, and it was known that Sikander Shah had had on his person a sum of nearly two hundred rupees. The cut on Syed's hand was such as might have been made by the little knife hanging to the chain at Sikander's waist. The Pathans had refused to make any statement but apparently there had been a short struggle in which the string-bed was broken, Shamsi Mia Syed wounded, and the Punjabi roused from sleep near by. Running to the help of his fellow watchman, the Punjabi must have fallen under the lathis of the murderers, and then, their bloodlust being at its height, knives had finished what the lathis had begun. The dung fire had burst into flame, consuming both itself and what it touched.

The three prisoners stood sullen and silent, hearing unmoved the evidence which, repeated later in the proper court, would certainly hang them. They made no answer, at first, when the coroner asked them if they had anything to say. He repeated the question somewhat testily.

Daud Khan fidgeted with his manacled hands, pulling at his richly embroidered waistcoat, and said nothing. But Mahomed Khan, clearing his throat, said in a hard voice, 'He who begs from men their wealth in order to increase his own, asks only for live coals.'

There was a burst of laughter and a little noise of applause in court as the words of the Prophet were heard and their dubious application to Sikander Shah immediately recognised. Daud Khan said boldly, 'Prison walls have holes,' and again there was laughter. The coroner commanded silence, and looked at Shamsi Mia Syed.

'For the third time,' he said, 'I ask you if you have anything to say?'

Cheered by laughter and their friends' applause, the Pathans were swaggering now. They stood jaunty and defiant, reckless of what would happen. Shamsi Mia Syed dipped his hands into a pocket and pulled out half a dozen walnuts. He threw up his head and cried loudly, 'All I ask is this, that I get leave to live till I have eaten these walnuts.'

'You will probably have time for that,' said the coroner drily.

'God is merciful,' said Shamsi Mia Syed, and with a quick movement tossed the nuts far and wide into the crowded court.

The Actress Olenina

THE NEW MOSCOW Repertory Company that came to London in June, 1914, was doubly unfortunate. Its endeavour to entertain the English with the work of dramatists so little known as Brusov, Blok, Gorky, and Sologub would have been courageous at any season, and in summer it was simply foolish-forlorn heroism. But as though holidays and hot weather were not enough to kill the venture, on August 4th Great Britain went to war, and in the enthralling days that followed even the scanty audiences who had previously found pleasure in watching the Moscow players were no longer attracted by the work of Gorky, Sologub, Brusov, and Blok; and after presenting *The Poor House* to an audience of twenty-six people and the programme-girls, the theatre closed its doors with a shudder and with relief.

On the following morning, a little after daybreak—for none had slept that night—the whole company, with the exception of Irina Markovna Olenina, their leading lady, went clamorous or tearful or jubilant to the Russian Embassy to demand the means of instant repatriation. When all the nations were at war they could find no peace in a foreign land—so it seemed, to simple minds, in the richness of their first excitement—but whether for good or ill they must stand on their own soil and feel about them the comfort of their own people. And presently they had their wish, and returned, by devious routes and ever-hesitant trains, to their native country, where most of them lived long enough to learn that the nearness of their own people was not always comforting.

But Olenina stayed in London till the first Christmas of the War.

It was her genius and her reputation that had kept their repertoire alive for six weeks. She was a remarkable actress and a woman of exceptional beauty. At the age of thirty or thirty-one she had nearly twenty-five years' experience of the stage, for she had made her début at the age of six, playing Cosette in a German version of *Les Misérables* at a small theatre in Vienna. She called herself a Russian, and certainly that was the nationality of her mother—a cabaret-singer for some part of her life—but that her father had also been Russian was not so well established.

Olenina had made herself reasonably at home in several countries. As well as on the Russian stage she had acted in France, Germany, Austria, and even, despite the conservatism of its theatre, in Italy. Nor was her experience confined to dramatic art, for as she said herself, in her more ingenuous moments, 'I am a great actress, but as a lover I am greater still.' It was her second husband, an Italian journalist who had seen her playing Camille in Vienna, and hailed her enthusiastically as *trovata di rose*, who had brought her to Milan and arranged her brief and solitary season there. It was not a success, and she left him within six months. 'Il était beau mais il était bête,' she said. Her experiences in love were seldom happy, for she never learnt by experience, but embarked on each new adventure with the passionate conviction that she had found contentment at last. It was said of her, indeed, that though she did not always go to church before going to bed, she never went to bed without meaning to go to church as well.

In London she had fallen violently in love with an officer in the Brigade of Guards, a Major Paignton-Boys, whose duty, for the moment, was not with his regiment but with the War Office. He combined ambition in his profession with a reputation for gay living, he was well-off and extremely handsome. He estalished Olenina in a flat in Upper Berkeley Street, and it was at his insistence as much as by her own uneasy inclination that she remained in England after the rest of her company had returned to Russia.

She was not happy for long. Her lover was absorbed in his duties at the War Office, but though the War interested Olenina also—to the exclusion of nearly everything else—he refused, blandly but resolutely, to discuss its progress with her. Because Russia was fighting on England's side she was fanatically pro-English, and praised the valour of England, its nobility of spirit and devotion to high ideals, with every extravagance of language and the whole range of her deep golden voice. But Major Paignton-Boys would not, overtly at least, share her enthusiasm. With boredom in his voice he said that the Allies were sure to win, and that there was nothing to fear from the strategy of the German High Command. 'We'll give them enough rope and they'll hang themselves,' he declared, and bade Olenina talk of something else.

This lack of *brio* on the part of one whose whole duty was the prosecution of the war—even though his duties were not in the field—depressed and puzzled Olenina, and her feelings were seriously hurt when he insisted on removing a large Union Jack that she had nailed to the outer ledge of her drawing-room window. His displeasure, and her disappointment, were even greater when one evening he went to her bedroom and discovered, beneath the ikon above her bed, an ingenious trophy made of the Allied flags and a photograph of Lord Kitchener.

He tore down the coloured silk and the well-moustached portrait. 'Good God!' he said. 'You can't do this sort of thing. You're not a shop-girl and I'm not a bank clerk. Try, for heaven's sake, to be reasonable and decent in your emotions.'

'But we are at war!' she cried.

'That is no excuse,' he said stiffly, 'for not behaving in essentially the same sort of way as we have always behaved.'

'Do your people, your English people, always crowd in the streets and cheer when soldiers go by?' she cried again. 'Are they always making long queues to join the Army, and singing when they go away to camp?'

'I wasn't referring to civilians,' said Major Paignton-Boys. 'War is a matter for the Army to deal with, and the less that civilians interfere the better it will be for everybody.'

But Olenina could not understand so stupid and cold a view, and because her lover would tell her nothing of the war she bought every day ten or a dozen newspapers, and read for hours their varying accounts of von Kluck's advance, and the advance into East Prussia, of French armies and Austrian armies, of the *Goeben* and the *Breslau*, and always, and whenever she could find them, stories of the multitudinous cohorts of the Tsar.

One afternoon Paignton-Boys came in and found her sitting on the floor, her back to the wall and a little afternoon tea-tray poised on her knees. But she was not drinking her tea; her cup was empty and unsoiled, the plates untouched; and Olenina, her face all wet and twisted, wept without thought of anything but tears and that which had prompted them to flow.

'My dear girl,' he said, 'what on earth is the matter?'

'I have been reading about the Russian soldiers who are coming to fight for you in France,' she sobbed. 'They are coming through England, and there will be a hundred thousand of them. Some came last night—my own people, my own Russian soldiers, they have been in London and I did not see them! They came down from Scotland in trains, and there will be more coming, every night, till a hundred thousand of them have come, and then the war will quickly be over, because Russia and Russian soldiers will always win!'

'Nonsense,' said Paignton-Boys. 'No Russian troops have passed through England, and none are going to.'

'But it says so in the paper!' cried Olenina. 'Look, it says so!'

'It quotes a rumour,' said Paignton-Boys. 'That means nothing.'

'Ah! You never tell me anything, so how can I hope that you will tell me now about this, about my Russians who are coming to London tonight and tomorrow night? But it is true, because the paper says so, and the papers know everything, everything!'

Refusing to believe Paignton-Boys's denials of the story, Olenina went every night for a week to King's Cross or Euston to see the late trains from Scotland come in, and to watch for the passing of her beloved countrymen. She saw no Russian troops, but plenty of English and Scottish soldiers, and in the company of the crowds who always thronged the station-entrances she found no little comfort: for their emotions were nearly as quick as hers, they were excited as she was, and, as she did, they showed their feelings in loud cheering and ready reception of the wildest rumours.

One evening, at King's Cross, she fell into conversation with a lean, somewhat shabby, somewhat unshaved young man who stood beside her in the crowd. A detachment of Highland troops were marching from the station, and as the crowd surged after them a short black cape that Olenina wore was half torn from her shoulders. 'Ah!' she cried, 'my *talmotchka*!'

The young man looked round. '*Talmotchka*!' he said, laughing.

'Why do you laugh?' said Olenina.

'Your *talmotchka*!' he repeated.

'You also are Russian?' she demanded with sudden excitement.

'How else should I know what *talmotchka* means?' he answered in her own language.

Olenina thrust her hand under his arm. 'Oh, come!' she cried. 'Let us talk together, let us talk Russian. I am tired of English, it is hard and flat and heavy. You came to the station to look for our own soldiers who are going to fight on this side, on the Western Front? It is true they are coming, isn't it? Someone Dunyasha knows—Dunyasha, my maid—said her brother had seen them. Perhaps you have seen them? Have you, oh, have you?'

Still talking eagerly, scarcely giving the young man time to answer, Olenina led him into a nearby public-house, a small and dingy place, and without noticing the curious glances they attracted, ordered two bottles of beer. She talked more and more.

Such was her joy in finding a fellow-countryman, so warm a feeling was engendered by this contact with her native land—here in London, on soil that still was foreign, however friendly it protested itself—that she was ready to weep, to dissolve in tears of love and piety, to behold in this shabby young man a personification of the spirit, the heart, and the strength of all Russia.

He was not ill-looking. He had fine brown eyes and thick dark hair. His teeth were white, his features animated. He was a waiter, he said, in the Imperial Hotel in Russell Square. His name was Glinka, and he had lived in London for eight years.

'But now you will be going home, to join the Army, to fight in the Carpathians, with the Grand Duke in East Prussia, perhaps on the Western Front? Soon you will be a soldier, not a waiter?' said Olenina.

Glinka had no such intention. He was, on the contrary, devoutly glad to be in a comfortable place like London, safe and far from the Carpathians and the Prussian marshes, and every night he contemplated with satisfaction his flat feet and varicose veins that would always exempt him from military service. But he was a shrewd fellow, and perceiving that this beautiful and wealthy and somewhat foolish lady had given her heart to the soldiers, he quickly pretended to be as fiercely patriotic as she was.

He was going home next week, he said. There was a ship sailing from Tilbury, from Newcastle—he was a little vague about this—but there would be many Russians aboard who, like himself, wished one thing only, which was to fight for their beloved land in this great and holy war.

He, Glinka, had been the first of these volunteers to enrol his name. He had gone to the Embassy and said, 'I want to go home, now, this week, to join the Army. I am a Russian and it is my duty to fight with my comrades in the Carpathians, in the Prussian marshes, anywhere you like to send me.'

Olenina was enraptured by this declaration. In a romantic vision she saw Glinka with his fellow-soldiers charging the enemy, head bent, bayonet out-thrust, those brown eyes shining. Through a mist she beheld him dead on the field of honour, a pledge of love, a sacrifice to Russia, and, emulous on the instant, eager to give with a generosity comparable to his, burning to offer her body freely as the soldiers offered theirs, she determined, in an ecstasy of self-sacrifice, to take him home with her—Glinka, the Russian soldier—and give him, the personification of Russia, before he died for Russia, such joy as she could.

In a voice trembling with excitement she bade Glinka wait for her. There was a telephone box in the public-house, in a sour-smelling narrow corner.

Paignton-Boys would be at his club. She asked for its number, and waited. When she heard his voice she said, 'Listen, Jack. I do not want you to come tonight. I have a *migraine*. I am going to bed. Yes, I am tired and not well. Perhaps it is a fever. Tomorrow, if you like, but not tonight—I am ugly tonight and very tired. Goodbye, Jack. Yes, good-bye!'

Then she returned to Glinka and said, 'Come home with me and we shall drink something better than beer.'

Glinka needed no persuasion. He had heard tales of the fantastic good fortune that sometimes, but all too rarely, befell a fine-looking young man, and he was ready to enjoy it if he could. On the way to Upper Berkeley Street—they caught a passing taxi—he embroidered his patriotic intentions with bright heroical words and convincing detail, and Olenina sat calmly in the expectation of sacrifice.

They entered the flat. Dunyasha, Olenina's maid, regarded the visitor with some surprise, and he, with obvious admiration of the richly furnished rooms, looked about him with unconcealed pleasure. Dunyasha was a sturdily built woman, about forty years old, with a confident manner and a well-marked moustache. Olenina told her to bring champagne. 'Bring two bottles,' she said. 'This is a fellow-countryman who is going home next week to join the Army. Very soon he will be fighting for Russia and for us. Bring three bottles of champagne.'

When Dunyasha had brought the wine, and set glasses on a tray, Olenina told her she could go to bed. 'I will look after the soldier,' she said.

Glinka drank greedily, and as he became a little drunk his manner grew more familiar. But Olenina scarcely saw him, scarcely heard what he said. To her he was Russia-in-arms, and in the calm that exists in the very centre of ecstasy she waited, blissful and impercipient, for the hour of her sacrifice. She saw Glinka's brown eyes, she saw a long grey line of Russian infantry advancing in the face of terrible gun-fire—and she saw herself, in the holy name of Russia, giving to her soldier what joy she might before he died for Russia.

Glinka drank another glass of champagne, and, coming closer to her, put his hand on her leg. 'Big eyes, fat thighs,' he said happily, and pinched her. Olenina, startled from her dream, moved away from him. 'You must have some more champagne,' she said, and opened the second bottle. She herself had drunk half a glass only. Glinka drank again, dipping his nose into the bubbles, and belched loudly. 'Better up than down,' he said.

Encouraged by the second bottle, his conversation became somewhat coarse, and with a leer he asked Olenina why she had invited him to her flat, and what she was waiting for now, since he himself was ready for anything. His appearance, as well as his language, had been coarsened by drinking. His eyes were a little red, his cheeks flushed, and his lips, half-open, were slack and heavy. Olenina shivered. Suddenly her ecstasy slid from her, like a falling cloak, and left her cold. Glinka bent over her, and, as she turned from him, kissed her hotly on the neck. She thrust him away, roughly, and he returned to his corner with an expression of sulky disappointment.

'Why did you ask me if it wasn't for that?' he grumbled. 'Why did you want me to come home with you?'

'Because,' said Olenina, ' . . . because you are going to fight for Russia,'—and because in a few weeks you may be dead, she thought, but did not say so.—'I don't know,' she said.

'You'd better make up your mind,' said Glinka, and putting his hand inside his shirt scratched his chest very comfortably.

Like a drunk man who, waking sick and sober, shrinks from the very smell of drink, Olenina shrank from the deed her imagination had so joyfully contemplated. I cannot, I cannot, she thought. And yet, she thought, it is still true that he is a soldier, that he is going to fight for Russia, and that, very likely, he will die for Russia. I brought him here for love, and if I do not give him love I shall have betrayed him, and being a traitor to him I shall be a traitor to Russia. Oh, what a coward I am!—But he is dirty, he is brutal, he would not understand. He is not *nice*!—But he is going to war, he is going to die.—Oh, why did I ever talk to him?

'Give me some champagne,' she said roughly.

Glinka filled her glass. 'That's better,' he said. 'We're going to have some fun after all, are we? Drink it up, there's plenty more here.'

Olenina stood up. 'Wait here,' she said. 'I shall be back in a minute or two.'

She went to Dunyasha's room, who slept in a closet on the other side of the hall. She left the drawing-room door open, and presently Glinka heard voices in argument. He shrugged his shoulders and filled his glass again. He was enjoying himself. He was not too drunk to realise the charm of his situation, and he felt reasonably sure that the night was going to end satisfactorily for him. Idly he wondered what Olenina and Dunyasha were talking about. Then he saw Olenina's bag, that she had left on a little table. He opened it, and found a purse containing three five-pound notes and half a dozen sovereigns. He hesitated, fingering the notes, and then, tossing one of the sovereigns into the air, caught it and put it into his pocket. He closed the purse, reluctant to lose sight of so much money but frightened to steal any more, and slid it back into the bag.

Olenina came in with a little frown on her forehead and a purposeful step. She took the purse from her bag and returned to Dunyasha's room. She was there for a few seconds only. Almost immediately she came back, and said to Glinka, 'You want to make love, don't you?'

Glinka whistled and made an improper gesture.

'Then come with me,' said Olenina, and led him across the hall to Dunyasha's room. 'Go in there,' she said, and shut the door behind him.

In the drawing-room again, alone, she drank a little more champagne, and stood frowning at her thoughts. Then she laughed. 'To live is to love and to love is to live,' she said, 'and when living is not a pleasant thing, why, *nos valets le feront pour nous—et pour la Russie, en effet!*'

A Sociable Plover

ONE

WE WHO are the shrivelled little bastard cousins of God—the last thin paring of his finger-nails, with the urge to create still beating against the hard and horny consciousness of separation from Him—we who have power beyond the scope and faculty of our neighbours, may come to know the pain of an impotence that never plagues and bedevils them. We, like God, need belief: the belief of those for whom we create. And without belief, we cannot. God Himself is failing, and if scepticism, neglect, and blank indifference can undo Him, how should I be immune? But that is no lenitive for the pain. He, perhaps, can find some recompense. There's none for me.

It was with a sullen knowledge of defeat waiting for me at the table that I went downstairs to my work-room, with the howl and bellow of the storm in my ears, for the house stood quite exposed to the north-west, and since midnight we had felt the walls shaking under the impact of a gale that drove from Labrador across the wild, white-tipped Atlantic—a graveyard torn up to show dead bones—and menaced with its fury the shelter of our thick-slated roof. Isobel had left me and gone into the children's room, where the younger one—a nervous, dull-witted girl—was crying; and I had slept and wakened, dozed and wakened again, like an angry, sleepy passenger in a railway carriage. My body, as I went downstairs, was as tired and miserable as my mind.

But, as always, I opened the door of my work-room with caution, quietly, with a little surge of expectancy. The big window looked out at a well-grown lawn I had levelled and sown seven years before: a lawn that was guarded on its western side by a thick, untidy hedge of blackthorn and beech, and to the north ran into some forty acres of thin heather grazed by a score of black-faced sheep. Below the lawn was a small meadow, and beyond it the ever-changing, bright-waved loch on which, for the last two or three years, I had taken my chiefest pleasure.

The new-made lawn had attracted an uncommon variety of birds to its bright sward. Snow-buntings came in winter, a chorus of small, clear voices rippling in the white drift of their wings; and black-headed gulls from the colony that nested by the marshy pool in the moor. Twice I have seen a greenshank parading on long pale legs, and once a dotterel looked at me with infinite surprise—or so it seemed—under his white eyebrow. Last year I was enchanted by a pair of snipe that, every morning for a fortnight, brought their young on to the lawn. They were, to begin with, intensely shy and cautious. One of the old birds, treading high-toed and hesitant, would first make a reconnaissance; and then, as if to signal that all was well, would begin to prod the green turf with its long beak. The two nestlings would follow, and they, unlike their parents, were utterly confident, wholly without fear, and ran about on tottering feet—two tufts of brown feather with bright eyes—while the old birds kept their nervous watch. The second parent (I never knew which was cock and which was hen) stayed always on the border of grass that fringed the moor.

I had, then, fallen into the habit of approaching my window almost as carefully as a scout crawling to a sky-line—but this morning I had no need to go as far. The window was a transparent drum-skin, reverberating the noise of the gale, and on the ledge was a bird like a lapwing in shape and size; one wing, aloft, as if dislocated—its feathers fluttering—was pressed hard against the glass. Its black cap was ruffled, and a round black eye stared into the room, and straight at me, with the intensity (as I first thought) of desperate fear.

I felt an absurd anxiety. I wanted, immediately, to free it from its obvious distress; and that I could not see how to do. Should I open the middle panel of the window, and coax it into the shelter of the room? But there, in a confinement it had never known, it would hurt itself in a frenzy to escape. Or should I go out and chase it from the delusive glass—chase it into the gale that might carry it, helpless, against a fence or wall where it could break a wing? I went nearer the window, now puzzling to identify the bird. I had never seen one of its sort before: of that I was sure. Its colouring was elegant: a pale fawn with a golden throat, black primaries with a black and white tail, a neat black cap with a blue burnish and a white eyebrow, and a curved black line running back from the eye. It was slimmer than a lapwing, perhaps a little larger, and its legs were dark.

I went closer still, and the shining circle of its eye held me in a fixed regard. Its expression had changed; or so I thought. It seemed now to be staring at me with a cold and dark appraisal. But that, I told myself, was ridiculous, and slowly I approached till I was only a foot or so from the window. Then the bird re-settled its fluttered wing, turned inwards—the wind under its tail lifted it like a fan—and looked straight at me with gleaming, slightly converging eyes. I felt a prickle of cold on my forehead, a little draught of cold under the arms, and foolishly—I heard the folly of it—I laughed. A nervous laugh that, by making me aware of myself, brought me to my senses.

From a shelf I took down a volume of Witherby's *Handbook of British Birds*, and soon found what I wanted. I wasn't to be blamed for not recognising my visitor, which was described as a 'very rare vagrant'. Only once before had it been seen, or recognised, in Scotland, and then as far from here as Orkney. I returned to the window, to compare it with the picture in Witherby, and now, with no apparent difficulty, the bird took off against the gale and flew to the far end of the lawn. It flew like a lapwing, and in the partial shelter of the hedge it settled, ran a yard or two, paused, and ran on: just like a lapwing. It seemed now a very normal sort of bird, and I went out to look at it again.

The wind met me with a buffet, and I leaned against it. The sky was a tumbled mass of fast-moving cloud, with here and there a pale blue gulf of vacancy, and the loch was a white-haired fury of grey water. A pillow of clotted foam had been blown against the boat-house door, and the jetty below it was smothered in white. I said to the bird, 'You've chosen a poor sort of day to come visiting,' and as if unaware that I was a only a few yards away, it poked suddenly at the grass—tilting its body on stiff legs, like a lapwing—to pull out a grub. I watched it for a few minutes, and went in again.

On Plate 122 in Witherby there was a very pretty picture of it: a Sociable Plover, beyond question, though according to the book it was smaller than a lapwing, and my visitor was certainly a little bigger. I felt extremely pleased to have so notable an addition to the guests of my lawn, and I thought of writing a short letter—to *The Times* or the *Glasgow Herald?*—to boast a little of my Plover . . . . But that might bring a dozen fervid ornithologists to the island, to pester me with their enthusiasm; which I did not want. So I put off letter-writing, as, for the last six or seven months, I have again and again put off writing of any sort; often with less excuse, or no excuse at all. No excuse but an overpowering sense of loss and hopelessness, of the unbearable tedium of writing when I know that none will read. Or only a beggarly few hundred now.

It was different when I wrote *John Gaffikin*, and sold 50,000 in Britain, almost as many in America. The second one did nearly as well, and the third was better than the first. Much better. And I deserved success, for I had found, with brilliant discovery, an idea of durable value and I knew how to realise it. None of your foot-slogging patient historical novels, covering ten years of narrative as slowly as the years and groaning under their load of costume, ornament, and quaint device, but a quick and sudden tale, lasting in time no more than a day or two, and embodying in action the temper and quiddity of its age. Each one, moreover, the tale of someone in the family I imagined, and have half-created, that holds (or should hold) like a knotted cord the growth and decline of England from the Great Armada to the partial dissolution of our power. There was an Elizabethan Gaffikin, a Gaffikin who made his fortune as a Puritan, and a Gaffikin who spent it under Charles II. Of them I wrote—that was before the war—and each time packed what I had to say into an acting-time of two or three days—no more—and got into three hundred pages the spirit, sentiment, and bowels of energy, falsehood or waste, that informed the age. I wrote well—they all admitted that—and I sold well.

But why can't I now? Since the war—since 1947, when I came back to civil life—I have written three others, of the same pattern, of the same family, and written better than I did before. With what result? A dribbling diminuendo of critical appreciation—but I don't give twopence for the critics—and a cascade of falling sales. 1940 was my best year, and that brought me royalties on 60,000 copies in Britain, 85,000 in America, and £15,000 for film rights. But last year I sold 2,300 copies here, and none abroad, of the best book I have written yet. Well, what in hell am I to do?

They talk—it's all talk and criticism now: no writing is regarded, except the first flatulent puffs of adolescence—they talk of the decline and decay, the sickness of the novel; but what's sick and decadent is the general public, too fatly fed and aghast in spirit to think, feel, act and choose for itself; and on the fringe of the multitude there's an etiolated frippery of homosexuals, and fellow-travellers with the homos, a swim of pop-eyed gudgeon living on the refuse and detritus that's carried by the Seine out of the sewers of French intellect into the dead water of the English Channel.

How can I write—how, how?—when no one reads? My last novel was my very best—and sold 2,300 copies. Now I'm in the seventh volume of the saga, and caught by the heels in apathy. The Romantic Revival is my background now, or should be; and how can I write of a flare of hope—even such foolish hope—in a gloom of accidie and no hope at all? Six other volumes I have planned, to make my tale complete, and I know that I shall never do it. But what else can I do?

Drink a little, and delude myself . . . I drank a little—not much: less than half a bottle of gin—and wrote two pages that I tore up before lunch came in. I have my lunch brought in on a tray, because Isobel eats with the children and a domestic table is more than I can bear. I still have an appetite—gin helps, perhaps—and that day it was cold roast beef, beetroot and boiled potatoes, a slice of apple tart. With a pint of beer. I slept for an hour in my big chair, before the fire, and woke to a sound of scratching on a window-pane. The wind had gone down, there was no more than a light breeze blowing, and in the quiet of a late-spring afternoon the plick-plack and urgent scraping of its beak on the glass had almost the compulsion of troopers at the door in the quiet before dawn. I woke and saw the bird against a background of glinting water, tall blue hill, and shining sky. The Sociable Plover on the window-ledge.

Its eye caught mine as mine turned towards it. Caught and held them. I was not properly awake, and perhaps that made me submissible to hypnosis. For I was, I think, hypnotised. The bird itself seemed to grow bigger against the lighted frame of water and bright sky, and the black circle (with a glint of red in it) of its unwinking, gleaming eye expanded till it was like one of those old, convex, sombre mirrors, in which I saw myself, infinitely diminished, and stretched upon a rack for inquisition.

I shall not say what the inquisition revealed. Some of it, I suppose, was true—if truth can keep its complexion ten years after the event?—but more, I think, was the hysteria that confession under torment must also elicit. Indecently, in response to that indecent imperative, I resurrected and exposed a dead, forgotten past. I lay in a quivering fear—for how long I do not know—and returned to normal consciousness in a cold sweat of exhaustion. The bird was still there, on the window-ledge, but now of natural size again; and its round and glittering eye seemed mildly inquisitive, innocently perplexed.

I went to the cupboard, and got a drink; and my teeth chattered against the glass. I sat on a hard chair and fought my defeated nerves for self-control. Suave and elegant, the Sociable Plover watched me, but now with no animosity in its gaze. I took a little more whisky, and the shining peace of the late afternoon began to assuage and mollify my remembered fear. The Plover, as though contented and at home, walked mincingly up and down the ledge. I could see more of his delicate and gaily brilliant colouring. His throat caught a golden light, and the white eyebrow under his luminous blue-black cap was a streak of bland irony. His back and wing-covers were dove-hued, and the dark of his belly shaded into russet. He was very beautiful.

I got up and went to the window, pretending now that my fright had been nothing but a nightmare; and hoping (with a shiver) to make a friend of my Plover. But he flew away, with a slow wing-beat and a creak in his wings, like a lapwing when it turns in the air to display its skill.

The next morning was fine, and the wind, that had died away at dark, now blew gently from the south, or south-south-west. Isobel made me some sandwiches, I put up my rod, and pulled out my boat. It was a perfect fishing-day—the temperature of the air about four degrees warmer than the water, with a good new hatch of fly, the terns hawking and showing where they were—and by one o'clock I had caught seven fine trout, the best of the basket just under two pounds. I went ashore on Rowan Island—three rowans, growing under a big rock, give it its name—to eat my sandwiches and drink my beer; and for a little while I was content. What were books, critics, and a besotted populace compared with this?

The loch was a dimpled blue—light-dimpled, pale corn-flower-blue—and the sharp hills of the outer islands rose beyond the contours of our own land like the ruined battlements of gigantic Gothic castles. Cirrus clouds drifted on the idle sky, and somewhere a rain-goose was hooting with sweet melancholy. A redshank on a half-green pebble nodded and said 'Chip-chip', a swan lifted vainglorious wings, bent its proud head, and swam past me with an elegant assumption of indifference.—Why should I care for popular esteem, I thought? What's the worm in my soul that torments my soul to look for fame? Why can't I stand up straight—straight in arrogant assurance of myself—and put my heel upon it? And having crushed it, enjoy all this with the full-throated appetite of innocence?—But innocence died long ago, I can't remember when. And that's part of the answer.

Then I saw the Sociable Plover. It stood in the water's edge—water half an inch deep, just covering its feet—and delicately picked its way. It paid no attention to me, but I grew most uncomfortably aware of it. I watched it for a few minutes and then, stuffing a remnant sandwich and an empty bottle into my fishing-bag, returned to my boat. I pushed off, and presently, with the island between us, began to fish again. I saw a rising fish, some twenty yards away, and with a thrust of the oars moved towards it. I cast within a foot of the rippling circle it had made—threw again—and there, hovering above my tail fly, was the Plover.

Savagely I cast at the bird—and missed by a rod's length, so quick was its movement. It began to circle me, with slow deliberate wing-beats, but side-slipping sometimes with sudden speed. I tried to ignore it, and with all the willpower I could summon, concentrated on fishing. I saw a black gnat on the water, and changed my top fly for a Pennell; but my fingers trembled and I had difficulty in tying the knot. It occurred to me—with a shock of occurrence: the shock of an idea flung like a pebble into my mind—that there was only one way to escape the bird's malignant eye and the persecution of its scrutiny; and without realising what I was doing I put down my rod and leaning over the side looked through a green transparency to the moss-carpet six or seven feet below. There, on the bottom, in the shadow of the boat—but then the shadow of the bird fell on the water, and I knew, with a sickened release from it, that the thought, the nascent intention, wasn't mine, but came from without. A pebble flung into my mind to unnerve and kill—and as quickly as I could I started the outboard motor, and at full throttle (the noise was comforting) headed for home.

Next morning, when I went down to work, the bird was on the window-ledge. I drew the curtains against it, and turned on the light. I had written a page or two the night before, and I settled to revision. But it was no good. Plick-plack, plick-plack on the glass, and then a scraping noise as if it were stropping its beak. I had to face it, and pulling back the curtains I looked it full in the eye from a distance of two or three feet.

Bold at first—pleased with myself for being bold—I drove my thought and enmity against it like a phalanx, like a pointed horde of imperatives bidding it to go and never trouble me again. But the phalanx split and dissolved, and the obsidian eye (with a glow of fire or garnet in it) came shining through, shining into my mind where gradually it lighted a growing belief that by yielding to its invitation, its command, I would find the happiness that had long eluded me. Down to the shore, it said, and out to the clear green water where the floor is carpeted with moss, and there's peace for ever in that quietness far below the air of a world that's poisoned by hatred, frustration, and fear. Down to the deep green peace . . . .

I felt conviction spreading through my thinking parts, faith welling from an unknown spring, and I turned to the door with the slow obedience of a sleep-walker—and in the long hall of our reconstructed farmhouse—the hall that once had been a cow-byre or pen for calves—I met Isobel. She, in a little cloud of literary confusion—but sun-lit, as in all her clouds—exclaimed, 'Oh, darling, you must help me. I was coming to ask you, is *Pride and Prejudice* by Jane Eyre or Charlotte Brontë, and do you think it's a good book to recommend to the Women's Institute for next winter's reading? I've got to go to a meeting tonight, and several of us have promised to suggest twelve really good books, that everyone should know, and I can't think of anything but *Vanity Fair* and

Gone with the Wind and the new one by that French girl which isn't suitable at all.'

I sat down and began to laugh—or did I cry? Both, I think.

'Torquil, what is the matter? You haven't been drinking already, have you?'

'Not a drop. But you have saved my life.'

I pulled her down beside me, and fondled her. To that she always responded, and as she was subject to me, so was I to her. Her mind was only half-furnished, but her body—and indeed her spirit—gave me continual delight. There were days when I avoided talk with her, but few nights when I did not go thankfully to bed.

Now in the long dark hall—the roof was low and the windows narrow—we sat enfolded, my head to her shoulder, and from her warmth and comfort I slowly drew sanity again to fill the gulf of madness that the abominable bird had dug. I held her close, talked nonsense that gradually became deliberate nonsense to please and make her laugh—and then, suddenly confident that with Isobel beside me the bird would have no power, I said, 'Come to my room and I'll tell you the books to recommend, and who wrote them; it's important to remember that.' But when we went in, the bird had gone.

It came again in the late afternoon, and next morning. I took to wandering, and from room to room carried a pen, a blotting-pad, and a sheaf of paper. In the drawing-room, spare bedrooms, a closet that I called my office and never used, I sat on unfamiliar chairs, the pad on my knee, and tried to think of Everard Gaffikin, a tall camp-follower of the Romantic Revival, and his disillusionment in France by the September massacres. To write of disillusion should have been easy, but the will to write had died, and in truth all I was trying to do was to keep my mind off that infernal Plover, its eyes off me.

The days became a hideously tormented, endless and ludicrous game of hide-and-seek. Rooms have windows, and from one to another the bird pursued me—sometimes anticipated me—scraped on the frosted panes of a water-closet if I sat too long. I dared not go out, though day after day brought good fishing weather, and every morning I woke in fear of daylight. Twice I found the Plover at the window of my dressing-room when I went in to shave; twice again I tried to out-stare him, and called for Isobel to come and help me when I felt my mind dissolving and his intention filling the void. Isobel—God bless her kind and silly heart—thought I had been drinking too much, and as she believed an author must drink a great deal to be an author, was neither perplexed nor unduly disturbed. She probably felt proud to think that an author's wife must share his unhappiness.

My spirit broke before hers showed any bruise; and when, after ten or eleven days of persecution, the bird came yet again to my work-room window, I took a half-empty bottle of whisky, and threw it with all my strength against the glass.

The Plover, unhurt, flew off; and then at last I overcame a curious, superstitious reluctance. I unstrapped my gun-case and took out one of the good pair I had bought with money that *John Gaffikin* made. I had not used them for three or four years, for I gave up shooting when I became more interested in watching birds than killing them; and they were smeared with vaseline. I cleaned one roughly with a handkerchief, put stock to barrel, and found a few cartridges . . . .

TWO

My name is Anne McQueen. I am a doctor, of the ordinary general sort—M.B., Ch.B., University of Inverdoon, 1947—and I live in Morissey because I am too sensible to be ambitious, because I have always loved the Western Isles, and in a rather unwomanly fashion I am very fond of fishing.

I took a good degree at Inverdoon, and the Gold Medal for Midwifery. My fellow-students said I owed the award to inside knowledge, because I was pregnant at the time. I had got married, in my third year, to a young man in the Royal Air Force. He was killed while flying on the Air Lift to Berlin, after the Russians had closed the roads, and in consequence of that, and, I suppose, of an old-fashioned sense of duty, I volunteered, after graduation, for service under the Allied Military Government in Germany. I didn't want to think that young men could serve abroad—and suffer and die abroad—while their girl-friends took their money and their kisses and did nothing, except roll in bed, to earn them.

So my mother took charge of the baby, and I had two years in Germany—about six months in Berlin—and then came home and did a course at the Rotunda—for midwifery really interested me—and two hospital spells, of six months each, in Manchester and Birmingham. Nothing I saw of industrial England inclined me to spend my life there, so I went home and looked for a job in the Highlands or Islands. I jumped at the chance of Morissey, and perhaps because no one else thought it worth applying for, I got it. And for five years I've loved every moment of my life and work here. Well, not quite, but most of it.

I'm putting all this down to show that I'm a normal woman, because the value of my evidence, for what follows, depends on my normality.

And I'm normal enough for anything, and sensible too. If I were writing an autobiography I could say a lot more to prove this, but for the present I'm only interested in the case of Torquil Malone. A bad man, but attractive.

He is a man of importance in the island, though he does nothing much, in a local way, to sustain his importance except spend a lot of money. But he is, or has been famous—relatively famous, by our standards at least—and that we respect. There is no one else here with a name that is known, or used to be, in London and New York and Los Angeles: not even our absentee laird who comes for six or seven weeks in the year, to shoot a diminishing number of grouse, catch a few sea-trout—I catch more—and take six or eight stags from the little stony forest that rises to the north-east and gives Morissey its romantic aspect; the rest of it is low-lying, gentle, and fertile. We have taller, bigger neighbours that are worth less on the rent-roll, and our nine hundred and sixty-three inhabitants give me enough to do, but leave me time, in summer, for as much fishing as I want.

When I first came, the older men and women were shy and reluctant to expose their ailments to a woman doctor; but in Germany I had acquired a sort of regimental, man-to-man approach, and though I have a good figure and long legs I am not aggressively attractive—not too insistently feminine—so gradually I won their confidence, and now, I fancy, they are almost unaware of my sex. Perhaps I have gone too far in suppressing or denying it. There is something inherent in my profession that makes it difficult for an ordinary man to speak directly to the woman hiding behind a Bachelor of Medicine—though often enough the woman wants to get out in front—and I, by the manner I have acquired, have probably made it more difficult. When I think of marrying again, as doubtless I shall, I'll have to take the lead and firmly conduct my young man to the bed-end. But I'm in no hurry, though sometimes I wish my little orphan had a small brother to play with. She seems happy enough at the village school, but she is very self-centred, like so many female children—and what, after all, has she got to do with the story I should be telling? Here I am chattering of myself, and my own affairs, when I should be telling what I know of Torquil Malone.

According to my day-book it was on May 23rd, just before lunch, that Isobel telephoned and asked me to come and see him. He had been drinking more heavily than usual—than his usual habit during the last six months or so—and now he had become violent. He had thrown a whisky-bottle through a window, and gone out with his gun. It didn't promise to be an agreeable interview, so I went immediately, without giving myself time to think about it. He lived three miles from the village, beside the loch.

Isobel was waiting for me at the roadside, looking self-important rather than distressed, as she should have been. She is a stupid woman, but very pretty. A minimum of intelligence, no nerves, and a lovely face and figure: a lucky mixture, I suppose, and perhaps I'm jealous.

'He's all right now,' she said. 'I mean he hasn't shot himself, and that's what I thought he was going to do after I heard the crash and saw him coming out with a gun. But I kept my head and didn't say anything to annoy him.'

'What did you say?'

'I just asked if there'd been an accident.'

I left my car on the road, and we walked up together. Their house was a re-built farmhouse with the farm buildings added to it, making three sides of a square with a paved court and a sun-dial where the midden had been. An attractive house, and very expensively furnished.

I found Torquil in his work-room, with a broken window to show where the bottle had gone. He was quiet and melancholy, full of self-pity, and—as I thought at first—gently raving.

'It isn't drink,' he said. 'Drink's been the salve and lenitive. Drink's kept me sane: drink and Isobel. No, the plain, undeniable fact—and you won't believe it—is that I'm haunted. Haunted by a fetch.'

'Is that what you were shooting at?'

'Yes.'

'Did you hit it?'

'Do you know what a fetch is?'

'No,' I said.

'I'll show you what this one is.'

He went to a shelf—two of his walls were lined with books to the ceiling—and taking down one of a set, showed me the picture of a pretty, dove-coloured bird with a black head, called a Sociable Plover.

'That's it,' he said.

'You've been drinking a lot, Torquil, haven't you?'

'Who wouldn't, who's persecuted as I have been?'

'But what is a fetch? Does it just mean a bird?'

He went into a long rigmarole of explanation—or lack of explanation—of magic and witchcraft, and I watched him a little anxiously, knowing that only an hour or so before he had suddenly become violent. His voice was low and monotonous, and his eyes were uneasy, turning to the window and back again. He had deteriorated a lot in a few months—and I, perhaps, was a factor in that—but in a dissolute way, that was now a coarse dissolution, he was still extraordinarily handsome; and I though of the uniformed photograph of him, in Isobel's room, that showed a head of brutal vigour and Roman formality: a severe and sculptured beauty. Now the lines were looser, the eyes duller, and the skin unhealthy: there was a little reddish patch, inflamed and pustular, on one side of the neck. But he was still a man to look at—as a man—with admiration, and his figure, though a belly pouted, showed the breadth and squareness of a soldier and an athlete. He was very sorry for himself, and his voice remained low and miserable.

'So you see what it is,' he said. 'Sometimes it's called a wraith, or apparition. It's the person himself, or herself, but not in his or her proper shape. No, never! It could be an animal, or something without apparent life. And it's sent—a "sending" is another name for it—by the person it is, or an agent who's taken control of him, for the single purpose of driving the intended victim to madness and death. It's the blackest magic that the adept knows.'

'How do you know about it?'

'There's not much,' he said, 'with which I haven't a surface acquaintance—or better.'

That was his natural, sometimes insufferable arrogance cropping out; and I was glad to hear it. If he retained some thing of his arrogance, he probably had the willingness to be cured, and could be persuaded to re-assert his sanity.

'Do you know,' I asked, 'who's likely to have sent the fetch? Can you think of anyone who hates you enough to want to drive you mad?'

'Forty,' he said. 'Forty at least. I haven't lived an easy life.'

Arrogance again. But his eyes, alert and frightened, turning to the window. He told me how often, how persistently, the bird had pestered him, and something of the death-wish it implanted and fostered in him. We went out to look for it, but could not find it. He had not hit it when he shot at it: that he knew.

I told him the best thing he could do was to go away for a couple of months. Leave Morissey and the bird—in which I didn't believe—and live for a while in London, Edinburgh, Paris or Dublin. Or take a long voyage in a cargo-ship. 'And stop drinking so much,' I said.

His lunch was brought in on a tray, and I went to eat with Isobel and the children. Two little girls, six and four, with pretty faces and futile minds. Their mother's children. If Torquil was suffering from melancholia, I thought, it was partly the fault of Isobel and her brood.

I had three or four patients to see in the afternoon, but I thought not so much of them as of Torquil. I knew too much of him for a detached, impartial, scientific view, but not enough for a whole and human understanding. I knew something of his background, and the reason for his arrogance; but not much of the life he had lived, except what he had told me, and part of that was mere boasting.

He came, as I did, from Inverdoon: a town large enough for gossip to be various, and small enough to ensure some accuracy in gossip. His father had been a Warrant Officer in the Navy, a man of twenty or twenty-five years service when, in the autumn of 1914, at the very beginning of the first Great War, his ship was torpedoed and he came to hospital in Inverdoon. With some thirty other early casualties he lay in a ward in the Royal Infirmary, and he and his fellow-patients—when to be wounded was still a distinction—were cossetted and comforted by many visitors. His most persistent visitor was a Miss M . . ., a lady no longer in her first youth, who was the fifth of five daughters of the Professor of Biblical History, a shabby and eccentric old man. Miss M . . . fell headlong in love with the robust and handsome sailor, and when he was discharged, unfit for further service, she married him in secret and brazenly brought him back to Inverdoon. Their marriage scandalised University circles and the Old Town, and shocked them more when Mr Malone set up as a bookmaker—Turf Accountant, he called himself—in Spitalgate, midway between Queen's College and the Cathedral, and soon prospered.

This I know because we lived next door; where my father was a butcher, not well-to-do, and the increasing wealth of Mr Malone was our endless source of envy and speculation.

Torquil was his only son, and when I came to Morissey—three or four years after Torquil and Isobel had bought their house and settled there—I quickly found that he hated, more than most things, to be reminded of his parentage and upbringing. To begin with, he openly resented my presence, because I knew too much about him and reminded him, every time he saw me, of what I knew. Then, for a while, he ignored me.

He had left home as soon as he left school, when he was seventeen, and gone abroad. For several years we heard nothing of him, but suddenly he jumped into fame with a first novel that became a best-seller and attracted a lot of serious attention when it became known that the author was only twenty-one and had already seen more of the world than most people do in a long life. From Inverdoon he had gone to Calcutta, as clerk in a shipping firm—that was true—but then the narrative, as it grew more various, became less dependable. He had, it seemed, been a journalist for some time, a reporter working in Shanghai and possibly Vancouver. It was commonly said that he had lived a wild life; and detail was filled in according to imagination. How he had acquired the book-learning and found the leisure to write *John Gaffikin* was a mystery for which two solutions were offered. There were those who said he had retired to a monastery—generally unidentified—for six months; but others, perhaps more plausibly, told of a rich woman who, having engaged him as her private secretary, gave him time to write and the freedom of her library: being impressed by his budding genius. Whatever the truth of it, *John Gaffikin* gave evidence of a more than academic knowledge of life, and made a small fortune for Torquil. In 1940, when he went into the Army, he showed again his remarkable aptitude for success, and was quickly promoted. So much I knew, and a little more . . . .

I did my work, and went home to supper. I read to Fiona, my little orphan, for an hour, and put her to bed. I settled down to my own book, and then the bell rang; and when I went to the door, there was Torquil.

I took him into my small sitting-room—furnished so cheaply, in such bare sufficiency, compared with the opulence of his house—and I saw with relief that he was sober; or in that settled, meridian state of drink that, for a drunkard, may be near sobriety.

He said at once, 'I've come to tell you how grateful I am for your advice. I've talked things over with Isobel—though she knows nothing of what I told you. She wouldn't understand—and I've decided to go away. I'm going tomorrow. To London first, and then, if I can find a slow cargo-boat, to South America. I've never been to South America. Perhaps I'll go up the Amazon.'

'Shall I give you a drink?' I asked. 'A small one? There's only brandy.'

'A small one for me and a big one for you,' he said. 'You've earned more than that today.'

He smiled as if he were wholly at his ease, and to be easy was his natural habit. But that was his way—he had the faculty of contradicting himself, and though he was often arrogant and brutally egotistic, he could suddenly show gentleness and a sort of innocence. He was usually, though not always, very gentle with Isobel: kind to her, and amused by stupidities that, if they had been treated with cold tolerance, would have got more than they deserved. In his utter absorption in fishing he was innocence itself—there's a fragment of my own portrait, I suppose—and to find him lying in a ditch with his field-glasses pointed to a flock of field-fares was to find not only innocence but humility; for in spite of his interest in birds, and the hours he spent watching them, he never learnt much about them, and admitted his ignorance.

But his arrogance could be embarrassing, and I was completely puzzled by his regular church-going till I discovered that he believed, quite firmly, in a family relationship with God. God, being an author too, was the chief of his clan: it was as simple as that. Of his own books he never spoke, nor encouraged others to speak; and that was pride again. They were there to be accepted, like islands in the sea, about whose creation one doesn't ask. And it's true that his novels are very good indeed, especially the early ones. The later ones don't gallop as they did, and haven't their freshness, their juice. But they're good—and he, though I can't tell how I know it, he, I'm sure, is intrinsically bad.

He talked for a while about his intended voyage, and then, with a change of tone, said, 'I've wasted, utterly wasted, the last six months. My life's been null and void. Boredom and blank despair: that's all I've felt. I can't even believe in myself and the worth of my own work—and that's like the fall of Lucifer, isn't it?'

'Don't tell me I'm to blame. I've heard that too often.'

'I'm in no state of mind to blame anyone. I haven't the force of will to discriminate, or the energy to decide. But you can't disclaim all responsibility.'

I could, of course—but not without a very embarrassing argument. The simple, unappetising fact of the matter was that I had once spent a couple of nights with Torquil in a Glasgow hotel, and then refused to have anything more to do with him. After my first year or two in Morissey, when he had ignored me, he began to show signs of interest, which presently became a specific interest. I was, I admit, attracted to him—as many women, in my circumstances, would have been—but also I knew how vulnerable I was. In my position I couldn't afford a scandal—that was obvious—and after one or two unpleasant scenes I thought I had convinced him of it, and found relief from a very pressing danger. But then I went to Glasgow, for a few days' shopping, and Torquil was there to meet me. We dined together, and in the remoteness, the anonymity, the irresponsibility of that vast hive of people, I gave in.

But two nights were enough. Oh, more than enough. I wasn't inexperienced, and I'm not unduly sensitive—but I'm not a troop of girls in a brothel, and that's what he needed. How Isobel has put up with him I don't understand; unless her stupidity is so dense, unfeeling, and imperceptive that it gives her a sort of invincible innocence. But Torquil and I quarrelled bitterly—noisily, vulgarly—and his vanity was wounded to the core. I left him in Glasgow, and went back to Morissey in profound relief; for the temptation he had offered was now gone for ever. But that he would not accept, or could not understand, and when, a week or so later, he came home, it was to parade in romantic despair and beg me to have pity on him. He made a great fool of himself, and hugged his disappointment as if he loved it. Perhaps he did. Perhaps it was a new experience, the first time a woman had disappointed him. He told me, in solemn anger, that I was ruining his life, and implied that no mere woman's whimsy should ever obstruct or exasperate a life that was held in trust for English literature. But he got no sympathy.

Then Isobel told me he was drinking heavily—more heavily than before—and I wondered, for a moment, if she was going to accuse me of hard-heartedness. She was so besotted with him, so convinced of his genius, that she might well have told me it was my duty to give him whatever small pleasure I could offer. But for once she was sensible, and said, 'It's my opinion that he's bored with this new book he's writing. He feels he ought to do it, and doesn't want to, so he drinks instead.'—And that, I've little doubt, was the truth of it.

But now, with him in my small and shabby room—on the verge of departure and still sorry for himself—I could say nothing of all this; and quickly turning myself into a whole-time medical practitioner—a calm and sagacious country doctor—I gave him good advice instead. I told him not to drink too much on the voyage, and wrote a prescription for sleeping-pills.

My professional manner soon bored him, and after another small brandy-and-water he got up and said goodnight. I wished him luck and a happy return; and closed the door behind him.

THREE

I could find no ship to take me to South America, and instead of the Amazon went to Kenya and South Africa. By sea—a dull voyage—to Mombasa, six weeks with a dim cousin in Nyeri, a trip to Uganda, a month with an old friend in Buluwayo, then a couple of weeks in Cape Town, and the voyage home; which was duller than the outward journey. All this was wasted time, except for a few hours. I got small enjoyment, and nothing else from it: no fertile thought, no propulsive or breeding view of humanity and its purpose. I dislike black men, and I found the African landscape either boring or repugnant, except for the luminous skies of Kenya, on which clouds lie like swansdown pillows, puffed-up and plumply patted on translucent satin that shows behind it coverlets of ever deeper blue. The skies of Kenya reveal a beauty that is quite incredible.

But the few hours of real value were spent at the Victoria Falls, where I discovered that I had no wish or will to commit suicide. I had been worried by the apparent ease with which that abominable bird had tempted me to look down, from my boat, into the cool, green, enticing depths of the loch; and, sorely perplexed, I had wondered if I harboured in my mind a secret thought of self-destruction. To test myself, I went deliberately to the Falls, and on either side of them stood, with intention, beside their superb and natural solicitation to death.

Nowhere on earth have I seen a more majestic spectacle than that vast descent of water turning with a roar to flocculence—the hypnotic, downward curve of solid water into a descent of floating whiteness that compels from the abyss a continuous, resounding bellow; and above the tumult of the enormous, broken stream a constant cloud, a vapour of air and water—and nowhere, in knowledge or imagination, can there be a stronger temptation to join the elements and enjoy the total dissolve, which they promise, of the wretched load of individual consciousness. But I stood, first on one side, then on the other, of that stupendous gorge—that break in the earth's crust, that breach of time and solid nature—and let the chorussed invitation of the waters to join them in dissolution fill my ears—let the sight of the burden of water transmuted by a great height into the weightless beauty of immaculate whiteness fill my eyes—and in the sober consciousness of my mind I felt no impulse to throw myself down. There was, within my deepest self, no thought, impulse, or hidden desire of suicide. That I knew, having faced the temptation of height and beauty and dissolving waters.

Of the rest of my voyage I shall say little. I behaved, on the whole, with a bourgeois common sense. I rarely drank too much, and only twice retreated from the common form of good behaviour: once in the darkest African parts of Kampala, once in Johannesburg, where I found opportunity for that sort of orgiastic pleasure which, I confess, has been a recurrent temptation throughout my life. But my average of behaviour was good, and though I got little enjoyment and less instruction from my journey, I came back to Morissey in a better state of health, both of mind and body, than when I left it. And Isobel I met with a new hunger of love: a love compact of gratitude as much as of desire—and every morning she was born anew.

But now I must speak in practical fashion, in a matter-of-fact, down-to-earth style of words, and admit that I was still a little frightened. For a few days I watched, nervously, for the return of the Plover. But he did not come again. The lapwings, the ordinary green plover, had by then diminished in numbers: there is a local migration that increases their number in the spring, reduces it in autumn. The migrants had gone, and by a rationalisation of my fear I concluded that my Sociable Plover, the fetch or sending, had gone with them. My nervous fear—the tension of fear—relaxed.

Superficially I was irritated by the presence of Isobel's sister Beatrice. She has two sisters, and I like neither of them. The eldest of the three is a lecturer in Economics at a red-brick university in the middle of England: a handsome woman of stiff and splendid presence who belies her appearance by the damp fervour of her belief in every dislocated idea that was thought 'progressive' twenty years ago. The middle sister, Beatrice, is an artist, a painter in the abstract style, and a Lesbian. She has, in that condition of life, the unfortunate advantages of a face and figure like Goya's—what's her name? The luscious aristocrat he painted nude, but when he painted her with a rag of clothing was denounced for his indecency—and when I first discovered the prohibitive temper of her mind I was savagely disillusioned. I was still, in a subdued and fretful way, resentful of her presence: that appeared to promise so much, and could give nothing. But Isobel was fond of her—fond also of Leonora, the stiff-seeming, soggy-minded lecturer in Economics—and twice a year we had each of them to stay with us for several weeks.

Beatrice was there when I returned to Morissey, and stayed three weeks. A few days after she left I had a dream that was more like visible and palpable experience than any other dream I have ever had: more real, in dreaming and in memory, than many days of open-eyed experience.—I was on the shore below the strip of meadow that fringes the loch, fishing thigh-deep in wading-boots, and Beatrice, watching, was sitting on a tumbled dyke behind me. Fish were rising, but not, as I thought, in a normal way. It looked as if they were being hunted by some larger fish. I was casting with a long line, to try and reach them, when Beatrice cried, 'There's something under the water!'

Then the surface was broken by a white and noble head, and with a ponderous assurance, with an ideal and perfect dignity—scattering the wetness of his fur with a shake and a shiver that surrounded him with a cloud of diamond drops—a great white hound came ashore. I retreated as he advanced, and our movement was slow, hieratic, as if in solemn procession.

Beatrice, in a foolish voice, cried, 'Oh, its a seal!'

But I, quite calmly, said, 'No, it's the Great White Hound of Cuchullin.'

It had a smallish head, shaped like a polar bear's, straight and heavy forelegs, a hound's body, and enormous, loping thighs. Its wet fur, round its neck and shoulders, was tightly curled as a Bedlington terrier's; but when I stroked it, it became smooth and wavy. I put my right arm round the hound's neck, and gave it my other hand to nuzzle. It was very gentle, but its teeth were as sharp as a puppy's.

Then I looked round, and saw the two children running down from the house. The elder was wearing fancy-dress that imitated the mask and skin of a panda—a dress she had been given for a children's party—and covering the hound's eyes I shouted to them, 'Go away, you mustn't make fun of him! You mustn't hurt his feelings!'

They went back to the house, and I clapped the hound on his shoulder. He was very friendly, and laid his nose in the crook of my arm. His eyes looked into mine with gentle confidence. There was no arrogance in his demand, but only trust, and I was conscious that I had become his servant. This knowledge gave me pleasure, and made me feel important.

Then the hound turned, and shook himself again, and slowly waded into the loch. He looked back at me, with the same confiding glance, and I began to follow him. But Beatrice, with a loud cry, seized me with angry hands, and pulled me to the meadow-grass. I struggled with her, and we fell. When I woke up, Isobel was in my arms and I pushed her from me, exclaiming 'Where's Beatrice gone? And where is the Hound?'

I got up and went to the window. The loch lay calm and empty, a silky, rippled grey, and I felt desolate, as though cheated of some great prize. As though a door to bliss had been closed in my face.

I could hardly believe the slow admission of my mind that I had been dreaming. Night after night I dreamt of my dream—by some deep division of my half-unconscious mind seeing it as a dream, seeing it in perspective—and this re-iteration made it, after every recollection, more oddly real. By dreaming of my dream, I turned it into something like actual experience; and this made me frightened to go near the loch-shore.

What emerged most strongly from an ever-thickening, impacted fantasy was the confiding look in the White Hound's returning eye—the look that bade me follow, and knew I would—and my consciousness that I had been willing to go with him and be drowned.

I felt, too, a mounting, quite irrational hatred of Beatrice for the part she had played in my dream. I could not endure to hear Isobel speak of her, and one day when Isobel was out and I found, among a little pile of letters that the postman had brought, a letter from Beatrice, I tore it across, unopened in its envelope, and threw the pieces on the fire. Then I began to wonder if I was going mad—and for the first time felt surprised to remember how immediately, in my dream, I had recognised the great water-beast as the Hound of Cuchullin.

Not for many years, not since I was very young, had I read anything of Irish mythology, and with something like consternation I realised that I didn't know if Cuchullin had in fact been attended by a hound.

I had on my shelves the old, massive volumes of the Eleventh Edition of the *Encyclopaedia Britannica*, and when I looked him up I discovered that he himself, Cuchullin, was the hound. He, the young hero, had killed the hound of Culann the Smith, and then served as watch-dog to the Smith till a whelp of the dead dog could grow to strength and maturity.—But why had I fetched him from the depths of my mind, and changed him, in the abyss of consciousness, to a water-beast? Had I been looking for a hero to redeem myself? It would, indeed, be a task for a hero.

I felt, increasingly, a disablement of mind or will that invaded and infected my physical parts. As I grew more frightened of going out and approaching the temptation of the loch—the temptation of waters that now were dark and seemed the deeper for their darkness—my arms and legs grew torpid and heavy, disinclined for exertion, and I spent most of the day, and every day, in bed . . . .

FOUR

There are some women who make such a fuss about having a baby that I could cheerfully knock them on the head, and shake it out. Mary McInnes is one of them. She has lain-in once a year since I came to Morrisey, and every time you would think she was the first woman who had ever submitted to the experiment, or else was about to be delivered of a Messiah.

I had spent all night with her, and was still in my dressing-gown, after soaking for an hour in a hot bath, when Isobel rang me up and asked me to come and see Torquil again. I was looking forward to a good breakfast, with a book propped on the tea-pot, and a day which, by tidy management, could be almost idle till my evening surgery. But Isobel was insistent, my breakfast was spoiled by irritation, and I was in a bad temper when I went to see him.

Isobel, to begin with, took me into her own small sitting-room, and closed the door with the portentous care of someone about to reveal a state secret. 'Torquil,' she said, 'has been drinking too much.'

'My dear Isobel,' I said, 'you can't expect me to register surprise and consternation when you tell me that.'

'No,' she said, 'I realise that he isn't like us, and doesn't behave like us. But great writers—he *is* a great writer!—can't be expected to find satisfaction in the ordinary things of life: the ordinary, middle-class measure of life. Torquil has often drunk too much, just to get out of the ordinary measure. But lately, for the last couple of weeks, he's gone too far. He's drinking in bed.'

'In your bed?'

'Oh, no! I wish he was. He hasn't slept with me for a fortnight. He's sleeping in his dressing-room, and he hardly ever gets up except to go downstairs for another bottle of whisky. He's too frightened, you see.'

'Frightened of what?'

'I don't quite know. I really mean, I don't understand. All I know is that he had a bad dream.'

I listened, with growing impatience, to her confused and meaningless story—in her incapacity to give a clear and reasonable account of what he was suffering, she looked extraordinarily young, innocent, and, from a man's point of view, I suppose, desirable—and interrupted her to ask, 'Does he know I'm here?'

'Yes, I told him you were coming. He was angry, at first, and then he said, "All right, I'd like to see her." He can be so sweet, he quite disarms you, doesn't he?'

I had never been in Torquil's dressing-room before. I had been to see Isobel in their bedroom, and that, by the opulence of its furniture, had slightly disgusted me. There was a double bed of inordinate size, with silk hangings, velvet curtains on the windows, a French sofa, a dressing-table of ridiculous luxury, and a wardrobe with an open door that disclosed hillocks of silk underclothes. I compared it with my own bare room—my skimpy chest-of-drawers—and felt a revulsion that may, in part, have been a mask for jealousy. But when I saw Torquil's dressing-room, and him in bed there, I was, in a quite simple, instinctive way, antagonised by the richness of its comfort. It was, absurdly, all in white—ivory, cream, or white—except for a quilt of gold satin and one great picture full and over-full of peaches, pineapples, purple grapes, a pheasant or two, and yellow plums—and staring from the general pallor, spectacular in its pride and luxury, there was the enormous, splendid skin of a polar bear, deep-furred, silky and resilient, with the cruel, proud head mounted to show its teeth in an eternal snarl.

Even in so rich a room it dominated, made the first impression, and with hardly a glance at Torquil—but I saw he had not shaved for two or three days—I was down on my knees to stroke the smooth white head and ask, 'Where did you get this?'

'It's more interesting than I am, isn't it?' he said. 'I've had it for a long time—and I still like it.'

'Well,' said Isobel, 'I had better leave you,' and went out, and closed the door.

'I've never seen anything that made me so immediately envious,' I said; and reluctantly got up. 'But you're the patient, not the polar bear. Tell me what's been happening.'

'In the first place, how glad I am to see you! I should have asked you to come and help me—oh, long ago—but I was too ashamed. It's very shameful, for a man of my sort, to tell a woman that he has been frightened into illness—frightened by a dream. But that's the truth of it.'

'Are you drinking a lot?'

'More than I have ever done.'

'Because you're frightened?'

'Yes.—And, of course, because I like it.'

He had, as Isobel said, a quality, a charm, that could not be denied and was capable of disarming the most unfriendly critic. I, at that moment, felt no touch or breath of friendship for him—a dissolute, unshaven man, stinking of whisky in a room of theatrical luxury—but as he sat up in bed and leaned towards me, and his voice deepened, as it seemed, in honesty and self-reproach, I knew that I must guard myself against the sympathy he would try to evoke; and perhaps could. I looked again at the skin of the polar bear, let envy run into my heart, and thought: Envy will keep sympathy at bay.

'You had better tell me,' I said, 'something about your dream.'

'It's going to be difficult,' he said, 'because it wasn't like a dream. It was much more like something that happened in another dimension of reality. An impalpable dimension, but not less real because of that.'

I listened to his story, and had to be told who Cuchullin was. I had never heard of him. I recognised, of course, some of the minor symbolism of the dream, and admitted to myself a little malicious pleasure when I realised, what was obvious enough, that at some time he had been rebuffed, or at least disappointed, by Beatrice; whom I disliked intensely. But I was fascinated and perplexed by the story as a whole.—He told it so well that, even to me, the Hound seemed to exist and have its own personality. It wasn't till he had finished, and I had given him a weak whisky-and-water—for telling the story had exhausted him—that I saw the obvious association.

I waited till he grew calmer, more composed, and then I asked him, 'How long have you had this rug?'

'Oh, a long time.'

'Where did you get it?'

I waited a full minute before he answered. Then he said, 'It was after the war. When I was in Berlin.'

'Does it remind you of anything?'

'Well, of course. Of Berlin. Of everything that happened there.'

'But of anything in particular? Among the things you remember in a general way, is it associated with any particular event?'

Again he was silent for a long time—I supposed he was thinking, jogging his memory—before he said, 'No.'

And now I must make a confession; for what I said next was not dictated by medical theory and a doctor's professional insight, but by the stark envy I had felt when I first saw the enchantment of that great, white, silky skin. I had wanted—absurdly, but quite positively, with a surge of adolescent or romantic abandonment to sheer physical desire—to undress and lie on it, naked; and I could hardly endure the knowledge that Torquil owned it. So I said to him, 'You ought to get rid of it. You know as much about the unconscious as I do, so I needn't go into tiresome explanation. But it seems probable that the rug is associated with something you want to forget—that consciously, perhaps, you have forgotten—and your compulsive dream of a Great White Hound, with its obvious likeness to a polar bear, is the work of your unconscious mind rebelling against a prohibition you have put on it. So get rid of the rug. It's a constant reminder—if my guess is a good one—of something of which you don't want to be reminded. So burn it, or give it away, and stop tormenting that part of your mind which, like the butt-end of an iceberg, lies out of sight and communication.'

'No,' he said, 'I can't do that.'

'I'll give you some sleeping-pills—you like nembutal, don't you?—but that's only a palliative,' I said. 'I want you to go for a good walk every day—get Isobel to go with you—and try not to drink anything before six o'clock. But what really matters, of course, is to find out what's frightening you, and eliminate that. We'll have to work by trial and error; and for a start I suggest—my advice is—that you get rid of the rug. Burn it, or sell it.'

At that moment, I believe, I had in my mind the thought, the hope, that I might buy it. But he disappointed me by repeating, 'No, that's what I can't do.'

'Then nembutal and healthy exercise are all I can offer you,' I said. 'I'll give Isobel the pills.'

It was not till a week later that Isobel telephoned again and said, 'Torquil is going to send away that white bearskin. He asked me to tell you. He's going to send it to London, to be sold for the Lord Mayor's relief-fund. I don't know what you said to him, and I don't know what it all means, but I feel much happier. It's a lovely rug, but I've never liked it—perhaps because he would keep it in his own room—and I'm very glad it's going. For the last two days he's been hardly human.'

I felt angry and self-contemptuous when I heard that my prescription—designed primarily for my benefit, not his—had been accepted, and my profit was to be nil. The rug might indeed be a clue to the psychological origin of his dream; it probably was, and the degree of probability, or my conjecture of it, was a reasonable excuse for the advice I had given. But the purpose of my advice had been to get the rug for myself. And, being defeated, I felt resentful of defeat and ashamed of the shabbiness of my motive. It was a very unpleasant moment.

I said to Isobel, 'You will need more nembutal, and I'll send you some. But keep the pills in your own room. And you must get him out of doors and make him take some exercise. Try to make him physically tired . . . .'

I avoided both of them for some weeks, and an autumn crop of gastric 'flu in the schools and rheumatic pains in the old, made that easy enough. But the tantalising thought, the damned enchantment, of that white luxury of arctic fur returned to me night after night as if I had been infected by the compulsion of his unholy dream. A dozen times I dreamt—of it, not him—and woke ill-tempered and self-hating.

It was shortly before Christmas that I read, in the *British Medical Journal*, a tendentious, kite-flying article on psychosomatic distempers in Melanesia by C.J. Patrick Ryan—and recognised Paddy Ryan, whom I had known in Berlin: an Irish doctor of ebullient temper and sometimes brilliant intuition whose gifts were often obscured by the triviality of his interests. He had a village appetite for gossip, an old woman's nose for scandal . . . and having remembered this, it occurred to me that he might have known Torquil, or something of him.

I sat down after supper and wrote him a long letter. I told him about myself, I spoke admiringly of his article, and presently said something of my interesting patient. 'A man you may have known in Berlin,' I said. I didn't go into details, I only said that Torquil was suffering from a neurosis about which I could do very little unless I knew more of the background in which it had been planted. 'And that's where you may be able to help me,' I wrote.

I was, I think, extremely tactful. I made no reference to Ryan's fondness for gossip, but spoke of his reputation for wide and judicious knowledge of men and their surroundings. I said, disingenuously, 'I remember how often people went to you and asked, "What's the truth of this story about So-and-So? What really happened to him?"'—Oh, there was substance in his reputation! He had a genius for gathering, sifting, and remembering the news of the day, and he never forgot a face or a good story. I flattered him, as was right and proper in the circumstances, but I went too far, perhaps, when I wrote: 'How much I would like to see you again! You must, I suppose, have leave from time to time, and when your next leave is due, think seriously of what Morissey can offer. I'll promise you brown-trout fishing far above the average, and if you're lucky a run of sea-trout in early July that you'll remember all your life.'

I addressed my letter 'care of the B.M.J.' and got no answer till the end of February; and that, when it came, was cryptic. He wrote: 'I never met Torquil Malone, but I know all that was said about him, and if you want the substance of it, read the Second Book of Samuel, chapter XI, and ponder the order, "Set ye Uriah in the forefront of the hottest battle." In his case Uriah and Bethsabe were Poles—and that, for the present, is all I shall tell you.'

He went on to protest an affection for me that he had never shown when, for several months, we had met three or four times a week; and finished his letter with an explosive, 'Bless you, dear Anne, for the invitation to fish! I shall, beyond doubt or peradventure, come to Morissey next June, when my leave is due, if I survive my next tour among black headhunters in the New Hebrides, and thereafter can discover the whereabouts of your island, of which I never heard till now. But love of you, and of sea-trout, will be my guide.'

The address he gave was 'Somewhere off Malekula, rolling heavily', and I guessed that when he wrote he was not quite sober. But I looked up the Bible my mother had given me—I had not used it much—and read some of the Second Book of Samuel. I read more than I first intended, for those ponderous great words, that thunder into meaning like boulders down a stream in spate, carried me with them, and the stories they told dismayed me with their news of the perennial wickedness of human creatures.—The eleventh chapter tells how King David fell in love with Bathsheba, or Bethsabe as Ryan called her, and slept with her. Her husband, Uriah, was a good soldier, and when David sent him up the line again, he went willingly, and was killed. And David got Bethsabe, who much preferred a live king to a dead colonel, or whatever Uriah had been. Well, I know others like her.

But it took me some time to digest Ryan's assertion—a vaguely drawn but seemingly confident assertion—that Torquil, in some sort of way, had played David to an unknown Pole; whose wife, by inference, he had coveted. And when I had digested it, it meant, perhaps curiously, very little to me. The Bible may be to blame for this: the Bible had told me of men's wickedness through all recorded time, and because I knew nothing of the people whom Torquil had betrayed and loved, he took his place, almost anonymously, in a long, long queue of sinners, and all I felt was a justification and stiffening of my dislike for him.

But dislike, in our times, when most of us have discarded the hard spine of morality and called our weakening 'progress', doesn't show itself in action. A day or two later I dined with Torquil and Isobel, and with a rather grudging pride considered the marvellous improvement in his health. He looked well and happy, and I could, I suppose, claim to have cured him—though I was doubtful if my medical colleagues would accept 'Remove the bearskin' as a scientific prescription. But I was glad to see him better, and rather against my will I was a little moved by the evident affection that still held them. They were going to Jamaica for a month. 'A reward to Isobel,' he said, 'for the persistency of her kindness and the loyalty of her devotion to such an utterly worthless creature as I am.'

She protested and contradicted, of course; and so would I if I had had the strength of mind to be truthful. I should have told them that his recovery began when he got rid of the rug, and it was my suggestion that made him give it away; but I let that pass. It was a lavish dinner, and I had drunk enough to be charitable for a moment.

But not for long. Jamaica, I thought! While I stayed in Morissey, through the cold, rain-swept, miserable last months of winter, he and Isobel would be revelling on hot white sands, in a bright blue sea, under a sky of golden glory, because he had been clever about investments. When he made a lot of money, in the late '30s, it was possible to save something of what you earned, and he had been clever enough to multiply his savings on the Stock Exchange. That's what I resented: his cleverness. I resented it more than his presumptive wickedness. Oh, I'm in no position to judge him! Only to record what I know of him, and what happened.

He and Isobel came back at the beginning of April, looking to us, still white and drawn by winter, indecently healthy. They were bright-eyed, sunburnt, deft and lively of speech and body: full of anecdotes, full of a newly won vitality. And we who had sustained a northern winter, and done our work in winter, were lack-lustre, pale of skin, and unhealthy of aspect. I liked him less and less, and saw very little of him until the second half of May, when, as usual in the beneficence of returning summer, my practice diminished, and I was able to spend two or three days a week fishing. Then, inevitably, we met on this or that favourite shore of the loch, ate our sandwiches together, and talked of fish and flies; or bewailed the difficulty nowadays of getting good gut and debated the best knots for nylon.

That he was now completely cured, I had no doubt whatever; and because I am not the sort of person who is everlastingly worried by what can't be explained, I no longer thought much about the mystery of a psychical obsession—a re-iterated or double obsession—that could be explained very simply in terms of witchcraft, but otherwise not at all. One day, indeed, when we had finished our lunch and the loch was so glassily calm that it was useless to think of fishing, we sat for an hour and watched the terns hawking flies, and listened to the creak of the lapwings' flight; and on a sudden impulse I asked, 'You haven't seen the Sociable Plover again, have you?'

'No,' he said, and looked at me with an expression of great gravity and resolution that was, perhaps, a little forced. 'I keep a good look-out, and so far there's been no sign of it. But if it does come back, I know what to do. It won't get the better of me again.'

I was surprised to hear his reply come so quick and serious. I had expected, I think, a throw-away, half-laughing disclaimer of any interest in so remote a matter; but so far from being remote, it lay on the very surface of his consciousness, and as if I had been wakened by some inexplicable noise at night, I felt, for a moment, the tense and hollow sensation of uncharted fear. Not fear for him, but an absurd fear that I too might be touched by supernatural things. I said nothing, however, except—in a voice of bluff scepticism—'I don't suppose you'll see any more of that bird.' And then: 'There's a fish rising off the point there. I'm going to put a fly over it.'

When I got home I found a telegram from Paddy Ryan asking, 'Can I be assured of friendly welcome and simple accommodation if I arrive June 15 for three weeks.' I went to Mrs Malcolm, in the village, who takes summer boarders 'just to oblige my friends', as she is careful to explain; and having persuaded her, quite easily, to put him up, replied to a London address, 'Both await you.'

It was on the morning of the 15th that I saw Torquil with a gun on his arm. I had had to deal with a boy who had fallen and broken his wrist, and on my way back, on a little rise of the road that overlooks his house, I saw him going down to the loch. He was carrying a rod in his right hand, and in the crook of his left arm a shot-gun. I could see it quite clearly.

I didn't stop. I felt that if I got out, and followed him to ask his reason, I should embarrass both of us as deeply as if I were to turn a corner and discover him in some gross indecency. I drove on; and have never ceased to blame myself.

FIVE

God alone—Who has made all—knows the intricacies of the human condition: the true state of us who are bound to history, in debt to the future, tied to our genitals, and lashed like a tiller in a storm to the impossible destiny of our salvation. I believe in my salvation, though I have been guilty of evil deeds. For also I have done good work that has served God's purpose, and my books have fortified many men and revived their appetite for life. That is my justification, and faith is my passport.

Mystery envelops us, but I have peace again. I drink a little, and sometimes more than a little; but only for the contentment and joy of drinking. Not for six months have I drunk for the cloudy comfort of drunkenness and the death of the mind in drink. I have gone back to work, and since we came home from Jamaica I have been working with my old, forgotten zest and with full confidence of the worth of what I write. This is the best of my novels, no doubt of that, and nearly finished now. Only two more chapters, and then I shall have done.

My eyes are wide open again, as they were in youth, and in the early morning I watch, in the birth of day, the birth of a new world. A new world every morning, and the scent of meadowsweet; and in the evening a rain-goose crying to the twilight. The great circle of the sky is our tent, and we, the nomads of inscrutable destiny, have rich pasture for the flocks and herds of our multifarious thoughts that graze on time and circumstance.

But I am wary in my happiness, my weapons are at hand. I shall not yield again to the maleficence of their witchcraft, and if their fetch returns—if from the summer sky that accursed bird drops down with muttering wings to tempt and call me to annihilation and betrayal of my good life—a gun will answer it. No parley with it, no hesitation, but true aim, a shot . . . .

SIX

My first sight of Paddy Ryan was, I admit, disappointing. I had been looking forward, with a growing eagerness that I knew to be ridiculous, to seeing him again, and the first effect of seeing him through the eyes, not through imagination, was to deflate—oh, not entirely, but enough to feel its lessened pressure—the gay balloon of my anticipation. I had forgotten that he was so comically ugly, or perhaps his ugliness had been modified and held in check by uniform, and now was released and amplified by his own choice of clothes. He wore a green and yellow tweed suit of a pattern that only a really big man could have carried, and a very small cap perched ludicrously above his deeply tanned face and great blond moustache. But he waved to me from the steamer with exuberant friendliness, and when he came down the gangway I was almost, if not wholly, comforted against my disappointment by the gleaming vitality of his eyes. I had forgotten they were so bright a blue: the very colour of speedwell.

We talked and laughed all the way home: talked incessantly, of Berlin and his new ocean-parish in the south seas, and of old friends whom I could scarcely remember, and, of course, of fishing. He had brought a whole battery of rods, and a bag full of reels and fly-boxes. We had fly-boxes open all over the tea-table, and whenever he stopped talking of Germany or the New Hebrides it was to ask if a Blue Zulu or a Black Pennell would be better, and what was the proper size to use? But when my little orphan came home from school—she is growing into a big orphan now—Paddy was kindness itself to her, and she took to him at once. I found him exhausting, to begin with, and it was with a feeling of drawing breath again that I drove him to Mrs Malcolm's, and left him there. But he was to come back to dinner.

I had gone to some trouble to give him, on his first night in Morissey, a really good dinner—to show him that we, in the Western Isles, knew as well as others how to live, and could enjoy a proper table—and Paddy Ryan won my entire forgiveness for the vulgarity of his suit, his comical face, and his unresting tongue by his appreciation of all I put before him. There was trout, and duckling, and a cheese soufflé. I was showing-off, and gave him two wines, white and red. There were flowers in the room, and I had a new frock—and Paddy, bless his heart, took notice of them all. I was almost in love with him when we took our coffee to the fire and settled down to talk of Bethsabe and Uriah the Hittite: of Torquil in Berlin.

I had been wondering how to start, when Paddy exclaimed, 'But tell me about Malone! Is he still here, and can I go and see him? I'll be discreet, I promise that. I won't say a word of what I know about him. Or, to be strict and accurate, of what I've heard. For some of the stories would be true enough, but others, it may be, were far-fetched. There was a lot of gossip, and I know it all. But I'll be very discreet.'

'About what, in particular, must you be discreet?'

'He was a man for the women—but he wasn't the only one, of course. And he had a job that brought him in contact with the Germans and the Russians too; and some thought he did a brilliant job, but others said he knew too much and went too far. That could have been jealousy, in some cases, for he was well thought-of by those high up, and everyone agreed that he was quite fearless. But there's one story I heard, and if it's true, then on that occasion he did go too far. Too far to be forgiven by any mortal judge, though what God's mercy can stretch to, none of us knows.'

'Why do you think the story true?'

'It was told me by a man I trust. A man who, though he hadn't legal proof in his hands—no action was taken against Malone—was in a position to form a just opinion of what had happened.'

'And that was—?'

'The old story, all over again, of King David and Bethsabe and the good soldier she was married to. Only he wasn't a soldier this time; he was an engineer. He and his wife were Poles, and she—I've seen her photograph—was a tearing beauty. The sort you see once in a lifetime. Well, Malone got them out of the Russian zone, and fell in love with her. He had a flat of his own, and he knew how to look after himself. Those who had been there said he lived in sinful luxury—on the very edge of the ruins of Berlin!—in a sort of whore's paradise, if you'll forgive me, of white silk curtains, and white rugs on the floor—'

'White rugs?'

'Or so they said, but that may have been exaggeration. They may have been piling it on a bit, with a memory of something they'd seen on a film. But whatever the furniture may have been, the girl was always there; and by and by her husband disappeared. The story was that he had made his peace with the Russians—thanks to Malone!—and gone back to Poland, to a good job there; for they needed engineers badly. And she, in the meantime, was happy enough in her whore's paradise; and who can blame her, after what she'd gone through?'

'Do you think she was enticed by the white rugs on the floor?'

'They're an attraction for some women; or so I've heard. But let that go, for I don't know if the rugs were fiction or fact. But what's true enough is that after five or six months she and Malone fell out.

It wasn't an open quarrel to begin with, but the sort of quarrel that smoulders for a while and then leaps up like a dull wood-fire that you help to a blaze by pouring paraffin on it. Well, there were two British officers there when the flames came out, and what she said, in the roar and heat of her anger, was that Malone, so far from finding her husband a good, comfortable job in Lodz or Poznan or somewhere like that, had sold him to the Russians, and they had sent him to a new hydro-electric construction camp down in the most godless, desolate country about the bottom end, or ends, of the Volga, where it runs into the Caspian Sea.'

'Is that true?'

'I don't know, but the man who told me isn't a liar by choice. And there's worse to follow. For the girl herself and her young son—did I tell you she had a child?'

'No.'

'But yes, there was a boy, about five or six years old—he'll be sixteen or more by now, if he's still alive—and he, they say, took after his mother, and looked like a cross between an angel and a Spanish gipsy. Well, a day or two later they both vanished, and were never seen again.'

'What happened to them?'

'The man who told me most of this—the man who ought to know—believes they went the same way as the husband. That, to oblige Malone, the Russians took charge of them, and because the Russians have a crazy idea of the proper pattern of life—sometimes it looks like logic, and sometimes like farce—they were probably sent down to the swamps and wilderness about the mouths of the Volga to join Uriah the Hittite.'

'Torquil can't have done that!'

'He was in the gravest sort of danger if the girl was out of control, and talking against him, and if what she was saying was true.'

'Can it have been?'

'The man who told me thought so and Malone, who'd been highly regarded till then, was removed to a quieter sector, and a month or two later went back to civil life. At his own request, of course.'

I had a bottle of whisky, which I hadn't intended to open, but we both fell into a sort of stricken silence from which there seemed to be no release; and to open a little wicket-gate of escape from the awful consciousness of what Ryan had been saying, whisky seemed the only thing. I gave him a Highlander's dram, and myself as much; and then I told him—not about the polar bearskin; of that, for some dark reason, I had no wish to speak—but the full story of Torquil's haunting by the

Sociable Plover, and Torquil's belief that it was something he called a 'fetch'.

That opened another sluice-gate, for in the south seas Paddy Ryan had dabbled enthusiastically in the magic and witchcraft practised in Melanesia, and with an Irishman's propensity to accept the supernatural—'to win freedom from the bondage of mundane causality by subscribing to a supra-rational volition,' as someone has put it—he had wholly accepted the possibility of magical 'possession', and was quite prepared to believe in the reality of fetches and sendings. He told several tales to substantiate his belief, and perhaps they were true. But I, by then, was tired-out and half asleep.

'In Scotland, too,' he said, 'you used to believe. Aren't there stories of haunted men who shot at a fetch with a silver bullet, and a hundred miles away he who sent the fetch was found dead with the bullet in his heart?'

'There may be,' I said, 'but I don't suppose Torquil loaded a silver bullet this morning.'

'You saw him this morning?'

'Yes, and he had a gun under his arm. To go fishing.'

'He'll have seen the bird again!'

'Or thought he did. But now, Paddy, I'm nearly asleep—'

'Then we'll meet tomorrow?'

'I can do all I have to do by eleven o'clock, I think . . . .'

We met, precisely at eleven, and went down to the loch. There was a light breeze and a broken sky. It was a good fishing day, and in spite of what I had heard the night before, my spirits rose. I had been tired-out by talk—helped, perhaps, by drink—and slept like a child. I had gone to see the boy with a broken wrist, a woman who had some trouble with her bladder, an old man with unseasonable lumbago; and to comfort people who had very little wrong with them, I had made up several bottles of medicine. I had done my work, I wasn't Torquil's keeper, and the loch was in perfect condition with a new hatch of olives on the water, and the terns and black-headed gulls hawking busily. In full consciousness of happiness we made up our casts, and within forty minutes had three twelve-ounce trout in the boat. We fished farther out, Paddy at the oars, and settled down to a long drift towards Rowan Island and the tiny holms beside it: always my favourite ground. Paddy made the day memorable by casting over a rising fish, hooking it the third time, and after a brilliant, running and jumping, reel-screaming little battle, landing a short, thick-shouldered, deep-chested two-pounder: a lovely fish with roseate spots and a belly like buttercups.

Paddy insisted on drinking to his success, and handed me a flask. I don't drink while I'm fishing, and don't like the idea of it; but for his sake—he was a good fisherman, very deft and quick, with a wonderful eye—I took a sip and passed it back. We were drifting by the stern, and the view beyond Rowan Island was growing wider. At that moment I caught sight of a boat which I recognised at once as Torquil's. He was about three-quarters of a mile away, and as I said to Paddy, 'There's Torquil, away down there to leeward,' he stood up, and with a curious gesture pointed to the sky.

Against the light wind we heard the faint puff of a gunshot; but before hearing it we had seen Torquil, standing in the boat, take a pace or two backwards and, most awkwardly, point again to something invisible. His gun—we could not really see it—must have been almost perpendicular, and from his ungainly, ill-balanced stance he toppled to the side and fell over. We saw the rocking of the empty boat, and a moment later we heard, a mere pout of noise against the wind, the second shot. And 'Row, row, oh row!' I cried.

Paddy took to the oars—Torquil used an out-board motor, but I had nothing so expensive—and pulled as hard as he could, the sweat starting on his face like dew in the morning. But we had a long way to go—more than three-quarters of a mile—and when we got there, nothing was to be seen but the empty boat, with Torquil's rod and net in it, and water on the bottom-boards that had come in over the side when Torquil fell out. It was drifting very peacefully, with the small waves lapping against it.

'How deep is it here?' asked Paddy.

'It's the deepest part of the loch. About eighteen feet. And he always wore heavy rubber boots.'

We rowed to windward again, to the place where, so far as we could judge, Torquil had fallen; and took cross-bearings on it. We peered down into the water, but it was deep and dark, and we could see nothing.

'It wasn't suicide,' I said. 'I saw him clearly. He was shooting at the bird, and lost his balance.'

'Yes,' said Paddy, 'he swung too far back and tipped over. I saw that too. But where's the bird?'

For five or ten minutes, with solemn perseverance and, half-consciously, a desperate wish to explain and justify Torquil's death, we rowed up and down and round in circles, looking for a dead bird in which Paddy firmly believed, and I still feared to believe. But we found nothing, and presently, returning to Torquil's boat, baled her out and with mine in tow started the engine. Sadly, speechless and bewildered, we motored home.

Paddy came with me to tell Isobel, but when she went into hysterics he covered his face and left us; and I had to deal with her. She wept in the very abyss of grief, and I, most unprofessionally, cried in her arms. For if she was grief-stricken, I was struck down by fear and remorse. But before giving way to my womanhood I had sent Paddy for my bag—my professional equipment and strength—and now it was Isobel's turn for sleeping-pills. I put her to bed; and Paddy gave me his flask. I was distraught, not only by the sudden death of a neighbour—oh, more than a neighbour—but by superstitious fear of a sort which, for most of my life, I have stubbornly and persistently denied, but which, I suppose, is native to some dark rivulet in my veins. I drugged Isobel to sleep, and then could not think what to do but cry on Paddy's shoulder; and it was he who took charge.

He had already told Simmers, the village constable, what had happened, and told him he must drag for the body. He had given him cross-references of where to drag, and before midnight (there is little darkness here in June) poor Torquil's body was brought to the surface. His two sidepockets were stuffed full of cartridges, and he still held his gun, the fingers of his right hand clenched on the small of the butt. His rubber boots were full of water, and he had a big flask of whisky in his hip-pocket. He carried weight enough to sink him quickly, and I hope he did not suffer much.

On the following day I saw nothing of Paddy till the evening; but all my patients—and I went back to practice like a runaway looking for sanctuary—all, every one of them, said to me, 'And isn't it like a judgment that the weather changed as soon as they found the body?'

The statement, if not the inference, was true. After midnight the light southerly wind blew up to a southerly gale, that roared in the summer air as loud and fierce as a winter storm. Paddy, as he told me in the evening, spent the whole day searching the lee shore for what the gale might bring to land; and found what he was looking for. He found the body of a bird which he could not identify, but which, he knew, was not a bird common to our shores.

There would be no legal enquiry into Torquil's death: of that we had already made sure. A simple accident had been the cause of death, and Paddy and I were witnesses to that. So the next morning we went to Torquil's house to discuss the funeral—to comfort Isobel if we could—and in some convenient interval to have a look at Torquil's bird books and identify the pretty body that Paddy had found. I, when

I saw it, remembered the picture Torquil had once shown me; but said nothing. In his superficial examination Paddy had discovered no injury to the bird.

Isobel was still in bed, but mournful in a calmer way. Her life, she said, had come to an end, but we spoke of the children—Paddy was very good in this respect—and insisted that her duty to them was now enlarged. We persuaded her to get up for lunch, and while she was dressing we went to Torquil's work-room and looked at his bird books.

We found, in Witherby's *Handbook*, the description of a Sociable Plover, and had no difficulty in identifying it with the bird that Paddy had found. There were two or three pages describing its field-characters, food, display and so forth, and in the paragraph headed *Distribution Abroad* we saw that the statement 'Breeds in S.E. Russia (Astrakhan and Samara Govts. to 56 N. in Perm. Govt.)' was heavily underlined; and on the outer margin, again in heavy pencil, the notation: 'O dear God!'

Our knowledge of geography, I am sorry to say, was inadequate. We couldn't see the meaning of this. Not till we found an atlas and saw that the province of Astrakhan covered much of the lower Volga. Then Paddy said, 'Of course that's it! But we must have positive confirmation.'

It was he who packed and sent the bird to some ornithological society from which, with great promptitude, we got the report: 'This is a young adult male Sociable Plover in perfect plumage. It is well nourished. Contents of stomach . . . (omitted). Cause of death uncertain, but minute perforation of skull in neighbourhood of hind-brain suggests it was hit by single pellet, not larger than No. 6. Pellet not lodged in brain. Its discovery in Morissey is of greatest interest because previously no specimen had been reported from Scotland except a single bird in Orkney (3 Nov. 1926). Its measurements are larger than the accepted normal maximum—wing 218 mm., tail 94, bill from feathers 36—and this, of course, adds to the importance of your discovery.'

Paddy Ryan stayed his full three weeks, and fished with great success. In his last few days, when the sea-trout began to run, he took from our little fast-flowing river seven fish weighing 22 lb., of which the biggest was 6½ and went off well pleased with himself. But I had no heart to fish.

I have reported what I saw and what I was told, but I have no explanation to offer. Torquil lies like a dark shadow on my memory, but thank heaven I have no time to brood over shadows. I am too busy with other people and their ailments to worry overmuch about my own affairs; and, as I have said before, I don't really resent the fact that some of the elements of life are insoluble in reason.

Paddy Ryan went to the London School of Tropical Medicine for a year's course before returning to the New Hebrides, and promised to come back to Morissey. He wrote several times, both to Isobel and me, and shortly before Christmas Isobel rang me up one morning and asked me to lunch.

I went, and after her usual gossip—but she was, I must admit, more sensible and balanced than she used to be when Torquil ruled her life and thought—she said, 'Paddy asked me to give you his love and show you this cutting from *The Times*. I can't see what it signifies, but perhaps you will.'

It was a small paragraph—one of those minor items of news that you find in no other paper, and that make *The Times* so fascinating—and it read: 'Reports of unrest in the Lower Volga basin, briefly mentioned some months ago, are apparently confirmed by an announcement in *Pravda* that full investigation has now been made into the counter-revolutionary demonstration that took place in June in the neighbourhood of Krasny Yar. The demonstration, it is alleged, was entirely the work of foreign agents, who have now made full confession. Apart from them, there was only one fatal casualty, a youth of Polish origin.'

In the margin Paddy had written, 'Do you think he was killed by a silver bullet?'—and Isobel demanded, 'Now what on earth does he mean by that?'

'I don't know,' I said. 'I really don't know.'

'I usually see a joke,' said Isobel, 'but I can't see that. But perhaps it isn't a joke?'

'No, I don't think it is.'

I found it difficult to keep my voice level and unaffected, but with a great effort to seem casual, I asked her, 'Does Paddy write to you regularly?'

'Every week,' she said, 'and sometimes oftener. He is a darling, isn't he?'

'Yes,' I said, 'a darling.' And I felt my heart contract, my bowels shrivel within me.